Secrets and Dreams

Aug. 2013

To John and Susan,

It's been a pleasure getting to know you — we hope it's the beginning of a fun friendship. Carpe Diem!

Linda Scarlett

Linda Scarlett

and

Marty Peterson

Secrets And Dreams
Linda Scarlett

Original cover art by Gregory Kammer
gregorykammer.com

Editor: Jessica Loberg-Marty

Copyright 2012 Lexington Publishing Company, LLC.
All Rights Reserved
ISBN-13: 978-1463685645
ISBN-10: 1463685645

DEDICATION

This book is dedicated to my husband, David Scarlett, the love of my life—and to my son Eric Crisafi-Scarlett, the light of my life—both of my men were the wind beneath my wings and my number one cheerleaders. David and I were blessed with thirty years of marriage—every night was date night. I was also honored to have thirty years with the greatest son ever—I miss their sweet presence, as they are both in heaven now.

Eric always thought that his Mom was the best in the world, wanting to do everything with me, which included hanging out with him and his high school football buddies—then later, even after he was married, he would call and wanted to just 'kick it' with me—what beautiful memories I have of a son who adored me, and who considered me one of his best friends.

David was a genius, and an avid reader—when I first started writing, and asked for his honest opinion about whether my writing was captivating, or not—David compared my mystery to a Dean Koontz style, and continued to encourage me to not only write Secrets and Dreams, but to write The Next Level and my Grief Program. To the world I am Linda Scarlett, but to David I was always, "Honey Baby Doll." He believed in me, adored me, and was always cheering me on—a Prince of a Man, and my Hero!

To the best men a woman could have in her life—I dedicate to you, Secrets and Dreams!

ACKNOWLEDGEMENTS

Being an Italian daughter of a King, I want to first acknowledge my heritage—that of Heaven! I thank God for the passion and the fire that He has ignited in me to touch lives through my writing, speaking, counseling and teaching.

Then, I would like to thank Lexington Publishing Company, whom it's been an honor to work with—not only because of who Jane Favor and Jessica Loberg-Marty are—simply amazing business women with huge hearts for God, but also for how much they believe in me, all my writings, and truly want to touch lives through my work. Our passions have collided, for which I am grateful and blessed. I thank them first, because if it were not for them, you wouldn't be reading this book!

Next, I would like to thank all of my family: my Dad and Mom, Michael and Norma Ricca who were my best teachers and biggest cheerleaders growing up—I love you. To my daughter-in-law, friend and cheerleader, Stephanie Scarlett-Ruybal, and my grand daughter, my Angel-Girl Bianca Crisafi-Scarlett. And to Stephanie's sweet new husband, Dom Ruybal who has been so good to me—Eric would have loved him. To my daughter, Michelle Crisafi-Scarlett and grand daughters— my Precious Jada Brown, and Brooklyn. To my brothers Mark and Lance Ricca, who both at different times in their lives were loving and supportive. To my sister-in-law, Tracy Ricca, who was always a friend and supportive, and to her and Mark's daughters, my beautiful and loving nieces: Jessica and Samantha Ricca. Also to Paul and Marta Hammack (David's Aunt and Uncle), who supported us tremendously through the three months that David was dying, and to their extended family who supported us as well.

Then, my list of 'family' would not be complete without the woman who designated herself as SOMH, 'Sister of My Heart,' Nohealani Stewart, and her husband Walter Stewart. Nohealani lived with me and David for the last month of David's life—she was our Angel!

To my amazing family of friends, both my long-time friends, and my newest friends: I want to thank all of you for loving and supporting me through a few of the darkest valleys in my life—you have all been here for me in so many different ways from comforting phone calls, to meeting at Starbucks for quick coffees, to having lunch and dinners so we could be together and stay connected, to coming over and hanging drapes and changing locks (Stephanie and Dom), and taking down my Christmas tree (Sheila and Mark) so I could move on… For all your encouragement, kind words, and unconditional love I will be eternally grateful, and I thank you with all my heart—Ti Amo!

Family of Friends listed in no particular order:

Marty Peterson, Stephanie and Dom Ruybal, Sheila & Mark Berndt, Dr. Daniel Deffenbaugh, Michele and Erika DeMaris, Jessica and Jim Hegarty, Linda Harris, Patty and Tom Clifton, Carl Christine, Norene & Ernie Antin, Gerry Eagle, Barb Nystrom, Holly & Marcus Hailey, Dawn Biladeau & Karen Fagerberg, Tracy & Sean Rierson, Dr.Chris and Angie Cotner, Jane Favor, Scott Kelly, Christine Stratton, Ron Hennig, Pete Lance, Candy McDaniel, Dr. Barbara Troiano, Dale Foster, Johnna Belarde, Palani Stewart, Brett Olmez, Ashley Noftsger, Christine Fontenot, Jade Christine, Liz Chaffin, Don & Georgene Yost, Bruce and Joan Lavers, Jay Kondo, Tom Connery, Adrian Van Meter, Jennifer and Ryan Rasar, Celeste Wright and Marci Pence, Mark and Linda Brunkhorst, Brian DeWall, Christy Storm, Nancy Gagnon, Leslie Brentwood, Josh Keller, Dawneeta Schmautz, Stan and Sharon Bloch, Diane Watson, Breauna Stockton from The Purple Café & Wine Bar, and Yvonne P. Adams and Stefanie McQuery from Whidbey Island Bank.

Many thanks also to all of my Professors, Pastors and Teachers from BCC, Seattle Ministry Institute and PCCCA who have inspired me, mentored me, and cheered me on to great heights! A Special thank you to my Mentors Dr. Jerry Cook from Seattle Ministry Institute, and Dr. Laura Bush from PCCCA.

I am so very humbled by the love and support of every person whom I have had the honor to know and love in my life—who collectively created a phenomenally beautiful patchwork of human beings that have loved me, helped me become who I am, and cheered me on to where I'm going! Carpe Diem!

Thank you ALL, for your amazing love and friendship!

Chapter 1

As I stood there all I could see was black, everywhere like a motionless black ocean, surrounding me and suffocating me. Suddenly a chilly wind jolted my body, whirling around me, sending shivers up and down my spine, echoing in my ears along with every gut-wrenching cry that came from the black ocean.

The bitter cold weather appeared out of nowhere in the middle of spring, as though nature was in sync with this pitifully painful day. The raindrops had a mysterious beat of their own—falling quickly and then slowly in the shape of giant teardrops, which began to join my tears as they disappeared into the sea of black. Having been there for hours, I was desperate to see anything besides black, anything besides rain. Finally through my tear-filled eyes I could see the blurry ocean begin to slowly separate as faces started to appear, one by one.

The faces were sullen, with pain and sorrow streaming from the windows of their souls. I've never seen that many eyes so full of pain, so filled with death. Slowly, out of nowhere a man's voice, deep and solemn, began humming in my ears until it got louder and louder, when conclusively and with clarity I heard him say, "Amen."

Father's funeral seemed to last for an eternity until the black umbrellas and black suits began to gradually separate, moving like an older film in slow motion—juxtaposed to how quickly and deeply the memory of a black ocean, and agonizing pain was being etched in my soul forever. The bitter reality that I would never, ever see my father again was settling into my soul, and death began to feel like a heavy, clinging coat that I could not remove.

Without warning I felt a strong, warm hand slip into mine. As I looked up I saw a pair of eyes that I will never forget—eyes that were strong and compassionate, yet what I felt most was that they were sincere. Behind those eyes was a handsome man who bent down slowly as he gently moved the hair from my face, stared into my eyes and whispered, "Gabrielle, they will pay, I promise." Then he quickly, yet ever so softly kissed my cheek, and walked away. Being somewhat taken aback by his gentle kiss, and unexpected words I wanted to chase after him, but I couldn't move—still so frozen from the shocking grief of burying my father. 'What did he mean,"They will pay?" They who?

Would pay for what?' I had never seen this man before, but deep in my soul I felt that I could trust him—maybe because my pitiable soul was in such a vulnerable state. The man disappeared as abruptly as he had appeared, but my thoughts of him lingered…

As I stood there in a zombie-like state of mind, a long line of people began walking towards me. Knowing that I needed to be strong, I wondered how I would face each one of these heartbroken people who loved Father so much when I couldn't even process this myself. I watched the parade of people coming closer, but instead of seeing them more clearly, they became one big blur, and their voices blended together as if they were humming in harmony.

My heart was already longing for my strong, loving father who was now becoming only a memory. Father and I were quite close, and had a relationship that most daughters could only dream about. Father had a unique way about him that demanded respect before he spoke a single word, but he was also a fun, loving man—contrasted with a very pensive, stern side. I had no fear of him, only admiration.

Father's stature was like that of an Italian masterpiece chiseled from pure marble, with facial features resembling a Roman god. His dark hair and dark eyes were so striking that one could just stare at him in sheer appreciation of his beauty. Father's attitude remained unscathed by his looks, because his demeanor was as beautiful as his visage.

Father was also a very serious and intelligent businessman, who was the head of a financial empire. He was in the shipping industry, and was also an independent ship owner who not only had his own fleet of cargo ships, but also chartered tankers for oil companies. The Pacific Rim was an excellent location for Father's businesses, and by the age of twenty-six Father had made his first million dollars. His tankers have always reaped immense profits, and from those profits Father's business became extremely diverse, allowing him to become independently wealthy. Father introduced me to his business at a very young age, and I've become increasingly involved each year, ever since I can remember.

Father's personality was wonderfully balanced with me, as he could be caring and tender, hysterically funny, or very, very serious. I remember experiencing one of Father's very serious sides years ago when he taught me how to drive. His voice was strong and demanding when he said, "You'll drive like a man, or you won't drive at all!" I sat up tall in the seat, and tried to muster up thoughts of just exactly how it was that 'men' drove, because when Father was serious he expected intelligent and immediate action from people.

I remember thinking to myself, 'Gabi, how do men drive?' I didn't want to disappoint him—I truly did want to drive like the guys, so my mind was rapidly drawing from the memories of all the times I had been in the passenger seat. 'Come on Gabi, think...how do men drive?' They seem to be very sure of themselves, they're very aggressive, they drive fast, and then I yelled out, "Here we go!" I floored it, and Father looked over at me with those piercing eyes that could look directly into your soul—then he smiled, and I pushed the pedal to the floor!

As nervous as I was, I couldn't believe that my foot was actually hard on the pedal, but it felt so awesome to be in control, in the driver's seat. I took great satisfaction in that single moment of 'Driving like a guy!' After a few weeks, Father told me I was a natural, and I would most definitely become an excellent driver. I did become pretty good—yes, just like one of the guys—if I do say so, myself.

Oh those guys, those brilliant, fun-loving and gorgeous guys! Father had an entourage of men that were constantly with him. They were not only his business associates, but excellent friends as well. 'The guys' did everything with Father, and have been involved in my life since I was young, because most of them had known Father for many years before I was ever born.

Shortly after I turned sixteen, the younger guys would let me drive their cars, however I wonder if they would have ever allowed me to touch them if I hadn't been 'Michael Deliano's daughter'. My Uncle Leon was older than most of the younger guys. He was also a great driver, and owned an awesome car, a BMW that was a real screamer. Uncle Leon is Father's younger brother, and is essentially a smaller version of Father, with the only difference being his hair. Uncle Leon had straight hair, while Father's was wavy, and Leon was three inches shorter than my father's six-foot-two. I will never forget how Uncle Leon was constantly talking about how he would surely catch up to my father's height some day, although he never did.

Then there was Jacob, one of Father's youngest protégés, and a promising new attorney to whom I was the closest. His car was the absolute best—a brand new Ferrari, definitely the fastest and most fun car to drive! When Jacob was younger, and somewhat of a gambler, he and his friends loved to bet on car races. Jacob oftentimes invited me to race with him, which I gladly obliged. He always left the others in the dust, claiming the winnings more times than I can count. I never understood why anyone would accept a race against Jacob, because they never won—I guess it's a guy thing.

Father had the greatest car of all, a Lamborghini, but it wasn't just any Lamborghini, it was a shiny, brand new, black Diablo—and of course, a convertible. From April through September it was the only car Father drove. While I did enjoy driving Father's Lamborghini, the black devil was a little too much car for me—Father on the other hand, couldn't drive it enough.

I remember one beautiful, warm spring morning when the pink dogwoods were in full bloom, the sky was an electric blue, and you could see forever. I was twelve years old, and had already learned to thoroughly enjoy my father's spontaneous sense of adventure. He was in one of his 'missing Europe moods', so we jumped in the Lamborghini, and headed north. We just kept driving…all the way to Victoria, B.C. We made that trip often, not only because it was a few hours from our home in Seattle, it was also beautifully scenic, and reminded Father of the many countries abroad that he loved so much.

We arrived in Victoria just in time for high tea at The Empress, one of Victoria's most famous English Hotels, after which we would always visit the renowned Butchart Gardens. While in the gardens the aroma was so exquisitely intoxicating, especially as we strolled through a patch of absolutely gorgeous, pink stargazers. As we were strolling, Father started a conversation that lasted for over two hours, I was so completely engrossed in his intense description of everything that it felt as though time stood still—Father was quite the storyteller who knew how to keep his audience marvelously captivated.

This particular narrative was about a very special photo that sat proudly on Father's desk—this was the first time he had ever wanted to talk about that picture, so I hung onto every word he said. Father started the story by explaining that it was a day, much like the glorious day we were momentarily engaged in. "It was a wonderful day like today, and it was your fifth birthday," he said to me. "'The guys' and I took you to a beautiful park by the lake. My gift to you was a very special charm bracelet that belonged to your mother when she was a little girl." Then Father explained that Uncle Leon and the guys each presented me with a carefully chosen charm to add to my bracelet. Father's memory, and the photo that sat on his desk for all those years, now had a special memory in my heart as well.

I will always remember how especially sweet all those exotic flowers smelled in the Butchart Gardens that day—so intensely sweet that I can still smell them, and as I breathed in deeply I realized that I truly could smell flowers, however, I wasn't in the gardens anymore...

I've never seen so many flowers at a funeral—it looked like an ocean of red and white roses for as far as I could see. Father's casket looked as though it was floating amongst them, literally covered with white lilies and his favorite, pink stargazers. The flowers are such a sweet remembrance of your life Father, and the fragrance you left behind—the thousands and thousands of flowers are definitely a reflection of the love that people felt for you.

My memories and thoughts of Father were coming in like the speed of light, and for a moment I forgot where I was, and for heaven's sake, what I was doing. I cleared my throat, wiped my eyes, regained my composure, and held out my hand to the next person in line.

Then, before I could completely focus on who was talking to me, I became mesmerized by the softest most sweetest, yet sexy voice I had ever heard. A woman, whom I didn't know, approached me from the side, and whispered in my ear—sounding like the combination of an angel, and a movie star. She spoke very softly, yet with intense sincerity in her voice she said, "Your father loved you very much."

As I turned to look at her through my tears, she slowly came into focus—a strikingly beautiful woman. She put her arm around me, squeezed me tightly, kissed my cheek, turned and slowly walked away. She seemed to be very upset, in a trance-like state, walking aimlessly as if she had nowhere in the world to go. But then, where does one go after a funeral?

I wanted to follow her, but at that very moment another hand slipped into mine, so I just watched her walk away. The little hand only rested in mine for a moment before it quickly pulled away and began tugging on my dress. Her sweet, small voice started saying something, but I didn't hear a word the little child was trying to say. All I could think about was that woman, who she was, and why was she so affected by my father's death. That brief encounter with a grieving outsider seemed very strange. However, everything seemed very strange to me today.

'Oh Father...I want you back—I hate this, I can't believe it's true—it makes no sense! I don't think that I can do this—I can't be strong. Who said I had to be strong? Strength...How can I have strength at a time like this? Where does it come from? Where did you get your strength? I feel so helpless, so small, and so alone. You were my Daddy…my best friend… my everything! And now…what am I going to do without you? You said I was strong, but look at me—I'm not strong, I'm weak, and I can't do this…I can't!'

I was in such an agonizing moment of grief that I didn't realize I was ignoring one of our closest friends, and quickly responded without thinking, "Oh, excuse me, I'm so sorry. Yes, I miss Father also."

Then, my brain was racing—I wasn't sure whether that was the correct response, or did she say something that warranted a completely different reaction? I knew she understood, even if I didn't reply correctly, because Mrs. Cardelli loved me as much as we all loved her. Most people just called her Mrs. C for short, but we of course, called her Mary.

Mary was a widow just like Father—and a lovely lady who lost her husband while she was still in her thirties. It seems like just yesterday, but it was actually fifteen years ago when Mary moved into our neighborhood alone, because her husband had just passed away. Mary loved Father as much as any neighbor could possibly love another neighbor. She was good and kind, with a smile on her face always, especially when she was giving, which she frequently did, because that's just who Mary was. She would bring us fresh flowers from her garden daily, and wouldn't let a month go by without baking one of her famous cheesecakes just for us. Mary also loved a good party, and she held some of the grandest in town. As a child I thought that Father was lucky to have Mary for a neighbor, but as I grew, it was I who felt blessed to call her a friend.

Mary walked over to the casket, stood there very still, and cried silently. I could tell that she was also praying, because every time Mary prayed she would lift her face toward heaven, then drop it slowly in reverence. After a few minutes, she placed the flowers she had in her hand gently over the lilies. Then, she remained poised in a most solemn position for quite a while, until something seemed to come over her—she lifted her head quickly, wiped her eyes, and then briskly walked off, fading into the sea of flowers.

'Oh Father, I know this sounds bizarre, but I wish you could have attended our own funeral, and seen how much you were loved. You touched so many lives, especially mine, and I thank you for loving me with that big ol' heart of yours.' While most of my friend's mothers were the center of their worlds, Father was the center of mine. He was all that I had yet somehow with the love and attention I received from him, I never missed having another parent. Father always made sure that I was well taken care of, and that important days were celebrated in equally important ways.

I remember my surprisingly lavish eighteenth birthday. Father out did himself from morning until night. Eighteen dozen red roses were delivered at precisely 8:11 AM, the exact time of my birth, as he never forgot a detail, ever! After the flowers arrived, while I was eating breakfast, I noticed something shiny on the floor in the hallway. It was a four-inch wide, very long, gold ribbon. I followed it down the hall, around the corner, through the large marble foyer, out the front door, down the steps, through the courtyard, and to the huge circular driveway. To my surprise, the ribbon was attached to my dream car—a brand new, cherry red Porche! The ribbon was not only attached, but there was the hugest gold bow on the roof of the car that I had ever seen.

After letting out a very excited scream, I ran back to the house to find Father, when I stumbled headlong into him in the courtyard—I nearly knocked the video camera out of his hands as we tried to keep each other from falling down. Father had been taping a video of his great surprise, which I should have known he would be doing. He always enjoyed watching my reaction to whatever present he gave me. After we both had a good laugh, I squeezed him tight, kissed his cheek, and then raced off to my best friend's house to show her my car.

Ashlee was one of the sweetest, most loyal friends that anyone could ask for, and she just happened to be as pretty on the outside as she was on the inside. Ashlee's waist-length, thick, natural blonde hair, and her huge green eyes, with long dark eyelashes made heads turn everywhere she went. Ashlee was always positive and happy so I knew that she would be excited for me—I had never met anyone like her, because most girls I knew were either selfish or catty, but not Ashlee—she wasn't wired that way.

Ashlee's life was quite different from mine in that both of her parents were deceased. Her mother died while delivering Ashlee, and Dominique, her father died in a plane crash, just six years ago when she was fifteen. Ashlee's inheritance left her a multi-million dollar teen, yet even with that kind of wealth it was a very hard and lonely time for Ashlee.

Besides great friends, Dominique was one of Father's business associates, and confidants. Dominique's life ended in a tragic accident when the 747 he was in went down in the freezing ocean. Father's entire company had been in Munich for a business trip, and then they all flew to Switzerland for a masquerade ball afterwards. Dominique however, decided to fly back to the states the next morning, a day earlier than everyone else. Any kind of death is hard to deal with, but one in which the body is never found leaves a person without a sense of real closure. Funerals are so, so sad.

One by one, the people kept coming—each with the best of sentiments, yet it was all I could do to stand on my own two feet, or utter a single word to either console them, or thank them for coming. I had never seen 'the guys' this distraught—even Uncle Leon, and Father's closest friends were crying like little boys. Little boys cry differently than little girls, as their tears just roll slowly down their faces—they don't make noise, or jerking movements like the girls.

Even though Uncle Leon was grieving, his demeanor was extremely worrisome and alarming to me, as if he had something else besides the funeral on his mind; he was acting nervous and visibly shaking, which was certainly out of character for him. Uncle Leon was usually such a pillar of strength so his behavior made me quite concerned. I motioned for him to come over, but as Leon started walking toward me, Jacob abruptly intercepted; he slowly picked up my hand, kissed it and lingered. Leon just kept walking. Jacob looked into my eyes, almost the way Father did as he said, "I am so sorry Princess—there was no one like Michael."

Jacob gently put his arms around my waist, and held me as though I was as fragile as a porcelain doll. I slipped my arms up around his neck, hugged him back and for a brief moment I felt lost in Jacob's embrace—realizing for the first time all day, that I was still a live, warmhearted human being. As I began to look around for Uncle Leon who was nowhere to be found, Jacob released me from his embrace, squeezed my hand, and as he walked off he blended into the mass of people who were still loitering, almost motionless by the graveside.

Time seemed to stand still, and I had no recollection of just how long we stood there, but as we finally started walking away, the oddest feeling came over me—I felt as though this funeral was not just an ending, but some dauntingly, mysterious new beginning, and I began to shiver…

Chapter 2

I was the last one to leave the cemetery, and the only one in that long, black, stretch limo with a driver I didn't know, except for the fact that he was very empathetic, and didn't make me feel rushed as he drove me back to the church. Feeling terribly detached from the world, I climbed into my car realizing how alone I was, and my heart sank as I started for home.

As I drove, I could see nothing on that canvas of life that I had so neatly painted before. Instead, my beautiful picture was blurring as the paints began running into each other in shapes of tears, and then quickly streaming off the canvas, never to return. It was an eerily blank canvas—crying out for something, anything—but nothing made sense. My mind began to spin out of control, so I quickly pushed the canvas out of my head, and concentrated on driving—I gripped the steering wheel tightly with both hands, stared at the street, and focused on the white lines, one by one…

Without warning the memories of Father began rushing into my head again at warp speed, and I could hardly stop them—not that I wanted to, but now each moment was literally flashing before me in little frame bits of time like it was yesterday. There I was, standing in a beautiful, pink dress—it was my tenth birthday, and Father was calling me Princess. He had requested that I escort him on a very important business trip to London, so we could spend my birthday together—he wouldn't dream of missing it for any reason, not even business.

After modeling at least half a dozen dresses for Father, I finally found the one that he thought was the most splendid of all. As I strolled out of the dressing room pretending to be a model Father grabbed my hand, took my arm above my head as he twirled me—smiled from ear to ear and said, "You look just like a princess." Yes, I definitely felt like a princess right out of the storybooks. From that day on, Princess became the name that Father mostly called me, unless of course he was upset with me, in which case it was always, Gabrielle!

Although I loved my sweet nickname, it didn't ring so sweetly in my ears after reading the article about Father's death in The Seattle Times. The article named me, 'The Ice Princess,' as his sole beneficiary. 'The

Ice Princess' conjured such an ugly, mean image in my mind—where in the world did they come up with that?

Suddenly the car came to a screeching halt. I sat there for a moment, shaken and scared, realizing that I had been on autopilot, and drove five blocks past the turn to my house. I quickly pulled myself together, made a u-turn, and speedily drove back. My mind was going crazy wondering when, or if I would ever adjust to this tragedy that had changed my life forever.

As I drove up the long, circular driveway to the house chills came over me. I knew that Father would not be there, and that he would never be home to greet me again. I could see the lights in his office, which usually meant that he was in there working late—however tonight was different. I had instructed the staff to leave the lights on in the lower level of the house, because I knew that I would be returning home late from the funeral. I also told the staff to take the night off, as I knew that they would also be very upset over the loss of my father, and I wanted them to be able to handle the grief in their own way.

Most of the staff had been with us for over twenty years. We were never allowed to call them 'servants,' because Father said that sounded like we owned them, or were better than they were. His philosophy was that no one was better than anyone else. I agreed wholeheartedly with his views about life, and had adopted them as my own. I made great strides in having Father's same type of attitude, and most of the time I did quite well, but my patience wasn't nearly as matured as Father's, which got me into quite a bit of trouble sometimes.

As I approached the garage door someone ran out of the house holding something in their hand. They were running so fast that I could barely burn a description of the person in my mind. Even though I couldn't recognize who it was, I was quite sure that it wasn't one of the staff, because they always used the side entrance.

I pulled my car into the garage as I was wondering who in the world would be violating our home, especially today. I jumped out of the car and ran to the back of the house as fast as I could run—usually I can't see well in the dark, but tonight my sight wasn't guiding me—I was running on instinct and sheer adrenaline. As I arrived at the back of the house, a black sedan with dark tinted windows came screeching around the corner, and then took off like lightening—unable to see the person, I bolted back to the garage, and through the house hoping to catch a glimpse of something!

Wondering who was in our house, my mind was going through every face I had ever met, remembering that offenders usually know their victims—I couldn't imagine anyone that we know, doing something like this! Absolutely no one came to mind—my brain drew a complete blank.

All I could think about was Father, and my last heart wrenching days with him—watching him lying in bed, and the life draining from his body with every breath he took. Father said things while in that state of unconsciousness that were bewildering, as though he was trying to confess secrets, or something—how silly, but they continue to haunt me...

My soul still aches from watching Father's beautiful body fade away so quickly at the hand of a virus, which didn't make any sense whatsoever to me—death is so hard to justify. And, the insidious way that the virus tortured his body—it was so hard to watch the pain, so hard to watch him deteriorate. Seeing Father's beautiful, thick hair falling out by the handfuls, and his definitive facial features that had become extremely distorted from being so horribly bloated was pure agony to watch. The most painful for me were his eyes—those gorgeous, big, brown eyes that were once expressive, and so full of life, became very dim, gray and lifeless. The man lying in that bed no longer looked like Father—he was a complete stranger. Then, as his body grew weaker by the day, he drifted in and out of consciousness all too frequently. Later his voice became so weak that he could barely talk, and his lungs filled with fluid that was continually choking him. I never left his side, because I wanted him to feel my presence, and my love for him until the very end.

As the last hour approached, I held him in my arms with his head close to my chest—I was so completely scared that my heart was pounding rapidly, feeling as though with each beat it would surely push itself right out of my chest. My hands were quite clammy, so I was continually drying them before I would touch my sweet Father's face, constantly reassuring him that I was right by his side. Part of me wanted to hang on to him, because I didn't want him to leave this world—the other part of me felt so sorry for how he was agonizing that I knew he would be better off if God would just go ahead and take him. What an awful battle to have raging inside me as my Father lay dying in my arms.

The last five minutes of Father's life were very painful for him, and horribly excruciating for me—the entire time I kept holding him tighter, and tighter wanting him to feel secure as he was leaving this world. I will never forget the very last minute of his life. My arms were wrapped around him, his head was cupped in my hands, and as his body was jerking, his eyes that could barely open would roll to the back of the sockets, and then shut again—although that lasted for only a minute, it seemed like hours to me. I reached across his chest, gently picked up his hand, and placed it inside of mine—I knew this was the last time I would feel life in his hand that was once beautiful, but now unrecognizable. My heart ached as I prayed silently. Before shutting for the last time, Father's eyes fixed on my eyes for a brief moment, as his weak and laboring voice slowly said, "I…love…you." The life inside my Father's body was now gone.

    I held him in my arms as I prayed for his soul, and then I started crying uncontrollably as I kissed his sweet face. Uncle Leon approached me slowly, gently unwrapped my arms that were glued to Father, and carried me out of his room—he held me tightly in his arms as I cried, and cried, and cried.

    The memory of Father's dying face with a tear running down his cheek, and those lifeless eyes will be etched in my memory forever.

    I suddenly escaped my painful thoughts, and became instantly enraged thinking that someone could violate our home. I sprang off the couch like a cat bursting with energy and started running through the house looking for some kind of clue! I bolted upstairs first, searching through all thirteen bedrooms, including Father's, but not finding anything that looked suspicious I ran back down the long spiral staircase. I jumped as I hit the last stair and flew over half of the marble entryway. Now, my adrenaline was pumping as rapidly as my legs—I ran even faster through the foyer, all the way to the ballroom where I stopped dead in my tracks—I became spellbound by the light that was dancing on the wall, reflecting the prisms in the chandelier, reminding me of all the grand parties we held in that room. I turned, and slowly closed the door, as if it were the cover of a good novel—not really wanting to close it, but wanting to re-read the last chapter, over and over again, hoping the book would never end.

    I made my way back down the hall, through the gym, the kitchen, the parlor, and finally to Father's office, which was my favorite room in the house, because this is where Father spent the majority of his time when he was home. Father held many meetings in this beautiful and spacious office that must have been at least two thousand square feet, because the huge, antique cherry table seemed extremely small against the surrounding fifteen-foot walls, covered with books. There were four huge, stuffed, burgundy leather chairs, which were arranged around the cherry table, placed strategically by the window with a view of the perfectly sculpted gardens. Underneath the chairs was a gorgeous, white Persian rug, which was one of my favorites that Father had picked up in Egypt on one of his business trips abroad.

Father's enormous desk was on the opposite side of the room, with a large, burgundy, leather chair behind it. Across from his desk there was a most comfortable antique, burgundy and black, Italian couch from Milan. Behind the couch was one of my favorite works of art that Father had recently added to his collection. I could stare at the Pieta for hours, an exquisite work carved from marble, of Christ lying in Mary's arms. Every corner of the room was decorated with such incredible detail, displaying pieces that Father gathered during his many travels. Father's office had always felt so comfortable to me, but tonight it felt very cold, and very different.

Suddenly I became compelled to run to the bookshelves. I didn't know why, so I just kept walking back and forth, running my hand along the books, while looking intensely at every little detail—yet nothing was missing. One would notice if something was missing in this house, because Father was extremely organized; everything had a place, and nothing was ever out of place. As my eyes scanned the other side of the room, I panicked as I realized that maybe the safe had been broken into; I actually ran to it, and then just stood there for a moment, staring at the picture. I could tell the picture hadn't been moved, but I wanted to check inside the safe just to ease my mind. It appeared that nothing had been taken from there, and after I thought about it for a moment, I realized that it would have been almost impossible to break into this particular safe without Father or my fingerprints placed on the reader, because without our doing that, the silent alarm would be triggered.

Feeling a little frantic again, I decided to check each drawer of Father's desk, but from what I could tell, nothing was missing there either. I quickly sat down in Father's chair, which was usually so comfortable—however, at that moment it felt like any other chair, except for the fact that it smelled like Father.

As I began to rifle through the few items that were atop his desk, I noticed a large envelope with a manila folder inside that was barely visible under the leather desk mat. Father had certain envelopes that belonged in the safe, and were designated as such, and this was certainly one of them, however I don't ever remember seeing it before this moment. How odd. Why hadn't Father returned it to the safe? Just how long has it been sitting here? He's been completely bedridden for exactly a week. Father would have never left something out that belonged in the safe, but then my sweet, sick father didn't know he was leaving this world, on that day.

Has that much time passed that I don't remember how long it's been since I've set foot in Father's office? Has it been a week already? I put the file back in the safe since my brain was in a fog, and I wouldn't be able to make sense of it anyway. Then I just sat there staring at the desk, because something else seemed different—I couldn't put my finger on it, but something was definitely different.

My eyes were stinging now, and began to feel heavy; my body felt weak and somewhat sick, so I laid my head on Father's desk, and before I knew it I fell asleep. Two hours had past when Maria returned home, found me asleep at the desk, and gently tried to awaken me. After convincing her that I was fine, and wasn't ready for bed, I also had to persuade her that nothing else was wrong, so as not to alarm her quite yet. Again, I sat there half asleep, staring at every inch of Father's desk, feeling in my gut that something about his desk just wasn't right.

The phone rang, and instinctively, yet cautiously, I answered. My voice was shaky as I said, "Hello" but there was no response, so I hit the cancel button immediately, feeling somewhat violated. I slowly placed the phone back in its cradle, while my eyes fixed on one spot to the right of where the phone unit was sitting.

I stared and stared. Finally…exhausted, I could no longer sit up, so I leaned back in Father's chair, closed my eyes, and all I could see was a black ocean of umbrellas with rain dripping from each one—people crying, flowers everywhere, and strangers staring at me. I started dozing off, but then suddenly my body jerked, waking me up. Happy to have been awakened from a dream that began with such grief, I tried to fight the urge to fall asleep again. I opened my eyes wide, shook my head several times, and sat straight up in Father's chair.

A tear streamed down my cheek as I turned my head slowly, looking at the desk once more, when my eyes kept returning to, and staring at the area behind the phone. "What is it Gabi? Come on focus," I kept saying out loud to keep myself awake—suddenly it came to me…'yes, that's it, that spot is empty!' There was a picture, which had been in that very place for years, in a beautifully carved, cherry frame—it was that special picture of Father, 'The guys,' and me on my birthday! Shocked at its disappearance, I searched the entire office, again and again, until I was satisfied that it was nowhere to be found.

By now the remaining staff members who had taken the night off had returned home, and were all sound asleep. I wasn't sure if I wanted to wake them, and get everyone involved right now, or if I should just let them sleep—but, since I figured out that the picture was definitely missing, I needed to know if they knew anything about it. I decided to wake them—there was no way that I could wait until morning to inquire about something this important. I quickly went to each of their rooms, waking them, and asking if they had seen the missing picture, or if they had moved it for some reason.

Feeling badly that I was somewhat interrogating our loving and loyal staff, I felt the most guilty as I approached Maria. She explained to me that she was the one who always cleaned Father's office, and would never have moved his favorite picture, ever. She also told me that the only time her fingers came anywhere near that picture was when she picked it up twice a week to dust Father's desk. I quickly inquired as to when the last time it was that she had dusted.

"Yesterday Gabi, yesterday!"

I ran out of her room, and flew up the stairs. I felt as though my heart were in my hands, panicking about whether I would ever see the picture that held such beautiful memories for Father and me. I threw myself onto my bed, with feelings of abandonment and anger, which quickly gave way to a brief moment of denial, thinking that Father's death hadn't really happened—surely, any moment now, I would awaken to hear his voice calling me. Then, as quickly as those thoughts came, they went—leaving me feeling very sad, and incredibly lonely.

As I sat there staring at the ceiling, my mind was going through the many faces of people that had ever been to our house, which happened to be hundreds! There was no way in the world that I could ever begin to single out any suspects! What was I thinking? I should have called Alex, and I should have called the police!

Alex had been up for many nights during Father's illness, and eventual death, and now was mourning the loss of his lifetime friend. Alexander Stone and my father grew up together, were best friends, business associates, and confidants. Alex's brother, Charles, was the captain of the police department, also very close to Father, and whom Father and Alex relied on in times of need.

How could I have possibly fallen asleep at Father's desk! Now we probably had no chance in the world of catching anyone! I knew that I needed to call Alex, but I couldn't muster up enough strength to do another thing. I finally laid down—my head spinning, my heart broken, and my body totally numb.

Chapter 3

I fell asleep the minute my weary head hit the large, well-worn, feather pillow. I started dreaming about something that was like no other dream I've ever dreamt before—it seemed entirely too real, and over-the-top disturbing. The dream started out when I was five years old. Father was taking me to meet my mother at a park by the river. This same scene kept playing over and over, like a movie that was on perpetual repeat, until the scene instantly changed in a flash—I stood there in the park, and yelled out, "Wait a minute…I don't have a mother!"

Being distressed, I awoke abruptly, sat straight up in bed, and quickly tried to analyze my extremely crazy dream, which must have been inspired by all the many fanatical happenings of my day. Exhausted, my body instinctively wanted to return to its sleep state, as it involuntarily threw itself back onto the bed. In no time I was asleep, only to revisit the same dream, which oddly picked up right where it left off—it was as if my waking up was a commercial break.

Father and I were walking hand-in-hand through that beautiful park on a clear, crisp, spring day with the smell of freshly mowed grass and sweetly scented flowers in the wind. The birds were continually singing as they flew from one blooming dogwood to another—I could hear the flowing river, which eventually came into view, as we got closer to an enormous weeping willow.

A woman was standing by the weeping willow in a long, flowing floral dress dancing to a beat of its own, while blowing in the wind. As we approached the woman I called her mother, which became so disturbing to my mind that the scene was continually interrupted, until the words came out of my mouth without feeling odd. It was as though my mind was an overlay on a movie screen, analyzing it frame by frame, and saying 'cut' each time it came to the 'Mother' part.

The entire time that I was dreaming about this particular scene, my subconscious mind could not understand why I was calling this woman Mother. I knew that I did not have a mother. The frame finally moved on, as I looked up at Father and said, "Who is this? Who is this woman?"

Father just kept looking at me sweetly, and smiling without ever answering me, which was very unsettling to my soul. I kept wondering why Father wasn't responding. As we got close enough to touch the woman, I yelled out to her, "Turn around…look at me!"

Suddenly the scene changed, and Father started calling the woman by her name. I couldn't hear what he was saying, because his words were being carried off with the wind. 'He's calling her by name, but what is he saying? Why can't I understand his words?' I began tugging on his hand so that he would look down at me. As soon as I had his attention, with pleading eyes I looked at him and said, "Father, please tell me what you're saying!"

He just looked down at me and smiled, as if I hadn't said a single word. Once again, as we got close enough to almost touch her, the woman started drifting, further and further away, her image quickly vanishing into the ripples of the water.

I was startled as my alarm went off, which felt like a very rude intrusion, blasting off at 5:00 AM as usual. As I awoke, instead of feeling rested, I felt incredibly strange. I sat on the edge of the bed, holding my head in my hands, wondering how in the world I was going to keep my life together. Everything was becoming a blur, and I didn't know which was worse—dreaming, or being awake. I jumped up, and literally tripped into the shower to clear my head before I made a phone call to Alex.

As soon as the words fell out of my mouth about the man that I saw running from our home, Alex told me that he and Charles would be there in a flash. Alex carefully explained why I shouldn't let any of the staff into Father's office, and then, in an even more demanding tone, told me not to let anyone touch a thing until he arrived. I knew that wouldn't be hard, because the staff didn't awaken until six o'clock—everyone except for Antonio, who managed the staff and would rise at the crack of dawn to plan the day for everyone. Antonio made sure that Father's house was running as smoothly, and precisely as a Swiss watch.

Father met Antonio and his wife, Maria in the mid seventies while he was in Spain on a business trip. It was a time of political unrest in Spain that was linked to economic pressures, which motivated Antonio to work three jobs. His favorite job was that of a maitre d' at a five star restaurant where Father frequented. Father was so impressed with Antonio, because of his excellent service and attention to detail, that during one of his trips there he invited Antonio and Maria to come to the states to work in our home. My father had a big heart, and loved to help people, especially hard working, kind people going through rough times. Antonio and Maria became part of our family. They never returned to Spain after they moved in with us.

Alex and Charles arrived in no time—Charles approaching with the usual entourage that one expects from watching detective movies. He began walking the grounds as Alex started questioning me in a fashion more like an interrogation than a concerned friend.

Alex was an ex-Navy Seal, and was everything that one would imagine a seal to look like. He was 6'4", had a muscular build with absolutely no trace of fat, and light brown hair that was kept quite short, which set off his large, dark brown eyes. While in the navy he mastered his incredibly disciplined life. He also became a security and surveillance specialist, which led him to develop the department of operations and security for Father's business, Deliano Shipping. I had the utmost respect for Alex, as did Father.

Charles made sure that his team dusted everywhere for prints. Then he took pictures of the room, and fingerprinted the entire staff. I saw the mortified look on Maria's face, as they were placing her thumb on the squishy, black finger pad—feeling embarrassed for her I blurted out, "For heaven's sake Alex, tell Charles to stop, Maria is innocent!"

Alex agreed with me, but explained that they didn't want any stone left unturned. In the meantime, Charles started rounding up his men, and as he walked off he said, "Gabrielle, I'll file the report, run these samples for prints, and be in touch."

The minute that Charles was gone, Alex started in on me again. I stared at him with a quizzical look, but before I could speak, he said, "Gabrielle, your father had a very high profile, and we would feel better if someone was here to…"

"Protect me?"

"Yes!"

"Why?"

"Gabrielle, please don't question me."

I knew better than to argue with Alex, but as he walked out the door, I rolled my eyes at him. He responded with that all too familiar stern look, reinforcing his muscle. I threw myself down into Father's big, burgundy chair—sitting behind his desk made me feel a sense of security. Then I started mulling over what Alex said, "'Your father had a high profile'—what exactly did he mean by that?"

This information was entirely too much to process, and my mind was on overload. I couldn't sit still any longer, so I jumped out of the chair and started pacing back and forth, back and forth, until I broke the pattern and was walking through the entire house like a zombie. Out of touch with all my feelings except for the immense pain I was in, I wondered what my life was about to become, and how I would go on now that Father was gone. My life, as I knew it, content and full of love had been changed in an instant. The person that I loved most of all was now in a grave, gone forever!

As I walked through the foyer, for probably the tenth time, I was startled as the huge Grandfather clock's chimes began to bellow, reminding me that Uncle Leon would be arriving in an hour. Leon and I always arranged our business meeting for the first Monday of every month—a time that we both thoroughly enjoyed. We decided to keep our scheduled meeting today, even though we knew it would be hard. There were pressing issues, and decisions that couldn't wait.

Leon arrived at twelve o'clock sharp, which was the precise time we had scheduled. However, Leon usually made his entrance exactly twenty minutes late, and since he was never on time, I had planned my morning accordingly. Being accustomed to his lack of punctuality I wasn't quite ready, so I told Antonio to have him wait in the parlor.

Leon didn't go into the parlor, and told Antonio that he would be in Father's office instead. Leon shuffled around, and then started pacing frantically—first sitting on the couch, only to pop right back up, as quickly as he sat down. Then he started pacing again, his eyes traveling around the room, anxiously looking for something.

As I walked into the office, Leon acted surprised, and ran headlong into the large coffee table that was in front of the couch. I asked him what was wrong, because I had been observing his behavior for a few minutes as I approached the open door to Father's office. He told me that he had lost something in the room, and desperately needed to find it.

"Good heavens Leon, what did you lose? When did you lose it? And what is so important that it has you this jumpy?"

"I lost it last…"

The phone rang, and as I answered it I was still looking to Leon for a response when I noticed that his face looked as though he had just seen a ghost. Alex was on the phone, ordering me to not go anywhere, not even with Uncle Leon, until detective Green arrived.

I blurted out to Alex, "Okay…alright…I won't move!"

Leon kept pacing frantically, and rubbing his hands together with great fervor—I looked at him lovingly, yet with concern in my voice asked, "Leon, what is wrong with you?"

He didn't even look up at me, but continued pacing, as I said to him, "You lost it last what? What were you saying?"

Leon looked at me for a moment, and then stared out into space, ignoring me. Feeling quite frustrated, and out of character myself, I yelled, "Last what? You lost it last what?"

"Oh...um...last week," he said in a quiet voice, as he looked down. Becoming very nervous, he started pacing again. This behavior was so out of character for Uncle Leon—I didn't quite know how to deal with him.

"What in the world did you lose Leon? You are acting so weird, what is going on in your head?"

Breaking his pacing pattern, Leon walked over to the window, and stared outside so intently, as though he was wishing to be anywhere else except where he was at this moment.

I had forgotten momentarily about our extensive entertaining, and what we did when we found things in the house, but upon remembering, I blurted out, "Wait a minute Leon, if you lost whatever it was, last week, then Maria would have found it, and put it in the lost-and-found basket! Come on Leon, let's check the basket! Now, what was it you lost?"

Reluctantly Leon began to tell me what he had lost. "An antique gold cigarette case."

"Cigarette case? Leon, you don't smoke!"

"I know Gabi, but I didn't use it for cigarettes."

"Then what did you use it for?"

"Well, actually it was a gift that I just received."

"And this person didn't know that you don't smoke?"

"Yes, of course they knew!"

"Then why did they give it to you? What did you use it for? And who was it from? Who would give you a cigarette case, when they know you don't smoke?"

"Geez Gabi, enough with the interrogation—alright?"

By this time I was very frustrated with Leon—he wasn't making any sense at all. I was also losing my patience—I pulled the lost-and-found basket out of the closet, and threw it at him.

"Leon, what's going on?"

Leon knew that I stayed pretty calm and composed for the most part, but once I reached my limit I was not a very sweet thing to deal with. We searched through the many things in the basket, but a gold cigarette case was not among them. At this point, Leon was beyond jumpy, and looked as though he was a drug addict who was coming out of his skin, needing a fix! He was so jumpy that he was making me nervous from just watching him, and since he was on my very last nerve, I was just about ready to slap him!

Trying not to pounce on him, I blurted out, "This gift must have been from someone pretty important."

He answered me with the same tone, "Yes, come on Gabi give me a break—that case came from your father!"

"My Father?"

"Yes, and it wasn't just a cigarette case, there was a very important list inside!"

"When did Father give it to you?"

"A few days before he passed away."

"What kind of a list was it, and why didn't I know about it? And if it was so important then why was the case out of your hands? And furthermore, why did you tell me that you lost it a week ago? Come on Leon, what's going on?"

By now, it was all I could do to not scream at him. I was holding back the tears, and my throat was getting so tight I could barely swallow like it always did when I got extremely upset. Because of the events of the past few weeks my mind was pretty dull, however as my mind revisited something Leon said, I instantly blurted out, "Wait just a doggone minute Leon! When I answered the phone, you were saying that you lost that case last…then you stopped talking, and started to turn as pale as a ghost. Were you going to say, last night?"

We've all played poker together for years, and Leon's face was always a bust—he was not a good poker player. Right now his face was telling me he knew something and he was extremely uncomfortable.

"Oh no! You weren't the person that came into the house last night, were you? The one I saw running to the back, and then screeching away in a black sedan?"

Looking quite surprised, Leon said, "Gabrielle, what are you talking about?"

As I started explaining the story, I wasn't sure how, or if he was involved, but he kept nodding his head, and acting like he had something else to add...then he blurted out, "I was only doing what your father wanted me to do!"

I trusted Uncle Leon with all my heart, as did Father, but I asked him anyway, "Were you the one I saw running out of here? And if you were, why Leon?"

Sounding very convincing, Leon calmly said, "No, it wasn't me running from the house, or leaving in the Lincoln."

My mind gave pause for a moment, and then I said to him, "Yeah, I guess it was a Lincoln...but how did you know that?"

Then the whole story began...

"Your father told me that on the day of his funeral, I was to meet with..." then Uncle Leon looked down, and paused, for a very long time.

I gasped as I said, "Meet with who?"

"Gabi, I don't want to tell you his name right now."

"Why Leon—why can't you tell me who you were meeting?"

"It's not important at this point. Anyway, my instructions were to give him the letter, and he would take care of..."

I interrupted him, "Wait a minute Leon, I thought you said it was a list, not a letter!"

"Well actually, it's both."

"Okay, so you were supposed to meet this guy, here?"

"Yes, because your father knew that everyone would be at the funeral."

"I see—then what?"

"Well, this guy and I got into a very heated argument regarding how to handle the information, which is exactly what Michael was afraid would happen. I knew what your father wanted, and this guy didn't agree with me. During our very animated conversation, a few things got moved in the office—I accidentally dropped the cigarette case, and knowing that everyone would be here soon, I told him to leave."

"Wow Leon, what did Father say in that letter?"

"Not now Gabrielle—I don't want to discuss it now. Anyway, I looked for the case quickly, but it was nowhere to be found, and then I left a few minutes later, because I didn't want the staff to come home and catch me here."

"So then, who was it that was running from the house when I arrived?"

"It must have been him—he was driving a black Lincoln! But what's confusing to me is why he came back here. He must have come back, and found the case! I knew that I should have stayed to look for it, but I was too concerned about the staff. Boy was that ever a bad judgment call on my part!"

"Yes Leon it was! But how did he get back in here without tripping the alarm?"

"I rushed out so quickly that I forgot to reset it. Oh Gabi, what are we going to do now?"

Surprised by his question, I said firmly, "Leon, what do you mean, 'what are we going to do?'"

"Did I say we? I meant, what am I going to do?"

"I think we have a bigger problem on our hands than what you're telling me, and I want to get to the bottom of this right now! I don't know if he found your cigarette case or not, all I know is that Father's picture is missing."

Leon's head just about snapped off his body as he quickly turned to look in my direction and make sure that he heard what he thought he heard. "Did you say that picture of all of us on your birthday, is missing?"

"Yes Leon, it's gone!"

"Oh no! Oh no, no Gabrielle! This is not good, not good at all."

"Uncle Leon, what is going on? You're starting to really scare me. I need to call Alex, so he and Charles can come back here and talk with you."

Leon interrupted me and yelled, "Absolutely not! Get them off this case immediately!"

"Why? I want that picture, and you seem to know who took it! And your case with that list, or letter, or whatever it is—don't you want them back?"

Leon headed for the door, "Gabrielle, I'll be back later, you stay put."

"No Leon, where are you going? What are you doing?"

"I have to find him before he…" The door slammed behind him. With the way Uncle Leon was acting, I knew that something was terribly wrong—I stood in the middle of the room, tears streaming down my face…

Just then, he stormed back in and said in a very stern voice, "Whatever you do, do not tell Alex and Charles, or anyone what I just told you, do you understand me Gabrielle?"

As he flew back out the door, I cried out, "Yes Leon."

Our family was very close with Alex and Charles, but as close as we were, we would never go against what the family requested, especially Uncle Leon. When Father wasn't home, Leon was in full charge of everything, both personally and professionally. Next to Father, Leon always knew what was best for the family. Somehow I had to convince Alex to call off the investigation.

Suddenly, out of dead silence there was a knock on the door, so forceful it sounded like 'King-Kong.' Antonio ushered a very large man in, escorting him right to my side. He actually placed him within my space bubble, making me feel slightly uncomfortable. Evidently, upon his arrival he told Antonio who he was, the importance of why he was here, and Antonio felt obliged to walk him directly to where I was standing.

This large man stuck out his muscular arm, which was attached to one of the most beautiful hands I had ever seen on a man. Father had great hands—that was one feature I was extremely attracted to in men. Then in a very deep voice he said, "I'm here to take care of you, my name is Detective Stephen Green."

"Take care of me?"

"Yes Miss, Alex sent me, and I'm not supposed to leave your side, until otherwise instructed to do so."

As he spoke, I checked him out from head to toe, a definite 'Rambo' character. I could tell he took his job very seriously.

"Okay Rambo! Just give me a little space. I'm going up to my room for a minute."

Chapter 4

Sitting on my bed, all I could think about was how badly I acted towards Uncle Leon. Something was obviously very wrong with him for his behavior to be so radically different than usual. And for me to call Alex before I called Uncle Leon was totally out of line on my part. Father always told me that when there was a problem to go to Uncle Leon first. I could feel my blood pressure rising as I continued to berate myself—what in the world was I thinking?

'Okay Gabi, calm down—just ask Stone to drop the case, and explain that you made a mistake. Yeah right—that's never going to happen! Come on Gabi, think, what should you tell Alex?' As I was going over the details in my mind, I remembered that nothing was mentioned to Alex about the cigarette case, that was a good thing, I guess. My train of thought was interrupted by the sound of heavy footsteps as Antonio was ushering Rambo up the stairs. 'Oh no, what does he want now?—I was in no mood to go another round with him.'

I didn't even open my door, I just yelled out, "Hey, Detective Green, I really need some space. Why don't you go pump some iron or something? The gym is down the stairs, third door on the left."

As soon as the words fell out of my mouth, I instantly felt horrible, thinking that I could say something so mean, but I was in such a sarcastic mood at the moment that I really didn't care.

Detective Green called back to me, "Thanks for the offer, but I'll remain right outside your door—let me know if you need anything."

'Okay, so he's polite—well goody for Rambo.' I walked over to the door, swung it open so hard that it almost knocked off one of my toes, glared at him, gave him a sickeningly phony smile, and slammed the door shut again. 'Well now, that was an effective and classy act—what is wrong with me?'

Knowing that I had to find Alex in a hurry, and knowing that I had to tell him a lie was making my behavior somewhat colorful at the moment. Lying was appalling to me, and I wasn't in the habit of doing it, so I was getting increasingly nervous.

I tried to call him at home first, "Hi Sandi, is Alex there?"

"No Gabi, he's at the precinct, but I think you can reach him on his cell. Are you okay?"

"Yes Sandi, I'm fine thanks, I'll talk to you later."

Sandi has been Alex's wife for twenty years, but due to a tragic accident, their marriage has been anything but pleasant. Fifteen years ago, they lost their three-year-old daughter in a drunk-driving accident, which almost took Sandi's life as well. She was in a coma for six weeks, and hasn't been the same since. The coma left Sandi with a few personalities that she slips in and out of, all too frequently.

Father and Alex were outraged by the outcome of the trial. The drunk driver received a punishment of only three years in jail, which is why Father founded the organization SDD, Stop Drunk Driving. This non-profit organization was one that Father donated several million dollars to this last decade alone for everything from educating the high school and college kids in our state, to their famous SDD Homes. These SDD shelters are for intoxicated people, where they can actually spend the night, and not leave until they're sober. They also had an SDD taxi service that anyone could call, and for a nominal price would either be taken to their home, or to the SDD shelter. Father was passionate about this cause as he saw first hand how drastically those who drink and drive irresponsibly, affected lives.

Father told me that poor Alex blamed himself for years. Consequently he immersed himself in work just to cope with the loss of their child, and the drastic, sad change in Sandi. Then, six years ago Alex seemed to become even more distant from Sandi, acting like he had no spouse at all by either working an extreme amount of overtime, or spending his off hours with Father and me.

I think the reason Alex and I have such a great relationship is because I was the closest thing that he ever had to a child, so he was almost like a second father to me. Sandi refused to ever get pregnant again. I'm not quite sure if it was Sandi, or if it was one of the other three personalities that made the decision, but either way, she never did.

After I hung up the phone with Sandi, I remembered that Alex had recently changed his cell number. I didn't have the new one yet, so I yelled through the door at the detective to give me Alex's new number.

"Hey Green, do you know Alex's new cell number?"

After he politely told me the number, I pounded it into the phone, and started hating myself for how awful I was acting.

"Hi Alex! Yes, I'm fine, but I have some interesting news!"

I sat there for a moment and wondered if I should tell him a lie or not. Then I analyzed the facts. 'Alex is already involved, this whole thing is starting to sound pretty weird to me, and maybe Alex could help me figure it out.' At the last moment I decided against the truth, and told Alex the story I had rehearsed—I was hoping that he was buying my ridiculous story, because I certainly wasn't.

"Gabrielle, where exactly did you find the lost picture? What was Leon doing at the house, and why was he running?"

I knew that Alex would be very inquisitive, and wouldn't accept what I was saying without drilling me. I was prepared for that, and kept repeating the same thing over and over again—only this time, I answered in an exasperated voice.

"Well Alex, the picture had been accidentally placed in a drawer after Maria dusted the desk. Leon came over to the house to find something he had misplaced, which he found, and then left the house in a hurry, because he was late for something."

"Late for what, Gabi?"

"How in the heck am I supposed to know what he was late for?"

"Gabrielle, what do I hear in your voice?"

"Alex, you have absolutely got to be kidding me! What you hear in my voice, is that we just buried my father after a horrible illness, and I am totally exhausted!"

"Gabrielle, I know you're spent—we all are, honey. Well, since you seem to be quite sure that Leon was our mystery guest—then, if you're satisfied with everything, I am too. Go ahead and send Detective Green back to the office—oh, and by the way, how was he?"

"A little over the top Alex, but I think he'll make a mighty fine Rambo Cop—is there anything else?"

At that, he said good-bye. I hated being a disgusting liar. I felt horrible for treating Alex with such disrespect, however in spite of my poor behavior, I did feel pretty good for pulling something over on "The great" Alexander Stone. That was a first, which tells me that he must have been extremely busy, or very tired, because normally he wouldn't tolerate that attitude from anyone, not even me.

Glad to dismiss my shadow, I threw open the door, and relayed the message from Alex to Detective Green. I thanked him for his services, and then nicely shook his hand. He probably thought I was a total and complete nut case, but at that point I didn't much care.

I quickly shut my door and started calling Uncle Leon, only to be diverted to his voice mail. I left three messages—each one getting more and more frantic! At this point I was very stressed, and very, very tired.

I hadn't eaten much of anything in the last five days. I was starting to feel like I was having an out-of-body experience—not that I'd had one before, but my body felt tingly and my mind was fuzzy, like I was disconnecting. I jumped into bed, and before I knew it I was sound asleep. I quickly fell into a deep sleep and started dreaming instantly.

As my dream began, I was very young—Father and I were standing in my bedroom. I looked up at him asking, "Where are we going Father?"

He looked down, and smiled at me as he walked to my closet, picked out my best Sunday dress, carefully put it on me, combed my long brown curls, and then placed the matching hat on my head. 'This must be a special occasion—Father is dressing me in my very best dress, with my fancy hat, and all.'

"Father where are we going? Are we going to a party?"

Father replied in a deep and quiet voice, "No, we're going to the park, Princess."

"Am I going to see Mother? Will she tell me a story?"

"Yes Princess, this will be the..."

My dream became terribly disturbing. All of a sudden I sat straight up in bed, my heart was beating, so hard and so rapidly I thought it was coming out of my chest. I was perspiring and my mind was racing like I was high on caffeine. I jumped out of bed so fast that I saw stars, and started pacing back and forth in my room. I couldn't get the details of the dream out of my head—it was all too strange. I've never dreamt about a mother before, so why now? 'This is making me crazy, what's wrong with me? Why am I dreaming about having a mother? I know what it is—I'm hallucinating because I'm so hungry—yes, that's it!'

As I ran downstairs to the kitchen, the dream was playing over, and over again in my mind. I stopped suddenly right in front of the cupboard, and stood there, staring at it, forgetting just exactly why I was standing there. After a moment, I remembered what I was doing. I quickly threw open the cupboard, grabbed a box of cookies, and started stuffing them into my mouth, one right after the other. I was barely finished eating one cookie, as I quickly shoved another one into my mouth—chewing faster and faster, staring harder and longer into space. I was so lost in my thoughts I didn't even notice Maria was standing very still on the other side of the kitchen, staring at me in shock.

"Gabi dear, slow down! Are you okay?"

"No Maria, I'm not okay, I am NOT O-KAY! But tell me, can a person hallucinate if they've been deprived of food?"

"Yes Gabi, yes! Crazy thoughts can come into your head when your body is depleted of nutrition, or if your body is run down. You know that!"

"Quite frankly Maria, I don't know what I know right now."

"Gabrielle, let me make you something good to eat. Put those cookies away!"

Maria warmed up some of her famous enchiladas, which I ate in no time flat! I thanked her for always taking such good care of me, and I rushed off to Ashlee's house.

I usually called Ashlee first, but I was still so lost in my thoughts about that bizarre dream—all I could think of was getting there. Ashlee was not only my best friend, she was a psychology major, and always had some good insight about weird thoughts.

When I arrived, I saw that Ashlee was just leaving with her date. As I started getting back into my car she saw me, quickly ran over, threw her arms around me, and gave me one of her very tight, 'I'm-so-glad-to-see-you' hugs! Feeling badly that I interrupted her night I said, "Ashlee, I am so sorry that I interrupted something—I'll just see you tomorrow."

"Gabi, look at me…what's wrong?"

"Nothing, absolutely nothing…"

Before I could finish my sentence, she walked over to her date, said something to him, and he left.

Ashlee ran back over to me with a look of dismay on her face as she said, "Gabrielle, don't try to fool me—I know you better than that! So besides the obvious, what's bothering you?"

"Ashlee, you didn't have to make him leave—and by the way, who was he?"

"I met him at school, but forget about him, let's go talk."

Ashlee changed her clothes into something more comfortable, and explained to Norm, her butler, that we didn't want to be disturbed. She sat me down on the couch opposite her, remaining silent for a moment as she stared deep into my eyes, "What is going on?"

"Hey Ash, thanks for caring so much about me."

"Gabi, like you've never cared for me?"

"I know, but just thanks."

"So Gabi, your eyes look troubled, and there's something in your voice. You sound like you're almost," and she paused… "Scared—talk to me."

"Ashlee, how do you feel about dreams? Can people dream about things that aren't true and are totally crazy—things that make no sense at all?"

"Gabi, I'm sure that anything is possible, and you know how strongly I feel about dreams, having studied them for years. Dreams are very interesting, sometimes through our dreams we deal with situations that we can't cope with while we're awake."

"But Ashlee, what if the situation that you're dreaming about is nothing that you're knowingly trying to cope with?"

"Many times we aren't aware of what has been repressed in our minds, and what we are subconsciously dealing with."

"Ash, this dream is just so bizarre, yet at the same time, it is so incredibly real. This is the second time I've dreamt the same thing within the last couple of days. I don't know whether it's because I'm stressed, exhausted, or because I've been taking tranquilizers. Or, maybe it's from not eating, or maybe…"

Ashlee interrupted, "Gabi, I know you hate drugs, but mild tranquilizers would not cause that! So…tell me about your dreams."

I knew that Ashlee was a great listener, and I really needed some insight, or advice, or something, so I explained the dreams to her in vivid detail. She never said a word, but kept nodding her head the entire time I was talking. When I finally finished telling my story, there was a dead silence as we both just stared into space.

Suddenly, we were knocked out of our trance-like state, and just about fell off the couches when my cell phone started ringing.

"Dang…that scared me! Sorry Ashlee."

"Me too…answer the darn thing!"

It was Uncle Leon, telling me that we needed to talk immediately. I explained to Ashlee that I had to leave, and apologized for ruining her evening. Ashlee was most gracious as she hugged me, and told me to come back later if I felt like it.

"Nice to see ya, Uncle! Why in the heck did you ignore my messages?"

"Gabrielle, get yourself in the parlor, and watch how you talk to me. Have you taken leave of your senses?"

"Excuse me Leon, but have you taken leave of yours? You tell me this crazy story then leave me hanging! And yes, I think I have!"

"You have what?"

"I've taken a rather large—no let me rephrase that, a rather HUGE leave of my senses, and I feel like I'm going crazy. For the last few days everything seems so surreal, and nothing makes any sense at all."

"Sit down Gabi."

"Leon, that look on your face is starting to scare me."

"Well, for the first time in my life, I'm not quite sure what to do."

With my heart beating so hard that I could barely talk, I screamed, "Leon, now you are definitely scaring me!"

Leon was wearing the same clothes that he had been in since yesterday, which were now extremely wrinkled—he was very pale behind his unshaven face, and I had never seen him look that unkempt or worried, which was so out of character for Leon.

He began to walk towards me, looking as though he was contemplating saying something quite profound.

"Gabrielle, I want you to know…"

I interrupted him, because I really didn't want to know anything else at the moment—my mind was on over load, and my heart was searching for something that made sense. As Uncle Leon stared at me, he looked like Father with those piercing eyes, which always meant that he had something serious to discuss with me. Leon's demeanor instantly went beyond serious to very solemn as he said, "First of all, I need to tell you something that is going to come as a shock to you."

"Leon, believe me, absolutely nothing could shock me today."

"I'm not so sure you'll think that when I'm through…"

I cut his sentence short, "For heaven's sake Leon, what could be so shocking?"

"Do you remember the strange man that came up to you at the funeral?"

"Leon, did you see that handsome stranger talking with me?"

"Yes, and he whispered in your ear, 'They will pay.'"

"Oh come on Leon, you're trying to really freak me out! How could you have heard that? You were yards away, and I didn't tell you what he said."

"I know you didn't, he did."

"Who is he?" I yelled.

"His name is Eric."

"How do you know him?"

"Gabrielle, I know this is going to be hard…but, Eric…is your brother."

I stood up and almost fell back down from feeling so light-headed. I could hardly believe what my ears were hearing. First my weird dreams, then this crazy story that Leon was fabricating—it was just too much to deal with right now. I walked over to Leon…held his head firmly in my hands…looked him squarely in the eyes and said, "Leon, I feel like I'm losing my mind—please be honest with me, and tell me the truth about everything, right now!"

"I know how hard this must be for you, but believe me Gabrielle, Eric is your brother."

"Okay, you got me! I'm shocked—I'm freaked out—I'm over the edge! Are you happy now? Why do you want to do this to me? And let me ask you this, how could he possibly be my brother?"

"Because he's your father's son."

"I don't believe you Leon—this is just too, too weird! Why are you lying to me?"

As he raised his voice, Leon said, "Gabrielle Deliano, have I ever lied to you?"

Looking sheepishly at him, I said in a very quiet voice, "No."

The story seemed somewhat believable. This Eric guy did look like me. We both had thick, dark hair, and the same dark brown eyes, and our skin was the exact same shade of an olive tone, and he must have been almost Father's height, which was about seven inches taller than me…

"Now I suppose you're going to tell me that I have a sister too! Was there another sibling at the funeral that I don't know about?"

Leon gave me a crazy look, so I knew that was a stupid question.

"Well, why did he just show up like that? Where has he been? And why didn't he tell me who he was?"

"Because there was entirely too much to explain, and he didn't have time to approach you before the service."

"How long had he known about Father's death?"

"He knew about everything as it was happening. Eric was the mystery man that I was meeting, and the one who was running from the house last night. That's why I couldn't tell you who he was at first, because there was too much to explain."

"Well there still is Leon—there's still an awful lot to explain!"

"I know Gabi."

"Let's start with at least something that I do know about, like what was he doing here. Why were you guys having such a heated argument? And how could he have been talking to Father all this time? Oh my goodness Leon, I just remembered something! Father kept saying the name, Eric to me those last couple of days, and I didn't realize what he meant at the time, because I thought he was delirious—was it the same Eric?"

"Yes Gabi."

"Do we have the same mother?"

"Yes, you do."

As soon as I heard the word 'Yes' fall out of Leon's mouth, I must have fainted, because when I came to, I was on my bed. Uncle Leon must have brought me up to my room and put me to bed, because I found a note on my nightstand from him that said:

Dear Gabrielle,

I'm sorry about the way I had to deliver the news about Eric, but things are happening so quickly. You need to trust me, and remember what I said yesterday about your father wanting this whole thing handled very differently. I'll explain everything later. I have some other extremely important issues to take care of, so I've instructed the staff to leave you alone. Get some rest Gabi. I'll be back soon.

I Love You,

Uncle Leon

My mind was racing now. I remembered the strong feelings I had yesterday about the funeral seeming like a mysterious new beginning—certainly having a brother would definitely be a new beginning, as well as mysterious. 'Oh my...I have a brother! Where has he been all my life? And why didn't he live with Father and me? Oh Uncle Leon, hurry back—I have so many questions, like how could we have the same mother?'

My mind started whirling, and I was beginning to feel very dizzy from this completely bizarre information! Did Uncle Leon say that I have a Mother or that I had a Mother? Everyone had a mother, but mine was killed in a car accident when I was five, and I don't remember much else. Father doesn't have a picture of mother anywhere. He explained to me years ago, that it was too painful to have her pictures out—he adored her so much, it only made him miss her more.

My cell rang, and startled me out of my dizzying thoughts. It was Sandi. "Is Alex still with you?"

"No Sandi, I haven't seen him since this morning."

"What do you mean you, 'Haven't seen him since this morning'?"

"Sandi, he was here early this morning, and then he left."

"Listen Gabi, he said that he was going to your house to finish up some case he was working on, so let me talk to him, NOW!"

"Sandi, I assure you that he's not here. Maybe you misunderstood where he said he would be right now."

"Listen, you little tart! How dare you talk to me like that! You, sitting in your gorgeous, mansion, on your little 'Ice Princess' butt! You don't deserve to be there, and if it wasn't for your father…"

"Excuse me, Sandi!"

Then she screamed out, "Because of you, Michael is…"

I interrupted her, because by this point I was ready to lose it. I knew that Sandi wasn't herself, yet I couldn't let her get away with what she was saying.

I blurted out at her, "Michael is what, Sandi?"

"Nothing, just nothing! Why did you call me, Gabi?"

"Sandi, you called me! And I don't know who you are right now, or what you're talking about. Alex isn't here, and I'm going to hang up."

Sandi was displaying one of her other personalities that we so often had to endure. I knew most of what she was saying never made any sense, but this is the first time that she had ever called me 'Ice Princess,' and that bothered me. I wondered where she came up with that name, or if she had read it in the newspaper article. 'What did she mean when she said that I didn't deserve to be here? And what was she trying to say about Father?' Even though I knew better than to try and analyze any of her crazy personalities, I couldn't help but wonder what she meant by her accusations. I was so bothered that I had to call her back.

"Hi Sandi, it's Gabi."

"Hi Angel Face, how are you doing?"

With that greeting, I knew right away that this was not the same Sandi that I had been talking to only moments ago. I also knew that she wouldn't remember a word that she had said, so I told her I was fine, and then tried to get off the phone as quickly as possible.

But, before I could hang up, she launched into something about Mrs. C. Sandi has always hated Mary, and all of her personalities were in agreement on that. She started criticizing how long Mary was standing by Father's casket, and that Father and Mary were just a little too close.

At that comment, I had to cut her off and hang up, before I blew up at her. Mentioning Mary's name did remind me that I hadn't heard from her at all since the funeral, which wasn't like her. I was concerned about how she was feeling so I called Mary, only to get a busy signal. 'I'll call her later.'

My bed looked so comfortable, and I was quite exhausted. Uncle Leon said to rest—that sounded pretty good right now. I slipped off my shoes, and climbed underneath the comforter, feeling a little chilled, and very tired.

Chapter 5

The dream began immediately. A black ocean separating slowly—revealing a beautiful woman dressed in a flowing, black formal dress, with her dark, curly hair falling loosely around her exquisitely sculpted face. Seeming to float amidst the fog, the woman began moving towards me, holding out her hand, elegant and manicured perfectly. With apprehension, I slowly lifted my arm. She gently took hold of my hand, and wrapped her long, delicate fingers around mine—I felt instantly secure in her firm and loving embrace. As I looked up to see the woman's face, I was shocked to see her dress instantly change from black to white. Her hair was also different—it was now much longer, and straight.

As I stood there trying to understand why everything was changing, my hand began shrinking inside of hers. Perplexed, I looked down at myself and noticed that I was also changing, and had become a skinny, little five-year-old. I kept trying to see the woman's face, but the flowing white dress kept blowing in the breeze, blocking my view. As we walked hand in hand, all I could see was her back. Her hand felt so warm, and so loving that I felt a sense of peace just walking by her side. As I glanced up, our surroundings had also changed. Now, to my surprise, we were walking in that beautiful park, where the dogwoods were in bloom—a clean smell filled the air, and the birds were singing joyfully. I especially liked smelling the freshly mowed grass, and the sweet-scented flowers.

I looked up at her again and said, "Where are we going, Mother?"
She replied in such a sweet voice, "To our special place, Gabrielle."
I quizzically replied, "Our special place?"
"Yes, Dear."
"Where is that, Mother?"
Then I heard Father's voice say, "Sterling, it's time."
I woke up so abruptly that my thoughts continued, as I lay there wishing that Father would go away so that I could be with this woman. These dreams and my thoughts of them, were becoming one—so much so, that I couldn't distinguish between where the dreams ended, and where my thoughts of them began. The line was starting to blur, and it felt so strange.

'Who was that beautiful, warm and loving woman, and why am I calling her Mother? For heaven's sake Gabi, what is wrong with you? Stop it—that was just a dream!'

I couldn't understand my feelings, or why I was having such bizarre dreams that seemed so incredibly real. I knew that Ashlee would have helped me sort through this weirdness if I could have just finished talking with her. 'If only Uncle Leon hadn't interrupted us with that phone call.' I really needed to talk to someone. Ashlee wasn't home, so I picked up the phone to call my sweet and understanding friend, Mary.

Mary's phone was busy again, which was quite odd. She had the call-waiting feature, and I had never heard her phone ring busy before. It was almost nine o'clock in the evening, and I usually wouldn't go to a person's house that late at night unannounced, but Mary was different—she was like family. I went to the back door—Mary was usually in her very large parlor, listening to music on that side of the house. The back door didn't have a doorbell, so I knocked hard several times, but no answer. Thinking that there was a slight chance that Mary was in the grand, front room, I started for the other side of the house.

I walked on the pathway through Mary's huge flower garden that stretched alongside the entire length of her house. As I started walking through the beautifully manicured section of roses, I noticed that one of her prize rose bushes had some branches that were bent, and a few roses were lying on the ground. I knelt down to fix the branch, and pick up a freshly bloomed rose, along with some of its missing petals when I saw fresh footprints. I knew they didn't belong to Mary—they were quite large. Seeing the bush broken was a little unsettling to me. I knew that Mary would never leave her garden in such disarray—not even for one day.

Being a little suspicious of the situation, I felt compelled to run to the front door—I quickly started pounding on it while ringing the doorbell at the same time. Only a minute passed, but it seemed like forever until the door opened.

Mary sounded a little frazzled as she asked, "Why Gabi, how are you dear?"

Quickly I blurted out, "I'm fine, but how are you?"

She answered slowly, "Ducky—just ducky, thank you."

The door was barely ajar, with Mary standing in the small opening so as not to let me in. She had the oddest look on her face, which gave me pause, mainly because I had never heard Mary use the word 'ducky' before.

Knowing that everyone grieves in a very unique manner, I was attempting to be respectful of her privacy, yet I was quite concerned about her very odd behavior.

"Mary, you don't seem like yourself—are you okay? Your rosebush has been badly broken, and there were foot…"

She interrupted me and said, "Yes Dear, I'm as ducky as ever, however I am a little tired, and I was just climbing into bed. You go on home now, I'll see you in the morning."

I kissed her cheek, and out of respect for her I started for home, however, something inside of me felt very strange as I walked off, holding the rose petals in my hand. 'Why did she cut me off like that? Why was she acting so weird? And why in the world did she say, "ducky"?' I guess that Mary was dealing with the stress of losing Father in her own way, but she just seemed so totally out of character to me—I had never seen her act even remotely close to the way she was acting tonight. But then who was I to judge? With the way I've been thinking and acting lately, not to mention, the weird dreams I've been having.

As I walked home I was thinking about how desperately I needed to talk to Mary, to Uncle Leon, to someone I felt close to—the only other people that I felt I could share my heart with were Jacob and Ashlee, but I didn't want to bother either one of them right now. Just as I was crossing the lawn and stepping onto the driveway Alex came screeching up in his car, almost hitting me, and before it even stopped he rolled the window down, and in a very stern voice said, "Gabi, what are you doing out here?"

I wanted to respond with a rude and sarcastic remark, however at the last second, deciding that this was not the best time to provoke him, I nicely said, "I went to Mary's house."

"What were you doing over there?"

"I wanted to talk with her, but she was going to bed."

"Isn't it kind of early for her?"

"Well yes, but her retiring early wasn't the oddest part of my visit—she was acting very strange. I guess she's just tired and stressed. But one thing that was really weird Alex, I found footprints in her garden—they looked fresh, and they weren't Mary's. It's obvious that whomever they belonged to, smashed part of her rose bush—look, here is one of the roses I found on the ground."

"Well Gabi, you said that Leon came running out of the house, maybe he ran over to Mary's. Maybe that's the meeting he was late for."

For a minute, I had almost forgotten about the lie that I told Alex. As I stood there staring at him, he cocked his head to the side, his eyebrows furrowed, and just as he started to speak, I interrupted him.

"Oh yes Alex! You're probably right, I'm sure that was it."

At that point I wanted to just disappear, poor Alex was going on the assumption that the story I told him was true! My bad! My very, very bad!

Alex could tell that I was deep in thought, as he walked over to me, put his hand on the top of my head and said, "Earth to Gabi, are you okay?"

"Yes Alex, thanks for checking on me, I'm okay. Hey Alex, are you finally going home now?"

"What do you mean Gabi? I've been home for hours."

"Sandi called here looking for you."

"That doesn't make sense Gabi, because Sandi has been watching movies all night in the parlor, and she told me that she didn't want to be disturbed, so of course, I honored her wishes and went downstairs to work in my office. I guess she took leave of her senses for a while."

"That's okay Alex, don't worry about me, I feel sorry for you."

"Well you don't need to concern yourself over Sandi and me, you have enough on your mind."

"You know Alex, you can always come over here and work out in the gym whenever you like, because Father would want you to continue doing that."

"Thanks Gabi, I will, but I'm not quite ready yet—the gym reminds me too much of Michael."

I hugged Alex very tightly and then kissed his cheek. He was such a big, loving teddy-bear type of a man, and I felt so sorry for him, having to deal with Sandi's abusive personalities on a daily basis.

"Good-night Alex."

"Good-night, sweet Gabi."

Even though it was late, I couldn't sleep, so I went into Father's office and opened the safe, wanting to review what it was that Father had been working on. There were many things inside that large manila envelope, including a spreadsheet, with huge amounts of money being transferred from one account to another. As I was trying to recognize the unidentifiable account numbers, I became transfixed on the sheet.

The phone rang, startling me, causing me to jump, and knock the phone on the floor—when I answered it, there was no response. Then I remembered the same thing happening last night, which made it seem a little more unsettling tonight. I paused for a moment before I again said, "Hello, who is this?"

There was still no response, but I could slightly hear someone breathing, then after a few long seconds a man's voice said, "Is this Gabrielle?"

I wasn't quite sure, but I thought that the voice sounded familiar, so I responded very slowly. "Yes, it is."

"It's Sonny!"

Sonny lived in Europe, and sometimes there were pauses in the connections. I remembered Sonny's warm embrace, and sweet kiss on my cheek, as he expressed his regrets at the funeral.

"Hi Sonny! How are you? I'm so glad to hear from you."

"Gabrielle, I am so sorry that I didn't have a chance to visit with you after Michael's service, but it was imperative that I return to Europe. How are you doing?"

"I'm doing okay Sonny, and don't worry about rushing off, because I know how busy you are. Father has always said that you were one of his right hand men, so please, no need to apologize. And just because Father passed away, doesn't mean that we stop taking care of business, because 'the show must go on,'" just as those words fell out of my mouth, I instantly questioned my sanity.

Sonny ran the import-export division of Deliano shipping. He was absolutely gorgeous, quite tall and sexy, with blonde hair and blue eyes, and he had the dreamiest voice I'd ever heard. His voice was so soothing that it was like medicine to my soul, and for a minute I got lost in it, and forgot what we were talking about.

"Oh excuse me Sonny, I got lost in your voice again!"

He laughed. He was aware of the affect his voice had on women, then he repeated what he had said to me, "That's right Princess, we can't stop running the business. That's why I called, I need to talk to Leon, is he there?"

"No, but he should be home any time—you can reach him on his cell though."

"I've tried quite a few times, but no answer, which is not like Leon."

"Yeah, I know Sonny, Leon has been acting pretty weird lately."

"Gabrielle, I must talk to Leon before the end of the night, it's an emergency!"

"Is there anything that I can help you with?"

"No Princess, but thanks for asking. Just make sure that he gets this message, oh and Gabi…"

"Yes."

"Now that Michael is no longer with us, I want you to know, that if you ever need me for anything, make sure you call. I mean it."

As I listened to Sonny's kind words, it was all I could do to not start crying. I didn't want him to feel like he had to console me, since he was in the middle of something quite important. I just said, "Thank you Sonny, I appreciate your support. I'll give Leon the message—take care."

I leaned back in Father's leather chair, closed my eyes, and started thinking about what Uncle Leon had said about that stranger being my brother. I remember how I was instantly drawn to Eric, and I wondered how he felt about me. Oh how different our lives would have been, if we hadn't been separated, and could have lived together as siblings.

Feeling somewhat dizzy again, I laid my head on the desk and began thinking about how none of this made any sense at all. My eyes, feeling very heavy, closed without warning. My drifting thoughts were that I hoped Uncle Leon could straighten everything out when he got home.

I have no idea how much time had passed, but to my groggy mind it seemed like only moments later that I was abruptly awakened by the sound of a car horn, which I figured was Uncle Leon locking his car! Not able to go back to sleep, I lifted my head up off of the desk, trying once again to make sense of the numbers.

A few minutes later the horn went off again, and then quickly turned into one continuous sound. After a minute of listening to that obnoxious horn, and overly anxious to see Uncle Leon, I wondered what he was doing. I flew out of Father's office, running through the foyer almost knocking Antonio down, and then bouncing out the door like a little kid, anxious to see my Uncle!

Uncle Leon's car was parked at the beginning of the circular entrance, on the opposite side of the yard. I wondered why it was way down there and as I approached his car, I yelled with excitement "Hi Uncle Leon! What are you doing?"

I could see Leon in the front seat, bent over fixing something. As I got closer to the car, the noise was so loud, it was piercing my already dizzy head, and I yelled at him to stop, but he obviously couldn't hear me.

I ran up to the car, threw open his door, and all I could do was scream at the top of my lungs. There was Leon, bleeding profusely from his head!

I kept screaming louder and louder, "Oh, Dear God! No, not Uncle Leon!" I pulled him out of the car and onto the grass as I yelled for Antonio. Frantically I searched for a pulse, which I found, ever so slight. Leon's eyes were shut, his breathing faint, blood gushing down his forehead into his mouth. I put his head on my lap, and kept wiping the blood out of his mouth with my blouse.

I don't know why screaming at him made any sense, but I began yelling, "Leon don't leave me, you can't die, you can't! Say something, please! Please, Uncle Leon…TALK TO ME!"

As Antonio approached, I told him to call the ambulance immediately! Even though I knew in my heart that Leon was slipping away fast, I was trying to hang on to any kind of hope that the paramedics could miraculously save him. After a few seconds, I could tell that he was dying. I started praying, silently and fervently, as I held him close to me. I was pleading with God to diminish the pain, and allow him to die in peace.

I held Leon's head with one hand, and as I held his hand with my other, I kept kissing his face, telling him how much I loved him. With Father gone, Leon was the only family I had. Now I was losing him too, which made me feel so vulnerable, and so lost. I held Leon tightly in my arms, my heart racing, knowing that he was slipping away—his body started feeling like Father's did at the end. Suddenly the paramedics screeched onto the scene, jumped out of their ambulance, and ran across the lawn with their equipment.

I ceased yelling, and spoke quietly in his ear, "I love you, Uncle Leon."

His almost lifeless hand gripped my hand with such a weak, little squeeze that I knew the life was leaving his body. I kissed his cheek again, and he started to whisper something so very quietly, that I could barely hear him.

"I got the li…"

"Leon, you got the what?"

He was hardly breathing and his hand was loosening its already light grip. It was all I could do to keep from crying my heart out. Leon was trying to communicate with me, and I was desperate to know what he wanted to say.

"What are you trying to tell me Uncle Leon? What?"

His voice was so breathy that I could barely hear a thing. I placed my ear so close to his mouth that it was touching his cold, dying lips.

"I got the lis."

"The list Leon, you got the list?"

His eyes blinked yes. Then I asked him, "Did you get the letter too?"

His eyes blinked yes, again.

"Leon, where is the list?"

My ear smashed down on his face as I wrapped my arm around his body so I could hold him tightly as he left this world. My mind raced back to what I was thinking as I held Father on his deathbed. My heart started breaking all over again, while at the same time I kept thinking that this must be a bad, bad dream. I knew Uncle Leon only had seconds to live, when I heard the tiniest, faintest sounds floating up to my ear.

"My pock…et…see…Er…ic…love you."

Those were Leon's last words. I motioned for the paramedics to stay where they were while I spent those last moments in a tight embrace, not wanting to let him go.

Maria must have called Alex. He came running over to me so fast it looked as though he was flying.

"Gabi! What happened?"

I could barely see Alex through my tears, and as I stretched out my hand that was dripping with blood, I screamed out, "UNCLE LEON DIED IN MY ARMS! Alex, he was shot in the head, and he died in my arms—just look at him, who could have done this? He's dead Alex, Uncle Leon is dead!"

Alex tried to remain calm as he said, "Gabrielle, did Leon say anything to you?"

Even though I was distraught, I thought for a moment before I answered his question. I knew that Leon didn't trust Alex for some reason, and I knew that I needed to honor his request for silence. I looked up at Alex with a very matter-of-fact face and said, "No, he didn't say a thing."

The paramedics seemed to be moving in slow motion as they took Uncle Leon out of my arms and placed him on the gurney. I could barely watch while they checked his vital signs once more before pulling the sheet over his head. Feeling paralyzed from the shock, I couldn't move as the ambulance drove off with my uncle, who, like Father, would never be coming home again.

Alex pulled me up off the ground and into his arms—his fatherly hug brought the warmth back into my cold, shocked body that was starting to feel frozen inside from these daunting deaths. Alex looked at me in a quizzical manner, and asked me again if Leon said anything at all.

Through my tears, I looked him straight in the eyes and firmly said, "No, he didn't say a thing."

Alex seemed puzzled, and looked somewhat defeated, as he kissed my cheek, shook his head, and placed his arm around my waist to walk me to the house. I told him that I needed to be alone. As I watched him walk away, I wondered what he could have done for Leon to not trust him any more. It was breaking my heart to lie to Alex and to keep him in the dark, because I knew that Father trusted him right up until the very last second of his life. My heart became so heavy that I chased after him, and yelled out, "Alex, wait!"

He looked so pitiful, as he turned and said, "What Princess?"

"Can I walk home with you? I feel so alone and so scared, and there are a few things that I think I should tell you"

He put his arm around me, and we walked to his house without saying a word.

Chapter 6

Sandi greeted us at the door with a big smile and said, "Gabrielle, you're such a sweet daughter to go for a walk with your father—aren't we lucky Alex?"

Alex and I looked at each other knowing that it wasn't really Sandi who was talking, yet neither of us knew the correct thing to say at that moment. Usually we could figure out what she meant, or where she was going with whatever her comments were, but tonight we were still in shock over Uncle Leon. This was the first time she had made such a bizarre statement, and I knew this was not the appropriate time to tell her about Leon, so I just said, "Hi Sandi, how are you?"

Well, that was apparently the wrong thing to say. As soon as the words came out of my mouth she said, "Young Lady, it's not proper to call your mother by her first name, and you know exactly how I am, you both just left here!"

I have never seen Alex unable to handle his wife, but this time, he was totally dumbfounded.

Then Sandi said, "Gabrielle, go on up to bed now—it's getting late, and you have school in the morning."

So as not to upset Sandi, and possibly awaken another one of her personalities, Alex and I played along. I knew once we went upstairs she would go to bed and I could sneak out. We've done a lot of weird things in our quest to keep Sandi pacified, but this was by far, the weirdest.

Alex said that he would turn off the lights in the hall after Sandi went to bed and the coast was clear. I sat on the edge of the bed impatiently waiting for my cue. The guest room was huge with a queen size bed, dresser and nightstands on one side, and a maple roll-top desk, large couch and coffee table on the other side, next to the floor-to-ceiling, river-rock fireplace.

I couldn't bring myself to sit on the couch—it reminded me of when Father and I were shopping for it in France. Father and I sat on that couch for an hour just talking about how much we loved and appreciated Alex, and how excited he would be to receive this awesome piece of furniture for his fortieth birthday.

I was becoming more and more annoyed with each passing minute. I started pacing back and forth—five steps one way, and then tracing the exact pattern, five steps back. Stepping a little too far to the right I stopped dead in my tracks when I hit a place in the floor that made a rather loud creaking sound—I quickly landed at the desk, hoping Sandi hadn't heard it! Admiring the handiwork in the beautiful maple desk, I began running my hands over it, when I noticed one of the drawers was ajar. I tried to close it, but the drawer was quite stuck, so I pulled it open to fix it. As it opened, I could not believe my eyes.

What I saw was so shocking that I let out a screech of disbelief, remembering what Uncle Leon had said about Alex. This was proof positive that Leon was correct in his accusation about Alex, which made me feel so confused and so betrayed. Numb, once again, I sat there trying to decide whether or not I should take the photo.

Moments later the lights went out—I could hear Alex slowly opening the guest room door. The plan wasn't for him to come to my room, so I quickly jumped away from the desk to meet him. I got to the door just as he was opening it—my heart was pounding out of my chest. It was all I could do to look at his face without slapping it. I knew that he was reading my disdain, but at that point I didn't much care. I motioned with my eyes toward the direction of the stairs, and then held my hand up in a motion that meant to stop, so he would just stay put.

Finding the picture made me feel not only betrayed, but also scared and confused. All I could think of was running away from Alex as fast as I could. I tiptoed to the stairs, and started creeping down them very slowly and very, very quietly. After I silently slipped out the front door, I ran as fast as I could, all the way home.

Chapter 7

It seemed like it took forever to reach my house, but when I arrived, I ran straight into Father's office—my only safe haven. Throwing myself into his padded, leather chair, I felt engulfed and so very protected in my cozy chrysalis that I never wanted to depart from it. My mind spun out of control so fast that I felt dizzy from losing so much in such a short time. My life was becoming increasingly complex with Father and Uncle Leon dead. Now that I couldn't trust Alex, nothing in my life made sense anymore, absolutely nothing.

I desperately needed to clear my head. I was so frustrated from the night's adventure with Alex and Sandi, I couldn't think straight. All I could concentrate on was that I couldn't trust Alex, and that I had to hide from "Sandi the Psycho," a name Alex called her when she acted 'Way out there'. Tonight she was definitely way, way out there!

My thoughts were running rampant. I was trying to figure out why Alex had Father's picture, and how in the world I was going to get it back. 'Oh Gabi, just turn your mind off for now before you go crazy—deal with all of this tomorrow.'

I closed my eyes, and tried very hard to clear my mind. After a few minutes, the insanity of the day subsided, as the thoughts of having to plan another funeral lay heavy on me. I started thinking of everything that needed to be done. 'I'll do the eulogy like I did for Father, oh, that was hard. Then I'll…' before I could finish my next thought, I reached for my Bible. I started reading the passage out loud that I had read for Father, "Show me my life's end, and the number of my days; let me know how fleeting is my life…"

As I finished reading, I was struck by the truth of how brief our lives really are, and how we should try to make a difference by doing for others, and by touching lives. What is our life worth, if we don't do for others, and leave a beautiful fragrance behind?

Father's life was such an amazing example of an unselfish life. He always reached out to others, helping them in any way he could. I remember the many times he told me our lives were but a vapor here on earth, and all that mattered was what we did for others.

I sat there thinking about the purpose of my own life, and searching my soul. I kept thinking about Father, and how I wanted to make a difference like he did—I began praying and pleading to God out loud, "Show me what you want me to do with my life, and please give me strength to get through the process of burying another loved one."

My mind was spinning from thoughts that were swirling around at warp speed. 'Let me see now, how should I dress Uncle Leon? Oh my goodness Gabi, it doesn't matter how you dress him, just put him in a nice black suit with a tie, or would he prefer a more casual look? Why in the world didn't anyone tell me that I had a brother? Who is he? Was he really my brother? Uncle Leon said he was, but where is Eric now? Father said to help Eric while in a state of unconsciousness, and I thought he was delusional! Oh Father, how do I help Eric? And help him do what?'

Maybe the answer is in that letter, or the list, or whatever it is. 'Think Gabi, where did you put that list?' I went over my every movement, remembering that I had slipped my hand into the back pocket of my jeans—I knew that I had put the list in that pocket, but now it wasn't there! I must have left it on the... I panicked as I ran out the door and across the lawn as fast as I could run.

When I approached the place where I sat holding Uncle Leon, I could see something on the ground, and hoped beyond hope that it was the list. I made a beeline for it, and sure enough, it was the list! As I was running, I saw something out of the corner of my eye, and noticed that the bushes on the outer perimeter of the yard were moving. It wasn't a windy night, so I stopped suddenly, staring at the bushes until they stopped moving. I started to feel a little uneasy, so I bent over, grabbed the paper and literally bolted back to the house.

Antonio was standing in the middle of the doorway to greet me. He asked what I was doing as I shoved him aside, and continued running straight to Father's office. Just before I closed the door, I yelled back at him to lock up for the night.

"Oh, and Antonio, please release the dogs in the front yard."

He stood there staring at me for a moment before he said, "Gabi, I've already brought them in for the night."

With fervor, and a fanatical look on my face, I turned around, and walked toward Antonio. I said very slowly and very sternly, "Antonio, let them out!" The second those words fell out of my mouth, I felt horrible, "I'm sorry Antonio, I'm just a wee-bit jumpy! I'd feel safer if the dogs went out for a while. You know, with Leon being killed and all."

"Yes Gabi, I understand. I'm sorry for questioning you."

The Dobermans were trained to attack anyone they were not familiar with. It may sound severe, but besides the alarm system, Father felt that they were another good source of protection.

As I walked back to Father's office I heard the dogs barking, which made me even more nervous. However, it didn't sound as though they were in attack mode. Either way, I felt safer knowing that they would be out there, and called Antonio to tell him that I wanted the dogs to stay out for the entire night.

I was feeling very insecure—usually when anything happened while Father or Uncle Leon were out of town, my first response had been to call Alex. Now I wasn't able to call him, evidently he couldn't be trusted. I didn't know Eric, but my instincts told me that I needed to find him. I remember how I felt when he looked into my eyes at the funeral. His eyes were so warm and so sincere; I felt that I could trust him before I knew he was my brother.

As I opened the papers that were creased from being folded in the cigarette case, I couldn't believe my eyes. The list wasn't just a list of people's names; it also had information about each person that went well beyond their addresses and phone numbers. One list appeared to be the names of everyone we knew. The other must be a list of, 'Oh no…' I recognized some of the names, and they were not good people.

There was also a second page. At first glance, it appeared to be a letter. After examining it further, I could tell that it was indeed a letter—it wasn't a short one either, it was three pages long. As I quickly breezed through the pages I couldn't believe what I was seeing, and what I was actually holding! It was a letter from Father, in his handwriting, signed by him, and addressed to me! The shock was so overwhelming that I felt as though I was in an altered state, each second passing in slow motion. I could barely look at what was in my hands, let alone read it. I just held the letter and cried for what seemed to be an hour…until I could regain my composure. I sat back in Father's chair, and started reading the letter.

April 2011
My Dearest Gabrielle,
If you are reading this letter, it's because I have passed away. With my death will come some confusing issues that will need to be dealt with, and some truths that will be hard to accept.

My Sweet Princess, you know how much I love you, and how I would never let anything hurt you. Well, that was the impetus for making the decisions that I've made. All these years it was very hard for me to not share this with you, but I felt it was for your best interest that you remain uninformed, until now of course.

Do you remember the story I told you, about the picture on my desk, of the time when we went to the park for your birthday? And do you remember that I told you I didn't want your mother's pictures displayed because seeing them was too painful for me? And remember that I never, ever called her by her name? Which, by the way, is Sterling.

'Sterling...that's the name that Father called the woman in my dream!'

Gabi, the reason it was so painful, was because your mother never died, but I had to allow you to think that she had, so we could protect her.

My mind was spinning...I had a mother, and she wasn't really dead? And her name was Sterling! Shocked out of my mind, I kept reading...

After she gave birth to you, she gave birth to our son two years later. His name is Eric. Yes, you have a brother! I am so sorry that you have been raised apart. If we could have done something, anything differently—we surely would have.

'Oh, Father—how awful!'

When Eric was six months old, Sterling decided to take him to a new park that she heard was beautiful, but didn't know exactly where it was located. She got lost and drove down a few wrong streets where she unfortunately witnessed an awful murder. The victim was a prominent, political figure who was murdered by an equally important group of, shall we say, bad men. To make matters even worse, this terrible deed was not done by just one 'family,' it was done by two families! Sterling was sure that they had seen her car drive by, and could have possibly seen her, because her windows were down when she let out a blood-curdling scream.

Since I led such a high-profile life, I couldn't chance that Sterling might be seen in a photo with me. Her life would be in jeopardy if her identity were to be revealed. So, with Sterling and Eric's lives in grave danger, Leon, Alex and I decided that it was best for them to leave the country. Talk to Alex about the details, and please don't be upset with him, or anyone for not revealing any of this to you. You must surely understand why we were forced to live in secrecy.

I stopped reading for a moment—this was such shocking news that I could hardly process it. 'Oh my dear, dear Father, this is such an incredibly sad tragedy.'

Uncle Leon always knows where Sterling is—Sonny keeps track of her, and calls Leon with updates. There are two remaining players in this old murder case that need to be taken care of, so don't worry Honey, we're almost there.

My darling Gabrielle, in my wildest dreams, I never thought this would have taken twenty years to resolve. We did everything we could do. Hopefully, Eric and Sterling will be able to come home soon.

I read, and reread that line at least a dozen times before it sunk in that Sterling, my mother may still be alive! I continued reading...

Please continue to transfer funds to Sonny—you will find the file in the safe. Make sure that you stay in constant contact with him.

Please forgive me if I let you down, or made decisions that you don't agree with—it was only to protect everyone that I love.

My dear, precious, Gabrielle—I love you with all my heart and soul. Thank you for being the best daughter that a man could ever dream of having—and thank you for loving me.

Yours Forever,
Father

P.S. Jacob loves you very much, and you have my blessing with him. He is loyal and like a son to me.

It seemed like an eternity passed before I was finished reading the letter. What an amazing secret, and what an incredible shock! 'Oh Father, it must have been so hard for you to live with such a secret.' My heart could not contain the host of feelings that I was experiencing. I kept saying aloud, "I have a mother! I have a mother and she's alive somewhere." The big question now was...where is she?

I was not only in shock, but I was literally scared to death. I felt like I was losing my mind—I didn't know what to do, or who to turn to any more. My own body was beginning to feel foreign to me. My nerves were raw, my heart was broken, and my mind knew no peace. My world had been shattered, and the meaning of my life drastically altered in an instant.

Father said in his letter that Uncle Leon was supposed to take care of everything, but how could he take care of anything now? 'Oh Father, your letter didn't explain what to do if I lost Uncle Leon.' After mulling over the details of the letter, again and again, and the events of the last two days, I felt queasy and extremely exhausted. I walked upstairs to go to bed, and I folded the papers, putting them in my dresser drawer that locks, for safekeeping.

The shocking news was so inconceivable I felt as though I was having another out of body experience. Exhausted, I lay down to go to sleep, but kept replaying each sentence in that letter, over and over again in my head. My mind was racing with questions that had absolutely no answers, yet my subconscious seemed to be aware of the woman's name, which is probably why I heard Father call her Sterling in my dream. Maybe my subconscious knows what she looks like also. Those were my last thoughts before I fell asleep on the couch.

I began dreaming instantly. A beautiful woman was standing motionless by the weeping willow on a very cold, very rainy day. Drenched from holding no umbrella, she stood there crying silently, wearing only a long, black coat with a hood that hid most of her face. I felt sad as I watched the tears streaming down her cheeks, and quickly blending in with the rain, yet I was distracted by her beautiful hands that kept lifting a white handkerchief to slowly wipe the pain from her eyes. The wind blew her hood back, and the rain started coming down so hard that her long, dark, bouncy curls quickly started to hang straight, clinging to her wet, sullen face.

She raised her head slightly as if someone had called her name. Then with a blank look, she stared straight out into space. She slowly reached out her hand—I responded in like manner to take it as I said, "Oh Mother...Father is dead!"

My dream lasted most of the night. I woke up disoriented and extremely depressed, which is not like me. I quickly ran upstairs to take a shower, hoping to get the image of the woman in black out of my mind. The aroma of freshly brewed coffee seemed to help clear my head as I made my way down the stairs to one of Maria's famous lattes. As she handed it to me she gave me one of those 'Sit down and talk to me' looks.

She ran her hand through my hair, looked sweetly into my eyes and said, "How are you doing this morning, Gabrielle?"

"Well Maria, you know something? I've had better days—much, much better days."

"Gabi, I can't tell you how sorry I am about your father, and now your Uncle Leon." She started crying. "How could we lose two great men, in such a short time?"

"Maria, sometimes life is so unfair, it doesn't make any sense at all. Why bad things happen to good people is beyond me, but the point you brought up is a very good one, 'In such a short time.'"

"Gabi, do you think something fishy is going on?"

Where did all these animal terms come from? Quietly, I said under my breath, "Fishy and Ducky."

"What Gabi?"

"Oh nothing, I'll be back in a while, I'm going to Mary's house to check on her."

Just as I was walking out the door, Alex arrived. For a split second I was scared of him. I knew he was a dishonest thief, and God only knows what else! But then, he doesn't know that I found the picture, so just be cool Gabi.

"Well good morning Alex, did you sleep well last night?"

"Good morning to you too, Gabi. No I did not sleep well at all last night. Sorry about Sandi's bizarre actions, but right now I've got something far more important to talk to you about."

"What?"

"Gabi, the results came back from the autopsy."

"I thought the results were already in, so what do you mean?"

"I ordered further tests."

"Alex, do you think that was really necessary?"

"I just couldn't accept the report stating that Michael died from a rare virus he picked up in Japan last month. I have a good friend in forensics that owed me a few favors—I had him secretly run some more definitive tests. Call me ignorant in the health field, but this Japanese virus made no sense at all to me. As it turns out, it's a good thing I did run those tests, because that is not what Michael died from!"

"Okay Alex, you're scaring me! What exactly did you find out?"

"The results revealed that he did have the virus, but that he absolutely did not die from it."

"Then what did Father die from?"

My heart sank as Alex said, "He was poisoned!"

"How in the world could he have been poisoned?"

"That's why I'm so concerned Gabi. This information does not leave the room—I mean it! Don't breathe a word of this to another living soul!"

I looked at Alex, then stared off into space, then looked back at him again with a blank face and said, "I'll stay quiet for now, but I want a minute-by-minute report on anything that you find out. Everyone is suspect to me now. I want my Father's murderer caught!"

His voice bellowed back, "So do I Gabi, so do I."

"Alex, I was on my way to Mary's house—I'll catch up with you later. Thanks I guess, for the information."

Since I was feeling completely confused on all counts now, and outraged that anyone could have killed my father, I began to feel my blood run cold, ice cold. How ironic that I felt myself turning into the 'Ice Princess' that the paper so blithely called me before. If my Father's been murdered, they haven't seen anything yet.

As I made my way through the backyard, and alongside Mary's house, I stopped to check on that poor broken rose bush. Mary must have fixed it. The branch was neatly pruned back, there were no more petals on the ground, and the large footprints were also gone.

Just as I was ready to ring the doorbell, Mary opened the door.

"Hi Gabi, it's so good to see you. I was really hoping to have seen you yesterday, but…"

"I did see you yesterday Mary, don't you remember?"

"No, I don't. When did you?"

I interrupted her, "It was about nine o'clock. You answered the door, and seemed very distant. You wouldn't let me in, and said that you were 'just ducky'."

"'Ducky'? I said 'ducky'? I think you were dreaming Gabrielle, I have never used that term before in my entire life!"

"I know you haven't, and that's one of the reasons why you seemed so weird to me last night. Well, at least you fixed the broken rose bush."

"Gabi, what rose bush? Honey, are you okay?"

"Mary, last night when I came by, I showed you rose petals that I picked up and… if you didn't fix the bush, who did?"

"Gabi, I haven't felt very good since I came home from the funeral."

I could tell that Mary wasn't well, and was pretty upset about Father, so I didn't dare tell her about Uncle Leon right now. I didn't think that she could handle it, and she definitely needed some rest.

"Mary, maybe I did dream that I came over here last night. You know, I've been a little out of sorts the last few days. Why don't we both get some rest, and I'll be back later."

I spent the remaining part of the day and many hours into the night doing research on any, and all types of poisons that I could find on-line. By ten o'clock I was quite exhausted, and I could barely keep my eyes open. I dragged myself up the stairs to actually go to bed before midnight, which was a first for me, lately.

Chapter 8

I woke up at the crack of dawn and stumbled down the stairs to the kitchen—Maria was cooking my favorite breakfast, eggs benedict. The table was set with beautiful, fresh flowers from the garden along with sounds of smooth jazz playing softly in the background.

"Good Morning Maria, everything looks and smells wonderful, as usual. I don't want to offend you, but could you bring my breakfast and coffee into Father's office? I have a lot of work to do this morning."

"Certainly Gabi."

Fighting back tears, and desperately trying to get back into a normal routine, I turned on my favorite 'news talk,' KIRO, like I always did to start my day. Even though my mind was spinning between not being quite awake yet, and overwhelmed with the shocking news of Father being murdered, all I could think about were two things: Who and what poisoned Father? And where could I find more pictures of that special day in the park? I slipped deep into my thoughts… 'Were there more pictures? Where would another memory of that special day be?' Suddenly the office door was forcefully thrown open, which was not Maria's style—so I was quite taken aback. As I looked up to talk to her, I noticed that it was Alex!

I could tell that he was in a probing mood. I was a bit nervous about him drilling me right now, so I acted like I was busy, "Alex, is this about Father, or can it wait?"

Just then Maria walked in with my breakfast and coffee, and Alex bit her head off as he said, "Put it on the table, and close the door behind you—quickly Maria!"

I was stunned at his behavior, and scolded him, "Alex, do NOT talk to Maria like that ever again. She is a person who deserves respect. Her job is to make sure that we are taken care of—she is not, I repeat NOT a servant. She is no less a person than you are, so please do NOT speak to her in that manner again! Now…what's so important that it's made you lose your manners?"

"Sorry about that, I'm just on edge these days. I'll apologize to her when I leave. There's something you said Gabi, I'm confused about, and now everything means something regarding Michael's case."

"What Alex? What are you confused about?"

"I talked with the paramedics this morning and they said that Leon was mumbling something to you. Gabrielle, you told me that he didn't say a word to you. Even the smallest clue could reveal some insight as to what might have happened to Leon and your father. It's very important that I know what he said."

"Alex, please just calm down, and trust me. What he said was certainly not germane to this case."

Alex just glared at me and said, "Gabrielle, what did he say?"

The phone rang before I could respond to Alex. It was Jacob. I was so excited to hear his voice I forgot Alex was in the room. After the funeral Jacob left immediately for an important business trip in Switzerland.

"Hi Jacob, it's so good to hear from you, I've missed you. You're back in the states?"

"Oh, you just landed at Sea Tac! Okay, you're going to drop off your car, and I'll see you in a little while, then."

After I hung up the phone, I had a big smile on my face. I was quite surprised to be actually feeling a little happy about something. I thought for sure that all emotions except for pain, had vacated my desperately sad heart.

I looked back at Alex and said, "I love you."

Alex looked at me with the most puzzled face and said, "Excuse me?"

"'I love you,' those were Leon's last words to me."

"That's it Gabi, that's all he said?"

"Yes, that's it! And I doubt those words will help you solve this case."

Alex looked down in disappointment, and then up at me as he forced a smile on his face. "So Jacob is back from Switzerland? Good, I need to talk to him also."

Alex's face drastically changed when he said, Switzerland. He had a look that I had never seen before—it was very strange, yet sad. I was becoming more and more afraid to be around Alex, and more and more anxious to be with the one person I knew I could trust, Jacob—I knew that Father trusted him also.

With that weird look still glued on his face, Alex walked over to me, grabbed my hand and said, "Switzerland does not have good memories for me, Gabrielle."

I don't know why I felt compelled to talk with Alex about something that was bothering him, but how could I not? We had always been so close, and I still cared about him. I asked him very kindly, "Why Alex, what happened in Switzerland?"

He was visibly disturbed as he started telling the story. "I remember the last time we all came back from Switzerland. We had been in Munich on a business trip, and then flew to Zurich for a masquerade ball—at the last minute we ended up taking our wives with us."

"Yes I know, I remember how much Sandi didn't want to go on that trip."

"No she didn't want to go, but then I convinced her that it would be an experience of a lifetime."

"And was it?"

"Oh yes, she made bloody sure that it was!"

"What do you mean?"

"During the Masquerade Ball, after what I thought was a romantic dance between the two of us, she stormed off the dance floor, practically ran into the French doors that opened out onto the verandah, and…" he paused.

"And…"

"As soon as Sandi stepped out onto the verandah, she lit a cigarette like she was in one of those old time movies—the kind where glamorous women smoked cigarettes in fancy cigarette holders."

"Well Alex, since she doesn't smoke, I'm sure that was embarrassing, but…"

He cut me off, "Gabi, it doesn't end there, it gets worse…much worse."

"For heaven's sake, what happened?"

"Well, when I saw her smoking, I walked over to talk to her, only to discover that she had become one of those other women. I could hardly stand to be near her—I decided not to torture myself, so I went back inside to enjoy the party."

"Oh Alex, I don't blame you."

"Well, after almost an hour, and many enjoyable conversations with normal people, I decided to go back out on the verandah to ask Sandi to join me. She was nowhere in sight, so I quickly made my way through to the other side of the room. I ventured into a room designated the 'smoking room,' where the door was ajar. Since Sandi, or whomever she had become for the evening had taken up smoking, I thought that she might be in that room, so I peeked my head in to see if she was there."

I interrupted him, "Was she?"

"No! No one was in sight, but there was a light on in a back room that was adjacent to that room. I could barely see in there, but I heard what I thought was…"

"Did you see her? Was it her voice?"

"Well, at first I wasn't sure, because her voice changes a little when she's in a different personality. I listened for another minute and heard a laugh. Sandi's laugh was one thing that never changed, and I could tell that it was definitely her laugh."

"So then what did you do?"

"At that point, I wanted to make sure that it was her, and that she was okay. I walked quickly through the room, opened the door wider, and well Gabi, how do I say this nicely?"

"I don't know Alex, what?"

"It was her—she was with another man!"

"What do you mean with another man? Do you mean having sex?"

"I do."

"Oh my heavens Alex, how did that make you feel?"

"I felt so betrayed, so awful, so hurt. There aren't enough words to describe the pain."

"What did you do?"

"Well, it's what her lover did that was so rude and so shocking. I couldn't tell who was underneath her at first, until she moved aside, but when I saw his face…it took every ounce of my self-control not to take out my gun and shoot him."

"Was it someone you knew?"

"No! He was a stranger, a complete stranger!"

"Oh my gosh, I can't believe that! Oh, Alex…how awful!"

"Anyway…he jumped up, threw his pants on, looked me square in the eyes and said, 'She's definitely not my type, you can have her,' as he bolted out the door."

"Alex, how did Sandi act while this was all happening?"

"She had returned to herself again, and I believe she was a little ashamed of what she had done. After I helped her get dressed, we walked briskly through the ballroom, and directly out the door without speaking to anyone. I asked the valet for my keys—I thought a brisk walk in the cool night air would be good for Sandi, and even better for my temper, which at that point was off the charts. The car was parked about two blocks away, but when we got to it, she wouldn't get in."

"Alex, for crying out loud, what in the world was wrong with her?"

"Sandi didn't want to leave until we said good-bye to Michael first. I had to lie to her, or she would have caused another scene. I told her that Michael had already gone home."

"Did she finally get in the car?"

"Yes, and she cried all the way back to the hotel."

"Oh Alex, I am so sorry."

"So am I. Our lives haven't been the same since."

Alex looked at me with so much pain in his eyes as he said, "Gabrielle, I don't know what came over me, or why I started talking about Switzerland right now, but thank you for listening. You've always been like the daughter I never had. Thank you for your sweet friendship."

Alex walked over to hug me. I didn't know what to say, so I just stood there with my arms straight down, glued to my sides. Just then Jacob arrived at the office door. Seeing me all wrapped up in Alex's arms, he gave me a most quizzical look. I looked back at him like, 'You've got to be kidding, he's like a father to me.'

Jacob has always been a little jealous of any man that I gave attention to, except for Father, but I wasn't attracted to anyone except Jacob. He knew that in his heart.

Jacob was one of the most handsome men I had ever met, in fact, he looked almost exactly like Father and Uncle Leon, except for Jacob had crystal blue eyes and a mustache. His eyes were like a deep pool, drawing me in for a sensual swim, his hands, his beautiful hands—when they touched me, it sent chills up and down my spine.

"Gabrielle, I missed you so much."

"Oh Jacob, I missed you more than you'll ever know."

"Are you okay?"

"Do you want the short version, or the long version?"

Jacob, who didn't have a narcissistic, or selfish bone in his body and who cared deeply about me, actually loved to listen, which is a rare quality for some men. So, his empathetic response came as no surprise to me, "The long version."

"I am so not okay that I'm beginning to think I'm okay—how crazy does that sound?"

"Gabi, you poor thing, this has been over-the-top, too much."

"Can we talk about it later Jacob, when we're alone? Did you drop off your car?"

Alex chimed in, "What's wrong with your car?"

"Nothing, I'm just getting new tires."

Alex walked over to Jacob, gave him a big bear hug and said, "It's really good to see you, I want to talk to you, but we can talk later." Then Alex turned and left rather abruptly.

Chapter 9

Jacob stared deep into my eyes, as I was lost in his. He put his strong, masculine arms around my waist, gently pulled me towards him, and kissed me with such heated passion I thought I would melt. Firmly and slowly, he ran his hands up and down my back, and as his body pressed up against mine I could feel that he was as excited as I was. Jacob and I had always been close friends, but now our relationship was growing into something much more than that. I had feelings I had never experienced before. I was falling, deeply in love with him. I could tell that neither one of us wanted to break from our kiss, or the embrace, but I desperately needed to talk.

As I slowly started pulling away from Jacob, I reached down and squeezed his hand while I said, "I really need to talk to you."

Jacob took my hand, brought it up to his lips, kissed it tenderly—then, he walked me over to the couch. "Sit down Princess. What's going on in that pretty little head of yours?"

"Jacob, so much has happened in such a short time. It's difficult to sort it all out."

"I know Gabi. I can't tell you how sorry I am that I had to leave so quickly after the funeral service, it made me feel like I abandoned you."

"Jacob, you didn't abandon me, I knew that you had to work—I'm just confused about so many things that have come to light in the last couple of days."

"Oh Gabrielle, I'm so very, very sorry about everything that's happened. How can I help with the things that are confusing you?"

"I need to ask you something about a picture."

"A picture?"

I stopped to think for a minute before I responded. I wasn't sure exactly how much Jacob knew, or if it was okay to talk to him about anything. These secrets were making me crazy—Uncle Leon telling me not to tell Alex something, and then Alex telling me not to tell anyone, anything! I had to believe that I could trust Jacob. I needed to believe in him—in someone!

I looked at Jacob with longing eyes, hoping to learn something about my past. I held out a photo of that day in the park, which I had finally found in an old album that Father had hidden in his closet. "Jacob, what does this picture mean to you?"

Jacob stared long and lovingly at the picture. The first words that came out of his mouth were, "Michael…I miss you so much."

I leaned over and kissed his cheek as I said, "I know Jacob; this is such an unbelievable nightmare."

Jacob took another picture from my hands and said, "So many things have changed since that time in our lives, and as I look at this picture I get a really weird feeling." Jacob ran his finger across the picture as he continued talking with a sad voice, "Yes, so much has happened to all of our lives…even since this happy memory. Dominique's death six years ago, Daniel leaving the group, now, the death of your father and Leon, it's almost beyond comprehension."

I looked quizzically at Jacob, not knowing if I should share with him what Alex had told me. I didn't want to keep any secrets from him, and Father said I could trust him.

I blurted out, "Jacob, Alex had forensics run more tests on Father. He was suspicious of foul play, and the tests revealed that Father didn't die from that virus he caught in Japan!"

Jacob stared at me with a wrinkled brow, as he snapped back with, "What?"

"I know Jacob, that was the same reaction I had. The findings revealed foul play, which was exactly what Alex had suspected."

"And what type of foul play was that?"

I yelled out, "FATHER WAS POISONED, JACOB! HE WAS MURDERED!"

Jacob jumped up, his eyes filled with tears, his body was so tense that his jawbone was flexing in his cheek. He stomped his way to the fireplace, and began hitting the mantle with his fist. "They did it. They finally got to him!"

"Who got to him? Jacob, what are you talking about?"

"Not now, Gabrielle—I'll explain later. Did Alex tell you what kind of poison it was?"

"No!"

"Did he say how long it had been administered, and by what method?"

"No Jacob, he didn't. I didn't even think to ask those kind of questions, I was just so shocked about the news."

"So, it's definitive that it was not the virus from Japan?"

"Yes! Alex said that it absolutely was not the virus."

"Gabrielle, I need to talk to Alex immediately."

"Jacob you can't. Alex told me not to tell another soul about this."

"Gabi, I understand about not telling anyone who could leak this to the public, but Alex didn't mean not to tell me! He couldn't have meant me!"

Jacob started pacing back and forth, shaking his head non-stop, obviously lost in his thoughts. I had to say his name three times before he turned to answer me.

"I'm sorry Gabrielle. Between the pain of losing Michael, and the anger I feel towards his murderers, it's all I can do to contain myself."

Jacob stopped pacing, walked over to me, kissed my lips sweetly, then took my hand and walked me to the couch, where he motioned for me to sit down. His hands were clammy and tense. I could tell he was trying very hard to overcome his angry feelings so that he could comfort me.

As I looked at the picture, I felt so sad knowing that the people who were in the park that day were people who loved me very much. It was even harder to accept that they were either dead, or they were possibly on some hit list! How could our lives have changed so drastically, and become so totally complicated?

The people in that picture looked so happy, but that was so very long ago, and I was too young to remember. 'Oh, how I need to hear something good about that day.' My thoughts became audible as I said, "Jacob, what are your memories of that day?"

Jacob looked at me with such sadness in his eyes. I said to him, "Can you sit down and talk to me for a minute? I'm so curious about the people in this picture. I need to know Jacob."

We sat on the couch, and as I thought about Father, a tear rolled down my cheek. Jacob wrapped his arm around my shoulder and pulled me closer to him on the couch. Then he said, "Look at us in that picture; look how young we were! You were five and I was thirteen—we were just babies. That was such a bitter-sweet day Gabi. I remember when St…" then he stopped and looked at me as if he was hoping that I hadn't heard what he was about to say.

I snapped at him, "Jacob, what do you remember?"

"Oh nothing, Gabi."

I knew he had to know about Sterling. I wanted to tell him that I knew about her also, but by the way he reacted, it seemed as though he was still sworn to secrecy to protect me.

I looked at him with eyes that longed to know the truth as I said, "Jacob, Father wrote me a letter explaining everything about the past. I know that Sterling is my mother, were you about to say her name?"

Jacob reached over, pulled me towards him, and hugged me so lovingly that it was all I could do to not melt in his arms, as he replied, "Yes Gabrielle, I remember when Sterling took that picture. May I see the letter that Michael wrote to you?"

"Yes, but I'm a little confused. Father told me that the picture was of my fifth birthday, the one when all the guys gave me charms for my bracelet."

"It was Gabi, but it was also the day that your father had Sterling leave the country. She wanted a picture of the group to take with her. Since Michael always did whatever he could to make her happy, he agreed to let her take a picture of everyone at the park, which was on the way to the airport."

"Oh, Jacob how sad, how incredibly sad."

"Yes, it was Gabi, it was one of the saddest days in all of our lives." As he held my head close to his, he said, "So Honey, what did Michael say in his letter?"

"Well, first of all Jacob, for some reason Uncle Leon said not to tell anyone about any of this. Now he's dead, which makes me very suspicious and cautious. Leon didn't trust Alex—why I don't know. Alex told me not to talk to anyone about anything either, but now I don't know who to trust, and…"

Jacob interrupted me, "Slow down Gabi!"

"…But Father trusted you, and even said so in his letter. AND I trust you. I need to be able to trust you. I have to believe that I can confide in you."

"Gabrielle, I know everything. I also know that we were all committed to keeping this family safe. Everyone in that picture complied until the day they died."

"Then why was Uncle Leon suspicious about Alex?"

"That my dear, is a mystery to me. I think you'll probably get the answer to your question after I have a chance to talk to Alex."

"Jacob, I really thought that Leon was way out in left field with his thoughts about Alex, until I found…"

In Jacob's nervous state of mind he cut me off in mid sentence, because he was overly anxious to read the letter from Father, "Gabrielle, please let me read that letter!"

I handed Jacob the letter. He grabbed my hands, held them tight, looked deep into my eyes and said, "If you don't know by now Gabrielle, I am so completely in love with you. I always have been, and I always will be. Your safety means more to me than my own life."

As Jacob read the letter, a tear rolled down his cheek. He kept nodding his head in agreement with Father. He looked at me with compassion in his eyes. When he finished reading it, he kissed my lips and said, "Every single word of this is true. It must have been so very hard for Michael to write, but I'm certain it was even harder for you to read. I'm sure that you were beyond shocked to learn that you had a mother, and a brother."

"Yes, this whole thing has been such a shock. I'm not sure what is real, and what's not anymore."

"Oh my sweet Gabi, I am so very, very sorry. Michael wanted this handled so differently."

'How odd, those were the exact same words that Uncle Leon said to me.' With that, I began to feel safe for the first time since Father had died. Jacob was so gentle and loving with me as he pulled me towards him, and just held me in his arms for the longest time. Being wrapped up in a security blanket of love gave me hope for what I had to face in the days to come. I looked up at Jacob with eyes full of tears, and in a very childlike voice said, "What does my mother look like?"

"Oh Gabrielle, Sterling is a strikingly beautiful woman. You look very much like her. She has long, dark hair that hangs in loose curls around her face. She has exquisite features, like an Italian porcelain doll. She is slightly taller than you are, and walks with such model-like poise. With her classy way of dressing, and extremely proper mannerisms, she is markedly set apart from practically everyone else that walks the face of this earth. She is also intelligent, witty, and…"

I interrupted him, "Jacob, she came to Father's funeral, didn't she? I saw the woman you're describing, she was extremely beautiful, and she spoke to me! Oh Jacob, that was her, she was there, wasn't she?"

Jacob looked lovingly at me, and answered with his eyes, before a single word came out of his mouth—but out they came. In a very gentle and loving tone he said, "Yes Gabrielle, she was there."

"Oh Jacob, she is exactly how you described her! I was taken aback by her beauty and her voice, because she sounded like…"

Jacob interrupted me out of excitement, "Yes, she sounds like a sexy Angel, if that's possible!" We both laughed.

"Oh Jacob, that is exactly what I thought when she whispered in my ear at the funeral, and I had absolutely no idea who she was!"

"I'm sorry Gabi."

"Don't be sorry Jacob. I'm not angry or bitter—how could I be? I found out that I have a mother!" Do you know what it's like to discover that the parent you thought was dead is really still alive? I understand why things ended up being the way they did, but now things are different. I need to find her!"

"Gabi, I'm afraid that we can't just go find her. The situation is much more complicated than that."

Being slightly sarcastic, the words fell out of my mouth, "I understand that it might be more difficult than finding her on Facebook, but I still want to locate her as soon as possible. I'm sure there is an element of complication to this whole matter, or Father wouldn't have kept it such a secret all these years, but…"

Jacob pulled me towards him, and kissed my lips so softly and so sweetly while I was talking—I got lost in him for a moment. While I was in his embrace, I wondered how I could possibly process one more ounce of information. These secrets were revealing not only my past, but my future, so I continued.

"Jacob, I know about everyone else in this picture except for Eric and Daniel, what are they like?"

"Eric is strong like your father, but also very different in his views on how to deal with the business. I'd rather let you get to know him yourself, and let you come to your own conclusions as to what he's all about. I will tell you this much about him, he's extremely intelligent and very loyal to the family, even though he and Michael have had countless disagreements on many occasions."

"Oh Jacob, he sounds very intriguing. I can't wait to get to know him! Okay, now tell me about Daniel."

"Daniel is or was, quite the 'negotiator'. He could collaborate any type of business deal with any kind of person, on any continent."

"Wow, that's amazing! I can hardly tell what he looks like in this picture, because of that shadow, but it looks like he's as tall as Alex—is he?"

"I think that he was about an inch shorter than Alex. He was an extremely good-looking German with blonde hair, blue eyes, and he always sported a mustache on his year-round tan. Daniel rarely came to the states, except for when Michael called an emergency meeting.

For the most part, your father met with him in Munich on a monthly basis."

"That's interesting…so tell me more about what he was like."

"Daniel was very loyal to this family. We all really felt the loss when Daniel decided to do something else. It's unfortunate, but he has been out of contact with any of us for so long that we really have no ties to him anymore."

"So Jacob, besides Daniel, if Father was murdered, and Uncle Leon was murdered, then that leaves only Eric, Sonny, and you in that picture. Are any of you in danger?"

"Gabi, at this point I think that we are all in danger, and I'm a little worried."

"Jacob, how worried are you?"

"I'm worried enough to call in the force."

"What do you mean by that?"

"I'll explain later."

The Grandfather clock started chiming. It was four o'clock, which reminded me of Maria's earlier instructions that dinner would be at six o'clock sharp tonight, and that we should all sit down to a nice, nourishing meal. I agreed with her, even though I didn't have much of an appetite.

After hearing the clock, I remembered a few things that had slipped my mind. I shouted out to Jacob, "Oh no, I got so wrapped up in this picture that I forgot Sonny called wanting to talk with Leon last night. He said it was an emergency, and that Leon needed to call him before the end of the night, last night! Oh Jacob, so much has happened, that I forgot to call Sonny and tell him about Uncle Leon!"

"I need to call him immediately Gabi! There is still so much more that I need to tell you, but I do need to call Sonny now. I also need to go pick up my car."

"I know your conversation with Sonny will take a while so why don't you call him now. You can use the phone in my room where it's private, since Maria needs to finish cleaning the office. I'll go pick up your car so we will both be in time for Maria's dinner at six!"

"Okay Gabi, but come here first and give me a hug." Once again, it felt so good to be engulfed in Jacob's strong, loving embrace. As Jacob was on his way up the stairs to my room, he yelled back down to me that he hadn't seen Paul since he arrived, and wondered if it was his day off.

I yelled up at him, "I don't know; I haven't seen him either."

I went into Antonio's office and inquired about Paul, our driver, and was informed that he left early because his mother had fallen ill. Antonio offered to drive me, which would have completely messed up his schedule, so I thanked him and said that I would have Ashlee take me instead.

"Good idea Gabi, but don't forget about dinner!"

"We'll be here, and please set a place for Ashlee."

When I pulled up to Ashlee's house, she was waiting on the porch with her new beau. Being polite once he saw me, he kissed her lips and quickly walked to his car. I was a little disappointed—I was hoping to meet him. She'd been seeing this guy quite a lot lately and all I knew about him was that they met at school. Understandably, Ashlee and I hadn't talked about much of anything except for Father's illness for the last month. We had quite a lot of catching up to do. "Hey, Ash!"

"Hey Grilla, let's roll!"

It sounded so cute to hear her call me the name she used to call me when we were in elementary school. Whenever she called me Grilla, it usually meant that she was in a really silly mood. I called her Ash most of the time, no matter what mood I was in. That's good, I thought, Ashlee needs to be silly, she's been pretty stressed with school lately.

We talked as fast as we were driving, the entire way to the dealership. We went from one topic to the next, non-stop. Then I said to her, "Hey, I need to talk to you about something that's even weirder than my dreams."

"Okay, I'm a very captive audience, talk away." That was Ashlee's little attempt at humor.

I told her all about what Sandi had done in Switzerland, and how perplexing it was to me that she could slip in and out of those personalities.

"You know what really gets me Ash? Sandi is a very intelligent woman, she was a nurse, and I just don't understand how someone that smart can go over the deep end like that."

Ashlee thought for a minute and then said, "You know Gabi, some people have no choice, but others definitely choose to live in that world, especially after a trauma."

"Will she ever get better?"

"That's the sixty-four million dollar question regarding most types of mental illnesses."

"You know Ashlee, I spent most of my life feeling sorry for Alex, but now I find myself feeling sorry for Sandi also. She's been trapped inside her head with that illness, while Alex has been…"

Ashlee interrupted me because she knew how close I was with Alex, and that I was probably about to say something that I didn't mean, so she said, "Just take care of yourself right now, Gabi."

I sat there silent for a moment, thinking to myself…'Oh Ashlee, if you only knew that Alex is the one who stole that picture of Father and me. I can't tell you anything else, and this is really hard on me to not be able to talk with you about everything.'

I turned the corner a little too fast and Ashlee almost fell into my lap, then we started laughing like we did when we were kids. That felt so good. It had been a couple of weeks since I had driven my car and I had missed it. I was debating whether or not to let Ashlee drive my car back home, or if I should have her drive Jacob's.

"Hey Ashlee, do you want to drive the Ferrari home?"

"Sure, but only with your permission, Princess!" She let out her cute little laugh.

We drove to the other side of the parking lot, looking everywhere for the car. Why is it that no matter where you start looking for whatever it is you're looking for, it's always in the last place you look? Murphy's Law, I guess.

After finally finding the Ferrari, I dropped Ashlee in front of it, tossed her the keys, and started to roll away. As I was looking at her in my rearview mirror I noticed that she was still messing with the door, so I backed up to meet her. She turned to walk toward me. 'That's odd, is it the wrong car?'

BOOM! The blast blew debris, smoke and flames high in the air as the car exploded!

I threw the car in park, as I screamed "ASH-LEE!"

I jumped out of the car. All I could hear was the roar of the fire, and debris falling all around me, as I was looking frantically for Ashlee. I couldn't find her until I heard her voice cry out. She was pulling herself up from behind the car that was beside what used to be Jacob's car.

I screamed out, "ASHLEE, ARE YOU OKAY? Oh, dear God Ashlee, are you hurt? I could have lost you!"

Shortly after the explosion Charles, Detective Green, Alex and Jacob came screeching into the parking lot in separate cars, along with the paramedics and two fire trucks. Even though Ashlee's injuries appeared to be minor, the paramedics hurriedly placed her on the gurney, loaded her into the ambulance, and took her to the hospital.

Jacob, seemingly scared for us, grabbed me, and pulled me aside yelling, "Gabi, what happened?"

I shook uncontrollably as I pointed to the burning car, momentarily speechless.

Jacob yelled at Alex, "That was meant for me, wasn't it?"

Alex snapped back quickly, "Well it was meant to scare the heck out of someone!"

"What do you mean, 'scare,' Alex? That could have killed someone!"

"Not necessarily Jacob, it was triggered by attempting to open the door, which means that the odds of the explosion killing the person opening the door aren't that good. If someone wanted to kill the person, it would have been triggered by the ignition."

"Man Alex, what is going on around here?"

"Jacob, between you and me, I think this is just a smoke screen—no pun intended."

"So you're not taking it that serious?"

"I didn't say that Jacob. I am taking this seriously! It's making me think a lot harder, and a little differently about Leon's murder."

"Alex, this is getting just a little too close to Gabi, don't you think? We need to talk."

"I know, but we can talk later, take her home now. I need to stay here, and help with the report."

Chapter 10

Maria greeted us at the door, accommodating and sympathetic. She could see that I was visibly upset, my voice shaky, and I wasn't really making sense. Jacob told her that we would be in Michael's office, and requested she bring us some coffee. I had a feeling this was going to be a very long night.

I sat on the couch, just staring into space, not wanting to say a word. Jacob sat on the couch opposite me, in the same condition. Maria brought in a large carafe of coffee and chocolate mint cookies. Looking at me with concern in her eyes she said, "Gabrielle, I don't understand what's going on."

"I don't either Maria. I really don't, someone else could have died tonight—none of this makes any sense to me at all."

I could see that Maria was horrified, so I stopped talking about it, and said, "Oh Maria, I'm so sorry we missed dinner."

"Gabi, no worries—don't even think about that!"

As she turned to walk back out of the office I said to her, "Thanks for the coffee and cookies."

She turned, smiled sweetly, and closed the door softly behind her.

At this point, I was feeling extremely frustrated about being left in the dark for so long, especially since everyone around me was dying, which made me feel quite vulnerable. I looked over at Jacob, who seemed to be miles away in his thoughts, and said, "I think it's time you filled me in on all those gaps you were talking about."

"Gabi, you've had so much information dropped on you in such a short time. I'm afraid you're already suffering from overload; your father, Uncle Leon and now this. Not to mention the news about having a mother and a brother! I don't think that I should keep heaping anything else on you right now."

I could barely contain myself as I started yelling at him, "I JUST WANT TO KNOW WHAT'S GOING ON! I DON'T HAVE THE TIME, OR THE LUXURY TO BE PROTECTED RIGHT NOW!"

Jacob tried to console me, "Come on Gabi, please calm down, it's okay."

"No Jacob, it is NOT OKAY! Alex thinks that Father was murdered, and I know that Uncle Leon was, and we can't trust Alex!

Do you understand that MY WORLD HAS BEEN TOTALLY TURNED INSIDE-OUT?"

"Gabi, Honey, you're still rattled from the bomb, please calm down."

"Maybe I am rattled Jacob, but heaven only knows what was going on tonight with that car bomb, and who it was meant for. I HAVE GOT TO KNOW WHAT'S GOING ON AROUND HERE, BEFORE SOMEONE ELSE THAT I LOVE, DIES!"

"Gabi, I think a little glass of wine would be much better for you right now than a cup of coffee. What do you think?"

"I THINK NOT!"

Jacob knew that I had reached the end of my patience. He sat down right beside me, handed me a cup of coffee, and kissed my lips softly. With his tender gestures, I knew that he was about to break more news to me. We just sat there, frozen in a moment of time. As I held the warm cup in my hands, enjoying the aroma of the coffee, the steam rolled between us like a scanty cloud drifting across the sky. Then he started talking...

I interrupted him before he started, "Jacob, please don't do this in story form—please just the facts."

"Geez Gabi, you sound like a cop."

"I feel like a cop right now, so come on, fill in those gaps. I've got some things to tell you also. Oh, and before you begin, I want to know what Sonny had to say that was so urgent."

"Gabi, the call didn't even go through. I rushed off to the dealership to get you, not knowing you were with Ashlee, and got so wrapped up in all this that I haven't had a chance to call him again."

"Well you better call him now, because he wanted to talk to Leon last night, before the end of the night. He doesn't even know yet, that Leon is dead!"

Jacob tried to call Sonny, but it still wouldn't connect for about thirty minutes. Finally it did, "Hey Sonny, it's Jacob." Jacob placed the phone on speaker mode.

"Hey Jacob, where's Leon?"

Reluctantly, yet anxiously Jacob blurted out, "Sonny, he died yesterday!"

"He WHAT?"

"Sonny, Leon was murdered."

"Oh no, Jacob, how? How did he die?"

"He was shot in the head."

"Are there any suspects?"

"Not really, Sonny."

"Jacob, this is beyond tragic; Michael dying, and then Leon being murdered! How is Gabrielle doing?"

"Leon died in her arms, but she's holding up okay."

"Oh Jacob, he died in her arms?"

"Yes. It's just too much for a person to lose two loved ones in such a short time. It's just too, too much."

Sonny paused for a moment, then slowly said, "Jacob, I've got some bad news for you also."

"What?"

"Sterling is missing."

"What do you mean, missing?"

"She was supposed to meet me in Milan yesterday, and there's still no sign of her! I tried calling Leon after she hadn't shown for a few hours…and…oh man, Jacob, I can't even believe Leon is dead. Why didn't Gabi call me?"

"Well, after Leon died in her arms yesterday, she could barely function, yet she kept herself together. Then today she was almost involved in a car bomb accident, and well, we're just having one party after another around here!"

"What do you mean she was almost involved in a car bomb accident?"

"I'll tell you later, but right now we need to find her Sonny, and I mean immediately. We all need to get together, here, in the states. We have too much going on right now with both Michael and Leon's deaths being suspect, and besides, you should be here for Leon's funeral service tomorrow."

"Wait a minute Jacob, did you say that Michael's death was suspect? Do they think that he was murdered also?"

"Yes."

Sonny didn't hesitate a second in responding to Jacob, "I'll be right there." Father's company had just purchased a small jet in the last few years, which was Sonny's main source of transportation between continents.

Jacob looked almost sick when he got off the phone. In fact, I remember seeing that same type of look on Leon's face.

"Jacob! How can Sterling be missing?" I yelled out, "NO! This is not right, it's not fair, what in the world is going on?"

"Gabi, with Michael and Leon gone…"

I interrupted him, "I know, you assume number one position in the business. That's an enormous responsibility, but..."

"Yes Gabi, it is. I have a lot to do now with Sterling missing, not to mention, trying to figure out who is to blame for these murders!"

"Oh Jacob, this is such a nightmare!"

"Gabi, there should have been a list with your father's letter, do you have that?"

"Yes I do, but I haven't really looked at it yet."

"Could you get it for me please? We need to contact some people on that list."

"Sure Jacob, I'll run upstairs and get it."

As I ran up the long spiral staircase, it seemed longer than usual. It felt like I was in slow motion. My thoughts kept repeating the same thing over, and over again. 'I just found out that I have a mother, how could I lose her now? This is so unfair...I just found out that I have a mother, how could I lose her now? This is so unfair...'

Jacob slowly sat down in Michael's chair. He knew what had to be done. Contemplating the monumental task that was before him, he immediately shifted into high gear, grabbing the phone, then his cell, talking with several people simultaneously. Normally Alex would have assumed this position, but because of Sandi, he and Father structured the business in this manner. However, should anything happen to Jacob, heaven forbid, Alex would be the next in line.

Jacob was now the director of a very large business empire, and responsible for thousands of lives. It was incumbent upon him to find a balance between who he was in his heart, and who he needed to be in this extremely powerful position. With the mantle passed to him, he immediately became the man that the Deliano Empire could depend on.

I ran all the way from my bedroom, down the stairs and to Father's office. I barely stopped before I hit the front of Father's desk, where Jacob was sitting. "Here it is! Here's the list Jacob!"

Jacob stared at me with that serious look again as he said, "Gabrielle, next time, you need to walk."

As he spoke to me in that tone of voice, my heart sank. I felt sad for a moment, but as soon as I gained my composure, I became a wee-bit angry. I couldn't, and wouldn't reveal how I was feeling inside.

"Gabi, when I couldn't get a hold of Sonny earlier, I called Eric. It didn't sound as though he knew anything about Leon's death, or Sterling being missing. Then, when I told him about Leon's death, he literally freaked out, lost it, and had to call me back after he contained himself. Gabi, Eric's beside himself, and was crying pretty hard while he was trying to explain to me what happened between Leon and him. I could barely understand him, except for the fact that he kept saying that he felt so bad about what happened between he and his Uncle."

At this point, I was trying to act as serious and poised as possible, so as not to make Jacob angry, "Yes, Uncle Leon met Eric here while everyone was still at the funeral, and I guess they had a pretty heated argument."

"Not just here Gabi, but yesterday before Leon died. Eric told me that Leon made a surprise visit to him, and pretty much beat the living daylights out of him."

"Why would he do that?"

"To get the letter and the list back."

"Why did Eric want those things?"

"We have a serious problem here, because Eric has his own thoughts as to what's going on, and how to handle it. Evidently he's been attempting to take care of matters by himself, without the approval of everyone else."

"By doing what?"

"I don't know, that's what worries me, and it also worried Leon."

"Oh Jacob, poor Uncle Leon, as usual he was only trying to protect everyone, and it's quite scary that Eric is so out of control like this."

"It certainly is, and you know one thing that Eric said, which is really perplexing to me, is that Leon kept asking him for the picture that was on Michael's desk, and Eric said that he didn't have it. The only reason that Leon finally stopped hitting him was because Mary made him stop."

"What do you mean, Mary made him stop?"

"They were at Mary's house."

"Why in the world were they there?"

"Because Eric was visiting Mary, and Leon found him there."

"But why was Eric at Mary's house?"

"Oh Gabi, I'm sorry, you wouldn't know that fact, would you?"

"Know WHAT fact?"

"Mary is their sister."

"Mary is whose sister?"

"Michael and Leon's."

I could not believe my ears. I could barely talk as I blurted out, "What are you talking about?"

"Well, when Mary's husband died Michael wanted to take care of her, so he moved her close to him. There was one major stipulation—she had to change her identity, because of the situation with Sterling. Of course Mary didn't mind. She wanted to leave the memories behind, and she wanted to be close to her brother, and to you. She could never have children, and you were the closest thing to a daughter that she would ever have."

"Jacob, so are you saying that Mary is my Aunt?"

"Yes she is. I know how hard this all must be for you."

"Oh Jacob, you don't know the half of it! But that makes sense now, why Mary was acting so strange the other night—it's because she was keeping me from seeing Uncle Leon and Eric! And that's why the rose bush was broken and there were footprints." My mind was whirling once again, "What's Mary's real name?"

"It's Sarah."

"Oh Jacob, my mind can barely get around all this. How many secrets can one family have?"

"Gabi, you need to…"

I instantly interrupted him—I didn't want to be told that I needed to do anything right now, and it was my turn to talk. "Jacob, I've got some pretty weird stuff to tell you too, but it doesn't compare to what you've been telling me. You know that picture that Uncle Leon thought Eric took- the duplicate snapshot that I showed to you of all of us in the park?"

"Yes."

Well that's the picture that was blown up, and sat on Father's desk.

"Yes I know. What are you getting at Gabi?"

"That's the picture that came up missing the night that Uncle Leon and Eric met here in the office. The night they had that pretty heated discussion, which apparently turned into somewhat of a brawl. So, for those obvious reasons, Uncle Leon thought that Eric took it, but…"

Jacob interrupted me, "So Eric didn't take it?"

"No he didn't! I found that picture the other night at Alex's house."

"WHAT!" Jacob yelled.

Finally the shoe was on the other foot. I knew something that everyone else didn't know, I told Jacob the crazy story about that night when Sandi thought I was her daughter, and how I was up in Alex's guest room, where I found the picture. Being somewhat shocked, Jacob told me that he thought Leon was on to something about not trusting Alex anymore, now especially in light of this news. However

Jacob didn't want to jump to conclusions before he talked with Alex. At that moment though, I didn't want to talk anymore about Alex. I was more curious about the rest of Eric's story.

"Jacob, where was Eric going after he left Mary's house?"

"Back to England."

"I thought you said that he and Sterling lived in Germany in the winter, and then Italy in the summer, so what was he doing in England?"

"Eric just graduated from Oxford, and he was going back there to wrap things up."

"Wow, I just keep learning all kinds of amazing things about my new family. So tell me, what did my little brother grow up to be?"

"A doctor."

"Isn't that something? A doctor, and he couldn't even save Father!"

"Gabi, Eric did all the research he could on that virus. It was pretty rare, and the whole time he had his suspicions about your father's death being something else. He's always been quick to try to blame the bad guys for anything that goes wrong, so we have to keep a leash on him."

Suddenly I remembered what Eric whispered in my ear at Father's funeral, 'They will pay.' He did truly think that the bad guys killed Father, I thought to myself. I yelled at Jacob, "So then tell me Jacob, who in the heck is killing my family? Where is Sterling? And why did Alex steal that picture?"

"Gabi, as much as I'd like to take the time to figure out the answers to your questions, and I will soon, I do need to make some calls."

Chapter 11

While Jacob was reviewing the list, I thought it was better to leave him alone for a few minutes than to just keep throwing questions at him every time something popped into my head. As I moved away from the desk, I walked slowly to the other side of the room, so as not to make Jacob angry again.

I sat down on the couch, melted into its soft and comfortable arms, and started to pick up my cup of coffee that had been replaced, without my knowing, by a glass of Merlot. I picked up the glass, twirled it, and watched as the tears ran down the inside of the glass. As I twirled it again, my eyes fixed on the tears—tears of blood. All I could see was the tears of blood running down Uncle Leon's face. The image was so vivid I could hardly stand it, and had to close my eyes. Chills came over me from those horrifying, all too new memories. Once again, an unbearable sense of pain swept through my body like piercing wind on an icy, cold day.

Jacob continued going through the list with a fine-toothed comb. He mentioned an entry that wasn't done on the computer, but written in by hand. It was Sterling's name with three phone numbers adjacent to it, the last one had an 'n' written by it, which Jacob assumed meant 'new.' He decided to call it.

I could hear Jacob dialing a number in the background. My mind was exhausted, and my eyes were so heavy they kept closing...

She stared at the ringing phone, thinking how annoying it was. 'If I don't answer it the first time that obviously means I don't want to be reached. Pretty much a no-brainer, guys!' Sterling returned to what she was doing, while basking in the sun, on the isle of Capri.

From out of nowhere came a blood-curdling sound as Mary ran into Father's office in a panic, throwing herself onto the couch, practically landing on me, screaming, "Gabi, why didn't you tell me about Leon?"

Having been awakened in such an abrupt manner, I hoped that I was consoling her properly. "Mary, I am so sorry, I was going to tell you, but I knew you were already upset about Father, and so much has happened tonight. I am so very sorry."

Then I remembered what Jacob told me about Mary being Father's sister, which meant that she was Leon's sister as well. I moved closer to her on the couch, put my arms around her and said, "My sweet Mary, I am so sorry about Leon. He was such a wonderful man, and we loved him so much."

Mary put her arms around me, held me very tightly, and sobbed like a baby. We sat in that same spot on the couch for an hour until she was able to calm down. I asked her who told her about Leon, to which she, reluctantly and quietly responded, "Alex."

I was upset with him for telling her, however it did make sense that he would. Alex must have known that Mary was Leon's sister, which prompted me to then explain to Mary that I knew about the secret as well.

"Mary, I want you to know that Father wrote me a beautiful letter, explaining in detail about the secret that you've all been keeping for so long. Then Jacob has been filling in the gaps. What I'm trying to say Mary…is that I know you are Father's sister—I know you're my Auntie!"

She looked at me through eyes that were filled with tears as she said, "Oh Gabrielle, I love you with all my heart. We were only doing what your father requested, please don't be upset with me."

"Mary, I could never be upset with you, and I understand that Father did what felt he had to do. I have no bad feelings towards anyone."

Mary, becoming much calmer at this point, held my hand and said, "Gabi, I'm glad you know everything. This has been such an unbearable burden, and almost impossible secret to keep from you."

I didn't want to interrupt her, but I remembered that someone needed to finish planning Uncle Leon's funeral.

"Mary we need to plan…"

In a firm voice Jacob interrupted me, he knew what I was about to say.

"Gabi, I'll take care of it."

I looked at him with loving eyes, relieved that the heavy burden of finalizing those plans was no longer mine.

Mary had completely gained her composure now, walked over to the desk where Jacob was still sitting and said, "Jacob, am I correct in assuming that you are now in control of…"

Jacob cut her off, "Yes Mary."

"Do you know where Eric and Sonny are?"

Jacob answered her very matter of fact like, "Everyone will be here very early tomorrow morning, and the funeral will be in the afternoon. Oh and Mary, even though Gabi knows the truth now, that doesn't mean that anyone else is to know."

Just as Mary started to ask Jacob another question, he stared at her in a business-like, yet stern manner. She responded by looking at him with respect, but not uttering a word—Jacob had the same amazing effect on people that I had only witnessed by Father. After seeing that, I thought to myself how well Father had trained Jacob. He will most definitely command the respect fitting his new role.

Mary gave me a hug, and told me that she needed to go home. I walked her to the front door, we hugged tighter than we had ever hugged before, and I told her how much I loved her. I felt so sad watching her walk away, knowing that she had lost both of her brothers in such a short time. It was all I could do to not run after her.

I went back to the office and found Jacob still sitting in Father's chair behind the desk, but now it was turned the other way, facing the window. I started talking before he turned back around, "Jacob, maybe we should…"

When I approached the desk, the chair slowly turned back around, revealing that Jacob was on the phone. As I motioned that I was going upstairs, he raised an eyebrow, then looked at me with that same stern look he gave Mary, and motioned with his hand for me to sit down.

Jacob had never treated me like this before. I knew that he had a tremendous weight on his shoulders, and he was trying his best to keep emotions under control. I sat down in the chair by the desk, albeit with butterflies in my stomach. I sat there wondering to whom he was talking with. He was mostly listening at this point, and his responses didn't sound very positive. Within moments he hung up the phone. As I sat there waiting for Jacob to speak, an overwhelming feeling of grief came over me again. My thoughts started drifting to the ocean of black umbrellas…

He looked at me very sternly for a few seconds before he spoke, "Gabi, that was Charles Stone, and he's on his way to talk with Alex."

"About what?"

"Well apparently, and unfortunately it was Alex's gun that murdered Leon."

"Oh, no! No, Jacob, I don't believe that!"

"I don't either, but something is definitely wrong with this picture."

"Jacob this is completely unbelievable, and cannot be correct. I know in my gut that Alex would never do such a thing. Even though it's weird that he has the photo, there must be some explanation for that, as well as the reason why Leon didn't trust him anymore."

"Slow down Gabi, no one said that Alex murdered Leon; only that his gun was implicated."

"Which means that he's a suspect!"

"Not necessarily. One test that they will run immediately is a paraffin test, which validates if someone has shot a gun within the last forty-eight hours."

"Jacob, how is Sandi taking this?"

"She doesn't know yet."

"Who is heading up the investigation?"

"Charles and Neil, a friend of mine."

"When will they be arriving at Alex's house?"

"After they run the paraffin test on Alex at the station, Charles will take Alex to his house, and the team will meet them there."

"Jacob, I'd like to talk to Sandi before Alex gets home. I also want to get that photo out of the drawer before anyone finds it."

"Okay, but I want you out of there quickly."

As I approached Sandi's house I could see her sitting in the swing on the porch, rocking back and forth, looking at something that she had on her lap. I couldn't tell what it was. She didn't see me, because she appeared to be looking down into her lap crying, loudly. As I walked up the porch stairs, she put whatever it was behind her back, and said, "Hi Princess!"

I could usually tell whose personality Sandi had taken on, by the way she greeted me, and right now, she was Sandi.

"Hi Sandi, how are you doing?"

"Oh…I'm okay," she responded, with hesitation in her voice.

"It looks like you've been crying, do you want to talk about it?"

She paused for a minute before answering, "I was just wondering what my life would have been like if my little girl hadn't been taken from me."

"Sandi, I am so sorry about Lily. I can't even imagine what it would be like to lose a child."

"No, you can't! Nobody can possibly know what it's like until a tragedy like that happens to them. The depth of the pain is almost unbearable. I think the only reason that I stayed sane, was because I had so much love and understanding from that grief support group. Those people were going through the same type of pain that I was going through. We shared stories, cried together, and got each other through our grief."

"Yes Sandi, those are remarkable groups. They help to make the situation seem somewhat tolerable when people share the same type of burdens with each other."

"Yeah, right up until the grief is so overwhelming, and the pain attacks again."

"Like now, Sandi?"

"Yeah."

At that point I wasn't sure if I should tell Sandi what was happening with Alex or not. She was in such a delicate mental state, and I was worried that the news might push her right over the edge again. I was still wondering though, what she was hiding behind her back.

"Sandi, are you holding something that you'd like me to put in the house for you?"

She looked at me funny, and then she brought her hand out slowly, revealing a tightly clutched fist in which she was holding a small photo. Before she turned it around, I thought that it was a picture of Lily, because that's what she said she had been crying about. I felt quite badly for prompting her to show me what she was holding. However to my surprise, the photo wasn't of her daughter at all, but was a picture of Sandi, Alex, my Father, Sonny, Daniel and Jacob. I didn't understand why she was crying about her daughter while holding that picture in her hand, but then, not a whole lot about Sandi made crystal clear sense. I had to think for a moment, because I knew I had seen that photo before.

"Isn't that the picture of you all in Europe, at the masquerade ball?"

"Yes, it most certainly is!"

"Sandi, why is that particular picture making you think about Lily?"

"Gabi, that's not exactly what I said now, is it? I said that I was thinking about what my life would have been like, if she hadn't been taken from me."

For a moment I thought that I was going crazy. That is the same thing she was saying, but for the life of me, I couldn't understand Sandi's thought process. I decided to attempt to get her mind off of her daughter, and back onto the picture.

"Yes, I'm sorry Sandi, that is what you said. You know, you look so pretty in that picture, and look at the guys, they all look so incredibly handsome!"

Then she blurted out, "That was the best night of my life!"

I was taken aback, because I remember the story Alex told me about that night in Switzerland. I became so engrossed in my conversation with Sandi, that for a moment I had forgotten why I was there.

"Sandi, I need to use your restroom—I'll be right back, and then we can talk, okay?"

"Sure."

I ran upstairs, down the long hallway, and then rushed into the guest room, closing the door, slowly and quietly behind me. I opened the desk drawer to retrieve the picture from the place I had hidden it—it was gone! Trying to maintain my calm, or what was left of it so as not to freak Sandi out, I continued to rifle through every drawer, until I was satisfied that it was nowhere to be found. I quickly ran back downstairs, because I didn't want to be caught upstairs when the police arrived.

As I approached the porch, I heard Sandi talking. I stopped to listen—it sounded as though she was talking to herself, but then she answered a question, which made me think that she was on the phone. I couldn't tell exactly what she was doing, but as I walked out onto the porch, her phone fell off of the swing. She could have just hung up on someone, or she could have been talking to an imaginary friend; either way, something didn't seem quite right with her, but I couldn't put my finger on it.

Sandi's face went blank, and I could tell she was becoming one of the other personalities. 'Oh not now—I don't have time to be sent to bed again!'

I sat down by her and said, "Sandi, I need to tell you something."

"And what would that be, little Missy?"

Her voice had changed drastically. I had to take the chance that she would hear and understand me. I knew it would be much better for her if she received the information from me about Alex, rather than from someone else.

I started talking to her slowly and calmly, "Sandi....Charles and Alex will be here soon...They are conducting an investigation into Leon's death, because the gun...that killed him...was Alex's."

She abruptly cut me off, screaming at me, "YOU AWFUL, AWFUL TART, HOW DARE YOU COME HERE, AND LIE TO ME LIKE THIS—ITS ALL YOUR FAULT!" Then she ran into the house and slammed the door.

As I hurriedly walked home, I was dreading having to tell Jacob that I didn't accomplish much—I certainly didn't want to see that look on his face again. At that point I was so frustrated I yelled out, "Geez Gabi, you totally blew it—you blew that all to heck!"

Approaching my yard, I could see that the dogs were out and in a playful mood. Sometimes I felt bad that I didn't spend much time with them. They felt more like protectors than pets. "Hi Rocky—hi Molly!"

Molly came charging at me with the ball in her mouth, wanting me to throw it for her. How could I ignore such a cute thing? 'Come on Gabi, you are alive in there, aren't you? Pick up the ball, and throw it for her.'

"Okay Molly, go get it!"

She barked from the excitement, and then charged after her ball trying to keep it away from Rocky. He didn't seem to care about the ball, but was more interested in keeping me away from where he had been digging. Father didn't like it when Rocky did that, and would always talk to him in a very stern voice upon discovering one of the holes he had dug.

'Poor dog, he doesn't want to get into trouble.' I walked over to Rocky, talking to him in a sweet voice, but he turned from me and walked towards the bushes, rapidly wagging his tail. By the way he was acting, I thought he saw a squirrel or a raccoon, or something, so I followed him over there.

Rocky started barking at me, and as I approached he became nervous, frantically trying to cover the hole with dirt. His nose was covered with mud as he looked up at me, trying to figure out what I was going to do, and then he put his nose back down to the ground.

"You silly dog, you just wanted to show me the hole you have dug, and nicely covered up. How strange though, I've never seen you cover a hole before. Do you have a special bone in there, Rocky?"

Rocky wagged his tail, and started barking, so Molly ran over to see what all the excitement was about. Before I knew it, they both had me on the ground, licking my face.

"Okay, okay you guys, that's enough!"

Rocky went back over to the hole that he had almost completely covered, and started whimpering.

"Poor dog—I'll get your bone out for you."

I moved the dirt out of the hole, hating that I was getting dirt under my freshly painted fingernails. I felt the bone, and it seemed quite weird—as I pulled it out of the dirt, I saw gold shining through. As more of the dirt fell off, glass appeared, so I continued rubbing the dirt off until I could see that it was a pair of gold-rimmed glasses.

Oh how odd, 'Where in the world did these glasses come from?' I pushed the dirt back into the hole and said, "That's enough playing for now, be a good dog, and go lay down."

I went into the restroom to wash my hands before I approached Jacob in the office.

"Well Gabi, was your mission a success?"

"Not really. I couldn't find that photo anywhere, however I did manage to tell Sandi about what was going on with Alex."

"How did that go?"

"That didn't go very well at all. She actually turned into someone else as she screamed and slammed the door in my face."

"That's no big surprise. So the picture wasn't in the drawer?"

"No, and I looked through every drawer in that desk."

"Neil is on that search team. If it's there, he'll find it."

"It's nice to have so much confidence in someone, not to mention the connections that you have. They must really come in handy, huh?"

"Neil and I have been in the same pack…"

I cut Jacob off, "Oh speaking of packs, Rocky and Molly were desperate for some attention, so I stopped to play with them for a minute. Rocky led me to a hole, where he buried this," I held the glasses out in my cupped hand, mortified that dirt was still underneath my fingernails.

"Nice nails Gabi. So who do the glasses belong to?"

The nail comment was unnecessary, but I was too tired to care at that point, "Well, certainly no one from this house. None of us wear glasses, not even the staff."

Jacob looked quizzically at me and said, "How odd."

I thought the same thing about Jacob's behavior, but only responded with, "Yes Jacob, how very odd indeed!"

Chapter 12

I placed the glasses on the table, and asked Jacob to sit by me on the couch. I was spent, and really needed some affection from a friend, however his reaction to me was quite different from what I was longing for. Jacob quickly started talking about the list, displaying no affection whatsoever, as he started speaking in a hurried business tone. I interrupted him before he could finish his sentence.

"Jacob, I don't think that I can deal with anything else right now. Will you put that list away, and can we please talk about Sterling for just a few minutes?"

Jacob's entire demeanor changed. He put his arm around me, and apologized for getting so wrapped up in his responsibilities. He momentarily forgot how painful, and mind boggling this whole situation had been for me.

He reached for my hand, kissed it, looked sweetly into my eyes and said, "What would you like to know about Sterling?"

"Everything! Where does she live?"

"Sterling and Eric lived in Germany until Eric went away to school. They chose Germany because Michael had many connections there, and Munich is where he conducted a lot of his business. Sterling spoke German, so it seemed like a smart idea, however, she also speaks Italian, which is why they also lived in Italy."

"That must be where I get my love for studying foreign languages—from my mother, but I'm only fluent in Italian."

"Gabi, you are very much like Sterling. You are both extremely talented women."

"You said that they lived in Germany most of the time, but where else did they live?"

"In Capri and Zurich."

"Where did they live in Germany?"

"In Karlsruhe, a quiet little city outside of Munich. They lived there for most of the year, then in Capri for the summer, and Zurich during the skiing season."

"So, where was she flying off to yesterday?"

"Milan."

"And now no one has heard from her?"

"No, and we're a little concerned about her, but don't worry, I'm sure she's okay."

"Oh no, Jacob! Sterling is alone out there. Father is gone, Uncle Leon is gone, and now Sonny and Eric are flying to the states to be here for Leon's funeral tomorrow. No one is there with her!"

"I know Gabi, this all seems so surreal that it's hard to think straight at times, but if we don't regroup, someone else could become a victim to whomever is stalking us."

"Stalking us? You have got to be kidding me!"

"No Gabrielle, I'm not. I'm bringing in some men to guard the house, and protect you, around the clock!"

With my palms becoming clammy, my heart beating as though it would pound right out of my chest, I cried out to Jacob "I don't like this, and I don't know how much more I can take!"

"Gabi, once Alex became suspect, the dynamics of this whole investigation changed."

"Because you think Alex could have done it?"

"Absolutely not! What this does mean is that someone close to us may have done it. And they're either not close enough, or not smart enough. We know unequivocally that Alex didn't do it, yet someone is trying to frame him."

"This is making me literally sick. What are we doing to find Sterling? When will we find her? When Jacob?"

"Soon, I'm sure."

"Did you ever think about the fact that maybe Sterling isn't missing? Maybe she's just shopping in Milan, buying up all the latest fashions, or she could be…"

Jacob interrupted me, "GABI, I would love to tell you that is true, but Sterling had specific instructions from Leon to go directly to Milan, where Sonny always meets her. She never showed."

"I know you're tired of talking about all this, and it's getting you irritated, but please give me just a few more minutes of your time. Tell me something else about her—I can't lose Sterling now Jacob, she just came into my life!"

As Jacob talked about Sterling a big smile came on his face, "She's a prolific writer, and a fantastic painter."

"She's a writer?"

"Well actually, she's an author."

"So you're saying that her work has been published? How can that be, since she's been in hiding all these years?"

"She assumed a pen name, and sent all of her work from Italy to New York to be published."

"Jacob, that is so exciting! What name does she use? Is there any particular genre that's her favorite?"

"She goes by Annasophia. She writes novels, mysteries mostly. I do believe that she's had a few very successful ones."

"Oh my gosh, she drastically changed her name, that's a big difference from Sterling Deliano, to Annasophia! Do you know the name of any of her novels?"

"I never have time to read anything fun, so unfortunately I don't know the names, or plots of any of her novels. I do know the name of her latest novel was called Obsessions."

"I've heard of that book! It was on the New York's, Best Seller list just recently!"

"Yeah, Annasophia is pretty well known for her work, yet no one really knows who she is."

"Poor Sterling, she isn't even able to receive credit for her own work. That must be awfully hard."

"Sterling doesn't care about recognition. She says she gets enough satisfaction in just knowing that her novels are successful. Remember Gabi, she knew that changing her name and identity, and moving was the only thing that would possibly keep her, and her son alive. She's learned to appreciate life differently."

"Jacob, you said that she's also a painter? Has her painting career been any where near as exciting?"

"She doesn't sell her paintings."

"So then, she doesn't paint very well?"

"Sterling has been studying the Renaissance Masters for twenty-five years. Her work looks a lot like," then Jacob paused for a moment… "Well, you be the judge, it looks like the painting on that wall, over the safe."

"Is that Sterling's painting?"

"Yes Gabrielle, it is. I remember when Michael brought it home."

"I do too, that was about ten years ago. Father was so proud of that painting—now I know why. After he hung the painting, we sat there and admired it for hours, getting lost in its beauty. Jacob, Sterling is quite an artist—look at that picture!"

"She certainly is Gabrielle. It's absolutely breathtaking, just like both of you."

Even though Jacob had just delivered a very kind and deliberate compliment, all I could think of was the fact that I was staring at something so beautiful, and something that I never knew was painted by my mother I walked straight over to the picture she had painted so long ago, running my fingers across the canvas, wondering what her thoughts were as she painted it. I marveled at how much it looked like a Titian, or a Raphael. The skin tones are so lifelike, and the bodies look so real. The clothing that hung from the body, draped to the floor with such incredible detail, I followed it down to the bottom of the painting where I saw her initials, SD. Something came over me, and I started to cry.

"How awful this must have been for her, living her life in hiding."

"Gabi, not being able to live with your father and you has been a hard thing for her, but she has really had a good life. Sterling has also never wanted for a single thing, Michael made sure of that. She seems to be coping much better with everything though, these last five or so years."

Sterling was sitting on her verandah, sipping an Italian soda, basking in the sun, and finishing her novel. She knew that her days of hiding would soon be over, and she could live a normal life. She closed her eyes—all she could see was... suddenly Sterling's phone rang interrupting her daydream...

"I wonder who it is this time."

Sterling went back to her novel that she was having a hard time finishing, thinking that endings were always hard to write, but never this hard.

While I was captivated by Sterling's painting Jacob was staring at the photo of the day in the park. He seemed to be lost in his thoughts—I could tell he was missing Father.

"What kind of food does she like?" He didn't respond. "Jacob, did you hear me?"

Jacob cleared his throat, and tried to hold back the tears, "No, I'm sorry, what did you say?"

"What does Sterling like to eat?"

"Her favorite food is Italian, and her favorite dessert is Crème Brulee."

"Well I think that Sterling and I are going to get along just fine."

"Yes, I know that you will."

"Jacob, I hear what you're saying about Sterling always following instructions, but I really don't think that she's missing. She's in Milan for heaven's sake, the fashion capital of the entire world, she's probably on a shopping spree, and having a ball."

"No Gabi, she wouldn't do that."

"Why not?"

"She has her own tailor."

"Well I guess that's safer for her."

"Yes, that's true, but Sterling doesn't like crowds anyway."

"A gal after my own heart. Or should I say, I sound just like my mother! So how close are Sterling and Eric? She must be very proud of her son."

"Actually, they are not that close. Eric is a little hard to deal with sometimes."

"So, were Eric and our Father very close?"

"They had a love-hate relationship. Eric is still young, and a little hot-headed, but he never went against Michael's wishes."

"How did Father feel about him not being in the business, and becoming a doctor instead?"

"Michael encouraged Eric to become a doctor, and told him that the business was always there if he changed his mind."

"Very interesting."

We both kept staring at the picture, "So tell me about Daniel. When and why did he fall away from the group?"

"Gabi, we can talk about Daniel in a minute, but I need to get something to eat. Do you think Maria could bring us something?"

"Of course she can, what do you want?"

"I'm not picky. Whatever she'd like to make is perfectly fine with me."

I found Maria reading in her room. I could tell that she was still quite upset about Uncle Leon and Father. "I'm sorry to bother you Maria, but could we have a little something to eat please?"

"Certainly Gabi, what would you like?"

"Whatever is easy Maria, I know it's late."

"Okay, I'll be there in a minute. Oh, and Gabi, you're never bothering me. You and your father have been a blessing to us for many years; you could never be a bother to me."

"Thank you, Maria."

When I returned to the office, Jacob was on the phone once again. I just stood there, watching his lips move, and got lost in the thought of kissing those lips, and for the moment all I could do was watch them. I had a strong urge to walk over, sit on his lap, hold his face in my hands, pull him close to me and kiss his lips gently, warmly, and forcefully…'Oh Gabi, stop torturing yourself.'

Jacob caught me staring at him as he hung up the phone, and he looked at me as if he knew exactly what I had been thinking—maybe he did. He cleared is throat, changed his facial expression and said, "That was the guy I had on the search team at Alex's house; he found the picture."

"Where did he find it?"

"Under the mattress, of all places, in that guest room."

"Wow, how did he get it out of there without anyone seeing?"

"Very carefully! I guess he almost got caught, we'll hear the whole story when he arrives in a few minutes."

"Well at least someone did something right tonight. I really botched the job—especially messing with Sandi's head the way I did. It was truly unintentional."

"Hey, none of that was your fault."

Jacob's friend, Neil, arrived with the picture just in time for our late night meal. Maria brought a platter of meats and cheeses, tomatoes, avocados, onions, olives and much more for the open-faced sandwiches that we all loved. I hugged her, and walked her to the door of the office, "Thank you Maria, that's perfect."

Neil put the package containing the picture on the desk and blurted out, "That was not an easy task Jacob; you owe me big time for this one!"

"I really didn't think we were keeping score, but if you want to get technical, you're the one who owed me this time, remember?"

"Oh man, Jacob, no one gets anything past you—not that I was trying!

We all made our sandwiches and wolfed them down, without realizing what we were doing. I opened the package and just sat there staring at the picture. Jacob and I had a glass of wine, and soon I was drifting off. He nudged me, and told me to go on up to bed. I willingly obliged, and walked slowly towards the office door as Jacob sat down in Father's chair behind the desk.

Chapter 13

I climbed into bed thinking that I would doze off immediately, but tonight I just laid there, my brain on overload, desperately trying to sort through my thoughts so I could fall asleep.

'Who could possibly have murdered my father, and why? Who shot Uncle Leon? I know that Alex couldn't have anything to do with this, so who is trying to frame him? Has Sterling really disappeared?' My confused and busy mind lamented over those thoughts that kept reappearing in a circular pattern, over and over again…until finally…I fell asleep.

My dream began on a gorgeous, crisp spring day. Suddenly a beautiful woman appeared in a long white, flowing silk and lace dress, with a string of white, baby pearls around her neck, and earrings to match. She smelled like Jasmine. Her long, thick, curly, dark hair was bouncing as she ran in slow motion through the park. A smile came on my face, and in my heart, as I realized that it was Sterling.

She reached out her hand to me and said, "Gabrielle, we don't need to hide anymore."

I took her hand, and started running with her alongside the river, past the beautiful blooming dogwoods and sweet-scented flowers. The weeping willow was also flowing musically with the wind, reaching out to touch us as we ran by. The birds were singing in the trees—the same song that was in my heart.

It was turning dusk now, the park was becoming laden with fog, and as it thickened I could no longer see where we were. Sterling's hand became very tense as she held on to me tighter and tighter. I looked up, shocked to see that her appearance had changed drastically.

Her Jasmine fragrance had changed to a spicy Organza. Her dress was now scarlet with a plunging neckline, and a slit up her thigh. Her hair was pulled up in an exquisite French-roll. Her long, sexy neck was covered with diamonds that matched the dangling diamond earrings, setting off her very succulent, cherry, red lips.

In the distance I could hear music playing. We drifted through the fog and we got closer to the sound I could see that it was a full orchestra playing the tango. I was mesmerized by the music, and the beautiful ice sculptures that started to appear through the fog. Suddenly Sterling dropped my hand, and drifted off with a man in a black tuxedo. While I stood there and watched them move through the fog their images became fainter and fainter. I kept thinking over and over, 'Who is that man? I can't see his face—who is that man?'

I began stirring in my sleep, feeling nervous and anxious. Suddenly my dream was rudely interrupted by the alarm clock. It was all I could do to drag myself out of bed and into the shower. I stood there, dripping wet and motionless, my mind grew numb thinking about another funeral—I could barely pull it together to dry myself off, let alone think about the process of getting ready for this heart-wrenching event.

The thought of another 'black' day kept going round and round in my head. I need to wear black—what should I wear to this black affair? 'Well Gabi, you have three black dresses—this shouldn't be too hard—just wear one that you didn't wear to Father's funeral. OMG! Are you kidding me...Gabi, this is ridiculous—why are you worrying about fashion, and what you wore to the last funeral?' I began to feel shallow and cold. 'This should not be an issue Gabi—just pick a dress!'

My mind felt paralyzed from the recent events, making it hard to even decide on something as simple as what to wear. I slowly walked over to the window as if in some sort of trance to check out the weather, which finally helped me to make a decision on what to wear. It was a beautiful day, with an electric blue sky and absolutely no sign of rain—certainly not the kind of day for a funeral, and much different from just days ago when Father was buried.

My choice of dress for the day was a short sleeve, plain, black rayon with a scoop neck and black, covered buttons down the back. This is one of my favorite dresses, but would probably end up being hated the same way I now hate the one that I wore to Father's funeral, just days ago.

Jacob was waiting for me in Father's office in the same black, Bill Blass suit that he wore to Father's funeral. I guess guys don't worry about clothes like women do—how nice that must be. I knew that Jacob had at least five black suits, so why did he choose this one again? 'Oh stop it, Gabi!'

Even though Jacob looked as strikingly handsome as usual, his attitude was something different altogether.

He looked at me sternly, as he said, "Sit down Gabi."

"Well, good morning to you too, Jacob."

"Mi scusi, Gabrielle, I've got a lot on my mind this morning."

'Excuse me' in Italian was his way of saying he was really sorry. We loved speaking in Italian to each other—it was just one of our sweet things we did.

"I know you do, mi amore. It just seems like we're losing us in all of this craziness, and I don't like the way that makes me feel."

"Gabrielle, we will never lose us, because us is what keeps me going through this heart-wrenching ordeal. Please don't ever forget that. I need to stay focused on the situation and tasks at hand. I can't worry about your feelings right now, even though I would like to."

"How selfish of me—I'm sorry Jacob."

"Gabi, let's talk about a few things. The guys will be here in an hour, and we need to go over the final arrangements for Leon."

Jacob had a very organized, methodical mind. Nothing could throw him off track, not that I was trying. Our personalities complimented each other. Where I tended to be more emotional, Jacob was extremely empirical. Although sometimes we clashed, for the most part we were a good balance.

Jacob handed me the file for Uncle Leon's service, "Here's the outline, and the list of who will be speaking."

After he finished reviewing everything, he looked up at me and said, "By the way, who is our driver?"

"Paul, of course."

"Why do you have Ashlee riding in the family car?"

"Come on Jacob, she's like family, and she's all alone, besides I need her."

"No, Gabrielle!"

"May I ask why?"

"There will be too much discussed in the car in too short a time, and we don't want to have to watch what we say."

"Then I'll ride with Ashlee."

"You'll ride in the family car, and you can see Ashlee when we get there; enough said."

As I started walking off, Jacob said, "Oh and Gabrielle, one more thing. I want you to know that you will be watched 'round the clock, as will Alex. There will be two body guards on you at all times, starting today."

"Do you think that's really necessary?"

"Gabi, please don't question me! Need I remind you that your father and Leon have just been murdered? Right now every one of our lives are in danger! There will also be nine other new faces at the funeral, that no one knows, and they will be watching every move that every person makes."

"Have you been up all night planning this, Jacob?"

"All night and all morning, my love."

I just about fell out of my chair when Jacob said those words to me—I longed for him to hold me in his arms, but I knew this was not the time.

Sonny arrived at noon as expected. As I walked up to greet him, I could tell that he hadn't slept either. He threw his arms around me, lifted me up in the air, put me back down on my feet, and kissed my forehead like he always did.

"How are you holding up, Gabrielle?"

"I'm okay Sonny, but this whole thing seems like a nightmare that I can't wake up from."

"We'll straighten things out soon. Don't you worry your pretty little head."

I looked around, but didn't see Eric anywhere. "Sonny, where's Eric?"

"He told Paul that he wanted his own car, so we dropped him at the car rental place, sounds pretty weird, huh?"

I was beginning to feel very conflicted about Eric's personality, so I wasn't sure if that sounded weird or not. Sonny rushed into Father's office to see Jacob. I walked outside to wait for Eric and stand in the sun—I really needed to feel the warmth on my face, if only for a few minutes. My cold, insecure body felt so warm, and comforted as I stood there soaking up the sun's rays…

I looked around, remembering all the happy times with Father. I could hear the birds singing in the trees and the water trickling in the fountain that stood in the middle of the courtyard. Father and I would sit here for hours planning trips to distant places—traveling was a passion for both of us.

As I stood there, wrapped in the sun's warm and secure blanket, my thoughts kept drifting back to the many vacations that we planned just to get away from the Seattle rain. Father and I had traveled to exotic places at least three times a year, including Jamaica, Tahiti, Hawaii, Mexico and the Caribbean. St. Thomas was one of my favorite places in December. Where else could one find a person dressed up like Santa, wearing only a red bathing suit, and a red Santa cap, running along the beach delivering drinks? The cove at St. Thomas was a beautiful island paradise with its warm, clear, crystal blue waters that I had been swimming in more times than I can count.

Suddenly, and out of nowhere it seemed, a car screeched up the driveway, jolting me instantly out of my thoughts. It was Eric in a black, convertible Mercedes. He looked as handsome as I remembered him at Father's funeral. I just wish that I didn't have such conflicted feelings about him. He seemed so sincere that day when he spoke to me, but since then, everything I've heard about him seems somewhat irrational. 'Oh, stop it Gabi, just give him a chance.'

"Hi, Eric!"

"Hello, Gabrielle, I'm so glad you're by yourself, get in."

"Where are we going?"

"For a short ride, so we can talk privately."

"About what?"

"Things."

"Eric, I'd feel more comfortable if we just sat in the car to talk. Jacob won't know where I've gone, and he'll get worried."

"For Christ's sake Gabrielle, who is Jacob to you, anyway?"

Eric shocked me with his language. I wasn't sure what to say, but I thought that if I was going to have any kind of relationship with my new brother I had better set him straight, right now!

I boldly stared him straight in the eyes as I firmly said, "Three things Eric: Number one, Jacob is a very, loyal business associate and friend—Number two, if we're going to have a discussion, it's right here, or nowhere—Number three, don't ever say that again."

"Say what?"

"Don't ever use any sentence with Christ's name in it, again! I don't like it, understood?"

"Yeah okay, I'll give you number one and number three, but get in!"

I looked at him with a half smile—half smirk and said, "Well, this is a great way for siblings to get to know each other!"

"That's funny! We're instantly siblings, yet we didn't even grow up together—weird concept, huh?"

Okay…so he's a wee bit weird; I can live with that. "Well brother, it was a necessity that we lived apart, wouldn't you agree?"

"Quite frankly Gabrielle, I wonder how much of a necessity it really was. I think that it may have started out that way, but lasting twenty years for Christ's sake?"

I glared at him for using that word again.

"Oops, I'm sorry, I won't say that again. Anyway, I lived without a steady father in my life for twenty years. Wouldn't you call that irresponsible?"

"Didn't Father come visit you a lot?"

"Not enough."

"Well Eric, what did you want to talk to me about?"

"Gabrielle, don't you..."

I interrupted him, "You can call me Gabi."

"Gabi, don't you wonder what Michael did with all his money?"

"He's a billionaire Eric, he did a lot of things with his money!"

"Well, did you ever investigate?"

"Investigate what, and why?"

"For starters, how about any of Michael's Swiss accounts?"

He was starting to make me nervous, but I tried to sound strong as I said, "I knew about everything, Eric."

"Everything Gabi, are you sure?"

"Well, I think I'm sure, but now you have me second guessing myself."

I remembered finding the file that was on Father's desk, the one he left out, which had a spreadsheet with huge amounts of money being transferred to accounts that I wasn't familiar with. Maybe Eric did know something, but what?

"Gabi, I can assure you that you don't know everything, because I just recently stumbled onto this little fun fact, quite by accident."

"Onto what?"

I was startled by a loud knock on the car door, as Jacob said in a demanding voice, "I need both of you in the office, now!" Then he walked off.

"That's a nice greeting," Eric said.

"He's got a lot on his mind, give him a break."

We joined Jacob and Sonny in the office, reviewed the details for the funeral service, and agreed on a time for the meeting afterwards.

Mary arrived just in time before the family limo was ready to depart. She climbed in very awkwardly, and fell before she got to her seat. That wasn't Mary's style, and I thought it quite strange that she had been so uncoordinated. She held her head in her hands and cried silently to herself the whole way to the chapel. I lovingly watched her every movement, worried that she might be weak from not eating.

The people came in groves, much like at Father's funeral. I thought it was a shame that Sterling couldn't be here with her family. I wondered how close she had been with Uncle Leon. The nine men that Jacob hired would have blended in much better if they all hadn't looked so Mafioso, which they weren't. Probably nobody else noticed, but I found it somewhat amusing.

Due to the nature of Leon's death, the casket was closed. The service went fine for the most part. I delivered another touching eulogy, but this time I could barely keep it together, although I highly doubt that anyone else noticed. I found it so hard to get the words out each time I mentioned how close Father and Uncle Leon were. Tears filled my eyes, blurring my vision as they rolled down my cheek, landing on my carefully written speech.

The pain in my heart from both of these untimely and sad deaths was so fresh. It took every ounce of strength within me to get through the entire funeral service, yet somehow I was able to do this final gesture of love for Uncle Leon, the same way I did for Father.

Later, Mary and I stood hand in hand at the graveside, watching as each person placed a flower on Uncle Leon's casket. Ashlee stood there and cried for quite a while, then quickly rushed to my side, to be consoled by Mary and me.

Alex and Sandi stood by the casket for the longest time. I watched Alex's every move, as did Jacob, Sonny, Eric and nine other men. Alex's body looked limp, as though he was feeling sick from grief. I could see the pain on his face and in his eyes, which had a constant stream of tears coming from them, rolling down his cheeks, and soiling the rim of his shirt collar.

I knew Alex very well, and I could tell that he was truly in an immense amount of pain, much different than Sandi whose face was distant and contorted. I couldn't tell if she was sad about Leon, or becoming one of the 'others.' As I watched them I did see Sandi lift her glasses to blot her eyes with a handkerchief. I guess she felt something, if only for a brief moment.

Alex left Sandi alone, and walked over to Mary and me, pretending as though he was expressing his condolences. Instead, he quickly and quietly said, "The priority at the moment is to discover who is watching this family, and more importantly right now, who has stolen my gun!"

I looked at him, silently nodding for him to bend down so I could say something. I whispered quietly in his ear, "Yes we do, and I want to talk to you immediately."

Alex forced a slight grin through the pain that was deeply imprinted on his face, and whispered back to me, "After the service?"

"No, after the meeting, we…"

Alex and I were interrupted as Sandi walked up to Alex, grabbed his arm and yanked him away. Alex looked back at me with a pitiful smile, which I mirrored. He knew I understood Sandi's bizarre actions.

Ashlee looked at me and said, "That woman is a piece of work."

Mary responded to Ashlee, "Honey, you don't know the half of it."

I told Mary to go on ahead of us, to get into the limo, and that I would be there in a minute. Then I turned to Ashlee and said, "They're killing…"

Ashlee cut me off, "They who?"

I felt like I was losing it, and I became a little frantic as I said, "They are killing the people in that photo!"

"What photo, Gabi?"

"Do you remember that picture on Father's desk, of me and the guys?"

"The one in that beautiful frame?"

"Yes, that's the one! Ashlee, people in that picture are dying!"

"Now wait a minute Gabi, that's a pretty illogical leap."

"Good grief Ashlee, I don't care how logical or illogical it is. It's happening!"

"You sound like you're convinced, and a little freaked out. Have you got proof?"

"Ashlee I am freaked out, not to mention the fact that I'm losing people I love! And remember, I'm in that photo also!"

"It just doesn't make sense Gabi, why would anyone want to kill your family?"

"Ashlee, it's a long story, but trust me, people do!"

"And who are these people?"

I felt like I was coming out of my skin—the burden of this secret was becoming too heavy for me to carry. I wanted to tell my best friend everything, but I knew my words must remain guarded.

"I can't tell you the story right now, it's entirely too long, and I'm sworn to secrecy. It has to do with something my family witnessed by accident, and people want them dead because of it. Ashlee, my mother has been in hiding for twenty years!"

"Your who?"

"My mother!"

"YOUR WHAT?"

"Yes! Ashlee my mother is alive, and she's been hiding for all these years."

"Gabrielle, do you know how bizarre this all sounds?"

"Yes, but it's true!"

"When did you find out about this?"

"Father left me a letter that explained who my mother was, and why she was hiding. You know that car bomb the other night, well…"

"Whoa, Gabi, slow down."

"I can't Ash, you've just got to hear this!

"I want to, but it's just so much to take in at warp speed like this."

"You're telling me! Anyway, I think that the bomb was meant for Jacob, and guess what?"

"What?"

"He was in that picture also!"

"Okay, and your point is…"

"Ashlee, they're dying!"

"Gabi, go do whatever you have to do tonight, then come on over to my house. Don't bother calling, I'll be waiting for you."

Chapter 14

As I walked into the office, Jacob was yelling at Sonny about not telling him Sterling's newest phone number. Then he smacked Sonny upside the head and said, "Come on Sonny, that's not like you, you're usually on top of things!"

"Hey man, how was I supposed to get something that I didn't even know existed?"

Although they were almost funny, I didn't want to get involved in the banter, which prompted me to tell them how I felt.

"Hey guys, did it ever cross your minds that maybe she didn't want anyone to have the number?"

Jacob scowled at me as he said, "Gabi, that wouldn't make any sense at all."

Sonny smirked and then let out a chuckle as he said, "Why would Sterling have a phone number that she wouldn't want anyone to have?"

Jacob smacked Sonny on the head again as he walked by him to grab the phone, "Let's try that number again!"

Sonny looked at Jacob in a quizzical manner and said, "What do you mean again?"

"Well, because I've already called this number earlier, but no one ever answered."

Sonny snapped back, "Well, if that was Sterling's number, she would have answered it immediately."

Jacob switched the phone to speaker mode so everyone could hear it, but it just rang, and rang, and rang... After letting the phone ring at least twenty times, Jacob finally hung up.

Sterling was exasperated once again as she heard her phone ring and ring. She knew that she had given her number to only one person, and the number on the Caller I.D. was not his number—it did reveal an 'out of area' number, which she of course, would never answer.

Sterling made a cup of espresso, and returned to the computer to work on her novel. Frustrated by her lack of concentration, she began to re-write the chapter she had just finished writing...

The meeting started at four o'clock sharp. The family met with Alex and Sonny first, so Alex could go home to be with Sandi. Then they met with my two bodyguards, and finally with the force, Jacob's 'mini army' that he had summoned.

I felt quite protected with this very experienced group of ex-black belts, ex-Navy Seals, ex-under cover FBI agents, and a few others with equally interesting and impressive backgrounds. Aside from Mary and myself, there were thirty-six men in Father's office—a single woman's dream. When Jacob calls in those who owe him favors, he doesn't miss a one. These guys were all 'men's men,' and treated Jacob with the utmost respect, as they did Father when he periodically gathered them from the corners of the earth. After Jacob presented the plan in explicit detail, they each took their briefs, and departed immediately.

Jacob asked me to drive Mary home, because she wasn't feeling well. Since I had asked him earlier if I could spend some time with her, he agreed that I should. I took Mary home; we had a nice talk. Then, I jumped into my car and drove quickly over to Alex's house. I would have usually just walked there, but I was going directly to Ashlee's afterwards. When I arrived at Alex's, he was standing on the porch just staring up at the stars. I walked up to him, wrapped my arms around his waist and said, "Alex, I'm so scared."

Alex put his arm around me, and held me tight as he said, "We need to talk about how Michael was murdered."

I was a little confused, and looked at him in dismay as a single tear rolled slowly down my cheek.

"Didn't you say he was poisoned, and..."

Alex interrupted, "Gabi, those two men that followed you here—they are your body guards, I presume?"

"Yes, you know the drill, they'll be following me everywhere."

"Good, you need them!"

"Geez Alex, I don't know how much more insecure I could possibly feel right now."

"Back to what we were saying, Gabi. Yes, he was poisoned, but it had to have been administered slowly. There was hardly a trace, and it would have been missed altogether if I hadn't asked my friend in forensics to run those tests."

"So what kind of poison was it?"

"He's an expert, and the only thing that's conclusive right now is that it was some type of venom."

"What do you mean Alex, like snake venom?"

"Yes, it's most interesting in that it was a combination of a neurotoxin, and a hemolytic venom, which means that one type destroyed his red blood cells, while the other type was paralyzing his nerves."

"Alex, I can't stand this; I can't believe that someone tortured and murdered my father! And why, Alex?"

"I don't have a clue Gabrielle, but I'm thinking that whoever killed your father, also killed Leon."

"Alex, that goes against everything you've ever taught me about detective work. Those deaths have drastically different M.O.'s."

"You're absolutely correct about that, however it's just too coincidental for me—both Michael and Leon dying in a span of two days. It seems like someone was just a little too anxious to move forward with their plans, which can make people get sloppy, and change their M.O. sometimes."

"Oh Alex, who do you think could do something like this?"

"Someone who knows this family very well. Either an insider, or someone who has been watching everyone for a very long time."

"Either way Alex, this is very creepy, and makes me feel so violated."

"This is a violation of everyone's rights. The biggest violation of all, is that Sterling witnessed something years ago, which completely took her rights away, for a very long time."

I began to feel numb as the words 'violation' and 'rights' fell out of his mouth. Looking down with tears filling my eyes all I could muster was a faint whisper, "Her whole, entire life!"

"Gabrielle, I am so sincerely sorry about this."

"Alex, this tragedy is like a never-ending nightmare, and now with Sterling missing!"

"What do you mean, Sterling is missing? Since when?"

"We found out while Charles was at your house yesterday."

"Why didn't you tell me?"

"Alex, I couldn't."

108

"Why? Oh never mind right now, just tell me what you know."

"All I know is that Sterling never showed up in Milan."

Alex placed his hand over my mouth, "Quiet Gabrielle, I hear Sandi coming down the stairs. I'll come see you later, what's a good time?"

"I'm going to Ashlee's for a while—come over at eleven o'clock."

I drove to Ashlee's house with my trusty 'tails' right behind me. The thought of my having to be followed like this, because someone was watching my family, stalking my family, killing my family, was entirely too much for me to deal with. My heart was pounding hard, my throat was tight, and I could hardly swallow. I wondered just how much more I could handle.

As I pulled up to Ashlee's house I felt guilty about wanting to lay this unbelievably crazy drama on her. I didn't want to complicate her life right now, but she would never forgive me if I kept all this from her. Contemplating every heart-wrenching detail that had come to light since Father's death I sat in the car, frozen with fear and trepidation. I had to literally talk myself into getting out of the car, and walking up to Ashlee's front door.

Her Butler answered the door, and showed me into the parlor where Ashlee was waiting. After a long embrace the two of us sat on the couch as I shared the entire story, while sipping a single glass of wine for over an hour. It was so good to have such a close friend whom I trusted with my life—one who could give me advice, and help me sort through all the craziness.

I explained my last dream to Ashlee in vivid detail about Sterling. How perplexing it was each time she met me in one outfit, and then went through a metamorphic change mid-dream. As we started to work through what Ashlee thought the meaning was behind the dream, I began crying uncontrollably.

"Gabi, I love you so much and am too close to this situation to be what you need from a counselor. You should be seeing someone professional, like a grief counselor. And, although you are opposed to drugs, sometimes they will put you on a mild tranquilizer for a while, just to get you through the rough spots. Right now your body is chemically imbalanced from all that stress."

I stopped crying long enough to say, "Absolutely not!"

"Gabi, grief is considered one of the highest on the list of stresses—it is something so unique to each person that it's quite difficult to work through with someone unless they have a professional counselor to help them. Grief is insidious—just when you think you may have worked through something, it can come back and hit you even harder. Grief also doesn't have any real clear-cut stages; it's more like cycles, because no two people seem to go through the stages in any particular order. All that said Gabi, most people are ill equipped to help you deal with grief. I would like to give you a referral to see someone."

I stood up crying so hard I couldn't speak, and shook my head in a 'no' motion, as I started walking toward the door. Ashlee stopped me, gave me a hug, and told me that she would come by tomorrow to check on me.

I was so upset that I don't remember driving home. As I walked down the hall, approaching Father's office Jacob was standing just inside the office door, glaring at me as though I had just committed a crime.

With furrowed brows and an edged voice Jacob blurted out, "Why did you go to Alex's house, and then to Ashlee's?"

"Jacob, why don't you at least give me a minute to get in the room?"

"Doggone it Gabi, I don't have a minute! What were you doing?"

"I needed to talk with my friends, Jacob! Don't you understand that? You haven't been much of a friend since you became..." I stopped talking before I said something that I would end up regretting.

Jacob's expression softened.

"Jacob, I'm really losing it, and I need some help!"

Jacob quickly walked towards me, threw his arms around me, and gave me a very firm hug as he sweetly kissed my lips. He looked deep into my eyes and said, "I understand what you're going through. I know this is very hard; it's hard for me too."

I interrupted him, "You have no idea what I'm going through! It's as though I'm in touch with myself and with reality at times, and then other times I am so NOT! I don't quite know who I am! Do you understand that even my identity has changed? I no longer have the role of Michael Deliano's daughter, or Leon Deliano's niece. Do you realize how different the dynamics of all my relationships are now?"

"Gabi, I wasn't aware of those feelings, and I'm sorry that I can't make them go away. The one thing that I do know is that there is a clear and present danger right now—I need to keep you safe, so you must take my lead."

"I'm sorry Jacob, I'm just so wrapped up in my feelings. I don't know what I'm doing, or even what day it is."

"I know Gabrielle, which supports the reason that I want you escorted everywhere, and would prefer that you stay home at night, because you're not as sharp right now, or as aware of your surroundings as you usually are."

"I understand. It's just that this all makes me feel like a prisoner, and gives me a trapped feeling. You know how I hate that!"

"I know, but for right now please just do what I ask. My only concern is that you're safe. Now I need to leave, so promise me…"

"I promise."

Jacob kissed my lips quickly yet tenderly, and walked out the door as he said, "I'll be in touch."

I was getting impatient waiting for Alex to arrive, so I called him to come over right away.

Chapter 15

Although it was only minutes, waiting for Alex was making me stir-crazy. With each tick of the clock growing louder and louder I grew more and more anxious, like a wild animal that had been captured, caged and wanted to break loose. With a sudden feeling of claustrophobia coming over me, and the need for fresh air, I sprang from the couch and ran outside to the courtyard to wait for Alex.

As Alex approached I was frantically pacing. He walked briskly over, and stood directly in front of me. With a serious, concerned look on his face he picked up our conversation exactly where we had left off earlier.

"Gabrielle, did you say that Sterling never showed up in Milan?"

"Yes, she never showed up. Now Jacob thinks that she's not only missing, but that she's been kidnapped. Alex, do you think she's been kidnapped? Please tell me you don't."

Alex put his arms around me, and hugged me tightly as he told me how he felt. He loved me like his own daughter, and couldn't stand watching me endure this pain.

"No Gabi, I don't think that Sterling has been kidnapped, and quite frankly, I don't think she's missing. I think that she may be…"

I interrupted him, "Hiding Alex? Do you think she's just hiding from everyone right now?"

Besides my father, I guess that Alex knew Sterling better than anyone else, which made me feel quite relieved to hear what he said next.

"Gabi, I don't know if I'd go so far as to say 'hiding,' but I definitely think she's avoiding everyone in general."

"Why do you think that?"

"At Michael's funeral, Sterling told me that she was finishing a novel with quite an intense ending. I remember the last time she was working on the end of a novel she was out of touch for days."

"Well Alex, that's somewhat of a relief, and I think we need to let Jacob know those facts, so he doesn't keep searching for her."

"Gabi, right now Jacob and Sonny are taking care of other issues that need their immediate attention while they're in Europe. If something was wrong with Sterling, we would know it."

"Then why did Jacob make me think that he was so worried about Sterling's whereabouts and safety?"

"He is concerned about her, but that wasn't the main reason he took off."

"Oh Alex, this whole thing just keeps getting weirder and weirder. I wish that Jacob wasn't being so hard-nosed towards you, or is that a smokescreen too?"

"What do you mean?"

"Well, ever since Uncle Leon said 'not to trust you', and then of course when I found the pic…" I stopped in mid sentence, knowing that I almost blew it. I immediately stopped talking about Sterling, and switched the conversation, "It's getting too cold outside, do you want to go into Father's office, and sit by the fire?"

Unfortunately, nothing gets by Alex, and as soon as were situated, he responded.

"What did you find, Gabi?"

"Oh nothing Alex, I'm just getting confused."

I sat there thinking for a moment, wondering if I should reveal the fact that I found the picture Alex had stolen, how my trust waned because of it, or that there was still some suspicion about his gun. For now I felt that I needed to keep the secrets tucked away about all that I knew. Suddenly I broke the silence.

"Alex, Jacob has just been a little leery about everything right now. We all know how much Father trusted you. I just wish we knew what it was that Leon was suspicious about, so that Jacob could believe in you again."

"Gabi, are you concerned about what Jacob thinks, or do you have some reservations of your own?"

Tears filled my eyes as I looked at him and said, "I do."

"Gabi, this is very hard for me to say, because I've always tried to protect Sandi, but I think this whole misunderstanding is because of her."

"What do you mean?"

"Well, Leon came to the house a couple of times while Michael was out of town to have me sign a few important documents. While he was there, we were discussing some very sensitive business issues, and we literally caught Sandi sneaking around, listening behind the door."

"Why on earth would she do that?"

"Why does Sandi do anything she does?"

"Isn't that the truth!"

"So, Leon told me that he wondered how many times she had been listening to us, and/or me while I was conducting business. He felt with Sandi being extremely unstable, that she might say something and…"

"Oh my goodness Alex, is that what Leon meant when he said that you couldn't be trusted?"

"I'm sure of it Gabi. Leon and I have always been very close, but since that day, he stopped discussing business at my house, and always asked me where Sandi was when he called. I'm sure that's what he meant, he just didn't have time to explain the extent of his logic to you."

"Oh Alex, that makes me sick. If Leon had told me the whole story rather than just saying, "Don't trust Alex," we would all be moving forward in a different direction."

"Gabi, Honey, don't blame Leon. His brother had just died. He didn't have time between that tragedy, and his own life being taken, to fill you in on what he knew."

"Maybe so, but I need to ask you something else then."

"Okay."

"Would there be anyone in Europe that my father would be transferring large amounts of cash to? Who had nothing to do with the business?"

"Why do you ask that?"

"Because Eric suspects something, and there is a file in the safe with account numbers I'm not familiar with. I haven't had a chance to…"

Alex interrupted, "Yes, there was an account that Michael was depositing funds into, which certainly was his…personal and private business."

"Do you mean, personal and private business affairs, or a secret?"

"Actually Gabi, it was both. Why don't you just give me that file, and I'll wrap it up for Michael. No need for you to worry your pretty little head about that one."

Alex was visibly nervous as he moved to sit on the couch opposite me, just staring at the coffee table with a worried look on his face and tapping his fingers on the table, faster and faster… Then, he started tapping his fingers on the empty antique cigar box that was displayed on the table, quickly going back to tapping the table again, driving me crazy with the fidgeting…

Not being able to keep silent, I snapped at him. "Alex, please stop that tapping! It's quite irritating. Tell me what you are going to do with those accounts."

"Don't worry about it, they are really nothing for you to worry about—trust me, I'll take care of them."

"Alex, I am worried about everything now, and I have a right to be. What does Eric know about those files that I don't know?"

"Eric probably found out that Michael had an account that he wasn't aware of—end of story."

"Everyone keeps telling me that Eric is very quick to assume the worst, and suspicious of everyone. I'm thinking that maybe his suspicions are really correct and that others might be wrong, which is beginning to make me paranoid! But then, if Eric is wrong, it creates a lot of problems that we don't need. Oh Alex, just go ahead and take care of that account—it will be one less thing for me to deal with right now."

As I grabbed the envelope out of the safe, Alex began tapping his fingers on the cigar box again. He stopped himself before I could say anything, and said, "Sorry Gabi!"

I couldn't tell if Alex was nervous about Sterling not being where she should be, or if he was upset about Leon's suspicions, or Jacob, or the 'private' accounts. I knew him very well, and he was definitely upset about something. I kept thinking that I wished he would quit fidgeting though—it was really getting on my very last nerve.

As I handed Alex the envelope, he looked at me with incredibly sad puppy dog eyes and said, "Your father and I loved smoking good cigars and drinking fine, aged port. I remember our many conversations, during some very cold, winter nights with the fire roaring, as we drank port, and smoked cigars that Michael had tucked away just for us. We had some wonderful conversations, and solved many problems in this room, sitting right here, on these very same couches."

Alex's sad eyes brightened as he began to smile from remembering those special moments with Father. He ran his hand along the top of the beautifully carved, antique cherry cigar box once again, and had thankfully ceased tapping on it.

I looked at him lovingly as I said, "That's an empty case now Alex—no more cigars, but would you like some port?"

As Alex shook his head yes, his smile turned upside down again as a tear rolled down his cheek. He opened the cigar box for old time sake—then as he closed it, slowly and gently another tear rolled down his cheek. In an instant though, his solemn mood was jolted as a shocked look began to cover his face. He immediately lifted the lid back up so quickly that I thought the whole box was going to fly across the room.

I blurted out, "Alex, be careful, that's Father's special..."

He cut me off with a very firm voice, "Gabrielle, what are these doing in here?"

"What are you talking about?"

"Sandi's glasses!"

"Did you say, Sandi's glasses?"

He pulled them out of the cigar box. I stood there in shock as I said, "Alex how did those get in there?"

"That's the question I'm asking you!"

"I found them the other night, but I didn't put them in there."

"Why did you take them from our house?"

"I didn't take anything. I found them in our yard. I showed them to Jacob, and he probably put them in there for safekeeping. Rocky had buried those glasses by the bushes next to the brick fence, and... oh no!"

"What Gabi?"

"I just remembered something! The night Leon died, those bushes were moving and the dogs were barking, but they weren't barking as if it was someone they didn't know. Oh Alex, could Sandi have been in the bushes watching us?"

"Gabi, that's a good question. If Leon and I hadn't caught her listening to us in the house, I wouldn't even suspect that she would be hiding in the bushes, but now I wonder..."

"I don't know, but that would make sense as to why her glasses were out there, and why the bushes were moving that night when there was no wind at all. Unless, she was walking over to our house, and dropped them on her way."

"That doesn't make sense Gabi, she would have picked them up."

"But what if she didn't know that she dropped them, or if she did know, maybe she just couldn't find them. Let's give her the benefit of the doubt. Maybe she was coming over here, saw someone that scared her and she ran, accidentally dropping them."

"Could be Gabi, but on the other hand...maybe she saw someone lurking around that she might be able to identify for us. I'm going home, I need to talk to her while she's still awake. I'll call you first thing in the morning."

Alex ran off. My mind began spinning, and my thoughts went way over the deep end thinking of what the implications would be if those were Sandi's glasses, if she was in the bushes, and if Alex stole that picture off of Father's desk! Then what kind of lunatics had we been calling our friends? My mind went so many weird places that it was making me dizzy. I said out loud, as if to convince myself, "Stop it Gabrielle, just stop it, because there has to be an explanation about Alex, maybe not Sandi, but Alex would never do…" then I remembered that stolen picture, and my mind took the plunge again.

Sandi was still awake when Alex returned home. He quickly gathered his thoughts, as he approached her gingerly and said, "Hi Sandi, I'm back—are you too tired, or can we talk for a little while?"

"Were you over at that little tart's house?"

With that comment about Gabrielle, who was anything but a tart, Alex felt like someone had just knocked the wind out of him. He took a deep breath before he began, "I need to have a serious talk with you Sandi."

In a very angry and husky voice, Sandi blurted out, "Answer my question first, Alex!"

He paused for a moment then said, "Who are you calling a tart?"

"You know good and well who I mean, Alexander Stone!"

Exasperated, Alex said, "I was talking with Gabrielle."

"Ah ha, you were at that tart's house!"

"Sandi, why in the world would you call her that?"

"And YOU total pig, you're protecting that little…"

Alex interrupted her. He knew they weren't going to get anywhere with her in that other personality, and he wasn't in the mood for the venom that was spewing from her mouth.

"Never mind Sandi, I'll see you in the morning."

Sandi ran into the guest room, slammed the door, and stood in the middle of the room, and stared at the door. She didn't like the way Alex was talking to her, and she began to panic.

Sandi sat down at the desk, opened the drawer, and the discovered that the picture was gone! 'Where's that picture—what did I do with it? I know that I put it in this drawer!' She hysterically went through each drawer, getting herself so worked up she broke out in a sweat.

She started frantically dialing the phone, only to get a busy signal. She let it ring, and ring, and ring…until finally, he answered.

In an interrogating tone of voice she said, "Where have you been?"

Alex could hear her talking from his room, and thought that she was just talking to herself like she did quite frequently, until he heard her yell out, "I CAN'T FIND IT!"

He walked quietly down the hall to the guest room, and stood outside the door, waiting to hear what she might say next. He thought that she was still talking to herself until she said, "No, they don't suspect him."

At this point, Alex became suspicious that Sandi really was having a conversation with someone. He quickly found the other phone, and listened in, just in time for her to say, "I'll meet you there tomorrow," and then a man's voice said, "Okay."

Alex was in complete shock, and wasn't sure what to think, but he knew what he had just heard. Quite perplexed, he walked slowly back down the hallway to the guest room where Sandi was. He opened the door and found her lying on the bed with her clothes on, pretending to be asleep. He spoke with a very loud voice, "What in the world are you doing, Sandi?"

She acted as though Alex had awakened her from a sound sleep. She spoke in a groggy-like voice, "What do you mean Alex?"

"I want you to get up out of that bed right this minute, and quit playing games. Who the heck are you right now, and who were you talking to on the phone?"

Sandi screamed out, "You S.O.B. Alex, I demand that you leave my room right now, before I call the police!"

Very calmly Alex picked the phone up, and handed it to Sandi. "Here, call them!"

Sandi grabbed the phone out of Alex's hand, and threw it on the floor.

Alex glared at her as he said, "Well you can keep your crazy butt in that bed all night, but when you get up in the morning, I'm on you like glue until you tell me what you're up to—do you understand me Sandi, or whoever you are?" Then he walked off, and slammed the door.

Sandi got up, and paced back and forth—she didn't know what to do. Every time she hit the creaking spot by the desk it reminded Alex of the night that poor Gabi was held captive in that room. Being in a frenzied state, she went through each drawer again, as if thinking the picture would miraculously reappear.

Chapter 16

I ran through the courtyard, and across the grass as fast as my feet could run. It was dark enough that I couldn't see who was chasing me, but I could tell that it was a man in a black tuxedo. I kicked off my shoes one at a time as I ran through the courtyard so he couldn't hear the click from my heels. All of a sudden he appeared from behind the fountain. Now he was right behind me!

He was so close I could hear him breathing. I looked back quickly to see where he was, and I caught a glimpse of something shiny in his hand! 'Oh dear God help me—it's a gun! Where are my bodyguards?' My heart was pounding so hard that I could hear it in my ears. I knew that I was falling behind as the man got closer and closer, and finally grabbed my shoulder, pulling me to the ground! I screamed out with every ounce of energy I had left in me, but my screams went unnoticed as I started to pass out.

I was sleeping so soundly that I barely heard the phone, and fell out of bed while reaching for it on my nightstand.

"Hello!" I yelled in a desperate voice!

"Gabi, are you alright?"

I was breathing in a heavy voice, "Oh Jacob…no I'm not alright! I was having the most awful dream—no, nightmare!"

"Are you okay?"

"I'm so glad you called…it was terrible!"

"I'm glad I called too, are you okay now?"

"Oh Jacob, it was so scary!"

"Would you like me to call back in a minute?"

"No, I'm okay now, please don't hang up."

"Well, I've got some strange news about the last two guys we were worried about from the murder case."

"What about them?"

"They were sent to Attica Prison, and quickly transferred to death row about three weeks ago!"

"Oh Jacob, how eerie is that? That was when Father got sick!"

"I know, and somehow we didn't get the news—or someone got it, and didn't deliver it to us."

"Jacob, Alex doesn't think that those bad guys have anything to do with the murders, or with Sterling's disappearance. I think you need to talk to him."

"Gabi, we're not leaving here until we find…"

I cut him off. "But Jacob, what if she doesn't want to be found? She did tell Alex that she needed to finish her book, and Alex said that she's done this before. Really, you do need to talk to Alex. He sincerely thinks that Sterling is okay. Oh by the way, how is Eric doing?"

"Well, after he heard this news he was pretty upset. He was sure that the 'bad guys' were behind all this, as did all of us, this particular time, but now…"

I interrupted Jacob again—I wanted him to know what Alex and I discovered last night. "Jacob, you know those glasses I found?"

"Yes."

"Well, Alex said that they're Sandi's!"

"What were they doing in the yard?"

"We don't know, but we're speculating that maybe Sandi was coming to the house that night of the murder, and maybe she saw something. Maybe she saw who killed Uncle Leon!"

"Gabi, even if she did, do you think that anyone would ever take her testimony seriously?"

"Oh Jacob, I didn't even think about that. If she did see something, it might be a crucial clue that we could use to find the murderer."

"Have you, or Alex talked with her yet?"

"Alex was going to talk to her last night, Jacob. Oh, and Alex said he's calling you, first thing this morning. Please talk to him!"

"Gabi, they just finished fueling the plane, gotta go—I'll call him before we take off. I love you!"

I barely got the words "Bye, I love you" out, before he hung up.

Boy did I ever need to hear those words from him. I jumped out of bed, took my shower, and figured out that I did not need a 'Shrink', nor did I need a 'PILL'! After talking with Jacob, I realized that being in love was all I needed to feel sane, safe and secure. 'Oh Jacob, I love you so much.'

As I walked into the kitchen, Maria caught a quick glimpse of me and said, "Only Jacob could put a glow on your face like that! Did you talk with him this morning?"

"Yes Maria. He's the only sane thing I have right now, in this crazy, crazy world of mine."

"Do you want your favorite coffee this morning, Gabi?"

"Yes, please! That sounds great, but nothing to eat, thanks."

"Gabrielle, I think you should eat something for breakfast. How about a little toast and orange juice?"

"Okay, Maria!"

I turned on the 'news talk,' and just sat there in a trance…having breakfast without even realizing, or enjoying what I was eating. Rather, dreaming of happier times when Father and I were planning a trip somewhere. After breakfast, I went into Father's office to go over some business files. Alex came running into the office with Antonio running behind him, and the bodyguards running right behind Antonio. If life hadn't been so tragic lately, that would have been quite a funny sight.

Antonio cried out, "Sorry Gabrielle. I told him that he should be announced first!"

"That's okay Antonio, thank you. Oh, and thanks guys, I'm fine, you can go back to your post!" We exchanged smiles as they walked off, and I addressed Alex.

"Please don't freak everyone out like that Alex. You know they've been given strict instructions to guard me."

"Sorry Gabi, but Sandi is gone!"

"What! When did she leave?"

"It must have been very early this morning. I caught her talking to someone on the phone last night."

"No Alex, she was probably talking to her imaginary friend. The other night when I was at your house, I heard her talking to herself, or so I thought. But then, when I walked out onto the porch, I wasn't quite sure. The phone dropped off the swing—it was all just really weird."

"Well, that's what I thought until I lifted the phone in the bedroom, and I heard a man's voice."

"Oh Alex, oh my gosh! She really was on the phone?"

Alex explained what he had heard, and we both felt Sandi knew something that maybe she was too scared to talk about. Alex called Charles, so he could put out an APB on Sandi. Within minutes, she was found traveling south on 405. She was twenty-three miles from the house, and we were sure that she was headed for the airport—when she was picked up she had a small carry-on suitcase with her.

Alex met Charles at the station. After the two discussed keeping Sandi in more restricted surroundings, Alex took her home. He was so upset with her he could barely contain his temper. He always treated Sandi with kid gloves, but at this moment too much was on the line. He was at the end of his rope.

Alex grabbed Sandi's arm firmly with his hand and quickly jerked her down onto the couch. He stood above her and said, "We are not leaving this room until you start talking!"

"What do you mean Alex?" she asked in a demure voice.

"I mean that I don't care which personality you try to hide behind. I will deal with whomever, and you will deal with me! Is that understood?"

Her voice changed to a husky sounding, younger, harder female as she said, "Go to HELL, Alex!"

"Well, that's not where I'm planning on going, but that's beside the point, and I will ask you one more time, is that understood?"

In the same voice she said, "Alex, you had better not touch me—you crazy, violent man!"

"I'm not buying this Sandi! You, of all people know that I'm not a violent man—I've never laid a hand on you!"

"Why that's not true Alex! You've been beating me for the last six years!"

Alex's face turned to stone as he looked at her with piercing eyes. 'Who is this woman?' He thought to himself. He knew that he couldn't make love to her for the last six years, because of what she had done. He knew he couldn't hit her either, although many times he would liked to have taped her mouth shut. He couldn't quit thinking about how she said with such venom in her voice, 'You've been beating me!' Her sick mind was playing such weird tricks on her. It broke Alex's heart. He just stood there staring at her—really staring at her. Then he sat down on the large stuffed chair, directly across from the couch that Sandi was sitting on—he crossed his legs, put his hands on his lap, and sat there in a most pensive posture. Soon, Sandi became uncomfortable, and started fidgeting with her hair, then with her clothing.

Alex looked directly in Sandi's eyes, and talked to her as though she were someone he loathed, "You know Sandi, I've got you all figured out. I don't know why it took me this long, but I finally understand your game."

Sandi looked at Alex with a quizzical and worried face, she responded in a child-like voice, "What do you mean?"

"I've been dealing with criminal minds and psychopaths for almost thirty years, and I didn't even see what was going on right underneath my own nose."

Sandi could hardly contain herself, so she got up and started pacing. Alex walked directly over to her, grabbed her arm tightly again, and jerked her right back down on the couch.

"Sandi, I don't think you understood me when I said we are not leaving until you start talking. I am not messing around here! Don't get up again!"

"You disgusting pig, Alex! I HATE you!"

"I know you do Sandi, and I should have realized this years ago."

"And I hate Michael too, because he made me stay with you!"

Alex looked at her with fire in his eyes, "Don't you ever talk badly about Michael again! Ever!"

"Screw Michael, and screw you! I want a divorce!"

Alex refused to act shocked about anything that Sandi said, because he felt that this was the only way to keep her talking.

"I'm sure you do want a divorce, and you can surely have one."

"If it wasn't for you Alex, I'd be happy."

"You mean, if you weren't married when you had that affair with what's his name, you both could have gone off together. Sandi, don't you remember what he said about you? He's the one that said you were a lousy lover, and I could have you! Did you forget that part?"

"You PIG, I'm not talking about him. I'm in love with…" Then she stopped talking.

"You're in love with who? Who Sandi? I know you're not stupid. Somewhere deep down in there is a smart lady. I don't know what game you're playing, but let's start over by you telling me who you were talking to on the phone last night."

"What do you mean?"

"I heard you talking on the phone! Who were you talking to?"

"Someone I just met."

"Okay, from what I'm hearing you say, you're in love with someone you just met, and you were going to meet him this morning, and you had to fly somewhere to meet him."

"Maybe."

"So where is he now?"

"I was going to meet him, and I don't have to tell you! Alex, I don't want to talk to you anymore."

"Well, that's just too bad. I told you that we're not leaving until…"

Sandi stood up so quickly that Alex could hardly get to the other side of the room fast enough. She grabbed a bronze sculpture that was on the coffee table and swung it at him with all her might. Alex grabbed her arm with one hand, and jerked the sculpture out of her hand with the other. Sandi started kicking him as hard as she could, and then started biting his arm.

Alex grabbed both of her forearms, squeezed them tightly, and placed her back on the couch. He planted himself firmly in front of her so she couldn't attempt that stunt again! Alex stood there for an hour without budging—the whole time Sandi was kicking the floor with her feet, and running into his shins in the process. Alex wouldn't give her the satisfaction of letting her know that she was irritating him. He stood firm.

Now acting like a little girl she said, "Alex, I'm hungry."

"Do I look like I care, Sandi?"

"Well, I have to go to the bathroom! You've got to care about that!"

"I certainly don't."

Sandi hauled off and kicked Alex as hard as she could. At this point he decided that she needed to be contained. He stepped over to the desk, and pulled out his handcuffs.

She looked at him with desperate eyes, and said in a sultry woman's voice, "You wouldn't?"

"I don't use these unless I have a reason to. You've given me quite a few reasons!"

"You jerk, you pig! How dare you!"

As Alex was putting the cuffs on her wrists and her ankles, he was saddened that their relationship had deteriorated to this, and it absolutely broke his heart. Their marriage had no love in it, and hadn't for many years; he didn't even like her any more.

His mind was racing back to the past, trying to find a time when they were in love, yet nothing appeared. His thoughts stopped for a brief moment. He remembered trying so hard to be the best husband he could be—he would bring her flowers, take her on romantic dates, but she never responded to any of his loving gestures.

Years ago, when Sandi lost her daughter, she became a completely different woman. Alex tried so hard to communicate with her and to love her, but nothing he did got through to her anymore. His heart was breaking as he thought about everything he had endured with her—now his patience and tolerance were finally gone, as she had vacated his heart for good. The thoughts were so painful for Alex—he was fighting to hold the tears back. Sandi was so busy squirming that she didn't notice his pain, nor would she have cared.

"You can't do this to me…I hate you!"

"Well I just did. Quite frankly Sandi, I really don't care for you either."

It was now quite obvious to Alex that Sandi was beginning to come apart at the seams, when suddenly she blurted out, "He made me do it!"

Alex looked at her with fire in his eyes, and with a deeply stern voice said, "He made you do WHAT?"

She recoiled into a fetal position, and started crying. Alex stood there without flinching, while she cried. Finally, after an hour, she suddenly stopped crying—in her normal voice she screamed out "He needed my help!"

"Who did Sandi? You're going to need a whole heck of a lot of help yourself, if you don't start talking to me."

"I don't know. He came to me a month ago, and said that there was a very important case he was working on. He picked me to help him. He knew that I would be a good detective, just like you. That's when I agreed to help him."

"Oh my gosh, Sandi, who is he? Did he come to you in person?"

"No! I mean, yes! Every time he came to me though, he had a disguise on; even his eyes were always a different color."

"Can you give me a description of what he looked like, at least one of the times?"

"I'm a good detective, and I can tell you what he looked like every single time I saw him, except for the very last time."

"Why not the last time?"

"He had a mask over his face."

Leading her on, Alex said, "That must have been the night you got him past the dogs. Is that right?"

Sandi nodded, yes.

Continuing to lead her on, Alex thought that this was getting worse by the minute. "So tell me Sandi, what did he look like the first time you saw him?"

"Well, he's about 5'9", or 5'10"; his height never changed."

"Good observation, Sandi. That's good detective work. What color hair did he have?"

"That first night his hair was brown, dark brown, and he had brown eyes. The second time I saw him he had auburn hair with dark blue eyes. Oh, and the first time... he had a brown mustache, and a long brown beard!"

"Did he have a beard and mustache the second time also?"

"Yes, but they were much shorter."

Then suddenly, it was like someone snapped Sandi into some sort of a trance as she stared straight into Alex's eyes and began talking in a rapid, but monotone voice, without any pauses.

"The second time his hair was auburn, but the last time I saw him, his hair was blonde. His nose was very big the first time, like a Roman nose or something, but the second time it was big and boxy, and then the last time his nose was on the smaller side. It kind of looked like a ski-jump."

"Good Sandi, this is good." Alex was writing as she continued in the same speech pattern.

"Oh, and I remember something else! The second and third time he came here, he was carrying a backpack. I thought that was a little odd."

"Sandi, each time that he came to you, what exactly did he want you to do?"

Then, Sandi snapped again, changing her posture and voice.

"Alex, don't be so darn pushy! Let me think for a minute! Well, it was a month ago when he told me about this case he was working on, and the first thing he wanted to know was..."

Sandi paused, and stared up at the ceiling. Alex clenched his jaw; he glared at Sandi, "WHAT DID HE WANT TO KNOW?"

She responded in a soft, child-like voice, "He wanted to know where Michael lived. He told me that he wanted to protect him."

"And you believed him?"

"Of course I did, this was an important detective case."

Alex's mind was spinning on one track, and on the other he was still battling with the guilt he felt for not recognizing just exactly how sick Sandi was. When did she get this bad? His gut was now telling him that it was because of her, that Michael's family was suffering these losses. For a few moments he was paralyzed by the thought that his own wife was the source of this agonizing pain. 'This is my fault! She's my wife...and because of her...oh man, it's all because of her!'

Quickly switching mind tracks he was back to analyzing this newly discovered piece of evidence. He realized that whoever was using Sandi knew how mentally vulnerable she was, making their dirty deeds a whole lot easier to accomplish. Alex started feeling sick inside.

In a very soft tone, he resumed his conversation with Sandi. "Go on."

"Well...the next time he returned, he asked me to hide a picture, which he came back later to see."

"What picture?"

"A picture of the whole group."

"Where did he get this picture?"

Sandi looked quizzically at Alex as she said, "I'm not sure."

Then she quickly stood up, and stared with this completely blank look on her face, as she escaped somewhere in her mind again.

"Sandi, look at me! What did he want with the picture?"

She stood there for a few moments before she spoke.

"Alex...I just thought of something. Did he talk to you about the case too? If he didn't then I can't really tell you, but if he did, then are you helping us now?"

"Yes Sandi, I am. So please go on."

"Well...wait a minute. Just wait...I need to think about this for a minute."

Alex was beginning to grow impatient, and wanted to just shake the information out of her, but he refrained from any aggressiveness at this point. She seemed to be staying with the conversation, and he needed to know more. Feeling nauseated inside, he looked at her, and gave her a half smile.

"Okay, take your time Sandi."

"Yes, well...I think I remember. I think he already knew who Michael was, but he wanted to know who Leon was, so I pointed him out in that photo."

Alex thought for a moment about what Gabi had been saying earlier, about finding a pic... and she didn't finish her sentence. Gabi must have known about the picture! Alex began fuming inside, and could barely contain himself as he quickly snapped back at Sandi.

"Where did you hide the picture?"

"In the desk! I hid it in the desk, but then it disappeared!"

"Sandi, what do you mean it disappeared?"

"Quit shouting at me, you pig!"

Calming himself down, Alex took a deep breath then said, "Okay, go on Sandi, finish your story."

"Well then, the last time I saw him he asked me to get him past the dogs."

"And what reason did he give you, that would make you agree to do that?"

Alex could tell that Sandi was getting tired and worn out from all the questioning. After repeatedly yawning, she groggily said, "He was bringing Leon and what's her name…"

"Are you talking about Gabi?"

"Yeah, the Ice Princess, that's who it was. He told me that he was bringing a surprise to Leon and that little tart, Ice Princess."

"Don't talk about Gabi like that, you know she's a lovely young woman."

"Go to HELL!"

Sandi's words began to slur, and her eyes kept fluttering, then closing and opening again, as her neck began to bob, and she let out a deep breath. Alex knew that she was falling asleep, and would be of no further help to him at this point. He went upstairs to get her sleeping pills, administered them to her, and then put her to bed.

As Sandi was getting extremely groggy she said, "I'm a good detective, aren't I Alex? I'm working a big case."

Then, just as Sandi was dozing off, Alex whispered in her ear, "Did he bring back my gun that you loaned him?"

Sandi's eyes could barely stay open as she spoke in a very quiet whisper, "No, he still needed it…." Then, she was out like a light.

Exhausted himself, Alex closed her bedroom door, stood against it and closed his eyes as his head rested back on the door. He kept thinking to himself over and over again, 'I knew she gave him my gun…I just knew it.'

After he was certain that Sandi was sound asleep, Alex called Jacob and explained what just happened with her. He also told him the reason why he didn't think that Sterling was missing, and asked Jacob to confirm his assumption with Sonny. He knew Sonny was aware of the fact that she had done this before.

"Alex, we'll be back in the states tomorrow morning. There had better be some darn good answers when I return."

"I'm on it, Jacob. I'm calling Charles at the precinct right now, to get in touch with the sketch artist. I want to give him all the descriptions of each face that Sandi described to me. When I'm done, I'll be on my way to Gabi's."

Chapter 17

Alex knew that Sandi would probably be sound asleep for at least a few hours, so he felt comfortable leaving her. When he arrived at Gabi's, Ashlee was just leaving.

"Hi Ashlee! How are you?"

"Hey Alex! I'm fine thank you. How are you doing?"

"It's been a long time, we have a lot to catch up on."

"I've missed seeing you too, Alex."

"As soon as we get this mess wrapped up, let's all get together, okay?"

"Sounds great, Alex! Take care."

After waving good-bye to Ashlee, I observed Alex making sure that the bodyguards cleared him first. He stood for a while at the door waiting for Antonio to escort him.

Chuckling under my breath, I stood in the grand hallway, arranging some flowers I had just picked from the garden.

"Good morning, Alex!"

"Good morning, Princess! You seem happy today."

"I am Alex. I'm almost done with this arrangement—please wait just a minute, and then we can talk in Father's office."

"I saw Ashlee as she was leaving. She seems to have that same smile on her face, is there someone in her life as well?"

"Ashlee thinks she could be in love with this new beau that she's been dating from school. You know what, with everything that's been happening lately, I haven't even had a chance to meet him. She hasn't known him that long, but she seems quite smitten."

"I know a lot of people who fall in love in a very short time, and actually do live happily ever after, Gabi."

"That is just so romantic."

"Princess, I don't mean to rain on your parade, but…"

"I know, we still have a lot of unpleasant issues to deal with."

"We do, we certainly do. Please don't ever forget that I love you, and Jacob loves you. We will be okay."

"Alex, if I didn't have you and Jacob, I don't think that I could make it."

He hugged me, and then said, "Well Gabi, I talked to Sandi."

"What happened? Did she see anyone that night?"

"Yes, but before I get into that story, I want to talk to you about the picture."

I looked down as I said, "What picture?"

"The one you were trying to tell me about, but then pretended like you were confused."

"Not much gets past you, Alexander Stone!"

"Well quite frankly, it probably would have, if I hadn't discovered what Sandi knew about it."

"What do you mean? I know you didn't take it."

"Of course I didn't, but is that what you thought?"

"Oh Alex, I wasn't sure what I thought, I just know that I found it in the desk the night that Sandi went psycho on us."

"Gabrielle, why didn't you tell me?"

"Please forgive me Alex, I am so sorry. Uncle Leon said that he didn't trust you, and then I found the picture at your house! I didn't know what to think!"

"Well, let me explain what I found out from Sandi."

It took an hour. Alex explained every detail of his conversation with Sandi, and that the suspicion had now shifted to a mysterious man, with many faces.

After waiting patiently for the longest time, Alex couldn't wait another minute. He called the station only to find out what he already knew—they were still working on the drawings.

"Don't worry Gabi, we'll catch him."

"You know something Alex?"

"What?"

"I can hardly wait until this is all over, so I can see Sterling, and get to know her. I have a mother, Alex! Do you have any idea how that feels?"

"Yes, I do, Gabi. I would be turning cartwheels if someone told me I had a child after all these years! I would want to spend every waking moment with them."

"I'm sorry, Alex, I didn't mean to…"

"Don't be sorry."

"Hey, are you hungry?"

"I'm getting there."

"Well, I'm supposed to meet Ashlee for lunch today. Would you like to go with us?"

"That's awfully nice of you, and Sandi will probably be sleeping for a couple more hours. I'd love to."

"Let's go right now then. I'll call Ashlee, and have her leave a little early."

"That sounds good Gabrielle. I think we all need a break."

"Yes we do!"

Ashlee was more than glad to leave a little early, and happy to see Alex again. We ate lunch at one of our favorite restaurants, and caught up on everything besides the tragedies that had been going on in my life.

Ashlee shared the good news about her being accepted for an internship with a prestigious group of Psychiatrists in Seattle, how she was going to buy a new car, and finally redecorate the house. It was so good to hear about the great things that were going on in her life.

She also told us about her new beau, Pierre, and how they had fallen, head-over-heels for each other. Ashlee was excited he was settling in as an intern Pharmacist at the local hospital, and he was someone who could actually keep Ashlee's interest. She really hated stupid, boring men.

Ashlee had never been attracted to guys with just looks and no brains. Pierre won her over with his incredible mind first, and then his handsome looks second, she said. What a colorful and fun life Ashlee was enjoying right now. I was very happy for her.

On our way home, Alex told me that he was glad to have spent some time with Ashlee. He cared about her a lot, but didn't get to see her very much. Sometimes I wonder why life deals us the hand that is does. Alex would have been such a great father, and Ashlee such a great daughter, yet they both lived such lonely lives; Alex without a child, and Ashlee without a father. I dropped Alex off at his house, and headed home.

It was such a beautiful day, so I decided to take a walk to Mary's house to see how she was doing. She was in her garden with her adorable, little red hat and red gloves on, tending her roses.

"Hi Mary!"

"Hello my sweet little Gabi. How are you doing today?"

"I'm coping. How are you doing?"

"I'm coping too. It's just so devastating, losing two brothers in one week!" Then she was crying...

"I know Mary, it's very, very hard. But I also know that they wouldn't want us to fall apart. They would want us to be strong for each other. One day at a time, Mary...we will get stronger."

Mary looked at me and gave me a little smile, and a nod, as she leaned over and kissed my cheek. Then she put her arm through mine, and said, "I hope so."

"Mary let's go inside, and have some of your homemade lemonade—that sounds so good right now."

As we walked arm-in-arm to the house, Mary lost her balance, and leaned on me so she wouldn't fall. I asked her if she was okay, and she said that she was slightly dizzy. I was really beginning to worry about Mary—these symptoms had been going on a little too long now.

"Mary, how are you really feeling, and what other symptoms do you have?"

"Oh, I'm doing okay, considering I've been so upset lately. Gabi, don't worry about me. People lose their balance all the time."

"Mary, you lost your balance in the limo also, that is just not like you."

"You noticed?"

"Of course I did. I think that you need a good physical; when is the last time you had one?"

"It's probably been about five, or so years."

"Well, I think that you need to have one just to make sure you're okay, and I'd like you to make an appointment, today."

"I would Gabi, but the internist I've been seeing for so many years, finally retired last year."

"Did someone else take over his practice?"

"Not that I know of."

"I see a great doctor that I'm sure you would really like. Let me give you his number, and I want you to call him first thing in the morning. Promise me that you will."

"Okay, I promise."

After we drank our lemonade, I walked back home slowly, soaking up the warmth of the afternoon sun.

I stood in the courtyard listening to the fountain, remembering how many times Father and I sat on that same bench talking about our dreams. As I walked over to the bench to sit down, my mind started wondering about what our lives would have been like with Sterling...

As Sterling stared out onto the ocean to admire the sunset, she realized that she had been so wrapped up in finishing her novel that she had neglected to check in with Sonny. She told Leon that she would be going on to Capri, and to pass that information on to Sonny, along with her new phone number. How odd, that he hadn't called yet.

After a while Sterling decided to call Leon's cell, but the call was forwarded to Gabi's voice-mail. Sterling hung up immediately, and dialed again. She looked at the keypad of the phone and dialed each number very slowly, only to be sent to Gabi's voicemail again! She hung up instantly. She thought that was very strange, so she called straight through to Sonny. Sonny was en-route back to the states, and couldn't answer his phone either, so she was diverted to his voicemail.

Sterling's message to Sonny was very short. "I'm calling to check in. I haven't heard from you, so I'm wondering if Leon gave you my message. I'm still working on my book, and I'll call you in a few days. Oh, and by the way, why is Leon's number forwarded to Gabi's voicemail? Ciao!"

Sterling was a little perplexed. She was always able to get a hold of at least one of these guys. Her head was spinning from writing those difficult chapters. Needing a diversion, she decided to call Daniel for some stimulating conversation.

The sun felt so good as I sat there on the bench in the courtyard, listening to the fountain, and thinking about what I would say to Sterling when I met for the first time. I wonder where we will be when we first see each other, and what we will talk about. 'I have a great idea—I'll read Sterling's latest novel. That will be a perfect icebreaker!' I jumped off the bench like a little girl who was going to get an ice cream, and started running to my car.

The bodyguards started running after me.

"Hey guys, I'm just going to the store real quick; you don't need to…"

"Follow you? Yes we do," they said in unison.

Chapter 18

Driving fast down my driveway, excited to read Sterling's novel, I was lost in my thoughts of what the story was about when out of nowhere Alex was in the middle of the driveway. I swerved quickly so as not to hit him—Alex jumped back, almost falling over as I flew out of the car concerned that I might have hurt him.

"Oh my gosh, Alex, I am so sorry! I was lost in my thoughts…"

"What do you have on your mind, Princess?"

"Look Alex! I found her book; I have Sterling's latest novel!"

I could tell that Alex was taken aback by my childlike excitement, and wasn't quite sure how to respond when Antonio interrupted them. He seemed a little flustered, "The fax machine has been ringing the whole time you were gone!"

"It's okay Antonio, I'll take care…"

Antonio interrupted me, "It just keeps ringing and ringing, like it did a couple weeks ago."

Alex put his arm around Antonio and said, "Thanks for being so concerned, it's probably from Charles."

I gave Alex a quizzical look and said, "What are you expecting from Charles?"

Alex motioned for me to come with him to Father's office. He talked quietly, explaining that he was waiting for the composite drawings that Detective Green was working on.

As we approached the office, the fax machine started ringing again. "Oh, I forgot to load paper in that thing! I noticed it was empty this morning, and then it just slipped my mind."

"That's okay, don't worry; it will stay in the memory."

I stood there staring at the fax machine as it started to print, anxious to see the composite drawings of a possible suspect. The first page printed, but had no face on it. It was a standard, form letter of some kind.

As I stood there waiting for it to finish coming through, I let out a heavy sigh, "Alex, this is not a drawing. I wonder what it is."

"Oh, Detective Green probably sent a cover letter with it first. He didn't need to do that, but he always sends cover letters."

"Alex, it doesn't look like a cover sheet…hold on a second…it's almost through printing."

I sat down to read the form. The fax machine continued printing, and Alex began looking at the drawings that were beginning to come through.

"Alex, this is odd. The form is dated two weeks ago. Boy, has it been two weeks since we've been out of paper?"

"Well, you haven't conducted much business in here since almost a week before your father's death."

"Yeah I guess so. I haven't sent a fax, that's for sure, or I would have noticed it before. I guess no one has tried to send us anything, except for this, which was dated back… Exactly two weeks ago, yesterday."

Alex was so intent on studying the drawings that were coming in, he was barely paying any attention to me.

"Alex! This looks like a form letter from the hospital. It says that Father never picked up his high blood pressure medication two weeks ago, prior to the date on this form…how odd. It says the medication will be returning to the shelf if they don't hear from Father within three days. What's that supposed to mean?"

"What Gabi?"

"Weren't you listening to me?"

"Sorry! I got lost in these drawings."

Exasperated, I read the letter to Alex again.

"That doesn't make any sense to me. Read it one more time."

"Alex, here's the bottom line: from what this says, Father never picked up his medication. However, I know that's not true. He had to take that medication every night. He was taking it up until almost the last night before he passed away. I remember giving it to him! I read each bottle very carefully, giving him about eight different medications, every single night."

"What other medications was he taking?"

"I can't remember the names of each one right this second Alex, they were for his illness. I didn't really pay attention to what else was in the other bottles. I would take the prescribed amount out of each bottle, and lay it on the tray. When it came to his blood pressure meds, I would look at it, to confirm that it was Minoxidil, take the pill out of the bottle, and put it with the rest of them."

"Well Gabi, maybe the pharmacy sent this letter by mistake."

"You know what Alex, I'm going to go upstairs and get that bottle, just to ease my mind. I know I'm not crazy. I know that's what I was giving him."

"Go ahead Honey…I'll be studying these drawings."

I ran up the stairs to Father's bedroom. The door was closed and I stood outside remembering how Uncle Leon had held me during those tender moments after Father passed away. Tears rolled down my cheeks, I felt the same pain that I was feeling just nights ago.

My heart became heavy as I opened the door very slowly, my eyes traveled around the room while softly saying, "Oh how I miss you Father." I walked over to his nightstand, opened the drawer, and saw all of the bottles lined up neatly in a row. Nothing had been touched since that night, except for the bedding that was cleaned and returned to the bed.

The sun was shining through the window and onto the bed as I slowly crawled into its warmth, laying there for a minute as I longed for my father. I closed my eyes, and tears rolled down my cheeks from the smell of Father that still filled his room. Memories of his smiling face were dancing across my mind, but then quickly disappeared as I remembered his face in the casket. I jumped up with the bottle in my hand, and ran down the stairs to Alex.

I couldn't hold back my tears as I walked over to Alex, with my arms stretched out for a hug. He gently wrapped his arms around me to console me. I leaned into him, weakened by the same feeling of grief that came over me the night Father passed away.

"I'm sorry Gabi, I should have gone up to his room for you. I wasn't even thinking."

I never like to be out of control, and lately it seemed like this stinging sadness was controlling me. I quickly composed myself, "Alex, there's a lot of things I'll have to go through that's painful about losing Father. Going around issues isn't healthy. Sometimes I will be alone, and that's okay. Thank you for caring."

"Well, is that the correct medication?"

I studied the bottle closely, and blurted out with excitement, "It sure is! I wonder why they sent that letter Alex. We have the meds, so it was probably a mistake."

I crumpled the letter in my hands and threw it away. Alex was once again, very engrossed in the drawings. As soon as he heard the letter hit the trashcan he said, "Gabi, did you throw that away?"

"Yes, it's obviously a mistake."

"Take that out of the trash, I want to look at it."

He finally put the drawings down to look at the form letter. As he was reading the letter, I started looking at the drawings.

"Boy Alex, there are some pretty weird looking characters here."

"I know, it's not that easy. Especially when we're trusting a mind like Sandi's to give us an accurate description."

I kept going through the drawings, and stopped at one of them that caught my attention. "Alex this may sound crazy, but this one looks kind of familiar."

"No, that wouldn't sound crazy, but what looks familiar about it?"

"I'm not sure. It's the short hair, the way it's styled, I think. Did Sandi describe it this way, or is this the artist's interpretation of what she said?"

"The artist has a few footnotes, read those."

"Well Alex, footnote number three explains how the hair was described, and I quote, "His hair is short, and it has dark brown roots with blonde tips, and spiky like a porcupine."

"Is that it?"

"Yes."

"That doesn't sound too far out, Gabi."

"No it doesn't, but it's kind of interesting."

"Why's that?"

"Well because it seems like in the back of my mind, I've seen hair like that just recently."

"Then sit down and think about it Gabrielle. Close your eyes, clear your mind, and think."

I sat there for a few minutes with my eyes closed. My mind was anything but clear. All I could think about was Jacob returning, and seeing Sterling for the first time. From out of the fog, I saw Sterling appearing in that beautiful red dress, dancing the tango with that man in the tuxedo. Then my mind went to the man who was chasing her, who also had on a tuxedo. I opened my eyes quickly, and said, "Alex, I can't do this right now!"

"Okay Princess, just relax. You probably don't know this person anyway."

I shook the bottle of pills I had been holding in my hand and said, "Well, we certainly don't need these anymore," as I tossed them into the trash.

"Gabi, I would like you to call the pharmacy. Talk to whoever sent this letter, and find out what prompted them to do so."

"Okay Alex."

I sat down at Father's desk, and dialed the pharmacy. As I was waiting for them to answer, I took Sterling's book out of the bag and became mesmerized. I stared at the title on the cover, and then began whispering over and over again, "Obsessions".

"Excuse me," Alex said.

"Oh nothing...sorry, I was just talking to myself."

Alex was sitting on the couch, intently studying the drawings once again while I was on the phone. He couldn't hear much of what I was saying, but I knew he could see my face turning white, and that I was confused and perplexed. Once I hung up the phone, I tried walking towards Alex, but was uncontrollably wobbly as I tripped on the Persian rug, nearly landing in Alex's lap."

As he picked me up he said, "Gabi, what's the matter?"

"I feel a little faint, Alex; I don't understand this—it doesn't make sense."

"What did they say?"

"I talked to the pharmacist, who told me that he was the one who actually fills Father's prescriptions, and it's his initials that are on the label."

"Okay, so what are you saying, Gabi?"

"Well, he still has the bottle. He said that those letters are sent out automatically after someone doesn't pick up their meds. AND, he still has Father's bottle of meds!"

"According to that letter the meds would have been returned to the shelf."

"I know, yet we have the bottle!"

"This does not make sense."

"The pharmacist knows Father, so when he didn't pick up the meds, he put them in a safe place."

"How did Michael get another bottle then?"

"That's what I asked him. The only thing he could think of was that maybe Father came in after the meds were tucked in the drawer, and unknowingly, the other pharmacist filled the prescription for him."

"That must have been exactly what happened. Good detective work Gabi. Problem solved!"

I knew Alex well enough, and could tell he didn't mean those words that quickly fell out of his mouth to protect me. He had a hunch about something, especially after watching him make a beeline to the trashcan to retrieve the pill bottle.

"Gabi, I think it would be best if I keep this letter and those pills, just in case we need them later. And hey, I have to leave now Princess. I need to go check on Sandi. I hired a nurse to stay with her, along with Detective Green until the case is closed. I don't trust her as far as…well, I could throw her pretty far if I wanted." He chuckled as he bent down to kiss me on the cheek.

"When will you be back?"

"In a couple hours. Are you feeling okay?"

"Yes, I'm feeling better now."

"And you have Sterling's book to keep you company!"

"Yes."

"Why don't you start reading it, and get your mind off of everything else for a while."

"Perfect idea Alex! Good-night."

I sat on the couch, and just stared at the cover of the book. I wonder how long it takes her to write a novel. I wonder where she gets her ideas. I opened the book, started reading, and immediately liked the name of the main character—Tiffany, what a great name!

The phone started ringing, and startled Sterling as she had just settled down with a cup of coffee to read through her finished work. She looked at the phone number and was excited—it was finally him!

"Hi Daniel!"

"Hello Sterling, sorry I missed your call earlier."

"That's alright. I missed everyone on the phone today."

"I heard about Michael's death. How are you holding up?"

"I'm doing okay."

"Just 'okay'?"

"Daniel, Michael's death was so unexpected—it was a complete shock! Even though the distance in our hearts became as distant as the miles over the years, we still loved each other very much."

"I know. I'm so sorry."

"Unfortunately, all the money in the world can't keep a relationship alive if two people can't be together. I have learned to live my life without him, even though I missed him terribly in the beginning."

"Did it ever become easier?"

"No. I just kept busier, until something happened in my heart. I think the same thing happened to Michael. Life happens to people, and if you're not together for that many years, you grow apart."

"Well, you know that you always have your friends."

"Yes, and you have been such a good friend these last few years. I have grown to depend on your friendship—thank you for being here for me."

"Are you ever going to be able to see Gabrielle?"

"When I saw her at Michael's funeral, I thought my heart would break. She is so beautiful, and I have missed her so much, but I can't just waltz back into her life. I couldn't help myself at the memorial service, I had to put my arm around her, and I actually said something to her."

"That was pretty brave."

"No, it was pretty selfish, and I shouldn't have done it. To answer your question, I don't know when would be the right time, or if there will ever be a right time. I know that she must be devastated about her father right now. She doesn't need anyone else adding to that grief."

"No Sterling, she doesn't."

"I didn't realize how much I missed all my friends until I was at the funeral. I miss you too Daniel."

"I haven't seen many of my friends lately, either. I've been ridiculously busy with this project I've been working on for months now."

"Is it almost completed?"

"Almost."

"Well, I just finished the novel that I've been working on. Maybe you can come to Capri when you're done."

"I'll call you in a few days Sterling; take care of yourself."

"I will. Bye Daniel."

Chapter 19

I sat straight up on the couch when Alex returned, walking abruptly into Father's office. I could tell that Alex had some news that he wanted to tell me, but I was far too eager to share what I had been doing.

"Hi Alex, this is great! Sterling's book is fantastic, have you read it?"

"No Gabi, not yet."

"Have you read any of her books?"

"To be honest with you Princess, I really haven't had the time."

"Well, she's an excellent writer. I'm so proud of her!"

"Sterling is very talented, indeed. Gabi, I need to …"

"Oh Alex, I really need to talk to you about something before Eric gets back tomorrow morning."

"Okay, you go first, what is it?"

"Well, remember when I asked you about that strange account? You said it was a story for another time."

"Yes, I remember."

"This is the time Alex. I need to know what that was all about."

"I have some other things to talk to you about, Gabi."

"Please, please Alex!"

Alex let out a very heavy sigh, as he said, "Okay."

I put Sterling's book down to give Alex my undivided attention. Alex put the envelope on Father's desk that contained the pills, letter, and composite drawings. He walked over to the couch opposite me, and began to tell me the story.

"I don't want to drag this story out by bogging it down with too many details, so I'm going to give you the facts, the hard cold facts, and how they were handled—okay?"

"Okay, but you're scaring me."

"I'm not trying to scare you, it's just that there's so much you don't know, and I'm afraid you won't be able to…"

"Handle it? Alex, I need to know! There have been entirely too many secrets!"

He reached over and grabbed my hand. He held it tightly as he looked into my eyes, and began telling the story.

"Your father fell in love with Sterling the moment they met."

"Oh my, Father never talked about Sterling. Where did they meet?"

"In Paris."

"That's so incredibly romantic!"

"Yes, it was, but let's not get away from the story right now. We can talk about how romantic it was, later."

"Sorry. Please go on."

"Shortly after Michael married Sterling, a woman from Michael's past sent him a letter. Michael was not someone who had many women. He had only been seriously in love with one other woman. Well, this other woman sent him a letter telling him that she had given birth to his baby."

"Oh my gosh, what did Father do?"

"Well…Michael was not happy with the news."

"Why? Didn't he want this child?"

"No, he didn't. This woman had lied to Michael, and told him that she was taking care of the birth control, when in fact she was not! Consequently, your father was extremely upset with her. He thought that every precaution was being taken, knowing that he wasn't ready for children yet. He then wondered if maybe it wasn't his child at all, and thought that she may have just wanted his money."

"What happened?"

"He went back there."

"Where?"

"To Germany, and demanded a paternity test."

"The results?"

"Well, this child that Michael did not plan for at all was definitely his. Since your father was such a man of impeccable integrity, he opened an account for the child, and has been sending money ever since."

"How long was he planning on doing that?"

"Until she turned twenty-eight, which was last month."

"Oh, Alex! Father had another daughter! I can't believe it! I can't believe all this! All these secrets!!! You know so much…did Sterling know about her also?"

"Yes."

"What's his daughter's name?"

"Tiffany."

"That's the name of the main character in Sterling's book!"

"Just a coincidence, Princess."

"Yeah, I guess there are hundreds of Tiffany's, and it's a very pretty name. Alex, you said that you were going to take care of that file for Father. How?"

"I have power of Attorney for…"

"That's not what I meant; I meant, what are you going to do to take care of it?"

"I'm going to set up the transfer of funds for her inheritance, but I can't really do that until next week at the meeting, and then there will be closure to this issue."

"I can't believe how weird this is. I didn't have a clue about what my life was really all about, until Father died! Now, all these secrets are creeping out, one by one, like peeling the skin off of an onion; it's just so weird."

"I know it is Gabrielle, and Michael wanted to tell you all of this in a much different way. Unfortunately, his untimely death left all these untold secrets; secrets that haunted him every day of his life."

"I feel so badly for Father—these secrets must have been so hard on him."

"If you only knew the half of it, Gabi. Michael had many dreams about all…"

I interrupted him, because I couldn't believe my ears. "Alex, my dreams have been so…"

"I know we need to finish talking about this, because it's very important to you, but right now we need to discuss the new developments in your Father's case."

I was just beginning to absorb the enormity of what had been the unknown only days before. My mind began to reel from the shock. The secrets and dreams were becoming my reality, and the lines between them so blurred that I could feel myself losing touch with my life. I felt like I was drifting into another dream as I said to Alex, "Okay, talk to me about Father's case."

His lips are moving, he's talking…'Pay attention Gabi, you're not dreaming…'

"First of all, I went to the pharmacy and talked to the pharmacist. He showed me the prescription bottle that he filled for Michael, and I showed him the one that I had. He said he didn't fill that one, and then he showed me the label where his initials would be if he had. There were no initials, which is against pharmacy policy."

I sat there motionless, in shock as Alex continued, "Then, after studying the bottles, he told me that this particular bottle wasn't even one of the pharmacies bottles. At that point, I told him that I would be in touch, and I went to pay a visit to my friend in forensics."

"Alex, you're scaring me again."

"Well, he ran a test on the pills, and found traces of the venom compound in them."

I threw myself against the couch, and as my neck jerked backwards, I screamed out, "Oh dear God, no! No Alex! Were those pills poisoning him?"

"Yes Gabrielle."

I jumped up, ran to Father's desk, dumped everything out of the envelope, onto the desk, grabbed the pill bottle and yanked the lid off.

"Gabi, what are you doing?"

"I want to look at these things…they killed my father!"

Just as those words came out of my mouth, I threw the bottle across the room, and started pacing frantically. I screamed, and then cried, and then started yelling at Alex. "Who gave these to him? Who? Who could have done this?"

Just then my cell phone rang, and I just stared at it, "I can't talk right now."

Alex answered it, and put it on speaker, "Hello, this is Alex."

"Hey Alex, this is Jacob…where's Gabi?"

"She's pretty upset right now."

"What in the world is going on there?"

Alex told Jacob about the latest developments, and then kept saying, "okay"…"okay!" Then, Alex looked at me and said, "You heard that. Jacob will be here at seven in the morning, instead of ten."

I let out a faint whisper, "Thanks Alex."

Sandi was fully awake now, and still handcuffed. The nurse walked over to Sandi, and asked if she could do anything for her. Sandi screamed at her, and told her that under no uncertain terms did she want anything from that "sleazy wench". Detective Green tried to talk to Sandi, but she wouldn't give him the time of day.

Then Sandi screamed at the top of her lungs, "Where is my husband?"

Detective Green told her that Alex would be back soon, and to just relax.

"Look, you piece of crap, I don't need to relax. I need to get out of here!"

Green knew the whole situation about Sandi, and he also knew how to handle people in these situations.

"Where do you need to go?"

"I have to meet someone, Green-Man!"

"Well, you'll just have to wait until Alex gets back."

"And then I can go?"

"Whatever Alex says, Sandi."

"Come on little Green-Man, if I don't get to meet him, I'll be left behind."

"Meet who?"

"You stupid piece of crap, do you think I'd tell you who I'm meeting?"

"Okay Sandi, I'm going to call Alex, and tell him that you're awake and ready to leave."

"You just do that you…cruddy-crud!"

Sandi was acting so ridiculous that it was all Detective Green could do to not burst out laughing, but this was all much too serious a situation to react to Sandi's nonsense, which could possibly set her off on some other crazy tangent. He called Alex, who arrived within minutes, relieving the two who had been on Sandi duty.

Alex started questioning Sandi again, and was absolutely merciless this time. He began to look at her like she was a criminal—he no longer saw this woman as his wife.

Chapter 20

I sat there, totally devastated, discovering the truth about Father's death. He had been poisoned, and now we had the evidence. My head was spinning—I felt like I was going to lose my mind. I desperately needed to talk with someone. I called Ashlee, but she couldn't come over for an hour, so I decided to escape into Sterling's book, until Ashlee arrived.

I picked up where I left off, at chapter four.

Max was so in love with Tiffany, but he knew that he couldn't have her. His obsession for her was becoming more and more intense. Thoughts of Tiffany consumed him. Her face was all he could see, as he lay awake at night, just longing deeply for her. He wanted to touch her beautiful silky hair and hold her body against his. He wondered if she had the same feelings for him. He fantasized that she did. Max could see the two of them together, dancing in the moonlight, and smelling her perfume as they glided across the flowery, decorated court.

I closed the book, took a deep breath, and looked up at the picture that Sterling had painted. Then I started talking to the painting, as though it could actually hear me.

"This story is so romantic Sterling—and this picture is so beautiful—you are incredibly talented."

After editing for the fifth time, Sterling was hopefully reading the final copy of her novel. She remembered that she had left out another very important part in the middle of the story, and debated whether to write that part in or not. Realizing if she didn't correct it her readers wouldn't quite understand the event at the end of the book.

On her way to the veranda to begin writing yet again, she made a detour to the kitchen. She was craving her favorite coffee drink, 'famoso espresso.' She quickly concocted it, grabbed her laptop, and stood in the sun for a moment before starting to write. She wondered when she would hear from Leon or Sonny, and why Leon's number was forwarded to Gabi's voicemail. 'Oh my precious Gabrielle—I hope we can be together soon.'

Antonio ushered Ashlee into Father's office where I was still reading.

"Hey Grilla!"

"Hey Ash!"

"Well, I'm yours tonight! I have the night off, because Pierre left for San Francisco."

"Oh yeah, what's he doing there?"

"He's taking a few days to visit his family."

"I didn't realize that his family was from California, but I guess I didn't even know where he came from, either. I'm just not too sharp lately. In fact..."

"Oh, don't be so hard on yourself. You've been through an unbelievable amount of grief and shock lately. It's a wonder you're not in a worse state than you are."

"Hey, are you hungry?"

"A little, why?"

"Would you like some of Maria's famous enchiladas?"

"Yeah, that sounds delicious...good idea!"

"Okay, I'll be right back. Make yourself at home."

As Gabi walked out of the room, Ashlee went to Michael's huge desk, and sat in his big, leather chair. She looked out at the smaller chair, which was facing the front of the desk, and pretended to be a Psychiatrist talking to her patient.

"Well Elizabeth...what exactly led you to do such a thing?"

"Aha, I see...aha...well, don't you think that maybe you should have asked before you just took Mrs. Wiener's dogs from her yard?"

"You don't? Well...you can't take things that aren't yours, even if you are just borrowing them."

"Okay, well I think that what you need is a big dose of..."

"Hey Ash, who are you talking to?"

Just as Ashlee said, "my patient," we both started laughing.

"Have a seat Miss Princess, and tell me what's on your mind today."

Ashlee pretended to look at her patient's file on the desk. She moved the envelope that Alex had left there, and then gathered the drawings together, as if they were records that fell out of her patient's file.

"Let me see here Princess Deliano, it seems like we've been seeing you for…"

Ashlee started shuffling the papers, and was putting them back inside the envelope. All of a sudden she had a strange look on her face, as she noticed something.

"Who is this Gabi? Why do you have this picture?"

"Which one, and why are you asking?"

"No, that's not how it goes Gabrielle; I asked you first."

"Okay, I'm lost, what are you talking about? You act like you're not my shrink anymore; I thought we were pretending…"

Ashlee snapped back sharply, "We were! But, what is this?"

"What?"

"This picture! It looks so much like Pierre, it's scary—what are these?"

"Oh, it must be a mistake. Those are just composite drawings of the person that was visiting Sandi. We think he may have a connection with at least one of the murders."

"Oh that! Just that! Geez, the resemblance makes me feel a little uneasy."

"Sorry Ash. I don't know that much about these drawings. A lot of guys look like that—well, maybe not a lot, but if you want, we can go see Alex."

"Yeah, I'd like to talk to him; why don't you call him first."

I called Alex and told him what Ashlee said. He was in the middle of questioning Sandi again, and seemed a little upset at the moment, responding in his less than nice manner, "Yes, I forgot those on the desk…sure bring them over…I need to show the drawings to Sandi."

I felt sorry for Alex having to go through such painful conversations with Sandi.

"Don't worry about it right now Alex—Ashlee was just concerned about one of the drawings looking like Pierre."

"Who?"

"You know, Ashlee's new beau!"

"Ah, that's right."

"Well, she's concerned that this drawing is being circulated as a criminal and could cause problems for him, because it does resemble him, she said."

"Come on over! You and Ashlee stay at the gate, and have one of your bodyguards bring them to me. I don't want Sandi to get upset if she sees you."

"No problem Alex, we'll be there in a few."

Detective Green was at the gate when we arrived.

"How are things going in there, Steve?"

"I've been out here for a while, so I'm not quite sure. Who's your friend, Gabi?"

"This is Ashlee…she's the one that was almost blown away from the car bomb the other night."

"Ashlee, this is Detective Steve Green."

"Nice to meet you, Detective Green."

"Nice to meet you, Ashlee."

"How are you doing after that bomb experience?"

"I walked away with only a few scrapes…I'm fine, thank you."

Just then Alex walked out onto the porch—seeing us, he quickly walked to the gate. As he was hugging me first, then Ashlee, I noticed that my two bodyguards were walking towards me.

"Is it really necessary that they follow me over here?"

Alex answered with a very stern, "Yes."

"Those poor guys really get a workout following me around!"

They all laughed, then Ashlee got serious as she grabbed Alex's arm and tugged on it.

"Hey Alex, what's up with that drawing looking so much like my boyfriend?"

"Ashlee, unfortunately those composites tend to look like a lot of people—don't worry about it. I need to get back in there with Sandi. I'll talk to you two later."

"But Alex…"

He turned around, and walked off rather abruptly. Ashlee complained to me as we walked away from the gate. Detective Green yelled, "Good-bye" winking at Ashlee.

When we got back to the house, Maria was just bringing the food into the office. I still couldn't get myself to eat at the dining room table. While we were eating, Antonio arrived at the office door to announce Mary's arrival. I walked over to her, hugged her tightly, and then asked her to join us.

"Oh, I can't Gabi, thank you anyway. My stomach isn't being very nice to me today."

"Well, when was the last time you had something to eat?"

"Yesterday, I think. Yes, it was yesterday for breakfast."

"That's ridiculous, you can't go without food like that. How does your stomach feel?"

"Nauseated."

"Did you make an appointment with my doctor yet?"

"Yes, I did! As a matter of fact, I see him tomorrow, Gabi!"

"Well, I'm glad about that. You're just worrying me lately. I will feel much better after I know that he's checked you out, and given you a clean bill of health."

"He's not going to just check me out. I scheduled a complete physical, and I have to go in fasting."

"That's good that you're having blood work done also, but I think you started fasting a little too soon."

"Very funny, Gabrielle! I can't eat after eight o'clock tonight, so maybe I will try to have a few bites of those delicious enchiladas."

"Good idea. Hand me your plate, Mary! Have you still been having headaches?"

"Actually they started getting worse yesterday. I've been taking aspirin round the clock for that, but I was told to not take anything, including the aspirin, after eight o'clock."

"Including your high blood pressure meds?"

"Yeah—including those, also."

"How has your blood pressure been since you started the meds?"

"It's gone down considerably, but I've also been watching what I eat, and getting plenty of exercise. Oh, and I've been making sure my body isn't depleted of potassium, which helps maintain a proper balance of the sodium a person has in their bodies."

"I'm so proud of you, Mary. You really take good care of yourself."

"Michael and I have always been health conscious!"

"Oh, I know how Father was about his health."

"Speaking of which, we both were constantly reading up on what was the best medication to take, or the best foods to eat to keep us healthy, and would quickly inform the other on our findings."

"Yes, I remember, but at that point I thought you both were just competitive, yet friendly, neighbors. I had no idea you were siblings!"

"Well, I'm the one that found this latest blood pressure medication that worked best on Michael, and me. Oh, my brother was so precious. Last week when I ran out of meds, I didn't want to leave Michael's side, but he knew I needed my meds. As weak as he was, he tried to open his drawer. Bless his heart—his little, frail arm took forever to open it, and his shaky hands could barely unscrew the lid on the bottle. He wanted to give me some of his pills, so I didn't have to go without. Since I only take half of what was prescribed for Michael, I've been cutting them in half, and..."

I started choking on a piece of enchilada that I was swallowing as Mary finished her sentence about the pills. After coughing up what had been lodged in my throat, I let out a blood-curdling scream...

"NO...NO! PLEASE TELL ME YOU'RE NOT TAKING FATHER'S PILLS!"

"Yes, I am...I just told you I was. He doesn't need them anymore, so..."

"Oh my gosh, Ashlee! Get your car, NOW!"

"What's going on Gabi?"

"Just get it, Ashlee! Mary, let's go!"

"Where are we going?"

"I'm calling Dr. LaBarca and having him meet us at the hospital."

"What's the matter with you? I don't want to go to the hospital. What's going on?"

"I'll tell you in the car...let's roll...NOW!"

Chapter 21

Alex had been questioning Sandi for two hours, with absolutely no cooperation on her part. He finally did what his heart really didn't want to do—he threatened to take her to the station, and hand her over to Charles if she continued to be unresponsive. As soon as she heard him say 'Charles,' she quickly changed her tune.

"Alex, I don't think he ever gave me his name."

"Let me get this straight. You never called him anything—he just arrived one day, and signed you up for this case?"

"Not exactly."

"Well then, what exactly did he do?"

"He called me first."

"When did he call you?"

"I don't remember. I need to look at a calendar."

Alex took hold of Sandi's hand, and pulled her over to his desk where there was a calendar of both his business activities, and their social schedule. She turned the calendar page back to the prior month, and studied it for a minute."

"That's the day."

"Which one?"

"It was the first Monday of the month."

"How do you know that?"

"Because…I remember that you were at your monthly meeting at Michael's, and then you took Michael to the airport."

"Yes Sandi, that's what the calendar says I did. How do you know that was the day he first contacted you?"

"I remember that he got here almost right after you left for that meeting, and he stayed for quite a while. I remember wanting him to go away, because he'd been here forever it seemed, and I had planned to watch movies all day since you were going to be gone for so long."

"Okay, so we've established the contact day, but you still don't remember his name? Where were you supposed to meet him today?"

"I don't want to talk to you anymore, Alex."

"You listen to me, Sandi! I am not going to tolerate this, and I will take you to the station."

"No Alex, don't do that to me, please."

"Then quit playing your games! Now…where were you supposed to meet him today?"

"The airport."

"And where were you two going?"

"I don't know."

"Sandi, you were going to get on a plane with a perfect stranger and you didn't know where you were going? You didn't even know his name?! I'm not buying it!"

Alex could tell that Sandi was tired, irritated, and beginning to get mouthy again—her attention span was quite short. "I'll ask you again, Sandi. Where were you going with the stranger?"

Sandi quickly snapped back, "He wasn't a stranger! I told you, I'm in love with him. And he loves me."

"How could you two be in love and going away together if you don't even know his name?"

She screamed out, "YOU DON'T BELIEVE ME? YOU PIG!"

"No I don't believe you, but I have an idea. If I show you some sketches, you might be able to identify him, and that may jog your memory about what his name is."

"Where did you get these, Alex?"

"You gave them to me."

"No I did not, Alexander Stone. That's a lie!"

"Well you didn't draw them, but you gave me the descriptions."

"When did I do that?"

"Before you fell asleep this morning—now quit wasting time, and look at these. Do you recognize any of these men, Sandi?"

He slowly held up the drawings one by one, so she could study them, hoping, waiting for some kind of reaction from her. "Well, Sandi?"

"Nope, not that one."

"Nope, not him either."

"Nope, don't know him."

Sandi looked up, wanting him to stop. She knew Alex was a master at recognizing when people were lying. She wasn't sure if she should chance lying or not, and quickly changed her strategy. "Let me see those again. "

As Sandi looked through each one of the three sketches she had already seen, she mumbled something about them, "They all kind of look like people I know."

"Stop playing games, Sandi!"

"What do you mean?"

"Either you recognize the face, or you don't."

"Don't get mad at me, Alex."

"Just keep looking."

After Sandi looked at two more sketches, she paused at the next one, which happened to be the last.

"I think I kind of recognize this one."

"Well either you do, or you don't, which is it?"

"I think I do?"

"What color hair did he have when he was in this disguise?"

"I think it was blonde."

"Sandi, how old do you think he was?"

"Maybe twenty-eight, maybe thirty-five. Oh gosh, I don't know!"

"Did he have moles, or any distinguishing marks anywhere?"

"None that I can remember, but he did have something on one of his ears. It was a very small dot, a tattoo I think."

"This is good Sandi, you've done very good. I have one more question tonight."

"Okay, then can I go watch a movie?"

"Yes, you can. I need to know what number you called to reach him."

"I don't remember."

"That's not an acceptable answer, Sandi. You must remember how you contacted him."

"I don't Alex, you PIG!"

"I can find it easy enough. You know that."

"I HATE YOU, ALEX!"

Alex opened the door, and summoned Detective Green to accompany Sandi to the parlor to watch her movie, and further instructed him to stay with her until he returned.

"I'll have Angela bring in some food for her, Steve."

Steve nodded as he said, "Hey Stone, where's your cell, it's not on your belt?"

Alex felt for his phone, it wasn't there, "I must have left it in the car—see ya later."

When Alex got to the car, his cell phone was beeping with a message. It was Gabi calling him in a panic, explaining what had happened to Mary, and for him to meet them at the hospital. Alex took off like lightening, and arrived only moments after the doctor finished running the tests.

155

After Alex and I explained what had led to this event, the doctor admitted Mary into ICU.

They quickly pumped Mary's stomach, flushed her system, and reported that they would be watching her vitals for the next twenty-four hours.

Ashlee went to the nurse's station to talk to a friend she knew, and told us that she would catch up in a minute. As Alex and I were walking down the long corridor out of the hospital, I slipped my arm through Alex's and said, "Alex, I remember who that drawing vaguely reminds me of."

"Who?"

"When I was at Ashlee's house, I saw her new beau from a distance a couple times. I haven't had the chance to meet him yet, but I remember thinking how different his hair was. I never saw him close up, but his blonde hair was short, and very spiky looking."

"So, you've never met her boyfriend?"

"No, and please don't tell Ashlee I said that."

As soon as Ashlee caught up to Alex and me, Alex told us to go home and wait for him. He had some important business to take care of, and would be over later.

Alex stood at the pharmacy window, and waited for the pharmacist to explain about a new medication to a customer, but after a few minutes, he interrupted them and said, "I have an emergency here, could you wrap it up?"

At that, the lady walked off, and the pharmacist told Alex how rude he had behaved.

Alex had entirely too much on his mind, but he was ashamed of his behavior. He apologized to the pharmacist, flashed his badge, and said he was working on a case—then he immediately held up a drawing.

"Does this man look familiar to you?"

With a quizzical look on his face, the pharmacist answered, "Yes, he does."

"How do you know him?"

"He's an intern pharmacist here."

"How long has he been here?"

"Oh, about a month."

"Where is he now?"

"He's gone for a few days, to San Francisco I think…to see his family."

"Does he fill prescriptions on his own, without supervision from you?"

"Most of the time he does."

"What is his name?"

"Pierre."

"Thank you. That's all I need to know right now. I appreciate your time. I'll be in touch."

As Alex walked off, he ached in the pit of his stomach knowing what the ramifications of this information meant. He called Charles at the station to put out an APB on Pierre. He knew full well though, that Pierre had a huge jump on them, and wondered if they could ever catch him before he escaped the country.

It was such a nice evening that we were sitting in the courtyard reminiscing, waiting for Alex.

"Hi Alex. It's so pretty out tonight…can we just sit out here for a while?"

"Okay."

Ashlee sat down on the bench, and Alex sat right beside her. I walked up to Alex, and put my arm around his shoulders.

"What's the matter, Alex? You don't look so good."

"I'm not, Gabrielle."

Alex pulled the drawing of Pierre out of the envelope, and said to Ashlee, "Is this Pierre?"

"Well, it does look like him, but Pierre wouldn't do anything wrong!"

Alex looked at Ashlee with furrowed brows, and a very sad face as he asked, "Did Pierre have any distinguishing marks anywhere on him?"

"Well, I wouldn't know about 'anywhere.' I haven't seen much, but he did have a little tattoo of a star on his ear."

Alex's body became erect, as it forced him off of the marble bench. With a clenched jaw, and sweaty palms, he escaped into his own world mentally, and began pacing back and forth in the courtyard.

"Alex," Ashlee cried out, "WHAT'S THE MATTER?"

Alex stopped pacing for a second, "How long have you known Pierre?"

"About a month."

"And he works at the pharmacy, you said, correct?"

"Yes."

Alex started pacing again, this time slower and shaking his head back and forth.

Ashlee ran over to Alex, and stood right in his path to make him stop pacing. "Alex, what is going on?"

Alex stopped, put his arm around Ashlee, and directed her back to the bench.

"Sit down. I have to tell you something and it's not good."

She sat down, a tear rolled down her cheek as if she had a gut feeling that something was really wrong.

I sat down next to Ashlee. Alex stood above both of us and slowly started explaining.

"I'm quite positive that Pierre is the man who came to Sandi in quite a few disguises. It's a long story, but they ended up working together to penetrate Michael's house."

I screeched, "What?"

"Well, unfortunately, when he approached Sandi, he played on her mental deficiencies. He told her that she would be helping him with a case he was working on to protect Michael. All the while, I'm afraid Pierre was using her to get close to Michael and Leon."

"Oh, I think I'm going to be sick," Ashlee said.

I moved to Ashlee, and embraced her in a consoling hug. Tears streamed down both our faces.

"Ashlee, do you know if Pierre really had relatives in San Francisco, or could he have high-tailed it somewhere else?"

"Obviously, I didn't really know him. I don't know what to tell you, but he never mentioned family at all, until he left."

My heart was aching for her, "Ashlee, I am so sorry,"

"I feel like such a fool."

"How were you to know? It seems like he fooled a lot of people."

"Well I hope he rots in the pits of hell, if he killed Michael and Leon!"

Alex put his arm around Ashlee to console her, and said, "Ashlee, Honey, I am so sorry."

He turned to me, and said in a very quiet tone, "I'm going to take Ashlee home. You both really need some rest."

"But it's still early Alex, I don't want to be alone."

"I need to get home Princess, and you both need some sleep. Remember, Jacob will be here tomorrow morning at seven."

I stood up on my toes, and gave Alex a kiss on his cheek. "Thanks for reminding me…I'll see you in the morning."

Then I hugged Ashlee, and asked her, "Do you want to stay here and talk? My turn to play shrink."

"That's okay, Gabi. I want to go home. I need to sort this all out on my own. Love you."

"Love you too."

Chapter 22

Pierre was relieved to finally be on the plane and going home. He wasn't sure which description might have been given to the police, so he took his chances on wearing the first disguise that he sported for Sandi. It always felt weird to wear the dark brown wig, beard and mustache, but even weirder to wear the big Roman nose—the nose was claustrophobic, especially when he needed to scratch. He couldn't help thinking of how badly he wanted out of this business for good. He kept practicing his exit speech over, and over again in his head.

Being a hit-man was not Pierre's dream for his life. He fell prey to some very rich men in high places who would pay him when they needed things 'taken care of.' He hated himself for being so desperate for money that he became something this deplorable. Then, his thoughts turned to his father, the type of man who wanted to 'make a man out of Pierre' by having him work for everything since he was twelve. 'He made a man out of me all right—a very rich man, who has done very bad things.'

At thirty-one years old, Pierre decided that this was truly the very last time—no more contracts! He looked at his watch, relieved he would be landing in a couple of hours. Soon he would receive the balance of his money, and be done with this, so-called, 'business.'

I went up to my room, took a long, warm bath, and climbed into bed. I couldn't sleep. According to the new schedule I've been keeping it's entirely too early, so I grabbed Sterling's book and started reading.

When Max snapped out of his daydream, he was even more depressed about Tiffany. His obsession was becoming worse by the day, and his longing for her was turning into desperation. Max kept telling himself that the other man in her life didn't love her the way he did. That awful man abandoned her, and he didn't deserve her! Max began plotting ways to dispose of the man who was in his way. He was extremely intelligent, and was devising a plan that wouldn't be suspect as a murder—not in the slightest. He was so driven by his obsession for Tiffany that he thought about his plans night and day, in-between his dreams of her. Max had watched her for years, had waited so long, and now was his chance to finally have her for himself.

I closed the book and started thinking about how sad it would be to love someone in the way that Max loved Tiffany, and not be able to have them. The book hasn't mentioned if Tiffany loves Max though... Then I turned my mind to Jacob, and the warm embrace we recently shared. 'Oh, I long to be in your arms again Jacob. I couldn't stand to be this much in love with you, for all these years, and not be able to have you.' With those thoughts in my head, I finally fell asleep.

Soon, I was standing in the middle of our Grand Ballroom—the light from the chandelier was bouncing off the mirrors, onto the floor in every color of the rainbow. The orchestra was playing, and everyone around me was floating across the floor to Aria, one of my favorite Mozart tunes.

I looked exquisite in my strapless and backless, long sequin gown. My dark hair was swept up off of my face, with only a single curl hanging down the side of my forehead, and barely touching my collarbone. My face was glistening, and my lips were like plump, red cherries longing to be kissed. I stood there in the middle of the floor, waiting for Jacob.

As the song ended, the orchestra quietly exited the room, but then the next sound that came from the stage was shocking. I turned to look at the orchestra, and to my surprise they were dressed in black leather, huge black combat boots, long hair, and piercings on their bodies in places they should not have been.

Suddenly, the sound got even worse...it was heavy metal with loud, screaming voices. I stood there in utter shock. I couldn't move, I couldn't talk...I was stuck there! The people that had been floating to the beautiful sounds of Mozart were now dressed in clothes that matched the band. They were not dancing anymore, but throwing their bodies all over the place—a most bizarre sight.

'Stop this, what are you doing? Get out of my house,' I kept thinking, but I couldn't get the words out. As I was trying very hard to form words to speak, I noticed a pathway that was slowly appearing, and the people were eerily moving aside. As the sounds from the band got louder and more hideous, I was overcome with frustration and anxiety. I looked down the cleared pathway and I couldn't believe what my eyes were seeing!

I screamed, but nothing came out! Jacob was walking towards me, dressed only in leather pants and a v-cut leather t-shirt with a woman draped on his arm. She was quite beautiful, with long, golden-brown hair, and huge brown eyes; she was dressed in an outfit that matched Jacobs, perfectly.

My eyes got as big as saucers as tears came flooding down my cheeks. The couple stopped directly in front of me, then Jacob pulled the woman close to him—they kissed in a warm embrace for a very long time, then pushing the woman away as quickly as he grabbed her, he started his introductions.

"Gabrielle, this is Tiffany!"

I actually screamed, which woke me up. My heart was beating at warp speed, as I jumped out of bed, and ran down to the kitchen—trying to regain my composure, I began talking out loud, "I'm hallucinating again because I need more food—I need to eat—where are those darn cookies?"

Mornings on the Amalfi coast were so incredibly beautiful, and such an inspiration, Sterling thought. She made a 'famoso espresso,' strolled out to her verandah, and started her computer. The ending wasn't as powerful as she had intended—and another edit began...

With the final copy on the horizon, Sterling began to realize how isolated she had been. She was starting to miss the conversations she had with her very close friend. She wanted to be with him, and started to dial his number, but then hung up—her mind was wondering if he was really just a friend, or much more. She kept thinking about the last time they were together—wanting to kiss him, knowing he wanted to kiss her, but neither of them would feel right about it in their hearts. He was the only one that Sterling felt she could share her past with, maybe that's why she felt so close to him. She wondered why he didn't seem very warm yesterday when they spoke, so she decided to call him.

Daniel's cell went directly to his voicemail.

When Alex arrived back home, Sandi was still watching movies. He went to her room, and immediately started packing her bags. After Alex finished packing, he called Dr. Monroe, Sandi's Psychiatric doctor. He apologized that it was so late. Dr. Monroe was sympathetic and said to bring her in immediately.

Alex gave Sandi a tranquilizer so she wouldn't be hard to deal with on the trip. After about twenty minutes, he gave her another one. When the pills took effect Alex told Sandi that they were going for a ride. She went willingly.

When they arrived at the clinic, the nurse informed Sandi that she was going to take a few tests. Alex released her to the doctor, saying that she would be in safe hands with Dr. Monroe. Sandi really liked her doctor and walked into his office with a big smile on her face. 'Oh that poor man,' Alex thought, 'maybe…she's falling in love with him now, too.' Dr. Monroe gave him the look that meant to leave now. Alex obliged by walking out…slowly, closing the door behind him.

Alex drove back home knowing that Sandi might not be coming back for a very long time, if ever. He felt relieved though, and in a sense he desperately longed for his life to be different.

Ashlee sat in her huge living room, just staring at the ceiling. A steady stream of tears rolled down her cheeks, as she kept thinking to herself, 'How could I fall in love with a loser? A monster? A murderer? What was it about him that I really liked, and how could he have been so convincing? I'm sure that it was his intelligence. He had such a brilliant mind! Just too brilliant, I guess.'

Then Ashlee started remembering everything he told her. 'He said he went to school at Berkeley, but then one time he said he studied in Germany. After that, he retracted and said, what he meant was, he went there for a vacation.' She remembered that sounding confusing, but now wondered what he really meant. 'I can't believe I blew that off. Maybe it means something!' Ashlee decided to call Alex.

"Hi Ashlee. Yes, I'm home now, in fact I'm just pulling into the garage."

"Can you come over?"

"Of course, is something bothering you?"

"Yes, I need to talk about Pierre."

"I'll be right there."

The Butler showed Alex to the living room where Ashlee was sitting, looking very sad and very lost.

"Thanks for coming Alex, would you like a cup of coffee?"

"That sounds good, thank you."

They sat down together on the long, beautiful, soft leather couch. Ashlee burrowed in and started talking instantly.

"I just can't believe that I fell for such a loser. What does that say about me?"

"It doesn't say anything about you, Ashlee."

"But I'm a psychiatrist, well almost, and I should understand people's minds. How could this have happened to me?"

"Well, this could have happened to anyone. Don't be so hard on yourself. When someone lies, how are we supposed to know what's going on in their head? You were taking him at face value, drawing your conclusions based on what he told you, like any other normal person would do. The biggest point here is the fact that you weren't seeing him as a patient, you were seeing him as a friend."

"Good point, Alex. But it still makes me feel so..."

"Used?"

"Yes! Oh, what I wanted to tell you was I've been playing the conversations we had, over and over in my mind. I don't know if this will help, but I remember him saying something that didn't mean anything at the time, just a slip of words, maybe. But tonight, I got to thinking about it, and it seems weird to me."

"What did he say?"

"He said that he went to Berkeley, and then he said he studied in Germany. Then, he quickly corrected himself saying that he went on a vacation in Germany. Does that sound strange to you, Alex?"

"Yes, and I do believe that gives us a little something more to go on."

"Do you think that maybe he didn't go to San Francisco?"

"Exactly, and with that slip of the tongue, he may have revealed where he really did go to school. If that's all the information you have for me Ashlee, I need to run. If he actually left the country it will be harder to not only catch him, but to extradite him as well."

"Alex, listen to me! You do whatever you have to do to bring that scumbag to justice!"

"Ashlee, I'm going to the station now. If you remember anything else, call me immediately!"

He kissed her on the forehead, and as he was walking off, he said, "Hey Ashlee, thanks for calling me, now get some rest."

After I finished the cookies, I was wide-awake, and fully recovered from my dream, or rather my nightmare. I couldn't even think about going back to sleep. I ran upstairs to get Sterling's book, and then settled down on the comfortable couch in Father's office. I opened the book to start reading, but when I read Tiffany's name in the first sentence, I slammed the book shut.

Now the name was triggering thoughts of my new half sister, and I wondered what she was like. I also wondered if Father had hopes of us ever meeting and having a real relationship. I wondered so many things about Father now. I wish I had all the answers, like he always did.

I put Sterling's book down on the couch, and walked over to the safe to retrieve the file on my sister. Maybe, just maybe there is more information in this file that could possibly help me locate her. I opened the file, and painstakingly went through every single sheet of paper, every receipt, and every hand-written, scribbled thought.

In the middle of a rather large document that was stapled together by way too many staples, I found an address for Tiffany Deliano. My heart skipped a beat when I saw her name in print. 'Oh, she lives in Zurich, what a beautiful place to live.'

This money goes directly to her, how interesting. Then as I turned a few more pages, I saw that Tiffany's mother had passed away quite some time ago. 'Oh Father, you must have felt so bad. Knowing your heart as well as I did, you were probably more involved in her life than just sending her money.'

"I've got to find her! I've got to find my sister! I know that's what you would have wanted, Father!"

I copied the address, and put the file carefully back in the safe. Alex would be taking care of it tomorrow, and I didn't want him to know I had been in the file. Finally feeling tired, I decided to go back to bed—now I was excited to fall asleep, knowing that when I wake up, Jacob will be here!

Chapter 23

Daniel was withdrawing such a huge sum of cash at the bank that the manager was called to handle the transaction. "Well, this is the second time in a month I get to see you, Daniel."

"Actually Lou, it's been exactly one month and five days, look at the date of the last withdrawal."

"Yeah, a month and five days, you're right. This must be a pretty big deal, huh? Five hundred thousand dollars is a lot of money! Just out of curiosity, it this for payroll also?"

"Yes, and finally, the project is almost finished."

"Hey Daniel, what kind of industry are you in that pays that kind of money in payroll?"

Avoiding the question, Daniel answered, "Lou, there's a lot you don't know about business, being a suit and all. I've gotta run, I'm meeting someone in an hour."

Lou shook his head as he said, "Don't spend it all in one place!"

Under his breath Daniel said, "How corny can a bank manager be?"

Daniel arrived at the airport a little early, so he decided to go into a new beautiful lounge that had just been completed. It was like a first class nightclub in L.A. or New York, with an unbelievable ambiance, including a stage for live bands. He had never seen a club like this in an airport before.

When the cocktail waitress asked him what he'd like to drink, he was so interested in the club that he started asking questions, one right after another. He wasn't surprised to find out that this was quite the hot spot for people to meet and gather, every night of the week. He wondered why he hadn't heard of it yet, but then, he had been so busy as of late, he hadn't had time for much.

As he sat there drinking his scotch, he noticed a babbling brook running through the middle of the club, directly under the dance floor. 'Amazing,' he thought. His eyes followed the water until it came to a small bridge connecting the club to a dining area. A little stunned, his eyes went back to the bridge, and stopped, fixed on a woman who was standing on the bridge. She looked so familiar.

Her face looked almost exactly like…Gabrielle! 'No, it couldn't be! It couldn't be, but OH-MY-GOSH she looks just like her!' The woman walked off the bridge and took at seat in the lounge. He stared at her for the longest time—he couldn't believe how much she looked like Gabi. Then, as she was pulling a cigarette from a silver case, the waiter walked by and must have said something to her. She smiled at him, and said something back.

With both of those gestures, Daniel knew that it absolutely was not Gabrielle. Gabrielle had the most beautiful teeth and smile, of which this woman was a little lacking, and Gabi would never smoke. Daniel shook his head in disbelief, looked away, and wasn't bothered by her looks any further. Shaking his head again, he thought that this sighting must have been triggered from the discussion that he and Sterling had about Gabrielle yesterday.

Daniel walked down the long concourse, then up to the gate to meet his client. They completed their business transaction, and Daniel was on his way to Capri. He dialed Sterling's number to let her know that he would be on a flight to Milan tomorrow, but there was no answer.

The birds were singing and it was a gorgeous morning, so I decided to wait in the courtyard for Jacob. My face was aglow in the sunlight, my hair was blowing in the gentle breeze, and my eyes were sparkling, intermittently filling with tears as I awaited Jacob's arrival.

Jacob and Sonny climbed out of the car. As Sonny jetted quickly into the house, Jacob walked up to me, took my hand and said, "I am mesmerized by your radiant beauty—let's go for a walk."

Completely smitten by his statement, I would have just walked off into the sunset with him—but reality set in… "It's good to see you too. Why didn't Eric come back with you?"

"He was coming back with us until he got a call regarding a new position at the hospital. He couldn't very well turn down the chief of staff. I told him we could take care of things and we'd call him if we needed him. Gabi, we really don't need him here right now. I've got a ton of people on this."

"Oh I know, I just wanted to talk with my new brother, and get to know him a little."

"There will be plenty of time for that."

I slipped my arm through Jacobs, and squeezed it tightly as I said, "I missed you, Jacob—I missed you so much."

"I missed you too. I could hardly stand to be away from you."

We walked through the courtyard, and over to the marble bench by the fountain. Jacob took my hand and gently pulled me down on the bench with him. He put his arms around me, and pulled me close as though he had been dreaming of holding me forever.

Jacob's embrace was so warm, and his arms felt so strong as he wrapped them around my body—then, as he started kissing me with such passion, I felt as though I was dreaming. After his mouth pulled away from mine, he tenderly began kissing my forehead, trailing down to my neck, then paused and whispered in my ear. "I need you, I have to be with you, Gabrielle."

I slowly pulled away, just enough to look deeply into Jacob's eyes and said, "I need you too. I want to be with you with all my heart."

He put his finger to my lips, and stopped me from talking. Puzzled, I looked at him with longing in my eyes. Sensually and slowly, Jacob backed away from me, got off the bench, and dropped to one knee. He took my hand in his, and said, "Gabrielle Deliano...will you marry me? Will you make me the happiest man alive?" He pulled out a small, white satin box, and opened it!

My eyes grew very large as they filled with tears of joy; looking at him, I smiled sweetly and said, "Yes Jacob, yes! It would be an honor to be your wife!"

As Jacob took the ring out of the pretty little box, I felt as though my heart was skipping beats—I needed to remind myself to breathe. I couldn't believe my eyes! The ring was a beautiful marquis, two-carat diamond solitaire, on an exquisitely sculpted white-gold band. When he slipped it onto my finger, I very slowly, and with deep sincerity said, "Oh Jacob, I love you too—this is absolutely gorgeous!"

"So are you, Gabrielle. I love you with all my heart. I always have, and I always will."

Jacob sat back on the bench, and we held each other in a warm embrace, until Sonny appeared in the courtyard, "Okay Jacob, times up! Are you done? Hope so—cuz you're on, man!"

"Boy oh boy—lucky for you, I am!"

Sonny walked over, picked me up, twirled me around, put me back down, kissed my forehead like he always did, and said, "Congratulations sweet Gabi; you're going to make a fabulous couple! I'm very happy for both of you!"

He looked at my hand and said, "That's a gorgeous ring! Did you decide on a date yet?"

"No…I'm still in shock!"

Then Jacob chimed in with, "It will have to be pretty soon. I don't think I can wait too much longer to share my life with you, every moment, of every day!"

We all had very large grins on our faces as we walked arm-in-arm into the house together. I ran quickly into the kitchen to tell Maria and Antonio the news. Jacob and Sonny went into Father's office to finish discussing business before Alex arrived.

Sonny looked a little concerned as he said to Jacob, "Do you think that asking Gabi to marry you right now was a little too soon, after her father passed away?"

"No Sonny. Michael knew that I was going to ask her. If he hadn't gotten sick, all three of us were going out to dinner, so I could surprise her with my proposal."

"Oh, I didn't know that."

"And Sonny, this is best for Gabi. It will help her to think about planning the wedding, instead of becoming obsessed with mourning for her father, and Leon."

"You're right Jacob. You're always right!"

"Hey, I wouldn't say that…but you can!" They both laughed.

Daniel was so excited to finally be seeing Sterling. He was debating whether to keep trying to get a hold of her by phone or just surprise her in Capri. He knew that she didn't like people to just show up unannounced. It was one of her pet peeves, as she enjoyed her privacy. He also knew that she truly wanted to see him, and he was extremely anxious to see her.

There was nothing in the way now, and he could see Sterling with a clear conscious. He had been dreaming about her for years. The feelings he had for her, in his heart, were becoming more and more intense. He wanted to be with Sterling so badly it was all he could think about. He decided to call her.

After the first ring, Sterling answered, "Hi Daniel!"

"Hi Sterling, it's so good to hear your voice."

"Yours too, did you finally finish that project?"

"Yes, it was one of the…"

She cut him off, "Well, it's finally over, so why don't you come to Capri?"

"How is your book coming along? Are you ready for some company?"

"Daniel, you're so thoughtful. My book is pretty much completed, and I am always ready for your company."

"Okay Sterling, then I'll see you tomorrow afternoon."

"Ciao!"

Jacob and Sonny approached Alex with their usual respectful greetings. They knew that Alex was Michael's closest and dearest friend and confidant. They were glad in their hearts the aspersions that had been cast upon Alex, were purely suspicions, and nothing more. Alex reviewed the latest developments regarding Pierre, with Jacob and Sonny, and then they made plans accordingly.

Jacob was concerned about how hard an extradition would be if they had to extract Pierre out of Europe, so he decided to track Daniel down.

Alex didn't agree with Jacob, and was concerned with his idea. Daniel had been away from the group for so long. Alex also wondered if Daniel would be willing to get involved. Even knowing Alex's concerns, Jacob had to take a chance.

Daniel was boarding the plane for Milan when Jacob's call came through. It had been a while since they had talked, so Daniel was reluctant to answer, but finally decided he should.

"Hey, Daniel, it's Jacob."

"Hey, Jacob! It's been a long time. How are you?"

"Well, I'm sure you're aware of Michael's death."

"Yes, I'm so sorry. He was a good man."

"And then, Leon."

"What about Leon?"

"He was murdered, two days after Michael died."

"WHAT?"

"Yes. Leon is dead!"

"Do you think it was from that old case?"

"Not sure Daniel. Michael was murdered also."

"Jacob, what in the heck is going on?"

"That's one of the reasons I called you. Have you got a minute?"

"I was just boarding a plane, but I guess I can take the next one. What's up?"

Jacob was glad that his relationship with Daniel hadn't skipped a beat. "Daniel, we think that the person who murdered Michael and Leon, could be on is way back to your neck of the woods. We're not sure if he's from San Francisco, or from Germany."

"Hey, there are a lot of miles between those two places. What's the deal?"

Jacob explained the story in detail to Daniel, and since Daniel was in such a hurry to get to Sterling, he was as pleasantly accommodating as possible, so he could keep moving forward. Daniel promised Jacob that he'd get on it immediately, and stay in contact with him. With that, he was off and running… and completely mortified.

Chapter 24

Sonny finally had a chance to listen to his voicemail messages. Sterling was one of them. He quickly closed the door to Michael's office, and dialed Sterling's number.

Sterling could see that it was Sonny's number on her caller ID, so she answered the phone.

"Well, hello stranger...you finally got my message!"

"Sterling, a lot has happened, and where have you been?"

"Sonny, don't go there! You know I was finishing my novel."

"A lot has happened!"

"What's going on? And where is Leon? Why isn't he answering his phone?"

"He's been murdered."

Sterling screamed and dropped her phone! Fumbling and shaking as she tried to pick it up, she could barely hold the phone, let alone speak, "What do you mean, murdered? How? When?"

"The day after Michael's funeral, Leon was shot."

"Oh, Sonny no...no...no! This is awful—just awful! So that explains why I didn't hear from you! You also probably wondered where I was. I am so sorry Sonny."

"We thought you were missing Sterling, until Alex reminded us that you sequester yourself sometimes when you're finishing a book."

"He's correct, but I did tell Leon where I was, and he was supposed to fill you in."

"Well, obviously he didn't and then couldn't! That's why we were worried until Alex reminded us of your M.O. while finishing a novel. That is the only reason we didn't call in the National Guard, Missy!"

"Sorry about that. I'm so sorry about all of it, Sonny. How's my baby? How's Gabrielle holding up?"

"Actually, she's pretty strong, and is doing as well as can be expected, after Leon died in her arms."

Sterling let out a cry, and then just sat silent for a moment.

"Sterling, are you there?"

"Yes. Oh, my poor Gabrielle."

"I need to tell you something else."

"What?"

"This is good!"

"Well after that awful news, just about anything will be good news."

"First of all, the remaining guys on that old case have gone to prison at last."

"Do you mean that I can finally?"

He was so excited that he interrupted, "Yes, you can finally live a normal life."

"Sonny, do you mean that I can come out of hiding? Are you sure?"

"Yes, Sterling…we're sure. And that's just one part of the good news."

"What Sonny? What else?"

"Michael wrote Gabrielle a letter before he died, and told her all about you and Eric. She knows the whole story."

Sterling fell onto her couch, and started crying, "That's the best news I've heard in a very long time!"

"You have your life back Sterling. You finally have your life back!"

"I don't know what to say, or what to do. For so long I wondered what it would be like to return to a normal existence, and now that I finally do have my life back, Michael's gone! What do I do now?"

"Sterling, you should probably go to…"

She interrupted Sonny, yelling, "WHO KILLED HIM?"

"Michael or Leon?"

"What do you mean, 'Michael or Leon'? Oh no, Sonny, was Michael murdered also?"

"Yes, Sterling, Michael was murdered."

"Oh dear God Sonny, is Gabrielle safe?"

"Sterling, don't panic—Jacob has everything under control."

I was so excited about Jacob's proposal I could hardly contain myself. I went up to my room to make some calls in private. I didn't want anyone to hear the giddy 'girlie talk.' I threw myself on my bed, like I did when I was sixteen, and called Ashlee first.

We had so much fun discussing wedding plans, showers, and my trousseau. We became so wrapped up in the plans that we forgot the tragedies, which had overshadowed our lives for so long. It was really good to feel happy again. After an hour passed, I told Ashlee that I needed to finish making my calls, and that Jacob would be taking everyone out tomorrow night to celebrate.

I called a few more of my closest friends, then I was quite tired of talking, and just lay there thinking about how happy Father would have been for me, and for Jacob.

Then my thoughts went to Sterling. Sterling would want to be at my wedding, she would want to be a part of the happiest time in my life—I know she would. 'How will I break this news to her though? What am I thinking...how will I break anything to Sterling? She doesn't even known that I'm aware of who she is!'

Since my thoughts had turned to Sterling, I looked over at the book that was lying on my pillow, Obsessions by Annasophia. Once again I was in awe of my mother's talents. The story was so incredibly captivating, reading it somehow made me feel closer to her. I ran my fingers along the cover, and couldn't keep myself from opening it again.

After the deed was done, Max had a clear path to Tiffany. Surely no one would ever trace this to him. Now he could be with the only woman that he truly loved—all he could think about was getting to her. As he packed his bags he knew that only one more night stood between them. He lay on his bed obsessing about her, longing to hold her in his arms, to kiss her lips with passion, to feel her body pressed against his and take her completely.

He dreamed of sweeping Tiffany off her feet, taking her on a cruise and proposing in the moonlight on some distant island. The smell of the sea, and the gentle warm breeze would surround them as he slipped the most beautiful ring on her finger. She would smile at him, and then wrap her arms around his neck, and kiss him with her soft, sensual lips.

Max saw someone looming behind a palm tree. He could no longer concentrate on Tiffany. His mind was worried that someone might be following them. Suddenly Tiffany disappeared, and Max saw a shadow with a gun coming out from behind the tree. Max started running away from the tree as fast as he could. The man with the gun kept gaining on him, but Max continued running. As Max was running, he wondered to himself if this was revenge for the awful deed that he had just done. He knew that this man had come for him, but he couldn't be without the woman he loved. Running as fast as he could now, each beat of his feet on the pavement accompanied a syncopated chant. 'Tif-fan-y I need you, Tif-fan-y I want you, Tif-fan-y I need you, Tif-fan-y I want you!'

My heart started beating so fast that I slammed the book shut, "Wow!"

'Sterling…this is good, this is really a good story, but I've got to get back downstairs.' I ran my fingers through my hair and glided downstairs, like I was on cloud nine. As I floated downstairs I started thinking about Tiffany again, and wondered if maybe my new half-sister would be happy about my upcoming wedding.

Tiffany waited and waited for Pierre. After a few hours she was finally tired of waiting, and just about to leave the club, when he showed up. He walked slowly over to her with a look on his face Tiffany didn't recognize. As he pulled her close to him she said, "What took you so long?"

"Hey, Babe! I had to put my face back on."

"So, how did it go?"

"I'm so tired of working undercover. This was my last job."

"Let's go somewhere quiet where we can talk."

"Okay Babe, let's go."

Chapter 25

By the time Pierre and Tiffany arrived at Pierre's house he was unusually tired. He was also very stressed from this last job. He desperately wanted out. Tiffany wasn't aware of what Pierre really did for a living.

"This must have been a pretty complex case, huh?"

"Yeah it was, but how would you know that?"

As Pierre was making himself a drink behind the bar, Tiffany was unpacking his suitcase, looking rather perplexed with each item she removed, "Well, first of all, you were gone quite a while, and look at all these different disguises you packed!"

Pierre flew out from behind the bar, grabbed Tiffany's hands, "Let's go out here and talk."

Tiffany looked at Pierre in a weird sort of way. She knew that he had rough mannerisms, and was a man of few words sometimes, but it still made her a little uneasy when he grabbed her quickly. They walked out on his spacious deck, and sat on the cedar bench. As Pierre stared out into space, Tiffany reached over to tickle him. He cracked a quick smile, took a deep breath and said, "It was a tough case, and I decided that I do want out."

"Well, can a person quit a government job, just like that?"

"I'm gonna try Tif. I want to start a new life, and I want to settle down with you."

"What are you trying to say, Pierre?"

"I'm trying to tell you that I love you, and I want us to move away somewhere together."

"That's sweet, but have you forgotten? I have a beautiful home in Zurich that I love. I don't want to move."

"Well, I need to move away from here to make a new life for myself."

"Then you can move somewhere in Zurich, and we could see each other there. Besides, I'm not sure that I'm ready to live with anyone right now."

"I don't know about Zurich, Tif. And what do you mean, you're not ready?"

Tiffany really cared about Pierre, but she wasn't quite ready for this type of a commitment.

"Let's just sleep on it, and maybe tomorrow you'll feel differently about Zurich."

Chapter 26

As I walked into Father's office I could hear Jacob on the phone—he was telling Eric about the latest developments regarding Pierre, discovering that he was the one who killed Father and Leon. He very firmly told Eric that Sonny would be there soon, and when he arrived to go with him to meet up with Daniel.

As he handed the phone to Sonny, his eyes met mine, and we were drawn to each other like magnets. Jacob cupped his hands around my face, and pulled me close to him as he kissed my lips. His hands moved from my face to my neck, and then around my back as he pulled me in even closer.

Lost in the moment, we weren't paying any attention at all to the fact that Sonny was in the room. After he hung up, he cleared his throat to let us know that we weren't alone.

I pulled away very sweetly from Jacob, and looked at Sonny to say, "Sorry, Sonny."

"No worries—absolutely no worries, Princess. I need to get back home to meet up with Eric and Daniel, so can we get together tonight for our celebration?"

"That's fine with me!"

"Hey Jacob, do you think we can trust Daniel?"

"I'm quite sure we can! He's always been loyal, until the day he decided to do something else with his life."

I looked at Jacob very quizzically and said, "What has he done with his life, Jacob?"

"Nobody knows exactly. He made his first million with your father in the shipping business, and then made some investments. I'm not sure what else he's been busy doing."

"Don't you think it's kind of weird that Daniel just quit like that? None of Father's other really close friends left him."

Sonny interrupted, to tell me what Jacob wasn't willing to, "None of Michael's other friends had a crush on Sterling."

"Seriously?" I asked.

"Oh, very serious. Daniel never said anything, but he would watch her, like she belonged to him. I never said anything to Michael—I didn't want to cause any problems, but I saw it, and kept a close eye on it."

Jacob voiced his disdain about the situation—quite irritated with Sonny for not telling Michael what he witnessed.

I looked at Jacob sweetly, as I said, "Jacob, it doesn't matter now anyway, Honey. Don't worry about it."

Jacob kissed me on the forehead and said, "Okay, I won't worry about it for now." Then he turned to Sonny and said, "Sure we can go out tonight—does that work for you, Gabi?"

"Absolutely!"

Eric tried to call Daniel, but there was no answer. He left a message, "Sonny will be in Munich tomorrow to help you catch that rat!"

Eric could hardly wait to complete his obligations with the hospital so he could leave for Munich tomorrow to catch the scum. Eric may not have seen eye-to eye with Michael on some issues, but he loved and respected his father nonetheless, and was determined to avenge his murderer.

Eric called to inform Sterling about his hooking up with Daniel. She was surprised and happy that he agreed to help. Then she told Eric that Daniel had planned on flying to Capri to see her in the morning. Eric was shocked that she was seeing Daniel, even if only as friends.

"What do you mean that Daniel is coming to Capri to see you?"

"He's a friend, he's visited me many times."

"What do you mean?"

"He's been flying to Capri for about five years, always flying to Milan first, for security reasons."

"That's not what I'm worried about Mother! I want to know why he thought he could come see you."

"We're just friends, Eric. For the last five years, he's been to see me twice a year and he's been nothing but a gentleman."

"Well I don't like the fact that this man has been seeing you at all."

"I've been so lonely. Do you know how often your father came to visit me?"

"No"

"Well he was here maybe, once a quarter, and only for a week-end at a time."

"That's it, Mother?"

"Yes, that's it! I needed a friend, and Daniel would come visit me."

"I thought that Michael…"

Sterling stopped him, "Eric please don't call your father, Michael. That's disrespectful! I'll call Daniel to let him know about the meeting."

"No, I'll call Daniel…this business isn't yours, Mother. I'll talk to you later."

Eric tried to call Daniel, but still no answer. He left a message saying, "I'm aware of your relationship with my mother, she won't be expecting you tomorrow, but I will be. Call me!"

This was the second time that Daniel had ignored his phone. He listened to the messages and for the first time in his life Daniel didn't know what to do. He was paralyzed in his thoughts. What have I done? I did it! It's over… no turning back now…it's done! What was I thinking, and what was HE thinking?

Since Sonny had to return to Europe tomorrow, Jacob and I decided on an early dinner. Everyone was dressed for the festive occasion, and escorted to dinner in the family limo. Dinner was exquisite, paired with every appropriate wine, from the hors d'oeuvres to the dessert.

At the end of the dinner Jacob ordered a bottle of Dom Perignon, and we all toasted as Alex and Sonny gave their speeches. Then Alex gave a separate speech, written from what would have been, "Michael's words as a father, to his daughter and son-in-law to be." The speech was so incredibly touching there wasn't a dry eye in the house.

I looked at Jacob and said, "Everyone wants to know the date, is August still okay with you?"

Jacob yelled out, "August it is!"

By now it was nine o'clock, and with everyone being mindful of Sonny's schedule, the limo was loaded and quickly on its way.

Back at home, as Jacob walked me up the stairway and to my room, we were deeply engrossed in a conversation about the wedding.

"Do you want a small wedding, or does it matter to you?"

"Well, it's really hard without Father. I guess Alex can walk me down the aisle, since Uncle Leon is gone also."

"What about Eric?"

"Gosh Jacob, I barely know Eric, and Alex is like a second father to me."

"Sorry, that's not what I meant—I just want him to be in the wedding, also"

"Absolutely! What about Sterling?"

"She will definitely want to be at your wedding—she adores you."

"This is all so strange to me Jacob. I lost Father and Uncle Leon, who have been my family forever, and now I have a new family that I don't even know. It will take some time to get used to. I feel like a little girl again, having a mother and a brother!"

"I know you do, sweetheart—I'm happy for you."

"Oh, and don't forget...I have a sister also!"

"Okay, right! And who would that be, my little Princess?"

"Tiffany!"

"Who in the heck is Tiffany?"

"Oh, Jacob! Oh my! That's a secret that YOU didn't know about."

"You got me Gabi! Who is Tiffany?"

I explained the whole story to Jacob. He was completely shocked. Since he wasn't even remotely aware of this secret, he said that whatever I decided to do in regards to Tiffany, would be fine with him."

"Jacob, Tiffany must be so lonely—her mother died years ago. Father was the only relative that she had."

"How do you know that?"

"I read the file, and Alex filled in the gaps like you did with Father's letter to me!"

"My poor little Princess...you've had so much to deal with lately. Are you sure you want to plan a big wedding?"

"Absolutely!"

Chapter 27

Alex dreaded the decision that was upon him. It made him sad knowing that the results of Sandi's tests did in fact, reveal that she was quite mentally ill. Due to the circumstances of her being so closely involved with the murder case, Sandi was kept in a secured room at the clinic until the decision was made whether she was capable to stand trial or not. Either way, she would not be coming back home. She was declared schizophrenic, and a danger to herself.

After the long process of committing Sandi was completed, Alex's eyes filled with tears as he slowly walked through the corridor, and down the stairs. He stopped for a moment on the way to his car to wipe his eyes so he could see as he looked back at the window where her room was located. Alex's heart sank when he thought about the woman that Sandi used to be. The woman he loved, and dedicated his life to was no longer competent, no longer knew him, and no longer loved him.

The drive home was equally painful, but he knew that he needed to buck-up before he arrived at Gabi's to retrieve Tiffany's file. He knew how important it was to transfer the inheritance funds for Tiffany, finally completing Michael's wishes. Not only did Alex have power of attorney for Michael, but also with Leon's passing, he was now the Executor of Michael's estate. Michael and Alex decided this fact years ago, not wanting any conflict between Gabrielle and Eric upon Michael's death.

Michael's Will also had a provision in it for Tiffany, albeit nothing that compared to what was available for Gabrielle and Eric. It was a substantial inheritance that would allow her to never have to work for a living.

Alex knew that Gabrielle and Eric would be made aware of Tiffany's share of the money during the family meeting at the end of the week. He was hoping that they wouldn't begrudge Tiffany what Michael thought was her share. Alex figured they would be fine, knowing Michael left both of them billionaires with equal shares in his business.

Alex wasn't quite sure how to break the news of Michael's death to Tiffany. She wasn't anything like Gabrielle, except for her looks. The resemblance was remarkable, except for their smiles. Other than that, they were quite different. Even though Tiffany was fairy intelligent, and did have a sensitive side like Gabrielle, Tiffany was strong-willed and mouthy. When Michael needed to tell Alex something in code, he referred to Tiffany as his 'S.C.,' 'Spicy Child.' Alex was the only one in the world that knew whom he was talking about.

Now, Alex had to deal with 'Ms. Spicy,' and he wasn't exactly sure how to approach her. He sat as his desk, and staring out across the office his eyes fixed on the painting that Sterling had painted for Sandi and him, years ago. Lost in his thoughts about the past, Alex remembered how close he was to the lovely Sterling. She was like a sister to him, and he missed her terribly.

He stared at the painting then he'd look at the phone. He stared at the painting again, wanting to call her, but he fought the urge. He knew she was finishing her book, and he didn't want to disturb her with any of his problems. He picked up the phone to call Tiffany.

Tiffany and Pierre were in bed ignoring her phone. Pierre kept pleading with Tiffany to move to Austria with him, and start a new life together. Pierre was madly in love with Tiffany, but she wasn't sure whether she loved him or not. She had only known Pierre for two months prior to him leaving on this last case. She really didn't think that she knew him well enough to run away with him.

Pierre knew nothing about Tiffany's life. She was not an open book. She revealed very little, even to her closest of friends, and that's how she liked it. She was determined that no one would ever hurt her again, and because of her mother's situation with Michael, Tiffany was very leery of trusting men. She knew what a lonely and confused life her mother led. She didn't want to ever do that to a child, so she lived a very guarded life.

Pierre was getting somewhat nervous, and anxious to get back to his apartment, clean it out, and move forward.

"Tiffany, I'm getting older, and I need to move on with my life. I want you in it, and I want…"

She abruptly interrupted him, "I told you I'm not ready, and why Austria?"

"Because I've always wanted to retire there."

"Call me crazy, but I didn't think you were anywhere near retiring, Pierre!"

As Pierre sprung out of bed, and quickly threw on his clothes, he said angrily, "Whatever Tiffany! I'm done with this conversation. Just remember that I love you."

He pulled her close, kissed her quick and hard, and then ran out the door. As he ran out Tiffany said quietly, "Don't hold your breath."

Pierre caught the next train to Munich—he couldn't get home fast enough—not only to pick up the first half of the money he had hidden, but to also remove any of his tracks. He knew with the finesse in which he worked, there was no way anyone would have traced him there. Pierre was a professional with as many different names and passports, as he had disguises.

The score from this last job added to Pierre's already huge savings. Now he had plenty of money to retire and leave this crazy, transient life behind.

As the train approached the Munich station, Pierre was gluing on his dark brown mustache, and adjusting the big Roman nose, hoping that he had never used this particular disguise on Daniel. He kept repeating his mantra "No tracks, no traces, fake faces." 'I can't say the same for that amateur, Daniel.'

Daniel was now in a state of panic and couldn't think straight. He decided to go back home rather than catch the next plane to Milan. On his way back home he remained in the back of the limo, lost in his thoughts…'Pierre you complete idiot! What am I going to do now? No amount of money can fix this one! You out of control, idiot!'

Daniel made his millions years ago with Michael, yet has been an unhappy person, living an incredibly empty life. When Michael moved Sterling to Europe Daniel fell deeply in love with her, albeit a one sided affair only. He kept his feelings well hidden. After the masquerade ball six years ago, he became completely obsessed with Sterling. He dreamed of one day, having her. That was the time that he knew he needed to pull away from the group, or his feelings would certainly be discovered.

Sterling was always very nice to Daniel and enjoyed his company, but she never thought of him as anything other than a friend. Daniel's mind misunderstood Sterling's kind ways, fueling his desires for her.

Tiffany sat there thinking about Pierre and just exactly what it was that she liked about him. 'I was attracted by his wit, and then his butt, or was it his butt, and then his wit? Well either way, I'm tired of both, and I'll be darned if I'm moving to Austria. He must be out of his mind!'

Tiffany's cell had been beeping, so she checked the caller I.D. to see who called. It was Alexander Stone. She began mumbling aloud, "I wonder what he wants. I wish I could just call Michael instead of having to receive messages through Alex. I know it's that Michael wants to talk to me, so maybe I'll just call him. No, that would be too risky. Nope, better not." She reluctantly pounded Alex's number into her phone.

"Hey Alex, it's Tiffany."

"Hi Tiffany, how are you?"

"I've been better."

"What's the matter?"

"MEN!"

"Anyone in particular?"

"No! Not after tonight!"

"Well that sounds pretty final."

"Totally."

Alex knew that Michael's death could have hit the European papers, but since Tiffany hadn't contacted him first, he felt certain that she wasn't aware of the news yet. "Tiffany, I need to talk to you about something."

"Geez Alex, you sound kind of bummed. What is it?"

"Tiffany…Michael passed away this week."

"WHAT did you say?"

"Michael passed away. I am so sorry."

"Oh no, no Alex…I loved Michael! He was the only family I had… now I have no one. No, he can't be gone! He just can't!"

Tiffany cried so hard she made herself sick. Alex had an equally hard time listening to her broken heart. He wanted to console her, but she was crying so loudly that she didn't hear a word he said. Finally, she cried out, "ALEX, are you still there?"

"Yes Tiffany, I'm here."

"How did he die?"

"He was poisoned."

"You mean that Michael was murdered?"

"Yes."

"Why? How? Who could have done this?"

"There is a lead and I'm following it as we speak."

Tiffany couldn't control her feelings as she yelled out, "ALEX…I'm alone, totally alone!"

"You're not alone. You have a half sister and brother, and you have me."

"I know that I have you, but I also know that my siblings probably won't acknowledge, or even want to know Michael's illegitimate child, whose been kept a secret all these years!"

"You don't know that, Tiffany. You don't know that at all. Gabrielle and Eric are fine people who will probably welcome you with open arms." On second thought, "At least Gabi will" he said under his breath.

"What am I going to do?"

"Don't worry about the money."

"Oh my gosh, Alex, it's not the money!"

"Michael said he would provide for you until you turned twenty-eight, and…"

"Didn't you hear me? That's not what I'm upset about. Yes, Michael took care of me handsomely with his money, but it's him I'm going to miss! Don't you understand? He's all I had!"

"I told you that you have a…"

"And I told you! What do you think they will think of me when they find out?"

"You'd be surprised. I'm certain that Gabrielle will surprise you."

"Yes, I'm certain she will be surprised also—I'm not the Princess that she is, and…"

"Stop it! I need you to be here by the end of the week."

"I can't Alex, I have other obligations. Why do you need me?"

"You were in Michael's Will also. I'd like you there when we read it."

"You mean…..he actually admits to the world that I exist?"

"Tiffany, please don't be like that. Michael has explained this story to you many times. He told me that you understood."

"Yeah I do, it just hurts sometimes."
"Can you get out of whatever it is that you've got going on?"
"I'll try, but I can't promise."

Chapter 28

Daniel was going out of his mind worrying about what the guys were going to do to him when they arrived. He was convinced that they knew exactly what he had done, and that they were going to take him out. He paced frantically as he was trying to figure out what to do. He wanted to hear Sterling's voice, yet he knew he shouldn't call. The passion he felt for her was stronger than ever. All he wanted was to be with her.

Debating whether to call Sterling or not, Daniel made a stiff drink and sat down at the bar. He looked down at his favorite book he'd been reading, Obsessions. Knowing he would feel closer to Sterling if he read that part, he thumbed through the chapters, frantically looking for it.

Max knew that once he was caught, they would put him in prison, then on death row, and finally he would be killed for his wrongdoing. He couldn't bear to think about not being with Tiffany. 'I did all of this to be with her; we must be together, we were meant to be together.' Max called Tiffany, and told her to meet him in the park—their favorite place. He poured himself a scotch, poured out a handful of pills, and threw them down his throat without a second thought... Then, he grabbed his gun, concealing it well inside his jacket. Tiffany met him in the park, under the old-fashioned lamppost. As she stood there in the moonlight, and in the lamplight, she looked more beautiful than ever.

Max could smell her sweet perfume as he approached her, and reached out for her hand—then he pulled her close, and kissed her lips. He wrapped his arms around her to hug her, and held her tightly, feeling her body press against his with each breath that she took. His mind was reeling as he rationalized what he was about to do. The gun felt so cold in his hand as he held it next to her warm body. 'Just do it'...he told himself, 'and you will finally be together...just do it, and you will be together forever.' With that thought, he finally pulled the trigger, and they both fell to the ground.

Daniel was breathing heavily as he put the pills in his jacket pocket and poured himself another scotch, upset that he couldn't get a direct flight to Capri until five o'clock in the morning. Not wanting to hang out at the airport he decided to get plastered at home, and leave the driving to his limo driver. He poured one drink after another, pining for Sterling, staring at a picture he had of her from years ago.

He piled up every book that Sterling had written. Then, he grabbed Obsessions and kept thumbing through it, as if waiting for a secret message to jump off the pages just for him. Reading her novels was the way that Daniel connected to Sterling when he couldn't talk with her. Now, he was becoming more and more depressed as he emptied the fifth of scotch he had opened, only an hour ago.

Between Daniel's remorse for killing Michael, and his obsession over loving Sterling, he couldn't stop the guilt that haunted his every waking moment. With the Scotch seeping deeper and deeper into his soul, his guilt became magnified; Daniel could hardly forget the horrendous deed he had done, and all he could think about was Michael, lying in a casket. He even tried thinking about dancing under the stars with Sterling, but nothing could get his mind off the dastardly deed he had done.

The bottle was empty, so he started popping pills trying to erase that, which couldn't be erased. After a considerable amount of time had passed with no different outcome, he decided the only way to rid his mind of this nightmare was to write about it. With his vision distorted, and his penmanship barely legible, he scratched his thoughts onto the paper in the form of a confession.

'I need forgiveness for the awful deed I've done. I can't bare the guilt that I feel for killing you Michael. I love Sterling as much as I loved you. I feel so...'

Eric picked Sonny up from the airport. They went to breakfast to discuss the particulars they would talk with Daniel about, both agreeing they didn't want Daniel to know anything about the family business. They wanted to keep the relationship strictly about the issue at hand.

Eric told Sonny about Daniel's current relationship with Sterling, and how he didn't approve of someone who tried to have a friendship with his mother, while Michael had been so far away.

Reluctantly, Sonny told Eric about Daniel's behavior towards Sterling that he had observed for all those years. Eric blurted out, "That son of a..." then stopped in midsentence. "How convenient this all was for Daniel, then."

As Sonny listened to Eric mirror what he, himself, felt in his heart, it stirred in him an intense desire to beat Daniel to a pulp.

As they pulled up to Daniel's apartment, they both agreed to put those feelings aside as they dealt with the issue at hand, to ask Daniel to help them catch Michael's killer.

They knocked and knocked on the door, but no answer. They thought they heard noises in the apartment, so they rang the doorbell many times, but still no answer.

Sonny blurted out, "He knew we were coming. What's the deal?" Then he pulled out his small leather case and picked the lock. They entered quickly, and closed the door quietly behind them.

They stood in the entry way and yelled, "Hey, Daniel! It's us. Why didn't you answer the door?"

There was no answer. They kept calling his name as they walked through the living room, and into the kitchen where they both stopped, dead in their tracks. They saw Daniel on the floor. He looked like he had passed out, so Eric bent down to feel for a pulse and check his breathing. As he rolled Daniel over his eyes were fixed, and staring at them. Sonny and Eric gasped, and looked at him in utter shock. There was no pulse. Eric reached over, and closed Daniel's eyes.

"Sonny, what happened here?"

"This is so bizarre, Eric! When did you talk to him last?"

"About eight hours ago. Oh man, Sonny, it looks like he killed himself."

"Why would he do that?"

"Look at this! It's a note!"

Sonny yelled out, "The thoughts I had about Daniel from way back were RIGHT ON THE MONEY! That conniving, Casanova killed my best friend!"

"We need to call the police."

"Wait a minute, Eric. Don't jump to conclusions until we check all the evidence. Oh my God! I blame myself for Michael's death! I'm the one that observed his desire for Sterling, and caught him many times, staring at her as though she were his own. I never told Michael, because I didn't want any problems between them. After Daniel left the group, I didn't think about it anymore. Oh my God, Eric! I feel..."

"Hey man, don't blame yourself."

As Eric looked down at Daniel lying on the floor, his body still warm, but lifeless, he spit on him, and kicked his leg as he said, "We don't need any more evidence. This confession is all the evidence we need!"

"We should call Jacob."

Jacob and I went to Mary's house to take her a 'welcome home' plant. We were so glad that Mary was better and that she hadn't become an unintended victim to the poisoning. Mary kept thanking me for saving her life, hugging me tightly, and stroking my hair like she used to when I was younger.

Mary's eyes were sparkling as she talked about how happy she was with the news of the wedding. The excitement kept her mouth moving as fast as her brain was thinking, which made Jacob laugh. I could tell he was enjoying the few moments of happiness we were sharing in the midst of the pain that had hovered above us for so long. This new beginning would be just the miracle that our family needed to breathe life back into everyone's souls.

As we were discussing my choice of bridesmaids, Jacob's cell phone rang.

"Hey, Sonny!"

"Nope! Not alone."

Jacob gave me that look, so I took Mary by the hand, and guided her into the house, then went out to be with Jacob, as he motioned me to come back.

He flipped open the phone so I could hear.

"What's up Sonny?"

"We just found Daniel…dead!"

"What? What in the world is going on?"

"Well, wait until you hear this! It appears he committed suicide. Whether it was intentional or not, we're not quite sure."

"Suicide?"

"Yeah, and he left a note. Actually, it was more like a confession."

"A confession? For what?"

"For killing Michael!"

Jacob yelled into the phone, "WHAT?"

Eric yelled over Sonny, "This sick piece of crap had it so bad for Sterling! He killed Michael to get him out of the way! How sick is that? Jacob, I so badly want to kill this creep…but he's already dead!"

"Eric, I want you to calm down. Don't touch anything. I'll be there soon."

Dumbfounded and speechless, Jacob and I went back into the kitchen to say good night to Mary. On the way back to my house Jacob was totally silent, and all I could do was cry.

"Why are you crying?"

"Because it's over, and the man who killed my father is dead, but it breaks my heart that he was my father's friend."

"Obviously he wasn't, Gabi."

"Well, he was a long time ago."

"That was a long time ago, and people change."

"Why did he kill him? What possible reason did he have to…"

Jacob interrupted, "It appears that Daniel was in love with Sterling."

"Oh my gosh, Jacob! This was a pre-meditated crime of passion!"

"Yes. He was obsessed with her."

I started crying, again—almost uncontrollably. Jacob pulled me close, and held me in his arms. He gently kissed my lips and said, "Honey, I need to leave right now, for Munich. You go to bed. You really need some rest, and I'll call you in the morning. I love you."

I squeezed his hand, and as I started up the stairs I said, "I love you too, please be careful."

Chapter 29

While Sonny was taking care of some business matters, Eric was waiting impatiently in the grand lobby of the hotel. He paced back and forth on the marble floor—the click of his shoes getting louder and louder, making him more and more irritated with each passing second. His thoughts went to Michael's funeral, and the words he whispered in Gabrielle's ear that day, "They will pay, I promise." 'Well, the killer paid by his own hand, but I would have kept my word, and killed him, if he hadn't done it himself.' Then his thoughts turned to Gabrielle again, and their last conversation. He missed her, and wanted to talk to her.

The phone rang. I recognized the number and answered, "Hello?"
"Hi Gabrielle, it's Eric. I have some news."
"Oh Eric, I heard… I am so shocked, but I'm glad it's over, and that you found the creep that killed Father."
"Yes, and he did the job for me. It's just so hard to wrap my mind around it though—we were trying to find Daniel so that he could help us with Michael's killer! Then it ends up that Daniel is the murderer! I'm having a hard time processing this!"
"I know Eric—it's unimaginable at best. Hey, are you going to be here on Friday?"
"I don't think so Gabi, I'm aware of what Father has in the Will. You've got Alex and Jacob to help you with everything."
"But, I thought we could get to know…"
"I want to get to know you also, but I really have to be present at the hospital right now."
"I understand."
"Gabi, there is something else that I wanted to talk to you about."
"What?"
"Remember when I asked you if you knew where all of Michael's money went?"
"Yes, and I know what you were talking about now."

"You know about the woman that Michael was sending money to?"

"Yes."

"How did you find out?"

"No, you tell me how you found out, first."

"Well, I just happened to be standing in the bank, earshot from the manager's office, when I heard him talking to a woman saying, 'Ms. Deliano…yes, Michael's funds arrived this morning, and were transferred to your account'."

"Oh my gosh, Eric, what a small world!"

"Yeah, but what I don't know is, whether this woman was married to Michael, or whether she just assumed his name, because she was a 'kept' woman."

"Well…neither is correct."

"Come on, I heard it with my own ears."

"Yes, you're right, you did hear it, but she was not having an affair with Father, because, well…she is his daughter!"

"What ARE YOU talking about, Gabrielle?"

I explained to Eric what Alex had told me about Tiffany's story. He said that he didn't have any ill feelings towards Tiffany…but time will tell. "How many men would fulfill an obligation like that?"

"Well, it all fits now, why Michael was in Zurich more often than made sense at the time. So…we have a half sister, huh?"

"Yeah, and I didn't know I had a brother or a mother either. The secrets just keep getting better and better!"

After I hung up the phone, I was upset with myself for not telling Eric about the news of my engagement. I wanted to call him back, but decided not to.

Sterling was sitting on the verandah, sipping a glass of port and admiring the magnificent sunset. Her thoughts were racing back and forth, between a time when Gabrielle was little and life seemed so perfect, to wanting to spend time with Daniel. Her thoughts of tying Gabi's beautiful hair back in pretty bows to match her adorable dresses brought tears to her eyes. Then, her thoughts went to Michael, who was a Prince of a husband, and how her life had been so perfect. Then...without notice, her life was taken away, because of someone else's awful, awful deed. Anger came over her.

She was for paying the price with her life, and the life of her family for something that someone else had done. She finally couldn't contain herself any more and yelled out, "We were all victims! How completely wrong is all this?" She was now agonizing over how to make all the lost time up that she lost with her daughter, and how she could build a relationship with her, especially from another continent! The phone rang, and Sterling could see that it was Alex, so she answered it.

"Hello, my dear friend."

"Hello Sterling, how are you?"

"I'm trying to figure out how to put all of our lives back together. And more importantly, how to even begin to get close to my daughter."

"That won't be hard Sterling. Gabrielle is such a loving, sweet woman. She wants to know you, just as much as you want to know her."

"Alex, do you think she would come here to see me?"

"I don't know why she wouldn't."

"I think it would be perfect if she could come here. We wouldn't have any interruptions and could talk for hours!"

"Sterling, I think that's a great idea." He paused for a long moment...then said, "I do need to talk to you about something."

"I can tell by your voice, something's wrong. What is it Alex?"

"I don't know how to tell you this."

"Tell me what?"

"Daniel was found dead this morning."

Sterling couldn't stop screaming, "How Alex, how?"

"It appears he committed suicide."

"Why, Alex? Why would he do that?"

"Well Sterling...it seems he was ridden with guilt, because it seems..."

"Guilt? Why?"

"Daniel left a note confessing to Michael's murder."

"No, Alex! That's not possible! Why would he say something like that?"

"He disguised himself to Sandi, poisoned Michael, and obviously Leon got in the way, so he got rid of him also!"

"None of this makes sense! None of it! Daniel was supposed to come see me today. Why would he have wanted to kill Michael?"

"It seems that he was in love with you. Sonny said he observed Daniel watching you for years."

"Oh, that is so creepy. I thought he was coming here because he was my friend. I just can't believe this is true! I don't understand this world! I don't understand people!"

"I'm so sorry, Sterling."

"No, I'm sorry. Michael, poor Michael…this is so awful. All of our lives were changed forever with the shot that I heard twenty years ago. I can still remember like it was yesterday. And now THIS! It has all become a never-ending tragedy! If I had only gone to…"

"Sterling, you stop it right now! Don't do this to yourself! You know this was not your fault."

Chapter 30

Tiffany tried to change her plans with the builders. They weren't budging though, but she was accustomed to the fact that being an Architect sometimes meant there were dates one must adhere to. Tiffany was disappointed that she wasn't able to spend time with Gabrielle right now. She was ecstatic though, to know that she actually had a family. Her thoughts drifted to Pierre, and how badly he wanted to live with her. She did miss Pierre, so she picked up the phone and kept calling him for an hour, only to receive a busy signal, over and over again.

Pierre was on the phone with a client, who was requesting another job—he was the absolute best in his line of work in Europe, and his client was a very wealthy, influential person who expected him to be at his beckon call. Pierre knew that it would be impossible to say 'no' to this man, so he agreed to do the job. And once again, after he hung up the phone he started rationalizing why it would be okay to do just one more job. His heart had become hardened. He had iced so many people already. 'What was one more?'

He was instructed to pick up the envelope next week, revealing who, when and where. Unfortunately, he never knew why, although he didn't really care why—it was just a job. He usually spent a month creating a profile on his mark, studying their habits, figuring out the best way to do the job. However this one was ordered much quicker. This made Pierre a little uneasy, but his client compensated him quite nicely for such short notice.

In the past, Pierre had used women to get close to his marks, and of course would make them feel as though he cared, when really he didn't. Now his heart was torn. He was truly, madly in love with Tiffany, and all he could think about was settling down with her. The bottle of scotch on the table looked pretty good to him, so he poured himself a drink, and began day-dreaming of the day, that he and Tiffany would move in together.

I walked down the long spiral staircase and through the marble foyer to Father's office. The Grandfather clock struck midnight. Even though I had heard that sound since I was a baby, for some reason, I nearly came out of my skin as it chimed.

What's wrong with me? I felt quite uneasy and unable to go to sleep. I picked up Sterling's book, but couldn't read either, and decided that I would finish the last few chapters tomorrow. Thoughts of my wedding were flying through my head at a dizzying speed. Every time I saw myself getting ready to walk down the aisle, I kept thinking about Father not being there for the happiest day of my life.

I walked over to Father's desk, pulled the chair out slowly, sat down even slower, and threw my head into my crossed arms on his desk. My heart was so broken. I felt as though my uncontrollable tears were actually blood streaming out of my tear ducts, directly from my heart. I realized how my world had been completely shattered by the loss of my father, who was the best father a girl could have ever hoped for. The absence of his presence made me feel lost, alone, and scared. If it wasn't for Jacob, I feel as though I would surely die. My skin was stinging as the tears kept streaming down my face…

Working through grief is truly hard. I know that I must go through it, not around it, but no one warns us, no one prepares us for this. My thoughts went from missing Father, to denial, to anger, then back to denial again. 'Oh, this is hard. I need to focus on the positive about 'life,' and start moving forward—at least attempt to move in that direction. 'Oh Dear God, please help me with this.'

Through my blurry tears I could barely see as I grabbed a pad and pen, and started organizing my thoughts about my new life—my 'new normal.' My thought process began changing from painful to promising as I began making plans to celebrate my father's life, instead of mourning his death. And, celebrate my own life as well—thinking about new beginnings, rather than dwelling on the past, and what I don't have.

My thoughts went from my wedding to creating a bed & breakfast out of a portion of my home that Maria and Antonio could manage. I went from one page to another, making lists, and more lists. Hope was filling my spirit. My vision became clearer and more exciting with each thought I penned. The very last page was a schedule of my plans to visit Sterling in Europe, then Eric, and then to finally spend time with Tiffany in Zurich.

The canvas of my life was now being filled with colors again as the spark within me ignited a new picture. As the clock struck two I knew that I had better stop painting and go to bed. Tomorrow morning I had a lot of things to do, and not a lot of time to do them.

Alex arrived as scheduled at 7:00 AM, and of course I was ready and waiting, although I wasn't quite as sharp as I would have liked. I summoned Maria to bring in more coffee and bran muffins.

After three hours of discussing business matters, I couldn't contain myself any longer, and blurted out, "ALEX…are we through?"

"Oh my goodness, Gabrielle! Are you losing interest, or just excited about something else?"

"Both!"

"Okay, just sign these papers. I'll take care of the rest."

I could hardly pay attention to what I was doing. I desperately wanted to tell Alex the plans I was making for my new life, which definitely included him.

"Are you in a hurry to go somewhere, Gabi?"

"No sir-ree…I'm in a hurry to tell you all about my plans!"

"Okay, let's hear them!"

"Are you ready?"

"Yes, Princess!"

"I think that you, Jacob and I, should move to Europe. We could live there for most of the year and come back here on the off seasons."

"Gabi, Dear, I'm still married and Sandi will be in a…"

"Home, forever."

"Yes."

"Alex, I don't mean to be cold-hearted…"

"You couldn't be if you tried."

"Well, Sandi checked out mentally, many years ago, and you haven't had a marriage since then, AND she is getting worse. You'll be able to visit her when you are in the states, if you still want to. I think she's better off when you're not around. Alex, she's quite mentally ill."

Alex looked down, his face saddened as tears filled his eyes. "I know…I know—Sandi left me a very long time ago."

"Oh Alex, I am so sorry; I didn't mean to hurt you."

Alex couldn't contain himself enough to talk, so he just put his hand up for me to give him a minute. I left the room to give him some space, and returned after a short time had passed. As I re-entered the room, I saw him standing by Sterling's picture, just staring at it through teary eyes.

"Please forgive me for being insensitive."

"It's not you Gabi. I'm just overwhelmed by all the events lately, and the fact that all our lives changed in an instant by the wrong doings of others—by their actions we all became victims. It's not fair or right, yet this type of tragedy happens to people every, single, day."

"You're thinking of Sterling's life, aren't you?"

"Yes, do you realize that if Michael hadn't been so wealthy, and couldn't afford to send Sterling and Eric to Europe, they would have probably ended up being dead also. You have all been so lucky in that regard."

"I've thought about all of this, these last few days. I don't think we're lucky, I think we're blessed! Well, do you want to hear the rest of my idea?"

"Yes."

"You know, with the talents that we all have, collectively, we should be able to do something—something really meaningful, and make a difference in this world!"

"I think you're right. Finish telling me your plans."

"You are such a good man Alex, you're a lot like my father. I want you to be happy, because you deserve it. You have been so loyal to everyone, and you never, ever complain."

"What a sweet compliment Gabi, but it's easy to be loyal to those you love."

"No, loyalty is an admirable character trait that most people don't have, even when they love someone. I appreciate your dedication to all of us Alex. I want you to have the best that life has to offer, for the rest of your life."

He walked over, hugged me, kissed my cheek, and said, "Thank you for loving me."

"So, I think we should move to Europe—live by Sterling, maybe…"

"In which country?"

"Well, I think Italy would be nice. We would maintain the house here, and live in it for part of the year. Between Italy, Germany and Switzerland, we will have quite an outreach for our philanthropic projects."

"Do you think you want to have a relationship with Tiffany?"

"Of course I do, she's Father's daughter, and she's my sister!"

"I think that's a great idea, but you know she's a bit of a challenge."

"Aren't we all?"

Alex laughed, "Very true."

Then I said with excitement, "You and Jacob could run the business from either location, so there wouldn't be a conflict in that regard."

"Yes, and Jacob will want to live in Milan, so I should live in Germany, and that's fine, because Eric is there."

"Okay! It's set then!"

"Well Gabi, we'll have to talk to Jacob—we have many details to discuss, but your overall plan seems like a fantastic idea to me!"

I kissed Alex on the cheek, and after he kissed my forehead, he said in a very kind yet concerned and fatherly voice, "When do you think you want to do this?"

Thrilled that Alex was on board, I blurted out like a little girl, "As soon as possible!"

"Before the wedding?"

"Well actually, I think that I want to get married over there!"

"What about all your friends that live here?"

"We'll just fly them over!"

Chapter 31

With the passing of time, comes the healing of hearts, and new beginnings that spark a deeper appreciation for life. This helps us to celebrate our loved one's life, rather than continue to mourn their death. A new joy fills my heart, as I pen these words in my journal, feeling differently as I begin to experience a new cycle of life—the cycle of hope!

I now greet each day as a blessing, rather than an expectation, and I feel like my life has a greater meaning. My life has a very special purpose, and a vision with a mission that I have never felt before—to truly touch other's lives!

I lifted my pen one more time to finish writing for the day, and wrote in real big letters, the words.

I WANT TO GIVE OTHERS HOPE!

My canvas was becoming more and more colorful each day, not only by my love for Jacob, but for my desire to spread a very special, 'life-giving' feeling. HOPE!

After Jacob returned from Germany, which was later than expected, we talked at length about the past. With each story, I become increasingly more comfortable with the fact of why Sterling had to leave, learning just how much Sterling loved and missed me, and how much she hated every day that she was away from me.

I was a little nervous, but also excited as I called Sterling! What a joyous conversation that was! We decided to talk only briefly on the phone, agreeing that communicating in person, at our mother-daughter reunion was far more important than sharing too many details of our lives over the phone. I was too excited to keep the one detail of my life from Sterling, though, my engagement to Jacob. We began making immediate plans to meet.

Quicker than most people could make dinner reservations, I made arrangements to leave for Capri! I would fly out in three days, which so happened to be my birthday. That was quite meaningful in itself, because Father never missed my birthday, ever, no matter where he was. And now I could spend it with my mother, keeping that very special tradition alive.

Before I left for Capri, I told Jacob all about my exciting plans for our lives, which he was certainly on board for, and immediately started making plans to move the majority of the business abroad.

The Deliano mansion was so incredibly huge that I invited Alex and Mary to live here also. I considered Alex like a second father, and thought that it was ridiculous for family to live in three separate houses. They all agreed, so Alex and Mary put their homes on the market. Alex helped Jacob make all the business arrangements, and I gave Mary the job of creating the Bed & Breakfast for Antonio and Maria.

Jacob took me to the airport, and told me he could hardly stand that I would be away from him for a whole week. We stood in the concourse with our arms wrapped tightly around each other as we said good-bye. Jacob kissed my lips, softly and sweetly, and then slowly walked me to the door as if not wanting to let go…

My anticipation and excitement about meeting Sterling seemed to make the trip feel like it was taking twice as long to get there than it should. When the plane finally landed, my stomach was filled with butterflies and my mouth was so dry that I could barely swallow. As I walked up the long jet-way to the concourse, my heart was pounding hard, and my hands were clammy. My thoughts were all over the board…'I hope that I say the right things, I hope she likes me, I hope she wants to be a part of my life, I hope she wants to be in my wedding, I hope it's okay that we move closer to her, and oh my gosh, I hope she wants a daughter in her life…maybe she doesn't!'

With that last thought in my head, I looked up, and saw Sterling standing there with a dozen red roses, and balloons tied to her wrist. In one hand she was holding a teddy bear and in the other a beautiful porcelain doll with long, curly brown hair.

My eyes filled with tears as I thought, 'Yes, she does want a daughter. She does want me!' My heart was overjoyed as I approached this gorgeous woman, who exuded love, poise and confidence. I stretched out my arms to hug her and said, "Hello Sterling!"

Sterling's eyes filled with tears as she said, "Hello my precious, beautiful Gabrielle!"

We hugged for quite a while, and then Sterling handed everything to me. She picked up my bag and said, "Andiamo!"

We talked like best friends all the way home in the back of Sterling's limo. I could hardly wait to tell Sterling how Jacob proposed, which was one of the first things we talked about. As soon as I finished a sentence, Sterling started another. Sometimes we were talking over each other in excitement. We were so engrossed in our conversation we didn't even notice the limo had been parked in Sterling's circular driveway for about ten minutes.

Finally, Sterling's driver came to her door, opened it and said, "Would you two like to go somewhere else?"

We laughed, Sterling told him "No" quite politely as she helped me gather my things. Then she turned to him and said, "Oh, we would like to go to dinner in a couple hours, Giuseppe. Grazie."

She took me on a tour of her enormous villa. I was in awe of every inch of my mother's gorgeous home—standing in each room, admiring the beautiful artwork she had painted. I wanted to know the inspiration for each piece, which she gladly described in great detail.

As I entered the large parlor, I was drawn to the intricately carved French doors with an inviting and spectacular view of the ocean, which came directly up to the edge of the verandah. On the huge wall to the right of the doors hung a picture that was as large as life. I stopped and looked at the picture, which was staring back at me, as though I was looking in a mirror. I was speechless.

Tears came to my eyes, "Is that me?"

"Yes, it's my favorite painting."

"Your work is exquisite! Your talent is as masterful as the great Italian artists—it is absolutely amazing."

"Thank you my dear, you are very kind, but I have only copied the techniques that the artists created. They are truly the masters, and I will forever be their student."

"But Sterling, you have your own gift as well."

"That gift is a talent that I was blessed with, because my most precious gift was taken away."

"What was that?"

"You!"

I walked to Sterling, picked up her hand and said, "And you are my gift."

Soon it was time to go to dinner. Giuseppe drove us to one of Sterling's favorite restaurants. Giuseppe also liked this restaurant, because there were a few shops that he liked to hang out in while Sterling was occupied.

Sterling ordered in Italian for us. Antipasto and pane for starters, then insalata and zuppa, and finally, pasta. I hadn't eaten this much at one sitting since Father and I had been in Italy a few years ago. After three hours of excellent dining and conversation, we decided it was time to leave.

On the way back, I asked Sterling what she knew about Tiffany. After comparing notes, we both felt sorry for Tiffany who had the misfortune of having no family at all. I told her I wanted to meet Tiffany, and hoped that she would want to be a part of the family. Sterling agreed that it was a wonderfully, sweet gesture.

"I know that is how Father would want it, don't you?"

"Yes, I do Gabi; I'm fine with whatever you decide. I too will welcome her with open arms."

After we arrived back at the villa, we sat on the verandah, and slowly sipped a glass of refreshing Limoncello. We sat there for a minute without saying a word, which was the first time silence had visited us since we laid eyes on each other. Sterling was staring out at the ocean, then looked back at me and said, "If, and when, you want to call me 'Mother,' I would love that."

I looked at Sterling, and smiling sweetly, said, "Thank you."

Before we knew it, both of us were nodding off. Sterling decided that we should retire for the night. She had a big surprise planned for me in the morning.

Tiffany hadn't heard from Pierre for a couple days, and was starting to miss him. She hoped he had finally got out of that under-cover government job, and was making a new life for himself and possibly her, except for the part of leaving her home. She called his cell phone, but there was no answer. She left him a message, "Pierre, you must be very busy planning your new life, but I'd like to hear from you when you have some time. I miss you."

Pierre had been scuba diving all day, and to his surprise he had only one message when he returned. He listened to Tiffany's message at least five times, and then just sat there staring at the phone, missing her more than ever. This new job was too intense, and there was entirely too much at stake to let his guard down while being softhearted with a woman right now. He desperately wanted to walk away from the job, but he also knew that this was one client that he couldn't refuse. He longed to talk to her...

Tiffany was so busy with her drawings that her mind was ignoring the ringing phone. She finally tuned in to it on the last ring, and answered quickly with an irritated voice, "Hell-ooo."

"Hey, Tiffany."

"Pierre!"

"I just had to hear your voice."

"I know, that's' exactly why I tried to call you."

"I miss you."

"I miss you too."

"I've been busy with another case."

"What? Oh, Pierre...I thought you were through!"

"I was! But this was something that I couldn't pass up."

"It must be paying well then."

"Let's say that it paid so well, neither one of us will ever have to work again."

Tiffany thought for a minute about her inheritance, and the fact that she didn't have to work either. She wasn't sure if this was the time to tell Pierre about her life, or not. She decided that it wasn't.

"Well, then maybe this will be your last job."

"No maybe about it, Baby. This is it!"

"Do you have any idea when you'll be done?"

"Probably in another couple of weeks."

"Geez, that much longer?"

"Yes."

"Well, can you come visit me?"

"Not this time, I need to stay focused. I have too much involved with this case."

"I understand."

"Well, I'll try to touch base with you when I can. You stay out of trouble."

"You too, Pierre!"

As we ate breakfast on the verandah, Sterling explained to me all about the fun-filled day of surprises she had planned. While I waited for Sterling to finish getting ready, I stood on the edge of the balcony, staring at the electric blue sky, listening to the waves hitting the cliff, thinking to myself that I didn't want to wake up from this dream. The crisp ocean breeze hit my face and I suddenly remembered that I wanted to call Tiffany, hoping that she would agree to see me.

When Tiffany saw who it was on the caller I.D., her heart skipped a beat as she quickly answered, "Hello!"

"Hi Tiffany, this is Gabrielle! I'm in Capri, and I'd like to meet with you, if you have some time in the next couple of days."

"Yes, I do have some time. Even if I didn't, I would make time to meet you, Gabrielle!"

I paused for a moment, because I remembered what Alex had said about Tiffany being a 'challenge,' and I didn't get that impression from her in the slightest.

"Great...how's Wednesday? I'll give you a call in the morning to make plans."

"Sounds good...I look forward to it. Thanks for calling, Gabrielle!"

As the limo pulled up to the curbside, I asked Sterling, "Where are we going?"

"It's a surprise!"

We talked all the way to the Airport, and the entire time we were in flight! Soon we landed in Milan, and drove to the famous Via San Marco, where we dined for an early lunch at Ristorante Santini.

After enjoying one of the best lunches I had ever eaten, I was whisked off to the premier Ettore Spa and Salon. Greeted with an oasis of pampering by a staff who truly understood the meaning of their mission: 'Restoring your body, mind, and soul.' Feeling absolutely wonderful, I was still in for more surprises—Sterling was amazing and FUN!

Chapter 32

Even though I had been shopping all over the world with Father, somehow we had never been shopping in Milan. Sterling knew this also, and wanted me to have an experience of a lifetime. The next stop was the world's oldest and most elegant shopping area, the Galleria Vittorio Emanuele.

The wedding boutiques were filled with the most elegant designer dresses. I tried so many on, I finally asked Sterling to make the decision between the two that she loved the most. Of course, it was the most expensive gown in the boutique, but $25,000 didn't really seem like that much for an exclusive design from the Vera Wang Luxe Collection.

The dress looked like something out of a dream. It was long, form-fitting, pure white satin, backless, and cut to the waist, with very tiny strands of pearls that draped across the mid-back from shoulder to shoulder. This exquisite dress and its five-foot long train looked as though it were designed and custom made especially for me.

Sterling picked up my hand, smiled sweetly and said, "It's elegant, classy, and fits you perfectly."

The main topic of conversation all the way back to Sterling's villa, was planning the big event. She requested that I allow her to do the invitations. Her excuse was, so the two of us could enjoy addressing them together and so they could be postmarked from Italy—a detail which, as Sterling explained, the guests would enjoy. However, while that was most certainly true, I found out Sterling really wanted to surprise me with the beautiful church she had chosen for me, and wanted to have the invitations engraved after I gave her my approval.

The next morning we were up at dawn, had a light breakfast on the verandah, and then were off to discover Sterling's surprise. What an amazing surprise, indeed—the rental of a beautiful villa on Lake Como for the wedding, and our guest's accommodations—a very elaborate and generous wedding gift that Sterling was excited to present to me. When we finally arrived at Villa Giorgio, I'm sure my expression was worth every single dime she spent on this amazing place to surprise me!

Villa Giorgio is one of the most beautiful villas on Lake Como, and is considered a national monument for Italy. It was once the residence of Vincenzo Bellini. Sterling offered the owners an incentive to rent both the estate and the guesthouse. She needed sleeping arrangements for thirty guests, which they agreed to do, even though they never rent out both houses at the same time.

This thirty thousand square foot villa, and the five thousand square foot guest house were set on the most beautiful grounds with eleven illuminating fountains, gardens, a pool, and the lake as a back drop. The frescoes, marble columns, Venetian chandelier, high ceilings, antique marble floors, and Tuscan furniture were most enchanting. And then…there was the billiard room, gym, and cinema! At every turn, I was in awe of this unbelievable 'Palace.' Villa Giorgio was also fully staffed, with a gourmet chef that Sterling gave explicit instructions to regarding the menus for the week, including the exquisite dinner, ice sculptures and wedding cake for the reception.

As we climbed back into the limo to head home, I was so overwhelmed by Sterling's love and generosity, I cried tears of joy. Feeling a little embarrassed, I reached across the seat and hugged Sterling, laying my head on my mother's shoulder, enjoying every second of our bonding moment. A sweet, angelic voice whispered in my ear, "I love you, my precious daughter."

I sat back in my seat, and told Sterling that I loved her also, and how much I appreciated the beautiful surprise, "I can't believe that I will be getting married in two weeks!"

"It doesn't seem possible, Gabrielle. Oh, and don't forget that I will be flying back for your wedding shower next week also!"

"Oh, Mother, it will be such an honor to have you there."

"It may be an honor for you, but I think most everyone else will be going into shock!"

Laughing I said, "Yes, I'm certain of that!" Then I got serious. "Mother, Ashlee has been my best friend forever, and I've already asked her to be my maid of honor. Will you please walk down the aisle with Alex, and give me away?"

"Oh Sweetheart, I would love to."

"I forgot to tell you that I talked to Tiffany this morning, while you were getting ready."

"How did that go?"

"We didn't talk much, but she sounded like she was interested in meeting with me."

"I'm glad, I hope you two really hit it off. Now that your father is gone, it would be good for both of you."

"It will be very strange though, talking about my life with Father, when he's her father also. She didn't have much of a life with him—it's just so sad."

"It's all very sad—and very hard, Gabrielle."

"I just can't fathom how all these secrets were kept hidden for so long! I know how difficult it has been on me to process this information as quickly as I had to: losing Father, finding out that I have a mother, a brother, and a half sister. I can't imagine how Tiffany is coping, having this thrown in her face at warp speed. I think if I wasn't well grounded in who I am, and if Father hadn't loved me so much, AND if Jacob hadn't proposed to me to get my mind off of the pain... Well, I'm not sure how I would have coped with all this!"

"You're correct on all counts, Gabi. First, you are truly blessed to have so many people in your life who love you so much. You are equally blessed to have such a strong character—it serves you well. You are also a sweet, loving and intelligent woman—every bit as lovely as your father described you."

I smiled, and squeezed my mother's hand as I said, "Thank you. I will never forget those words you said to me at Father's funeral, 'Your father loved you very much.'"

"I'm so sorry Gabi, I should have never done that. I was just in so much shock, and I wanted to console you any way I could. I knew that I could never reveal who I was—not then anyway."

"Please don't be sorry. I know that because of what you whispered in my ear that day it made my subconscious work on what would someday be revealed. And, although I had no idea at the time, what any of my dreams meant, I believe that it helped my mind cope with the truth as it unfolded. So, please don't be sorry."

A tear rolled down Sterling's cheek as she said, "Oh, I've missed you Gabrielle. Loving you from afar has torn at my heart every minute, of every day. I think that's why I buried myself in the novels, and the paintings."

I hugged her tightly, kissed her cheek and said, "Thank you for loving me, Mother."

Sterling kissed my cheek and said, "Let's get busy with the invitations."

The next morning, after having breakfast with Sterling, I flew to Zurich to meet Tiffany. We didn't have any trouble picking each other out of the crowd, because we definitely looked like sisters. In fact, we almost looked like twins except for Tiffany's smile.

I walked up to Tiffany, introduced myself and then leaned forward to hug her. Tiffany paused for a second, and then leaned forward to hug me back. I could tell that Tiffany's heart wasn't quite as open, and loving, but that's okay, we'll get there…

As we approached Tiffany's car, I wasn't surprised about her choice; it must be in the genes I thought as we got into Tiffany's brand new, canary yellow Porsche. I was glad to see that she had something nice, knowing that Father had surely provided that for her.

We were instantly drawn to each other, and talked all the way to Tiffany's house, seemingly without taking a breath. We talked mostly about my life. Tiffany didn't want to let her guard down too soon, but I sensed that, and even though I was usually the listener, I felt comfortable with being the talker, as we began our bonding process.

Tiffany designed her house, both inside and out, and it was absolutely gorgeous. Her taste was impeccable. I also loved her choice in artwork; the Italian Renaissance period, which was my favorite and appeared to be Tiffany's as well. I walked slowly through each room, admiring every piece and discussing the history of them with her, who happened to know as much as I did, much to my surprise.

After the grand tour, she opened a bottle of excellent champagne to celebrate our finding each other. We toasted to a great sisterly relationship then we sat on the verandah and talked until late into the night. It was obvious that the hard-hearted Tiffany wanted more than anything to have a family.

I fell in love with my sister at first sight. Then with every part of the conversation Tiffany endeared herself, closer and closer to my heart— I was truly happy that I found her. We built an incredible bond that night, one in which I was certain Father would be pleased about.

The next day I flew to Munich to see Eric, and disappointingly discovered, when I arrived he was only available for a couple hours, since he was unexpectedly scheduled in surgery. After a quick embrace, we sat down at the table, and immediately Eric started talking—he seemed to have an agenda as he began speaking in bullet points.

"Besides getting to know each other, we need to make some major changes in the Deliano business. I don't want Ashlee involved in our family affairs. We need to make sure that Tiffany understands her place in this family, and…

I quickly interrupted, "Excuse me Eric, but I thought we were going to have a friendly, catch up visit. I thought you wanted to hear what was going on in my life, but instead you are barking out orders."

Eric didn't let me finish, as he got a little louder, "Gabrielle! I do want to hear about your plans. I'm laying the ground rules first, so there will be no misunderstandings between us."

It was all I could do, to let him finish his explanation before I laid my second set of ground rules out for my new brother.

I stood up, looked down at him, and stared intently into his eyes, as I said, "Okay Eric, my turn. First of all, I love that you're my brother, and yes, we do need to get to know each other. However, YOU need to know something about me, so there will be no misunderstandings, period!"

"Sit down Gabi."

"Don't tell me what to do."

"Alright, stand then."

"Do not ever mistake my kindness for weakness. I am my father's daughter. If you knew anything about Michael Deliano, you know that he had the kindest of hearts, but he was also strong, determined, uncompromising, and no one—I mean no one, told him what to do or how to do it. In other words…don't screw with me! If I wanted to, I could take this entire Deliano Empire for myself, and exclude whomever I wish—don't give me reason to play the card that Father left with me."

As Eric started to stand up, I placed my hand on his shoulder, lightly pushing him back in the chair as I said, "Make no mistake, Eric—you screw with me—you lose, got it?"

Eric stood up, looked me straight in the eyes and said, "Hmmm, Michael's mini-me—Interesting!"

Hoping that he didn't want to escalate the banter, I stared right back, and said, "Alrighty then, now that we have that settled, let's move on. "

I was pleasantly surprised that his next words were, "I'm glad that you and Jacob are getting married—he's a good guy."

Just as our conversation was becoming cordial again, Eric's pager started buzzing.

"Gotta run Gabi, I'm needed in surgery, now!"

He kissed me on the cheek, then moved towards my ear and whispered, "Don't screw with me either," as he winked and walked off.

On my flight home, I stared out the window—my mind was reeling from the new relationships that had been thrust upon me. With juxtaposed emotions: thrilling and exciting—anxious and disconcerting, I was quickly filing them in the mental folders that each belonged, de-cluttering my thoughts while I was in the midst of the happiest time of my life.

This truly bizarre new beginning was taking on the form of a complex analytical model, which I was adept at—'So bring it on little brother. Father, I promise you right here and now, that I AM your mini-me. I am proud to be the woman that you groomed me to be, and I will never let anyone, I don't care who they are, screw with me, or the dreams you and I had for the Deliano Empire—not even you, Eric!'

Chapter 33

A week had flown by, and the parties for Jacob and me were quickly upon us. The guys took Jacob out for his bachelor party, which put most 'guy' parties to shame. It was done highly tasteful, yet extremely exotic, hosted by an all-female cast who were dressed in every costume imaginable. The limo drivers were even women, dressed in French maid costumes, as were the servers at the private dinner club.

Champagne was flowing from fountains, and expensive cigars were being smoked in every corner of the grand room, Jacob was being roasted by nearly everyone there. After dinner the chandeliers were dimmed as a gorgeous, brown Clydesdale came walking through the room with a beautiful woman on the horse's back. She was in a costume that made her appear as though she had no clothes on, wearing a blonde wig that flowed from her head to her toes, portraying Lady Godiva perfectly.

Alex and Jacob left the party at one o'clock in the morning, both falling asleep in the limo on the way home. Paul, their driver had to wake each of them up, and walk them to their front doors.

I was excited about Jacob's party, and wanted to hear all about it, so I was waiting up for him when he arrived.

He walked up to me, threw his arms around me and said, "Hi, Lover!"

I perched my lips to be kissed, but Jacob grabbed my arm, pulled me towards him, and said, "Let's go to bed!"

I was so shocked at his comment that I sucked my lips back in so quickly they made a funny noise, which caused me to break into a coy giggle. I quickly changed my demeanor to serious and firm, as I said, "Let me walk you to your room, Jacob."

Jacob hung on me as he said, "Okay, I'll wait one more night…"

Relieved at Jacob's quick change of heart, I said, "No need to be sorry, just go to bed." I opened the door to the downstairs guest room where he had been staying.

I walked slowly up the stairs feeling badly that I had to talk so firmly to Jacob, but then quickly changed into my nightgown, and climbed into bed. I could barely keep my eyes open.

I fell asleep the second my head hit my pillow. The moon was shining brightly onto the enormous verandah as shadows skipped across the antique, marble dance floor. The sweet-scented flowers were draping down the trellises, and the orchestra was playing Fur Elise in the background.

Jacob and I were dancing in our wedding attire. Jacob so handsome in his black tux, and I looked so beautiful in my white silk gown.

The fog kept separating and returning as Jacob twirled me across the dance floor. My spirit seemed to be floating to a paradise island, as my head and my heart were singing with the orchestra. My feet weren't even touching the ground and I wondered if I would feel like this forever.

Then, from across the dance floor, a woman came towards me. The fog was so thick I couldn't see her face She kept floating closer and closer in slow motion, and as the fog began to clear, I could see that it was Sterling dressed in the same gorgeous, sexy, scarlet dress that she wore before.

Sterling had her eyes fixed on a man who was dressed in a tuxedo. He began walking towards her from the other corner of the dance floor. They kept moving towards each other in slow motion—so slow that it looked as though they would never come together. Sterling's face went from happy to being anxious, to looking horrified!

"What's the matter Mother?" I shouted.

Sterling answered, but I couldn't hear a sound. Her face was now frightened as she turned to go back to the corner that she came from. Then, when I turned to look back at the man in the tuxedo…he was gone. I looked at Sterling only to see a flash of red take off in the fog. Then I heard screams that got louder, and louder, and louder…

I started to chase after her screaming, "Sterling…where are you? MOTHER…where are you?"

I sat straight up in bed, my heart beating out of control, and as sweat dripped down my forehead I yelled out, "No!"

Relieved that I was only dreaming, I sat on the edge of the bed, and tried to clear my head of that nightmare. I thought about going to talk to Jacob, but decided against it, because of his intoxicated condition, so I just lay back down and drifted off.

The next morning, I was awakened by the sound of someone tapping very quietly on my bedroom door. "Come in," I said in a very sleepy voice.

The door opened slowly, and it was Ashlee. "Good morning, Princess. I've come to take you to breakfast."

"Ashlee, what are you doing here this early?"

"I told you that I would be here at eight o'clock, and it's eight-thirty. Maria had me wait downstairs for you, but finally told me to come up and get you!"

I jumped out of bed, "Sorry I'm late! I really didn't sleep well last night. Let me shower real quick—can you give me twenty minutes?"

Ashlee laughed, "Sure Princess…you just take your royal time."

We both laughed, as I ran to the shower. Just as I was getting into the shower, I heard my cell phone ring, "Hey, Ash would you get that please!"

Ashlee answered the phone, "Hello, Ashlee speaking, may I…"

There was dead silence on the other end, then a dial tone. A few minutes later, the phone rang, and the same thing happened again. Ashlee didn't recognize the number, so she put the phone down.

He hung up the phone and sat there puzzled. He knew all of the numbers that Tiffany had, and wondered why this one was written on a sticky, and put on her computer screen. Why in the heck would Tiffany have Ashlee's number? This didn't make sense at all. His curiosity was driving him to panic, but he didn't have time to figure it out. He was in the middle of a job, and couldn't take his mind off his work.

Ashlee and I had one of the greatest days we've had in a long time. One of Ashlee's bridal presents to me was a day of pampering and shopping. We started with an outrageous breakfast of Eggs Benedict,

Belgian waffles and Mimosas. Then on to a day spa for facials, mesages, manicures and pedicures. After that enchanting experience, Ashlee took me to Victoria's Secret, and bought me a dozen bras with undies to match, and all styles of lingerie—something different for an entire month! I argued about accepting so much from her, but she insisted and said it brought her great joy to be able to give back to someone who had done so much for her.

We could barely walk with all the bags, so we took a couple of breaks before we made it to the limo. As I was just starting to relax from all the hustle and bustle, Ashlee brought out her 'To do' list to finalize the details for my bachelorette party.

Antonio and Maria greeted Sterling with love and respect, as though she were a Queen returning to her home from a long journey. Jacob greeted Sterling with his usual, hug and kiss on her cheek. The two of them already had a great relationship, and she loved him like a son.

As Sterling and I walked through the house, I could tell that she was reminiscing silently as we went through every room. Sterling slipped her hand into mine as we walked through the foyer and then into Father's office. When Sterling saw the picture that she had painted for Father, I could tell that the memories were pouring in, as her tears were pouring out. She walked over to the couch to sit down. I sat by her, and put my arm around her knowing how hard this must be.

"I'm sorry, Mother. I was afraid this might be very hard for you."

"I had no idea it would feel like this. I thought that I might never see Michael again so I was nurturing a hardened heart for the last several years. Little did I know, I truly would never see him again."

I looked Sterling in the eyes, held her hands, and said, "Mother, this it not easy, but we will get through this…together."

Sterling sat up straight, wiped her eyes and said, "I'm so sorry my sweet Gabrielle, you shouldn't have to be consoling me, you're grieving too. And poor Mary, how is she doing?"

"She's much better now."

"Alex told me all about how we almost lost Mary also, what a godsend you were Gabi—you saved her life!"

"I wish I could have saved Father's life also."

Sterling put her hand in mine, "Come on—show me your bedroom."

We walked hand in hand to my room. As we walked up the stairs I could tell that Sterling was remembering the romantic nights with Father—my heart ached for her.

We entered my room—Sterling stood at the doorway, her eyes slowly scanning every inch of the room before she walked past the threshold.

"Your room is lovely."

"Thank you. And as you can see, I collect porcelain dolls. That was so sweet of you to bring me one."

Sterling looked at me lovingly, as she said, "I know you do."

"Well of course you would, because Father told you everything—how stupid of me."

Sterling looked at me adoringly and said, "Gabrielle, nothing about you is stupid."

"Oh my gosh, Mother, look at the time! We've got to get ready for the party! I'll have Antonio bring your luggage up here, to the guest room next to mine."

Sterling said softly and sweetly, "The floral room."

"Yes, the beautiful floral room. Did you decorate that room?"

"Yes…but oh, so many years ago."

Tiffany arrived at five-thirty, her arms literally overflowing with presents. Sterling was still upstairs, so I had a chance to talk with her for a few minutes before she came down. I gave her a quick tour of the downstairs. She was impressed, and taken aback with the similarities in taste that she and Michael had.

She turned to me and said in an excited voice, "Michael, I mean, Father's house is everything that I pictured it would be!"

"Wait until you see Father's office. He collected so many beautiful pieces from everywhere—it's my favorite room!"

Just as we were walking through the foyer towards the office, Sterling came down the stairs. Tiffany just stood there with her mouth half open, staring at her as though she were a gorgeous, perfect Angel floating down from heaven.

"Tiffany, this is Sterling, my mother."

Tiffany stretched out her hand to Sterling and said, "It is such a pleasure to meet you. Gabi has told me so many wonderful things about you, which are obviously all true."

Sterling squeezed Tiffany's hand tightly, and reached over with her other arm to hug her, "It's a pleasure to meet you Tiffany. Michael has told me some very nice things about you and they seem to be obviously true, as well. You are as lovely as he described, and you do look enough like Gabi that you two could pass for twins."

Tiffany said, "That is quite a compliment, thank you."

I looked over at Tiffany and wondered why Alex thought that she was such a "challenge." I had seen nothing but loving-kindness since we met. The three of us sat in Father's office and talked until it was time to go.

Paul was standing by the limo, waiting to drive us to Ashlee's house. As the three of us walked out, Sterling grabbed my hand and pointed to where the Porsche was parked. "Is that the beautiful car that Michael got for your eighteenth birthday?"

I was surprised at her comment, as I blurted out, "Yes, it is!"

"He sent me a video of you following the gold ribbon to the car, and then your great reaction—I laughed when you ran into him as you were running through the courtyard, trying to find him!"

"Oh, Father was taking that video for YOU—I remember that like it was yesterday!"

"Yes, I have a whole library of Gabrielle Deliano movies! You're quite a popular movie star in my home."

"Oh Mother, all those times when I thought Father was just trying to capture a "photo op," he was actually sending moments of my life to you!"

When Tiffany heard what Sterling and I were talking about I could tell that she felt like she should leave us alone for a minute. I saw her walk over, and climb into the limo with her presents, looking out the window and watching us as we continued talking. 'How thoughtful she is…'

While walking to the limo, Sterling stopped abruptly, hugged me and said, "Gabrielle, we are finally together. Let's enjoy each moment that we have, right now."

I hugged her back, and then took her by the hand and walked to the limo. As I climbed in, I smiled at Tiffany and started explaining, "Sorry, we got caught up in the…"

Tiffany interrupted, "The moment! Gabi, don't ever worry about me; I'm just so glad to have every 'moment' that I can with a family… my new family."

Sterling reached over, patted Tiffany's leg, and smiled.

Within minutes we were at Ashlee's house. I shouted out like a little girl as I said, "We're here!"

Tiffany was shocked at the sight of so many cars. "Gabi, look at all the cars! My goodness, a lot of people love you!"

"I love a lot of people! Speaking of which…oh Mother, I wasn't even thinking, we should have picked up Mary!"

"Sweetheart, I talked to Mary on the phone while you were getting ready. We had a great visit. She said that she was going early to help Ashlee, and not to worry about her."

"Okay…I just wouldn't want her to feel left out—I love her so much."

"I know you do, and she loves you. She also knows that you have a lot going on in your life right now so don't worry about any of us. You just enjoy your day!"

I walked through the door and the band that was set up in the foyer started playing as white, pearlized balloons came floating down from the top of the stairs. When I walked through the double-doors to the Grand Parlor, everyone was standing there holding a glowing white candle that shone so brightly in the dark room—the sight was breathtaking. I just stood there enjoying the moment…

Being the creative type, Ashlee had turned a large stuffed chair into a throne with white tulle and white baby's breath draped all around it. She walked me over to the throne, through an aisle of calla lilies, and told me to be seated.

The room was decorated with white, everywhere. There were ten round tables, which seated ten guests each, decorated with white linen, and white roses. White tulle flowed from each corner of the ceiling to the center of the room, with baby's breath intertwined inside, making it look like something out of a dream.

The white china had a beautiful little gift that was wrapped, and placed on each plate for the guests. On each table, there also was a tall, white, round candle, and ten smaller candles around it, all glowing brightly.

I sat in my chair, feeling so blessed to have such a wonderful friend who created this enchanting, dream-like event for my very special occasion. Ashlee told me that each person was going to come up, one at a time, tell me what I meant to them and give me a wee-bit of advice. Each of them came, most bringing tears to my eyes, as they shared their sweet, pearls of wisdom.

After they spoke, each woman sat at her designated table, placing her candle in the holder to join the others. Ashlee told Sterling and Tiffany beforehand, they were exempt from this exercise. She knew that it would be awkward for them.

The room was so beautiful that I could hardly believe my eyes. Before I walked back to take my seat at the table, I walked over to Ashlee and hugged her tightly, then I turned to everyone and said, "I want to tell you all what Ashlee has meant to my life."

When I was through talking about Ashlee, I walked over to Mary, and said, "I have a secret to tell all of you, my dear friends!"

I quickly told them the whole story about who Mary really was, which left every mouth open and every eye filled with tears. Then, I walked over to Sterling, had her stand up. Before I introduced her to the whole crowd, I said, "And if that secret wasn't big enough, listen to this!"

Standing, tall and proud, I told the story about Sterling, and how I couldn't wait to share my life with my mother. Before I was finished talking, every woman there was crying, almost uncontrollably, then they all stood and started clapping. After Mother took her seat, I went to Tiffany, and explained her story as well, which received the same reaction from everyone. The energy in that room was electrifying and it lasted well into the night...

Chapter 34

The next morning Sterling, Tiffany and I packed our suitcases for our trip back to Europe. Mary couldn't leave yet, because she finally had an offer on her house, so Ashlee and Mary made plans to fly out together in two days. Ashlee didn't want Mary to make the trip alone.

Jacob and Alex rode with us in the limo, and everyone was discussing the gorgeous Villa Giorgio on Lake Como that Sterling had surprised Jacob and me with. The car was abuzz with last-minute decisions and details, all the way to the airport.

The men ushered the girls to the concourse in a whirlwind, and finally relaxed as they sat back down in the limo to go home. Alex was very concerned about something. He hadn't wanted to burst Jacob's bubble during this happy week, but decided that he better update Jacob now, to keep him in the loop.

"Jacob, I need to discuss something with you that isn't really very pleasant, so I want to apologize ahead of time."

"Don't worry about it, there will be a lot of unpleasant issues that we'll still have to deal with about this whole situation. I'm aware of that."

"I know, but I didn't want anything to rain on your parade right now."

"What's on your mind, Alex?"

"Well, if Daniel was disguising himself as Pierre, to Ashlee, I could understand her not recognizing who he really was, but what about Sandi? Don't you think Sandi would have recognized him?"

"Not necessarily Alex. It's been a long time since Sandi has seen him, and she's not very sharp."

"I know, but there's something else that I'm curious about. Sandi told me that Pierre asked her to tell him who Leon was when they were looking at the photograph. Does that make any sense to you?"

"It was probably a smoke screen, or maybe he didn't even say that."

"Yeah, you're right."

"Alex, it's finally time to put this all to rest, and move forward with our lives!"

"Echo that!"

After boarding the Deliano Jet, we were served champagne and a delicious, five-course meal. We had our lists on our laps and were comparing notes as the plane took off. With the wedding only a few days away, and all the guests arriving tomorrow, we had plenty to discuss.

When we arrived at the house, Sterling's staff rolled out the red carpet for me. I was waited on, hand-and-foot, like royalty. As I was being treated to every imaginable pampering, Sterling and Tiffany were making sure that all the details were being properly attended to.

Two days later, we left for Lake Como. My spirit floated, enjoying every breathtaking sight along the winding roads that were lined with trees—each turn revealing a spectacular view of the lakes and islands. When we arrived, Sterling had pre-arranged the same type of pampering treatment for both, Tiffany and me that she had presented upon my first visit. After our mani's, pedi's, mesages, and salon treatments we felt as though we were movie stars living in a dream. The concierge offered us a cool, raspberry iced-tea as we left to begin our tour of the grounds.

Strolling down the cobblestone sidewalk through the gardens to the lake, I was in my own little world. I took in every beautiful sight, sound and smell. My dear family knows I'm a "Carpe diem" kind of girl, so Sterling and Tiffany fell behind, allowing me the space to capture and embrace the beauty of the moment.

As I approached the private Cathedral, I stopped...dead in my tracks...staring at the outside walls, and admiring the strength of their structure. The walls not only supported the building, but the centuries-old ivy seemed to be part of the walls, flowing down from their very tops, to the bottom, vanishing into the sidewalk. The sturdy Cyprus tree, whose roots were so intertwined with the structure, gave it an illusion of not knowing where each of them began, or ended.

Walking inside, I stopped by the door and closed my eyes, feeling a sense of security as the smell of old wood, incense and burning candles surrounded me. I opened my eyes and looked at the beautiful stain-glassed windows casting intricate shadows on the inner walls. My soul soared as I, once again, felt a deep sense of peace and joy in my life.

Sterling and Tiffany came up from behind me, Sterling said, "Doesn't this cathedral have character like none other?"

I leaned over and kissed her cheek, "Yes, it most certainly does— Thank you, Serling…I mean, Mother. It feels like I'm walking through a dream."

At dinner, Mother surprised me with a charm for my bracelet. I opened her present and tears filled my eyes as I realized what the charm was—a perfect replica of the church we visited today, and I would be married in tomorrow.

"Mother, this is amazing- so intricate. How did you get this done so fast?"

"I have a lot of friends, and we work miracles for each other when we need to!"

We all laughed, as Tiffany handed me a small present. "I asked Sterling if there was anything special that I could get for you, so I…"

I interrupted her, "You have already done so much for me, Tiffany. I didn't expect anything."

"I know you didn't, but I wanted to do this. I've never had a sister, and this is fun."

As I opened the present, my lips began to quiver slightly, I tried very hard not to cry—it was a charm of two girls holding hands.

"That's us," Tiffany said.

"Yes, that is definitely us!" I leaned over, and kissed her on the cheek.

Mother announced that the men would be arriving soon, and she wanted me to be out of sight, in keeping with the tradition of the groom not seeing the bride beforehand.

"But Mother, there's one more day, until I'll be married!"

"I know, and that's one extra day he'll have to want you even more!"

We all laughed, and went to our adjoining rooms to finish talking.

The next day Mary and Ashlee arrived, bursting with so much excitement they could hardly contain themselves. The men were sight seeing, and the guests were everywhere!

Ashlee and I told Tiffany all about our friendship. Every crazy thing we had ever done together. Tiffany laughed so much, she was crying. We all bonded wonderfully, even though Tiffany didn't feel comfortable enough to share about her own life, quite yet. Everything was going well between the three of us, until Tiffany asked Ashlee if she had anyone special in her life.

Ashlee was looking for clues from me, not knowing how much she should reveal to Tiffany about her boyfriend, the alleged killer of Michael, which understandably made Ashlee feel terrible, and not comfortable discussing.

I knew this, and interrupted, "Well, Ashlee was dating a guy just recently, but he was absolutely not her type! Next question."

Tiffany read my response, so she left it alone. "Okay, well I'll tell you about the man in my life then."

I blurted out, "Tiffany, I didn't know you were seeing someone! You never mentioned anything!"

"I know. It's just that I'm slow to open up and trust people. Believe me, this is fast for me!"

I felt as though Tiffany was trying to make up for stepping into something about Ashlee, I assured her "You don't have to talk about anything that you don't want to talk about."

"I know. I don't feel like I have to—I want to."

She sat there like a little girl in third grade, cross-legged, sharing stories with her friends. She started out by saying, "First of all, he has a very exiting position as an under-cover agent for the government."

Ashlee and I gasped, "Wow, that is so cool, does he actually go on assignments?"

"Yes, he does. In fact, that's where he is right now."

The knock on the door startled all three of us—Sterling knocked hard, and quickly opened the door. With a worried tone of voice she said, "Excuse me for interrupting, but Gabrielle, our shoes haven't arrived yet, and I'm a little concerned."

"Didn't they come with the dress?"

"No!"

"Everything has been so perfect. We had to expect that something would go a little wrong. What should we do?"

"Let me think...what size shoe do you wear?"

"A seven."

"That's good! So do I!"

"You didn't happen to bring an extra pair of white satin shoes did you?"

Sterling thought for a moment, "No, I only brought one pair of white satin shoes for the wedding, and then a different pair to wear to the reception. The rest of the shoes I brought wouldn't be appropriate for the wedding at all."

I quickly looked at Tiffany, "What size shoe do you wear?"

"An eight."

"Well, that might work if…"

Sterling interrupted, "No, I'll just wear the other shoes to the wedding, you can wear my white satins."

"Sounds like a plan; let's go try them on!"

As Mother and I walked off, Mary and the girls decided to go visit the guys.

Chapter 35

Early the next morning I was awakened by a loud knock on my door—when I opened it, the Concierge was standing there with twelve dozen red roses, holding them all very carefully in his arms. I reached out, and took the note off of the bunch that was the closest to me, and read it aloud, "Good morning my Bride, soon to be my wife! See you at the altar. I love you, Jacob."

The Concierge was grinning from ear to ear when he said, "That was very sweet Miss, where would you like me to put these?"

I took some of the flowers from his arms, and I pointed where to put the rest, "Thank you, thank you so much for delivering these... Yes, he is very sweet, and very romantic."

I tried to tip him, but he said, "I've been well taken care of by your fiancé."

What a most glorious way to start my day! I was excited to show Mother the gorgeous roses that were quite a sight, but thought it best not to wake her yet.

I decided it would be a good time to get my shower out of the way, before others started coming to visit. I tripped into the bathroom, before even having my coffee, which I never do—but then, I never get married every day either—the coffee can wait. I pulled back the shower curtain, and was surprised to see a beautifully wrapped present. I retrieved it, and ran back to my bed to sit down and open it. How mysterious...

There was no card attached, but after receiving the flowers, I was suspicious that it was from Jacob. I tore the paper off—it was a box from Herrods! It's got to be from Jacob, he knows that's one of my favorite stores.

I opened the lid so fast that it flew across the room. I pulled back the tissue and there were two porcelain dolls, a male and a female, made to look as much as possible like Jacob and me in our wedding attire. 'Oh, what beautiful dolls to add to my collection, how incredibly sweet.'

I was tempted more than ever now to wake Mother, but I thought that might be rude. I decided to take my shower.

As I was drying my hair, I heard another knock on the door. It was one of Mother's friends who was taking care of the reception and needed some advice. Since I was letting her sleep, I took care of the situation myself. Giorgio wasn't sure where the band should stand. I explained they would be best positioned with the lake behind them as a beautiful backdrop.

Then Giorgio asked, "Where should we put the fog machine?"

Not certain of what Mother had in mind, I hesitated, but then said, "Well, it needs to be out of sight, and the only place to hide it would be under the ledge of the verandah that hangs out over the lake."

"I'm sorry to have bothered you, and please don't tell Sterling. I don't want her mad at me for interrupting you."

I wasn't sure why this was such a big issue, but could see that Giorgio didn't want Sterling upset with him for anything. Realizing what influence my mother had over people, I agreed, "Don't worry Giorgio, and thank you for taking such good care of all the details."

Sterling finally woke up, and could hear Gabi stirring around. Just as she was about to knock on their adjoining door, there was a loud knock on Sterling's main door. She could see that it was a person who worked in the lobby by the way they were dressed. She threw on her robe, and answered the door.

The man only said a few words, "Are you Sterling Deliano?"

After she said "Yes", he handed her a note, and walked off.

There was a puzzled look on Sterling's face as she opened the note, and read it.

You must be a goddess, for I have never seen anything so beautiful. I surrender myself completely to you. My life is yours to do with what you will. Tonight, when we dance, our bodies will be touching so closely—you'll feel the love inside me—I will give that to you over and over again. I can taste you, and I want to be inside...

Shocked, and feeling as though she was reading something that was private between Gabi and Jacob, Sterling quickly re-folded it, and knocked on Gabi's door to give the note to her.

"Good morning, Princess! Happy Wedding Day!"
"Good morning, Mother!"
"Did you have a good sleep?"
"The best I've had in a long time. How about you?"
"Good, really good." Then as Mother walked into my room further she could see the flowers, everywhere, "Oh Gabi, the flowers are beautiful!"
"Did you know about them?"
Mother smiled sweetly, "Yes."
"Then you must have been the one who put the…"
"Dolls in the shower, right again! Jacob is so romantic, and so thoughtful. I am so happy for you. I already love him like a son. Oh, I ended up with a note that Jacob sent to you also; it just arrived.
Mother handed me the note, as I read it I looked at her and said, "Wow, this sounds a little different, he must be very…"
She interrupted, "Excited to be with you!"
"I guess."
"I'll get ready, and then we'll see you in a while to help you finish with your hair and veil."
At eleven o'clock sharp Mother arrived back at my suite with Ashlee, Tiffany, and Aunt Mary. Then Bianca, Jada, Brooklyn, Michelle, Stephanie, Nani, Patty, Samantha, and Jessica arrived—my other very close friends, and bridesmaids.
We all went out on the spacious verandah for a beautiful and delicious brunch. I thanked them all for everything they were doing to help my dream come true, and presented each one with a lovely and unique present I had picked especially for them.
Tiffany stood up, and said that she felt like the luckiest of all. She had been blessed with the kind of sister that most people only dream about. She also thanked everyone for accepting her, and being so kind to her in such a short time. Tiffany explained her excitement about having a real family, which included Sterling, an aunt, a sister, and a brother.
As the word, brother fell out of Tiffany's mouth I remembered my conversation with Eric. I tensed up with a gut feeling that he was going to present me with as many challenges as he did everyone else. Thinking of what I would do if he did, ignited cogitation and strategy

on a distant track in my mind—with no one aware of my thoughts, I just smiled and nodded.

Mary looked at me and smiled back, 'bless her heart, this was a lot of secrets to carry around—what a burden that must have been for her.'

My heart began—to feel true happiness once again. I knew that Father would be happy knowing—that the tragedy of his death was actually an opportunity for new beginnings, and new relationships between the people that he left behind.

We sat at the table talking for a few hours, laughing and having a great time. Finally, Ashlee looked at her watch and said, "Okay, it's three o'clock. We all have to be at the church in two hours."

With that statement, everyone scurried out of the room except for Mother. "I want to talk to you before we leave for the church."

"Okay, let's sit out here—the view is so gorgeous."

"Gabrielle, I love you with all my heart, and you are a beautiful woman. You are beautiful inside as well as outside. Since we haven't lived together as mother and daughter, I feel like I want to share a pearl of wisdom with you, in private—from my heart to yours."

I was so touched by my mother's words that a tear ran down my cheek as I said, "Please…share."

"I'd like to tell you something about beauty."

I looked straight into my Mother's eyes, and smiled as she opened her heart.

"Please don't ever take your beauty for granted, or use it to manipulate others. I know that you wouldn't, but sometimes it can be tempting. Outer beauty is a gift that you had nothing to do with, and it should never, ever be used for gain, or for manipulation. Remember Gabrielle—true beauty, the kind that comes from within, lasts forever. No matter how many wrinkles you get—and trust me, you will get them, or how much your body changes—and believe me, it does. If you have a pure heart, and truly love people the way we're supposed to love, that will continue to shine through, and your beauty will never fade. A person's beauty is also measured by the lovely fragrance they leave behind—and by that, I mean how you touch lives each day—blessing people with small acts of kindness, or precious and priceless, loving words. Having them feel uplifted after seeing or hearing from you—that the fragrance of beauty you leave behind."

Tears continued to slowly run down my cheeks, "Thank you, Mother—those were very wise words I shall never forget."

Mother kissed me on the cheek and said, "I love you, Angel," then she went to her suite to finish getting dressed.

Chapter 36

The scene on my verandah was electrifying. The weather was perfect. The birds were singing and the sweet flowers spread their scent through the gentle breeze. Enjoying each beautiful moment I stood there motionless, taking in the sights, the sounds and the smells. I closed my eyes, took a deep breath, and recorded this magnificent memory in my mind forever.

Soon Mother arrived with the photographer. The three of us agreed that taking the photos outside on the verandah would be perfect. The backdrop of the lake with the sun going down, looked like something one would see on the cover of a travel magazine—it was absolutely breathtaking.

Ashlee arrived soon after we had taken a few dozen photographs, and could tell that I was ready to get going. She quickly helped gather everything I needed as we rushed out to join the other women in the limo. As soon as we arrived at the church, all the women were quickly ushered in so that no one would be seen before the men arrived. My heart was racing—I wasn't sure if it was because I was excited, or upset.

Ashlee looked at me. She could tell that something wasn't quite right. "Hey Grilla, what are you thinking?"

"Well, I'm....."

Ashlee interrupted me, "You're nervous, and it's because you're getting married..."

"No, I feel shaky, like something else is wrong."

"Nothing is wrong, everything is right. You're getting married today—to the man you love...the man of your dreams!"

"I know Ashlee, but something just feels weird."

"Come here, Gabi. Let's go to that corner, where we can talk alone."

As we walked to the side of the room, Tiffany started walking over, but Ashlee put her hand up and mouthed, 'stay there.'

"What's the matter with you, Gabi?"

"I don't know. I just can't shake this weird feeling."

"Did anything happen to make you feel like this?"

I looked down and thought for a minute, "No...not really."

"Well, I know you have enough food in you—I saw you eat today!"

"Thanks Ashlee, you make me sound like Miss Piggy."

"Well, at least I know you're not thinking weird because you're starving."

"Something is just bothering me, I feel......"

Ashlee interrupted, "Good, we're getting somewhere. What? You feel what?"

"Well, Jacob sent me a note, and it just didn't seem like something he would write."

"What does it sound like?"

"Kind of...horny."

"Well gosh Gabi, what do you think he is?"

"I know, but it just didn't sound like him. It made me feel kind of weird."

"Do you want me to read it?"

"Well, later maybe—I think we're almost ready to start the ceremony, besides I folded it up real small, it's in my shoe."

"Well, give it to me. Let me see what's bothering you so much."

I bent down to take the note out of my shoe and handed it to Ashlee, suddenly the organ started playing. Ashlee held the note in her hand, and started arranging my veil. All my girls walked over to me, gave me a hug and said, "Here we go!"

The water was a lot colder and not as clear as he thought it would be, which made swimming into the cove quite a challenge. His scuba gear got caught on some branches and he had to cut it lose.

As he showered and climbed into his next disguise, he was most anxious for this night to be over. He watched carefully from his balcony. He needed to time his entrance perfectly; too soon, or too late, and others would know that he didn't belong with that party. As he put the syringe in his pocket, he kept saying over and over to himself, "This is my last job—my very last job!"

Alex and Mother met me at the back of the church. Mother whispered in my ear, "Don't forget Sweetheart, I will need to go to my room and change, because these are the red shoes that I brought to wear with my red dress, not this white satin!"

As she pulled up her dress to show me, we both laughed as she said, "This is quite the fashion faux pas!"

I looked down at the beautiful high-heel red sandals that poor Mother had to wear with her white satin dress just so I could have her white shoes. I smiled at her and said, "I'll remember," and then I sweetly kissed her cheek.

When the wedding march began, I slipped my left arm through Alex's arm, and my right arm through Mother's arm- looked at each one of them, smiled and said, "I'm ready."

As the doors opened, Jacob's eyes grew as big as saucers. He knew that Gabi was beautiful, but his expectations of what his bride would look like, paled to the reality. She was not only gorgeous, she was breathtakingly sexy and sensual, and he couldn't take his eyes off her as he said under his breath, "Totally HOT!"

It seemed as though I was floating down the center aisle, everyone staring at my every move. The rose petals seemed to be floating in slow motion as I drifted past them while they were in mid air. When I finally arrived at the altar, Alex gave my hand to Jacob. Jacob took it with so much love that I could feel it, all the way to my heart.

The ceremony was traditional and beautiful. A friend of Mother's, a professional opera singer, sang Ave Maria—that was one of Jacob and my favorite songs. Her voice, echoing through the church, sounded like an angel's voice, filling the heavens. It sent chills down my spine, as I stood motionless, in the moment.

After we were announced husband and wife, Jacob lifted my veil, and kissed my lips tenderly and sweetly. Then, intertwining his fingers with mine, he took my hand, and walked me out of the church and down the long walkway. As the beautiful Renaissance music started playing, two hundred white doves flew out of the steeple—glorious sights and sounds, on the most glorious day of my life!

The white limo was decorated with white carnations along the front hood, the roof and the tail of the car. In the back window, written in white paint, were the words, 'Just Married'. The two lines of cans that were to drag behind, were painted white with silver trim. Locked in a romantic embrace, Jacob and I rode back to the villa for the party—Jacob kissing me so romantically that all I could think about was how wonderful our first night alone was going to be. I pulled away for a minute because I wanted to talk, "Jacob, I haven't had a chance to thank you for the beautiful roses and the dolls! That was so sweet and thoughtful of you."

He kissed my lips and said, "You're welcome, my love."

"And that note......well, I ....."

"What note?"

"The note you sent."

"You mean the one that came with the flowers?"

"No. The one that someone gave to Sterling, to give to me."

"No Honey, I didn't send you any more notes other than the one that came with the roses!"

I looked at Jacob a little quizzically, "I wonder who it was supposed to go to then? Boy, am I ever glad you didn't send it."

"Why?"

"It was very weird, and kind of creepy. Mother thought that you sent it, so she brought it to me, but the guy from the lobby, actually told Mother that it was for her."

"Well, maybe she has a secret admirer."

"Maybe she does…"

As we pulled up to the reception, the line had already formed. Everyone was waiting to congratulate the bride and groom.

The sun was setting behind the draped tulle and twinkle-lights. The effects of the fog rolling up off the dance floor made for a very sultry, sexy and beautiful ambiance. The scene was quite surreal. It had an appearance that one was walking into a fantasy-like dream, a dream that was intensely alluring and romantic.

I looked around for Mother, but then remembered she was going straight to her room to change. I wanted to tell her that the note was meant for her. 'One of her friends must have a rather large crush on her.'

There were so many people coming through the line, we were feeling a little tired from talking so much. My estimate of two hundred twenty-something guests had really turned out to be two hundred and eighty-three, when all was said and done. I could see Mary getting a little antsy to start the dancing, and watched her walk over to the band, telling them to start the first dance.

Jacob gave me that alluring look as he put his arm around my waist and ushered me to the center of the dance floor. As we started dancing the fog got deeper and thicker, and with the lights twinkling, it was absolutely mesmerizing.

After the first dance, everyone anxiously became a part of this most awesome scene. I kept looking over Jacob's shoulder to find Mother, but she was still nowhere in sight.

I was watching Ashlee take her shoes off to dance, and saw the note that I gave her, fall out of her left shoe. She picked it up, and went to throw it away, but then I watched her open it—I guess she decided to read it.

As Jacob twirled me around, I finally caught sight of Mother in the corner, and I was relieved. "Oh Jacob, there's Mother! She looks beautiful—look at her!"

Jacob looked over at her and said, "Sterling is definitely hot."

Mother was stunning in her red dress with a slit up the side, and her long dark hair pulled up and swept off her face. Then, I really looked at her....Mother looked so shockingly like she did in the dream I had about her, I started to feel uneasy.

Ashlee opened the note and started reading it. After she read the last line, she read it over again, and stood there in shock. Then she read it a few more times, because she couldn't believe her eyes. She crumbled it in her hand, her heart started beating hard, and she started feeling sick inside.

Suddenly, from out of nowhere, one of Jacob's friends, a guy whom Ashlee really liked grabbed her, and took her out on the dance floor. I watched her being twirled around, and for a minute it looked like she was having fun, but then I caught a concerned look on her face, that gave me the impression that she was looking for me.

Trying to get Mother's attention, I kept watching her, hoping to make eye contact with her, but she was looking somewhere else. Finally I saw Mother look in the opposite corner across the verandah, smile, and walk towards someone.

When I looked in the direction that she had been staring, I saw the figure of a man in a black tuxedo, who was also staring back at Mother. 'Who is that? I can't see his face.'

My mind went fuzzy for a minute, and then it recalled something from my dream. 'Oh…my…gosh! I couldn't see his face in my dream, either!' Then I got worried. Mother and this strange man kept moving towards each other through the fog. 'Are they moving in slow motion, or does the fog just make it appear that way? Who is it? Who are you meeting, Mother?'

They continued to move slowly towards each other, as if drawn like magnets. When they finally met, he put his arms around her, and they started dancing closely, as if they knew each other well.

My concerns lessened as I saw Mother dancing close to him; 'Maybe that's the man that sent her the note, and maybe he's been a secret admirer—how romantic.'

'He is so incredibly romantic—he must be one of Jacob's friends, Sterling thought,' as he held her in his arms.

As they danced through the fog, he held her closer, and closer—tighter, and tighter. Their faces were very close, he moved his lips in the direction of hers, then he quickly moved to her ear, and whispered, "Obsessions can kill."

Feeling a little uneasy and worried from hearing those words Sterling began to pull away, but then wondered if he knew about her book. 'Maybe he liked it, and is trying to start a conversation. But… how could he have possibly have known that I wrote that book?'

He held Sterling, as if he didn't want to let her go. She started feeling very uncomfortable, and tried again to pull away, but his grip on her was now becoming threatening. Then, he pulled the syringe out of his pocket, and while holding it concealed in his hand, he began to slip off the needle cap as Sterling said "Are you Jacob's friend?"

He looked in her eyes very romantically, as he said, "Yes."

Just as he was answering her, Ashlee screamed from across the foggy dance floor, "Pierre!"

When Tiffany, who was standing on the opposite side of the dance floor heard that name, she automatically looked up. She couldn't see him clearly through the fog, but her mind told her that it couldn't be Pierre. 'He doesn't know these people, and why in the world would he be here?'

Pierre looked in the direction that his name was called, and through the fog he thought he saw Ashlee, but seeing her there didn't make any sense at all to him. He started feeling nervous inside. It was unnerving to hear his name when he was in the middle of a job. Then he heard his name being called from a different direction, Tiffany yelled out, "Pierre, what are you doing here?"

Pierre looked in the direction of Tiffany's voice, and saw her standing there, looking at him in disbelief. His immediate thoughts were that someone was messing with his mind... 'This scene can't really be happening.' Then, both women called out his name again and were moving towards him from opposite directions.

He flashed back to when he called the mystery number Tiffany had, and Ashlee answered, which made him start to freak out and panic. Pierre's head was spinning. He was losing control of the situation. He started to put the syringe back in his pocket, while he kept trying to continue dancing with Sterling.

As Ashlee quickly worked her way through the fog, and the dancing crowd, she grabbed Sonny who was watching over Sterling. She pointed at Pierre, and screamed, "That's Pierre!"

The music was so loud, that Sterling didn't hear Ashlee, but observed Sonny approaching her quickly, knowing that he was probably overly concerned about Pierre dancing so close with her. Sonny pushed Ashlee out of the way as he grabbed Pierre, pulling his arm up, and behind Pierre's back. Then Sterling screamed as Sonny grabbed her so quickly she didn't know what hit her. He threw her, as carefully as he could, away from Pierre.

As Sterling stood up, she firmly said, "What's the deal Sonny? He was just dancing close."

Then she looked down, and saw that her dress had been ripped. The slit that went up the side of the dress had torn all the way up to her waist, which was indecent and embarrassing. She ran back to the villa to change her clothes.

"Clear the floor and turn off that fog machine!" Sonny yelled.

In a split second, Sonny had a death-grip on Pierre, as he moved his arm up, around Pierre's neck. Then he grabbed Pierre's other arm, to pull it back, so that he wouldn't be able to grab anyone else. As he pulled his arm up tightly to his neck the syringe dropped out of Pierre's hand, onto the floor.

Sonny looked down, saw the syringe, and looked back up at Pierre with fire in his eyes. No one but Pierre could hear Sonny, as he whispered, "You dirty scum bag, you were going to kill her, the same way you killed Michael. This time you lose, you disgusting piece of trash!"

Sonny's grip was so tight—his initial reaction was to snap Pierre's neck, but he resisted the temptation. He knew that dead men can't talk, and he wanted answers.

Tiffany stood there in shock, just staring at Pierre who was speechless and helpless in Sonny's arms. By now Eric, Jacob and Alex had their guns pulled and pointed at Pierre. Ashlee came running over and said, "That's Pierre, that's him!"

Alex looked at him and said, "Yes, this is Pierre." Then, under his breath he said quietly, "But not for long."

The scuttle happened so quickly, and the guys managed the whole situation in such an orderly way that no one but them, really knew what was going on.

Chapter 37

Sonny didn't want anyone to be suspicious, so he told the guests to continue the party. He and the guys took Pierre to their villa. Knowing that Pierre killed Michael and Leon made them crazy inside. Each was planning their own way of killing Pierre in their minds.

Tiffany came running over towards me, and Ashlee who was watching the guys usher Pierre away, blurted out, "What's going on Gabi?" Then she turned to Ashlee, "I heard you call Pierre's name. How do you know Pierre?"

"How do you know him," Ashlee asked.

Tiffany looked quizzically at me, and said, "He's the guy I've been dating. What do they want with him, Gabi?"

"You were dating that scum?" Ashlee asked.

Tiffany was trying very hard to not explode, as she blurted out, "Excuse me Ashlee, but..."

I interrupted quietly, I knew this would be quite a shock for Tiffany. "Tiffany...Pierre is the man who killed Father."

Tiffany looked at me, then Ashlee, and then watched in shock as we both nodded our heads in a yes direction, and looked down simultaneously.

Tiffany cried out, "No, that can't be true!"

I put my hand on Tiffany's shoulder and said, "I'm afraid it is."

Tiffany couldn't accept what we were saying, "No, I don't believe it, he works for the government—he's an under-cover agent—he's a good guy!"

"Is that what he told you, Tiffany?" Ashlee asked.

"Yes, and I know that's what he really does."

"No, I'll tell you what he really does!"

Ashlee explained how they met, where he worked, and what he wrote in a note to Sterling, which was exactly the same lines he had used, in a note he wrote to Ashlee.

Then I interrupted, confirming what Ashlee was saying by telling her how Pierre used many disguises to get close to our father.

"It just sounds so bizarre...I can't believe he did anything like that! How does he know Father? Why would he want to kill him?"

"Well, when they found Daniel..."

Tiffany interrupted me, and in an angry tone of voice said, "Who the hell is Daniel? What does he have to do with Pierre?"

I looked at Tiffany, and felt sorry for her. Learning about secrets was hard. I took hold of her hand as I said, "Tiffany, Daniel was an associate in Father's business a long time ago. They found him dead, with a note saying that he had murdered Father. They assumed that Daniel did the actual killing, but evidently, he had hired Pierre to do the job."

"But Gabi, why?"

"I don't have all the answers, Tiffany. But one thing we do know, is that Pierre did kill Father."

Tiffany stood there for a minute just thinking. Then she asked Ashlee, "When did you first meet Pierre?"

"It was about two months ago," Ashlee said.

Looking hurt and betrayed, Tiffany turned to me, and asked in a little girl voice, "He had many disguises?"

"Yes, Sandi gave multiple descriptions of him. One was with a brown wig, mustache and beard, and…"

"Oh dear God… he did lie to me! That slimy scum is a bloody hit man!"

I looked at her with sad eyes, as I said, "Yes, he killed our Father."

I could tell that Tiffany was in shock, and so outraged by the news, all she kept saying was that she wanted to shoot Pierre. She began running towards the villa as fast as she could run on the grass in heels and a dress. I grabbed Ashlee's arm and said, "Let's go!"

Mother finally returned from changing her clothes, and caught sight of Ashlee and me as we were headed toward the villa. "What is going on—where are the guys?"

I turned to Mother, and hugged her tightly, as I said, "Oh Mother… I think he was trying to kill you!"

"Who?"

"Pierre!"

"Who is Pierre, and why would he want to kill me?"

"The guy you were dancing with!"

"Gabi, wasn't he Jacob's friend?"

"No, he wasn't!"

"Oh my gosh, I thought he was! He was acting a little weird, but…"

I interrupted, "I should have seen this coming! I saw this in a dream, Mother. I already saw this. This is all my fault!"

Mother pulled away from me, and grabbed my hands as she said, "Gabi, this is NOT your fault! You didn't know. I was the one who should have known better—I shouldn't have accepted a dance from a complete stranger."

"Mother, he's not just a stranger, he's a murderer!"

"Gabi, where did they take him?'

"They took him to their room and they're going to..." I paused and looked down.

"They're going to what?"

"What do you think? Pierre is the man who murdered Father, and Uncle Leon!"

"He can't be! I thought it was Daniel who...."

"No, Daniel hired Pierre to kill Father, and they think that Uncle Leon just got in the way."

"Oh Gabi, this is such a nightmare."

"I know! I know!"

"He told me that he was one of Jacob's friends. Oh Gabi, he was so weird! I don't understand what he was doing here."

"Mother! You're not listening to me! He was trying to kill YOU!"

"For goodness sake Gabrielle, this doesn't make sense. If Daniel hired Pierre to kill Michael because Daniel was obsessing over me, then why would Daniel have hired Pierre to kill me?"

I looked at Mother and then stood there, frozen in my thoughts for a minute before I could say, "This does not make sense! Why would he want to kill you?"

As those words fell out of my mouth, we both looked horrified as we were thinking the same thing. I looked at Mother and said, "This couldn't have anything to do with that old case, could it?"

Mother looked like she was going to faint as she said, "Oh no, it's not over yet."

"We assumed that he killed Father for Daniel, because Daniel was obsessing over you, and wanted to be with you. It makes no sense at all, that Daniel would have Pierre kill you!"

"Gabi, a sane mind would come to a logical conclusion, but I don't think we're dealing with people who are thinking straight. Pierre could have just become obsessed himself."

"No, I don't think so! My gut tells me that it's something all together different."

Walking quickly toward the villa, Mother said, "Gabi, listen to me… we have got to talk to Sonny before he takes him away—we need to find out who sent Pierre here."

"I have never felt such hate or such rage, Mother. I'd like to rip him apart with my bare hands for killing Father!"

"I know. I'd like to put a bullet through him myself!"

As we all started running, I looked at Mother and said, "Will they turn him over to the police tonight?"

Mother reached over, and grabbed Ashlee and me by our arms, stopping us both rather abruptly. Tiffany kept walking faster and faster, as anger was raging within her. Mother looked at Ashlee, then back at me and said, "They will find out what they need to know, then Pierre will be taken care of in the appropriate manner."

I winced as I asked, "What will they do to him?"

Mother looked at us long and hard, then replied, "The man doesn't exist anymore. No one will ever find him, or even a trace of him, ever."

I yelled out for Tiffany to stop. When we caught up to her, I told them all to come to my room so the guys could do what they needed to do. The girls wanted to go to their suites first, which gave me a minute to gather my thoughts.

Standing on my verandah, listening to the waves crash against the rocks, I lifted my hands to the sky, took a deep breath, closed my eyes and felt the strength that had been stolen from me by grief…come flowing back into my body like adrenaline on speed. I was no longer in a weakened state from grief, rather a heightened and renewed sense that I had never felt before. As I exhaled, I said, "Gabrielle is back!"

The wedding celebration continued for hours. Meanwhile Alex convinced Jacob to leave, so he and Gabi wouldn't be late for their flight, and assured Jacob that he could take care of the situation at hand.

As Jacob rushed off, Alex whispered in Jacob's ear, "Let go of all of this, and be with your wife tonight! Go enjoy your honeymoon…you only get one!"

Feeling torn, Jacob knew Alex was correct with his fatherly advice. Jacob gave Alex a big bear hug as he kissed his cheek and said, "Thanks man."

As the Deliano, private jet lifted off for Paris Jacob toasted me with one hand, and held me tightly with the other. I could barely finish my champagne before his hands began caressing every inch of my body. He quickly pulled me towards him, pressing his lips firmly against mine—then, a sensual kiss…evoking surrender. Lost in the passion, erotic thoughts rushing in, tingling sensations running throughout my entire body, I was captivated. My only thoughts were that of lying naked in bed with my lover, and finally giving myself to him, completely.

The men were relentless, as they questioned and tortured Pierre for hours. None of his disguises could hide his looks as well as the disfigured face he now had. After working him over, and breaking his ribs, his breathing became labored, and blood was oozing from his ears, and his mouth.

The first words Pierre uttered were, "What did she do?"

Sonny grabbed his hair, and jerked him backwards as he said, "What did who do? You scum."

Barely able to speak, he said, "Ster…ling."

As Sonny pulled his neck back harder he said, "Nothing…she did nothing."

At this point Pierre could barely talk, so his words became a whisper as he slowly said, "Then why…did Stephano…want her?"

As soon as the name, Stephano fell out of Pierre's mouth, Alex looked at Sonny in horror. Then they both looked at Eric, and they walked to the other side of the room. Each one of them knew that Stephano was the head of the largest Mafia organization in Europe.

Alex's heart was beating so hard it felt like it was coming out of his chest. He looked at Sonny, then at Eric and said, "Put this creep back together as best you can."

"No! Are you out of your mind?" Eric snapped back.

"Just put him back together—temporarily!"

Then Sonny chimed in, "Since Stephano ordered the hit…we need more information!"

Alex looked at Eric and said, "Just do it!" Then he walked out the door.

Alex was so concerned about Sterling that he bolted to her room, wiping the blood off his hands only to find her in the courtyard watching him rid himself of the evidence. He stopped rather abruptly, as if slamming on the breaks.

"Oh Alex, was he really trying to kill me?"

"Yes, he was."

"Then, it's not over, is it?"

"I'm afraid not."

"Oh, dear God! Alex, it's really not over, and my baby will be coming back here!"

Alex put his arms around Sterling, and pulled her gently into his big, strong chest as he said, "Sterling, don't worry…please don't worry. We will take care of the situation quickly. Jacob and Gabrielle will be on their honeymoon for a month, which should give us plenty of time to clean this mess up before they return."

With hope in her eyes, Sterling looked up at Alex, and said, "I have confidence in you, Alex. I will keep dreaming of the day that these secrets will no longer keep my family apart."

Alex slowly dropped his arms from the bear hug embrace that he had Sterling in, and picked up her small hand that became lost in his. The moon was shining brightly, the trees were casting long shadows, and the wind was gently whistling as the two walked hand-in-hand silently into the night.

Coming Soon!

Volume 2

The Sequel to
Secrets and Dreams

SECRETS AND OBSESSIONS

LINDA SCARLETT

SECRETS AND OBSESSIONS
Chapter 1

Cruising along the Amalfi Coast was usually an inspiring experience for Sonny, but not tonight. He was driving at warp speed, racing to the plane—racing to safety. He looked in the rearview mirror at three women whose faces were scared, filled with daunting uncertainty. He knew it was his responsibility to transport them safely, and his heart felt heavy. Sonny knew better than to get intimately involved in the lives of the people that were in his care. He was unusually compassionate for a man. Should empathy catch his heart, it would surely cloud his judgment.

Sonny's mind was racing as fast as he was driving. All he could think about was hiding Sterling in a safe place—away from the world, away from Stephano. With his teeth clenched, and his hands gripped tightly on the leather steering wheel, his foot became like lead quickly accelerating past one hundred. Feeling as though part of him was the car, and another part of him completely out of touch, like the car was driving itself, Sonny knew that he was "losing it" for the first time, ever. He also knew that he needed to slow down—his mind and the car—before they both spun out of control.

"I know this is the correct decision," he said quietly under his breath. As those words left his mouth the tension seemed to go with them, and both the racing machines began to slow down. Alexandria was the only place where Sterling wouldn't be recognized. She had no connections to anyone in Egypt, except for Taylor.

Sonny was certain that Sterling would be excited to see her best friend. He also knew that Ashlee and Tiffany would absolutely freak if they knew their destination. Trying not to let those thoughts affect him, Sonny kept reminding himself the only thing that mattered right now was keeping all three of them safe.

He contemplated other options, but his mind repeatedly and quickly returned to thoughtfully dissect the chosen plan. After completing each maneuver in his mind, he felt confident that it was the very best decision—it was also his final decision.

As Sonny's thoughts became resolute, his tense body started to relax, regaining control of both his mind and the car. Now, loosening his tight grip on the steering wheel, he began slowly rubbing it to enjoy the clean smell of the leather. Smelling the leather reminded him of the first time he drove his brand new car along the coast. There was a bright, full moon just like tonight. His thoughts continued to drift as he watched the shimmering light bounce from the moon, to the water, and onto the windshield. The beautiful calm that this part of the country usually held for him was anything but serene tonight.

A wedding in Italy seemed like something right out of a fairytale. Now, being in Paris for my honeymoon far surpassed any of my childhood dreams. Having never given myself to a man, my erotic and passionate feelings, while foreign, soon found themselves in the bliss of becoming one with Jacob. The amazing and euphoric act of making love all night kept rewinding in my head until I could hardly contain myself. I rolled over on top of Jacob to wake him up. We spent most of the morning discovering each other, over and over again…

After finally prying ourselves away from the hotel room, Jacob and I walked hand-in-hand down the Champs Elysses. I was bursting inside as the reality of my new beginning had finally hit me. I felt so loved, and so happy again for the first time, in a long time.

Our sumptuous day began with a delicious brunch at a quaint, French sidewalk café where we splurged on Strawberry Crepes and Eggs Benedict. Then, we set out to see the sights. I love floral gardens, and the fond memories of when Father and I went strolling through the Butchart Gardens in Victoria, B.C. In memory of Father, our first stop was to the famous Luxembourg Gardens□ the second largest park in Paris. The Medici Fountain was my favorite site, from which Jacob had to drag me away, almost kicking.

Afterwards we walked along the Seine, downstream from the Eiffel Tower where we held hands and kissed for what seemed like an eternity. I'm sure the sight of "lovers in love" is certainly nothing new to the scenery in Paris, but I could tell that everyone who caught a glimpse of us appreciated the exuberance that we radiated.

I felt as though I was walking on air as we strolled hand in hand. Jacob's beautiful, strong hand felt not only warm and loving, but incredibly strong. I felt as though he was not only my lover, but my protector as well. I drew his hand up to my mouth and kissed it, in that same second Jacob literally swept me off my feet, threw me over his shoulders and quickly walked to the front of our hotel.

I could tell my kiss triggered his sexual desires, which also triggered the speed in which he wanted to get me back to our room. I giggled and started kissing his ear as I ran my fingers up and down his spine, driving him crazy. The front door of the hotel was quickly upon us. Jacob slowly slid me down his chest. I felt why he was in such a hurry.

I twirled around several times as we strolled through the lobby of the famous and opulent George V. This hotel was not only luxury at its finest, but also a romantically architectural work of art that left a person awestruck walking through the lobby. With marble columns, 18th century tapestries and the grandeur of yesteryear we felt the beauty of the Renaissance coming alive before us.

In the middle of the lobby I grabbed Jacob's hand and did a hop-shuffle dance with my feet, which meant I was excited. Jacob squeezed my hand, and tugged me toward the elevator. The door barely closed before he was on me with a kiss, while his hand slid up my thigh. He began to slam the stop button, but I gave him that look…'not here!'

We ran like kids down the hall to our Suite, threw open the door and tore off each other's clothes all the way to the amazing shower enclosed with mirrors on all sides. With the water cascading down my back, my dark hair seemed to be flowing with it, and looked more strikingly beautiful than ever. Jacob's eyes lovingly looked at me from the top of my head, down to my thighs, butt, and…

As he bent down to kiss my shoulder he wrapped my long, dripping wet hair around his hand and slightly pulled on it for me to meet him in a passionate embrace, and deep, steamy kiss. Standing in the middle of what seemed to be a luxuriant waterfall, with the water flowing all around us, Jacob pressed up against my breasts. His breathing was heavy, his legs strong. He brought me closer and closer into him until we were one - the water continued to engulf us.

Prior to today, the beautiful Villa on Lake Como had always been one of Alex's favorite retreats where his soul healed and his body refreshed. Not so much today.

He walked back into the room where they had all been torturing Pierre beyond recognition and almost to his last breath, trying to convince him to talk. A whole different feeling came over him, one of complete disquietude. His thoughts went from his best friend, Michael, being poisoned to death to Leon's bizarre and bloody murder, to rescuing Sterling the moment Pierre was in the act of attempting to murder her! Now, hating every scream that echoed from this tortured and dying man, Alex was tempted to put a bullet in-between his eyes. It took everything in him to refrain…

He sat down in a chair trying very hard to bring his thoughts together, and trying even harder to drown out Pierre's maddening screams. Knowing Pierre had murdered his best friends made Alex sickened to even be in the same room with him, let alone allow him to live. He would gladly have put Pierre out of his misery for good, but he knew that without the information about Stephano, it would definitely not be a smart move. Alex needed answers from this scum, and he needed them now.

Feeling like he was frozen in an incredibly bizarre nightmare he couldn't break loose from, his mind began jumping from thought to crazy thought. He quickly took control and landed on the task at hand. Breaking his silence, Alex yelled out to Eric to make Pierre stop screaming.

Eric yelled back out of frustration, "Shut the hell up!" As quickly as the words fell out of his mouth, he had wished they hadn't. Sure enough, Alex jumped out of his chair, walked over to Eric and smacked him so hard upside the head that his ear started ringing.

"Sorry Alex!"

Alex just stood there and stared at Eric, as if he would burn a hole through him. "Don't you yell at me like that again!"

"Sorry man."

Stressed and against his will, Eric had been trying to put Pierre's badly beaten body back together for the last few hours. At the moment of Alex's comment, Eric had been regretting that he was a doctor; he would rather let Pierre die than wrap his ribs, clean his wounds, stitch him up in multiple places, and bring him back from the brink of death. The entire time that Eric had stood over Pierre's wretched, horribly beaten body all he could think of was how much he hated this man for taking his father's life. Even though Eric was trained to save lives and honored the Hippocratic Oath, he would have much rather let Pierre die, than lift one finger to save him.

Eric knew that if he didn't put this miserable excuse for a life back together and in short order, they wouldn't be able to find out more information about why Stephano had hired Pierre. It was sickening to him, that he was actually saving the man who not only killed his father, but who had also come to kill his mother. At that point, Eric was so done with this whole gig; however, to appease Alex he put another compress on Pierre's forehead, and then smacked it hard as he walked off.

Needing to get away from this intense scene for a minute, Eric motioned to Alex that he was going outside; he needed some fresh air, and a few minutes alone. Alex was deep in thought, and nodded to Eric without realizing what he was doing. His mind was bombarded with memories of Michael, and all the good times they had. He remembered how hard it was for Michael to send Sterling away. However, her life was in too much danger after witnessing the murder of a statesman. And of course, it couldn't be just any statesman—it had to be one that was tied to the biggest "mob family" in town.

Again, without realizing what his body was doing, he started shaking his head back and forth as his thoughts continued. Twenty long years Sterling stayed in hiding, and to think that after all this time, tonight she was in the hands of the same man—the same man—who murdered her husband! His head was still shaking back and forth, and his brows were furrowed, as he spoke out loud, "Why now and how is Stephano tied to this? Why would Stephano hire Pierre to kill Michael, and then come after Sterling?"

His head still shaking back and forth, his heart heavy, he realized the monumental burden that awaited him; not just finding Stephano, but keeping everyone safe from him. Unaware of his actions, Alex's head stopped instantly as Eric walked in.

He watched Eric move slowly toward Pierre as if he were in slow motion, drifting through a thick fog. Suddenly, a shot from a gun rang out so loudly Alex jumped straight up and out of his chair. He couldn't see who shot whom, but Eric was still standing, so Alex rushed to his side.

"What in the world are you trying to do?"

"Calm down, Alex. I just want to make sure that this miserable creep knows I am NOT Dr. Nice-Guy!"

Trying not to be too smart aleck, or insensitive, Alex said, "Oh.. KAY! Good tactic Eric, that was really good. Now, the whole darn place knows you're Dr. Death. Smart move… NOT! Give me the gun."

Alex took the gun and walked back over to his chair. No more comments were needed, or it would surely instigate unnecessary conversation. Back to business as usual, Alex picked up his cell to make sure that it was on—seconds later it starting ringing.

Still wrestling with thoughts of the matter at hand yet being lured by the enchanting scene before him, Sonny's mind had two reels playing at the same time in his head.

A smile came over him as he remembered his first drive along the Amalfi Coast. He was completely awestruck by the majestically panoramic view of the Mediterranean. His soul was satiated with the all-encompassing scenery: The luxuriant hills, beautiful landscape, breathtaking vistas, the picturesque fishing villages, and the remarkable architecture. This place had become such a huge and powerful part of his memory—a place of solace where his mind always escaped in times of mental despair. However, tonight with the responsibility of three women's lives in his hands, the drive seemed incredibly long. Its beauty had all but vanished.

Sonny knew the roads intimately well. Tonight he was driving by instinct since he had traveled them many times for Sterling. The hard part was staying focused on the monumental task of boarding the jet and landing in Alexandria. He was afraid to ponder, for even a moment, what would happen if he made one wrong move.

Before he knew it, the car was screeching around the corner of Via Foria—the last street, and the longest stretch to the airport. The jerking movement of the fast turn jolted the women out of their private worlds. Instantly, Tiffany and Ashlee started crying as if someone simultaneously flipped the same switch on in both of them. Sonny glanced at them in the rearview mirror. They both looked up at Sonny with pitiful eyes, and pouting lips.

The shock of this whole situation was almost too much for even Sonny. The thought of Sterling being in the hands of a murderer, and that murderer being the same man who killed her husband sent Sonny's adrenaline skyrocketing again. His thoughts rapidly shifted to Gabrielle and he pushed down hard on the pedal.

We took a nap after our shower, and when I awoke I noticed that Jacob was gone. I got dressed in my sexiest outfit to greet Jacob in, and then turned on my laptop to quickly conduct business while my lover was away. We agreed that we wouldn't do any business while on our Honeymoon, but since he was gone, I needed to quickly check on the surprise I sent to him.

Having not checked my emails in three days, there were over 200 loading! I scanned the list of senders rapidly, hoping to locate where the package was before Jacob returned. Hurriedly reading the incoming names and subject lines, I saw one from Father that was still remaining. Before we left for Italy I put all of Father's emails in a folder. 'I KNOW I did! I grabbed every single one of them, reading each one as I transferred it to the file. How did I miss this one?'

Hmmm… 'That is NOT what I think it says! No…it can't be! How could it be? Am I dreaming? Stop it Gabrielle! Just stop it! But it says, From: Michael Deliano To: Gabrielle. And it's dated: TODAY!'

My mind was whirling. Bouncing back and forth thinking that I was either dreaming again, or I was obsessed about losing Father! 'NO! This can NOT be real!' Then, before I could analyze my grieving behavior, I clicked on the email. It was sent TODAY!

About the Author

Linda Scarlett is a passionate, Italian woman with a zeal for life that is unique, fun, and ultra contagious! Her vast life experiences, which include: traveling to Europe, a love of anthropology, years of being a counselor, teacher and mentor, are what make the creation of the characters for her novels, both rich and engaging. Linda is well educated, calling herself a 'forever student', and well-traveled with a love of foreign lands, cultures and people, which is why she also wholeheartedly embraces her non-fictional works as well—expressing many human emotions and experiences.

Linda lost her 30-year-old son to a tragic accident, and then her husband of 30 years to cancer. Linda understands grief, and has also written many pieces on the subject. Some of these works include: Grief Connection (a grief program), The Lady in Black - Cries of a Widow's Heart, Forever Changed and The Pain. She is also a Counselor/Life Coach, Teacher & Trainer, Real Estate Broker, Professional Business Consultant and a sought after Lecturer and Keynote Speaker.

Linda makes her home in the Seattle area where she enjoys the robust and diverse culture, and creative community with artists of all disciplines. She is a mother, grandmother, and amazing friend—some even call her their 'Angel'.

Made in the USA
Charleston, SC
29 May 2013